HONORÉ DE BALZAC

Old Goriot

TRANSLATED BY

MARION AYTON CRAWFORD

PENGUIN BOOKS

Melbourne · London · Baltimore

Penguin Books Ltd, Harmondsworth, Middlesex

U.S.A.: Penguin Books Inc., 3300 Clipper Mill Road, Baltimore 11, Md
[*Educational Representative*:
D. C. Heath & Co., 285 Columbus Avenue, Boston 16, Mass]

AUSTRALIA: Penguin Books Pty Ltd, 200 Normanby Road,
Melbourne, S.C.5, Victoria

AGENT IN CANADA: Riverside Books Ltd, 47 Green Street,
Saint Lambert, Montreal, P.Q.

—

Made and printed in Great Britain by
R. & R. Clark Ltd, Edinburgh

—

This translation first published 1951
Reprinted 1953

Introduction

Old Goriot is one of Balzac's finest novels, revealing all his virtues and showing few of his faults – he had both on a grand scale. The work is quite complete in itself, and requires for its enjoyment no knowledge of any other volume of the *Comédie humaine*, the great series to which it belongs. At the same time, the immense fertility of the author's mind, the breadth of his sympathies, and the range and multiplicity of his interests that sought an outlet in the whole vast undertaking are reflected in this small part of it; so that it gains by being part of a major plan. That plan envisaged nothing less than the writing of the whole history of Balzac's age in living speech and dramatic action.

The scheme was not preconceived. When in 1828 Balzac wrote the first novel to be published under his own name he was unaware that he was beginning the great epic work of his age, but as he wrote novel after novel he found them group themselves together as scenes of public and private life in Paris and the provinces, and the ground-plan began to take shape.

By 1834 when *Old Goriot* appeared, at first in serial form, the plan was more or less elaborated, and Balzac was using the general title *Studies of Nineteenth Century Manners*. But it was not until 1842 that the title *La Comédie humaine* was found, when arrangements were being made to publish a collected edition of the novels he had so far written; and it was then that Balzac wrote the famous *Preface*, explaining the vast scope of his undertaking, and leaving the public to judge if *The Human Comedy* was a presumptuous title for it.

He conceived of the creation of between three and four thousand characters drawn from every stratum of society, and every trade and profession, reflecting the whole of life in every aspect, and every sphere of human activity, as it was known to the three or four generations with whom a man of his own day might come into contact – men and women who lived through the civil wars of the French Revolution, when Napoleon was Emperor, in the France of the Restoration: an epoch of amazing changes in social conditions and in values of every kind. Balzac was not content simply to hold the mirror up to the times, but was concerned to expose the motive forces that drive men and women throughout their lives, and show how the framework of society constrains these forces and is itself affected by them, to analyse the evils of society and discuss the principles on which society is based.

Of these proposed three to four thousand characters Balzac succeeded in creating some two thousand, in twenty-two years of intensive work at relentlessly high pressure, working fourteen, sixteen, eighteen hours a day for months on end, choosing the night to work in, when he would be free from interruption, and stimulating his tired brain with cups of strong black coffee. In those years, apart from numerous essays, short stories and plays, he wrote nearly ninety volumes, of which almost every one is a novel of the first rank. Many other novels were in process of creation in his teeming brain. He prepared a list in 1845 enumerating the titles of novels of the *Comédie humaine* which had already been published, and those that had still to be written: the list contains a hundred and forty-four titles. Five years later Balzac was dead, worn out by his excesses of work.

It was characteristic of the nineteenth century that it developed a historical sense and set men in their natural circumstances, against their proper background, and in relation to one another. Balzac greatly admired Walter Scott, whose novels were then sweeping the Continent, and he imitated his method of bringing a historical period to life by means of exact, detailed description and analysis. In his documentation of his characters and his remorseless fidelity to the truth revealed by observation, Balzac

6

was a forerunner of the Naturalist School of Flaubert, the Gon-
court brothers and Zola.

The nineteenth-century French critic Taine has said that the
novels of the *Comédie humaine* constitute a Record Office filled
with archives. Brunetière examines them as historical documents;
as realistic documents, in their truth to the details of everyday life
(which Balzac's predecessors had kept out of the novel as being
vulgar and uninteresting), and in their introduction of classes of
men hitherto ignored by literature; and as scientific documents,
because Balzac regarded the novel as an instrument of scientific
inquiry. He remarked that the differences between a soldier and a
labourer are as considerable as those that mark out the wolf and
the lion, and was concerned with the description and classification
of men and women as 'social species', as well as with their variations from the class as highly specialized individuals.

Balzac was interested in noting people's surroundings – the
architecture and lay-out of their houses, their furniture, the pictures hanging on the wall, the food they ate and the clothes they
wore – not merely in order to pin them down to a place and a
time, but also because he regarded the surroundings as both an
extension of personality and a moulding force. Madame Vauquer
is her boarding-house – you cannot imagine one without the
other. From the tiger's stripes and the horse's hoof you can deduce
the conditions of life which these characteristics were evolved to
suit, and the creature's natural habitat. Similarly Madame Vauquer
is a product of her boarding-house as well as being the creator of
it, and a glance at her tells you what her kitchen is like, and her
dining-room furniture, and her boarders. It is no accident that
Old Goriot is dedicated to a zoologist. The Theory of Evolution
was very much in the air at that time, and Balzac was interested in
the theories of Darwin's precursor, Lamarck. Darwin himself was
to produce the *Origin of Species* in 1859 – nine years after Balzac's
death.

Balzac had the scientist's urge to discover law underlying the
apparent disorder of the universe. There was more than one

scientific bee in his bonnet – as well as sociological and philosophical bees – and they all buzz energetically in *Old Goriot*, as in most of his works. He was interested in Gall's system of phrenology, in Lavater's work on physiognomy, in Mesmer's theory of the transference of a magnetic fluid in the hypnotism of one human being by another, in the problems presented by the phenomenon of premonition, and he had a new theory of the omnipotence of the human will. These are all concerned with the action of mind on body, or of one mind on others, matters which are still the subject of scientific speculation and inquiry to-day, and matters which, of course, are of the liveliest interest to anyone concerned, like the novelist, with the study of human beings.

Balzac's psychological observations are of extreme acuteness and penetration, and all that the science of psychology has discovered in its immense advances in the hundred years since Balzac's death has done nothing to invalidate them. Of course Balzac was here proceeding not by the careful piling up of evidence, hypothesis and verification of the scientist, but by the intuitive knowledge of human nature and flashes of insight of the novelist, which when the novelist is a genius is a much swifter and not less sure method. It is a measure of the authenticity of the characters he creates that conclusions drawn from them are felt to be valid. One never for one moment feels that they are puppets set up to demonstrate the truth of his theories.

It is characteristic of Balzac that he uses both his magic power of divination and the laborious method of the scientist in his work. '*All is true,*' he cries at the beginning of *Old Goriot*, writing the words in English for greater emphasis, and he goes to endless pains in careful and exact delineation to persuade us that all is indeed recognizably sober fact. But the facts are all lit by his blazing imaginative insight; the truth is shown to be all drama. Balzac paradoxically seems to have possessed, and been able to use simultaneously, the power of detached, objective analysis, and the intensest emotional sympathy with the object of his analysis.

Madame Vauquer's boarders as described are loathsome creatures, but it is with impassioned understanding that the man who describes them discusses the storms and stresses of life they have endured, as well as the qualities of their own natures, that have made them so. No apparently dull person living an uninteresting life is ever dull or uninteresting when examined by Balzac. In this power of double vision Balzac far surpasses his medical student Bianchon, who is moved to tears by the dying Goriot's cries for his daughters, but delighted by the fact that his case is medically unusually interesting, and enthusiastically discusses every symptom, every detail of the treatment, every stage in the progress of the disease, thus contributing to make Goriot's deathbed almost unbearably realistic. Yet Bianchon is perfectly sincere and truthful when he says he has not lost sight of the patient in his interest in the disease; and it is Balzac's power of identifying himself with Goriot and poignantly expressing Goriot's inmost feelings, more than the realistic treatment, that makes the scene almost unbearably harrowing.

At times Balzac appears to overdo his realistic painting, and to dwell at what seems unnecessary length on the sordid side of life. He has also been accused, on the other hand, of over-dramatizing his characters, and seeing reality, as it were, in an apocalyptic vision. Baudelaire said that Balzac's characters were all geniuses, chock-full of his own vitality, and endowed with his own ambition and determination.

The beginning of *Old Goriot* is often cited as an example of Balzac's genius for description, which does not suffer from the fault he sometimes fell into of losing himself in a mass of details which become formless and tedious. No novel ever had its setting more exactly visualized. In page after page of minute particularity he builds up the boarding-house in all its concreteness, and then brings living, breathing personalities on the scene, and in his exposition shows us what has brought these people here, what their pasts have been, or may have been, what their hope, or lack of hope for the future, and what their relations are with each

9

other. All this is done with the greatest vividness of perception and warmth of feeling.

The novel is given a unity sometimes lacking in others of the *Comédie humaine* by the fact that throughout it we are following the fortunes of the young student, Rastignac. We see Paris through his eyes, share his delight in its pleasures and his disgust at its disgusting aspects, and his interest in his fellow-lodgers. We are introduced with him to the fashionable salons of Paris, and laugh with amused sympathy at his highly-coloured ambitious dreams, at his social blunders and the adroit way he extricates himself from the situations in which they land him. We live, in fact, at the growing-point of Rastignac's mind. We watch his experiences alter and mature him, his faults and virtues grow and develop. We follow his constant arguments with his own conscience, and his efforts to decide what he wants from life, and how he is to set about obtaining it. The novel is a history of the transmutation of character in contact with life, and not of Rastignac's character only.

In Rastignac's first year in Paris we are told 'he acquired an inkling of the way in which human beings are packed in strata, layer above layer, in the framework of society', and this structure of society is also a theme of the novel. We are shown a cross-section of these close-packed vividly-contrasted strata, and shown how the driving force of the human will can bring a man to the top of the dense mass. Vautrin, the anarchist, the disciple of Rousseau, expounds his ideas and discusses the methods by which the ambitious man succeeds. Rastignac rejects Vautrin's temptations in the end, but he remembers his doctrines and is influenced by them.

It is not surprising that Vautrin, the devil's advocate, should insist that men are to be used as a king uses his soldiers, by those strong-willed enough, ambitious enough, to crown themselves lords of their fellows; that he should declare that there is no such thing as moral principle – only circumstances exist, which can be turned to one's advantage. In his eyes the rich are not worse than the poor, nor women – always at odds with the law and with their husbands – better than men: all are corruptible. The constitution of society, however, favours the rich. Paris is a slough, and the only way to escape the mud is to ride in a carriage. Such sentiments are natural enough in Vautrin's mouth.

But Rastignac notes that Madame de Beauséant, in an unguarded moment when she was speaking from the heart, gave him very similar advice – he must use men and women ruthlessly if he wanted to succeed. The more coldly he calculated the further he would go, and on the way he would discover the corruption of women and the miserable vanity of men.

In fact, a powerful indictment of Parisian society, and of the methods of those who have risen to be its leaders, is framed by the testimony of character after character. 'Paris is a slough,' echoes the Duchesse de Langeais. Delphine declares that half the women in Paris, while leading apparently luxurious, carefree lives, are racked as she is with constant anxiety about money, and, unlike her, are prepared to go to any lengths to obtain it. Balzac is careful to say, speaking with his own voice, that women are compelled to commit such faults by the demands of society as it is at present constituted. Although Rastignac is irresistibly impelled to seek success, he is constantly reminded of the hollowness of the life of luxury as well as being shown its splendour, and he is left in no doubt that success can be achieved only at the cost of his integrity.

Rastignac, both in himself and in his experiences, is to a certain extent, in this novel, a projection of Balzac himself. Balzac had actually known what Vautrin forecast for Rastignac – years of obscurity, in poverty and hunger, observing that it was always the others, never himself, who were acquiring riches, women, success, luxuries and the lavish windfalls of life. Balzac, like Rastignac, had been a poor law-student in Paris, who lived in sordid surroundings and longed for luxurious ones; like Rastignac he had known the joys of exploring the city and learning its ways and gradually becoming a citizen of the capital. He knew the

11

effect produced by possession of a little money jingling in the pocket, and all the ways of raising money, and the reason why a student who has no socks or hat may yet possess a resplendent waistcoat, all from personal experience. Like Rastignac, Balzac had been befriended by his tailor and had later made the man's fortune by a witty remark about his trousers which made him known to fashionable Paris. He had a favourite sister, called Laure, who was his confidante. Like Rastignac he had a burning desire to penetrate the fastnesses of the Faubourg Saint-Germain. Unlike Rastignac he was gross and plebeian in appearance and, in his youth, awkward in manner and shy in society. Like Rastignac he felt within himself the power and a blazing ambition to succeed, yet for a very long time was not certain in what direction to exert his strength, nor what his ultimate goal was.

Yet this resemblance does not prevent Balzac from wittily showing up and laughing at Rastignac's little vanities and foibles. He also faithfully reflects a certain lack of imagination and insensitiveness, shown in the fact that Rastignac never for a moment considers Victorine's feelings – for him she is only a temptation which he eventually resists; shown too at the beginning of the story in Rastignac's obtuse remarks in Goriot's presence about Goriot's daughters' lack of regard for him, made at the very moment when he is constituting himself Goriot's champion against the boarders who bully him.

It is worth remarking, too, that Balzac, who is reported as being a notable snob, underlines the different snobberies of Delphine, Madame de Beauséant, and the Duchesse de Langeais, and that a certain vulgarity of taste that Rastignac remarked in Delphine's house is the very same vulgarity of taste that Balzac is himself accused of possessing.

The fact that Rastignac comes to the battlefield of Parisian civilization still fresh and unspoiled and wrapped in the influences of his family life in the country, and that he constantly casts glances back at the serenity and peace of that life, gives charm to the whole story of *Old Goriot*. The letters his mother and sister send him are a complete revelation of the sweet and tender natures of the women who write them, and of the graciousness of their perhaps narrow and frugal mode of living, in the traditional manner of the family of the petty nobleman in his château. Although these women are in the background of the story, appearing only in their letters and Rastignac's thoughts of them and Vautrin's references to their circumstances, their influence permeates the novel. In them and in Victorine, Balzac gracefully solves what in a tell-tale phrase in the *Preface* he calls 'the difficult problem of making the virtuous woman interesting'. Balzac was answering an accusation that he loved to depict the seamier side of life, and that all his great characters were great rogues. He replied by pointing to the long list of his 'good' characters, and saying that it was his task to paint every side of life.

The character of Goriot, at least, is an instance of a great character who is not a great rogue. The theme which gives the novel its title is a sombre one. 'My bourgeois novels are more tragical than your tragic dramas,' Balzac once exclaimed to the Romantic writers of his day; and he appears here to have deliberately chosen to show that a working-class Lear may exist, whose story is not less terrible or less affecting than that of Shakespeare's great king. It is a triumph of Balzac's art that the old, retired vermicelli-manufacturer, who has sunk to being the butt of his unfeeling fellow-boarders, who feels out of his element and uncomfortable at his daughters' elegant dinner-tables, should capture our affection and respect as surely as he captures Rastignac's, and that his tragedy is felt to be a tragedy of heroic proportions, even though he may be, as a boarder remarks, just one of the unnoticed many who die every day in Paris.

Yet Goriot has his immoral, not to say blasphemous, side. To spare either of his daughters a tear he says that he would sell Father, Son and Holy Ghost, and this is the more striking in that Goriot is a truly religious and God-fearing man; the moving passage in which he soberly and reverently tells Rastignac that when he became a father he understood God the Creator is only

13

one of those in which this is made clear. He readily condones his daughters' deception of their husbands, and whole-heartedly wishes Nucingen's gout would attack him more severely and kill him. He is quite unconcerned about the plot to murder young Taillefer, and sees no reason why Rastignac should go to warn him or his father. It is by such points as these that Balzac emphasizes the obsessional nature of Goriot's love of his daughters.

Obsessive passions of all kinds – ambition, avarice, a collector's mania for collecting – held the utmost fascination for Balzac. Even a virtue driven to excess becomes a vice, and such excesses not only invariably drive the obsessed victim to destruction, but are never without endless consequences for other people. This is a theme that Balzac develops in a hundred variations in his novels.

'Everyone has his own fashion of loving. Mine does no harm to anyone, so why should people bother about me?' Goriot asks Rastignac. But much later in the story Delphine says to him, 'If I am in the depths of despair now, it is perhaps partly your fault. We are so young when we marry – what do we know of the world or of men? Our fathers ought to think for us.' The remark is heartlessly unkind, but there is some truth in it. Goriot has abdicated his parental authority. His indulgence of his daughters is a form of self-indulgence with disastrous consequences both for him and them.

> The gods are just, and of our pleasant vices
> Make instruments to plague us.

In an hour of dreadful clarity just before his death Goriot perceives that he has committed a sin, that he bears direct responsibility for the evil effects his over-indulgence of his daughters all their lives has had upon their characters. He realizes that his daughters have been the instruments of God's vengeance upon him, and that they themselves will suffer God's vengeance for their sin against their father, perhaps through their own children. His fault, in fact, has endless repercussions.

14

But though in one aspect Goriot's passion is a kind of madness that drives him to destruction, the thesis that it is wonderful and admirable, that in it Goriot touches the sublime, is also maintained by Balzac. He calls him 'this Christ-like father'. Vautrin truly says that for Goriot his daughters are the clue by which he makes his way through the labyrinth of creation. Rastignac admires him with the generous enthusiasm of youth for true nobility.

It is the infinite complexity with which good and evil are intermingled in human beings and in human affairs that never ceases to interest Balzac, and in his best work the good or evil he studies is of a quality and intensity not so superhuman as to be incredible, but rare enough to raise the characters to the level of the characters of heroic tragedy.

Vautrin is clearly a character from a different type of play, and the atmosphere of melodrama he introduces into the novel is highly enjoyable or very regrettable, according to taste. Balzac follows the precedent set by Milton in taking great pleasure in his great villain: it is an obviously satanic rôle that Vautrin plays. The flames of hell play luridly about him. His strong smell of brimstone is mingled somewhat oddly at times with the flavour of Rousseau and of Fenimore Cooper. The scurvy treatment Balzac deals out to him, however, when he lets him fall a victim to Mademoiselle Michonneau's plot is evidence of a real, though temporary, lapse of artistic conscience on the part of his creator, which it is very strange to find in such a well-constructed novel.

The character, and the lack of scruple Balzac sometimes shows in dealing with him, are thought to be a legacy from Balzac's early days as a writer. At the outset of his writing career, driven at first by the need to earn money and gain his independence, Balzac wrote quantities of the most sensational novels. He catered, in collaboration and under a variety of pseudonyms, for the market for melodramatic novels that had grown up in England and on the Continent, partly as a consequence of the new fashion set by the spooky horrors of Ann Radcliffe and her imitators. There was no literary crime that he did not commit at that time, his pen was at the service of anyone who cared to pay for it, and he was later to regret it, and pay for it dearly in the occasional crudities of even his finest novels, and especially in the faultiness of his style, which was permanently affected by his years of hasty, unconsidered writing.

All Balzac's major characters are highly articulate, and the vigour with which they express their often subversive views has undoubtedly done some damage to Balzac's moral reputation. Characters as different from each other as Goriot, Vautrin, Madame de Beauséant, Delphine, hold the stage in turn, and expound to Rastignac at some length their philosophy of life, and principles or lack of principle, explain and justify their actions, with the utmost eloquence and force. In the course of the novel Balzac remarks on the fact that deep feeling can animate the heaviest clay, and give a man like Goriot a great actor's powers of expression and of evoking responsive sympathy. Whether this is universally true or not, it is certainly true of Balzac's characters. When they are swept by strong emotion they speak the language of dramatic poetry.

The persuasiveness with which they speak is, to some extent, due also to the clearness with which they see their situation, and their relations with other characters.

'You love me only by a convention which is a kind of good manners in men,' Delphine says to Eugène. And the fact that this is true, and that she sees it, and has the courage to say so, strikes through all the artificialities of the situation. We have here no glamorous hero and heroine of fictional romance, but adult human beings of recognizable flesh and blood. That being so we easily accept much that is romantic and fairy-tale in the story – for example the episode of Eugène's first attempt to play roulette, which ends so successfully.

Eugène's passion for Delphine begins by being a made-to-order passion, and even later when it is strong enough to eclipse the influence of his family Eugène is, at heart, under no illusions about the shallowness and frivolity of Delphine's nature, and the force of the snobbish ambition which would lead her to trample her father's body underfoot to go to Madame de Beauséant's ball. Yet the strength of her hold upon him is made entirely credible.

Eugène, understandably enough, readily finds excuses for Delphine. It is perhaps a black mark against Balzac, morally speaking, that he too finds a very generous and all-embracing excuse for her, when he is considering the inconsistencies of her treatment of Eugène. 'Women,' he says, 'even in their greatest deviations, are always true, because they are yielding to a natural sentiment.' Balzac has a creator's compassion for and understanding of the frailties of his creatures, especially women, and especially women who have been the victims of men, and ageing, forsaken women. The women of his own day found that in his novels a champion had taken up the cudgels on their behalf against the wrongs society inflicted on them, and they formed a large part of his enthusiastic public.

Balzac has nowhere in the novel shown greater skill than in the success with which he has kept our sympathy with, and even affection for, both Delphine and Anastasie, while showing up their failings in a high light. The two sisters are carefully differentiated in both personality and fortune, and in the degree of their lack of feeling for their father. The failure of both to be present at their father's death-bed is, of course, inexcusable, but the different circumstances that prevent their coming are most skilfully led up to, and shown to be the inevitable result of their previous actions, and of the shortcomings of their characters, which in turn, though inexcusable, have been shown to be completely human and understandable, and due, in part, to their father's spoiling of them.

It was a stroke of genius that made Eugène fall in love first with Anastasie, and displayed Anastasie early in the story in such a happy attractive light in the amusing scene when Eugène calls on her and finds Maxime there, and sees Goriot leave by a side door and Monsieur de Restaud arrive. She is then in complete command of the situation, and at the height of her fortunes, which by a later turn were to make of her an apparently hard, callous woman, ready to turn her father's very death into cash for the sake of her lover, and finally crush her beneath a weight of sorrow and regret. Anastasie is as much a victim of an obsessive passion as her father.

The clearness of sight with which the characters occasionally regard each other, and the fact that we see them through each other's eyes, often gives their presentment an astringency which enables us to swallow a good deal of sentiment. Goriot is a character who, if he were not always presented with complete sincerity and conviction, might easily appear mawkish at times. He is very effusive in his expression of affection and joy, when he and Delphine and Eugène spend their first evening together in the rooms he has helped Delphine furnish for Eugène. But Delphine's remark to Eugène that when her father is there he monopolizes her attention, and that it will be very tiresome sometimes, throws a strong light upon the situation. We realize that the remark does indeed contain the essence of all ingratitude, while still sympathizing with Delphine.

Again, if the scene where Goriot demands that Eugène should give him the waistcoat on which Delphine has shed tears is touching as well as absurd, it is at least partly because it has such a moving effect on Eugène.

If Balzac has been accused of occasional sentimentality he has also been accused of cynicism in his conception of love. It has been said that he could not paint the highest and most subtle forms of love. In this novel he remarks how rare true love is, as rare as true charity, both the highest form of generosity. Elsewhere in the novel he makes love a matter of gratitude. Whatever may be the truth about his power to conceive of and paint the highest form, in the *Comédie humaine* he certainly paints every other form of love, and many of them in this novel, and also of every other passion that exerts a compulsive force on human beings, with the power to alter lives and decide destinies.

A great force that Balzac was the first to paint, and that no one since has ever painted on so vast a scale, and one that plays a vital part in modern society, is that exerted by the desire to gain money, and the power and the amenities of life, that possession of money brings. There was nothing Balzac did not know about money, and financial operations of all kinds. His disastrous business experiences as publisher, printer and type-founder may have taught him much. But he learned far more, no one knows how, through his astounding faculty for assimilating vast quantities of knowledge of all kinds, and especially technical knowledge. No novelist depicted more exactly or more variously the different fashions in which a man may gain or lose large or small sums of money; or calculated in exact figures in more detail the income required to keep up various styles of living. The cost of living often looms as large in the thoughts of his characters as it does in the daily life of his readers. Money is indispensable to the young man who wants to get on. 'I cannot do without the tools they cultivate the vine with in this country,' Rastignac writes to his mother. And Delphine, wishing to give Rastignac not money but the things her money has bought, tells him that fine rooms and their contents are the weapons of the times, comparable to the swords ladies girded their knights with in olden times, and the armour they gave them. 'Money is life. Money is all-powerful!' Goriot cries, and it is not the least part of his pain that he knows that in dying he is leaving his daughters at the mercy of rascals who will strip them of every penny of the fortune he has spent his life building up for them. We are told the precise facts of Nucingen's swindling scheme for raising money. We follow closely the successive changes in Goriot's, and in Rastignac's, financial circumstances. We note the cost of everything, from the rent paid by each of Madame Vauquer's boarders and the market value of the pears she serves up to them as dessert, to the sums a fashionable young man must pay in Paris to his tailor and his laundress.

It would be interesting to know how the cost of living in the first quarter of the nineteenth century in Paris compares with the cost of living in mid twentieth century London, but it is not easy to compare them because of the changes in the value of the franc and the pound, both in their purchasing power and in relation to one another. In 1793 the franc was stabilized and became worth about tenpence in English money, a value which it held, more or less, from that date up to 1914. The livre was of the same value as the franc, which later replaced it, and the crown, now obsolete, was worth three francs.

Old Goriot is several times referred to as a 'drama', and is full of theatrical comparisons and allusions, and although, of course, Balzac's concern in so referring to it was to distinguish it from a 'romance', and not to imply its fitness for the stage, it has been remarked that the piece observes the dramatic unities of time, place and action much more closely than is at all usual in a novel. The time is the short space of a few months from December 1819 to February 1820; the place is always Paris, and usually the Maison Vauquer — we only leave the Maison Vauquer to go with Rastignac to the theatre or to a fashionable salon, and its squalor is constantly in Rastignac's thoughts when he is in luxurious surroundings, we are never allowed to forget it; the various themes are interwoven with the naturalness and apparent inevitability that betray consummate skill. In connection with this last it is particularly noticeable with what adroitness Balzac dismisses, towards the end of the book, the characters that have shared the limelight with Goriot — Vautrin disappears in a blaze of fireworks, Victorine goes out of Eugène's life to become a wealthy heiress, Madame de Beauséant exiles herself to Normandy, Mademoiselle Michonneau and Poiret make a fitting exit, so that at the end all our attention is focussed on Goriot and his daughters, and Eugène.

Then the characters are scenically observed, and they have their exits and their entrances. They come on the stage of the Maison Vauquer dining-room, or Goriot's bedroom, or Madame de

Beauséant's drawing-room, in pursuit of their own everyday occasions, and the groups they form so naturally always have a dramatic purpose and advance the action of the story, as well as exploiting a dramatic situation. Long passages of the novel might be bodily transferred to the stage with little or no alteration, to form exciting scenes moving at a very rapid pace; for example the scene when Rastignac calls for the first time on Madame de Beauséant, or the great scene when Goriot is preparing to leave the Maison Vauquer for ever, and his daughters arrive in succession, each with her tale of woe, while Eugène eavesdrops next door. There are many others.

The characters, too, are as clearly heard by the reader as they are vividly seen. Each has his individual and authentic voice, and speaks in his own idiom, which accurately reflects his personality, and the peculiarities imposed by his education, or calling, or experience of life – this is true even of the minor characters, such as Madame Couture, who say little. One could never be in doubt as to who was speaking, if all other indications were removed. One is always conscious, too, of *all* the persons present, and of their attitude towards what is being discussed, even when nearly all the talking is being done by one character. But if a tragedy were made from *Old Goriot* it would have to be a tragedy on the Shakespearean model, full of scenes of comedy and broad farce; and in losing the author's voice much more would be lost than in the case of most novelists. Balzac has the comic gift of making a remark aside to his readers, and he himself feels such amusement at the funny aspects of his characters and their situations, and such tenderness for their pathetic side, that he doubles our appreciation of them. His laughter is never cruel, nor his cynicism bitter.

Something has already been said about the subtlety of his psychological comment; and the wealth and variety of his knowledge on all kinds of subjects enables him to turn a searchlight on his characters from many different standpoints. There is no possibility of sitting back to read Balzac in a lazy, half-awake

21

fashion. He sends his reader's mind off chasing ideas in every direction, occasionally, it must be confessed, with the results obtained by a kitten chasing a ball of wool, and the most careless and indifferent finds he has no option but to become an active participant under the stimulus of Balzac's indescribable vitality, vivacity and wit. He calls on his readers to enrich his narrative by their memories of the classical and modern writers, the painters, sculptors and composers to whom he constantly alludes; and by his and his characters' references to operas and plays then being performed in Paris and novels being read, to men of note and notable events of the time or the immediate past, he both gives his readers a sense of participation in the things that occupied people's minds at that time, and relates the private history of his characters to the general history of their period. Rastignac's temperament is compared with Bernadotte's. Goriot has laid the foundation of his fortune during the disturbances of the Revolutionary period, and we are told how. Madame Vauquer has seen Louis XVI have his sad accident, and the Emperor fall and come back and fall again, and she takes it as all in the natural order of things since her middle-class boarding-house remained unaffected and undisturbed.

Balzac's many-sidedness in itself gives a translator a number of problems to solve, and these are added to by the variety and individuality of his characters. In this novel the characters range socially from the ex-convict Vautrin and Madame Vauquer's servants and boarders, to the aristocrats of the Faubourg Saint-Germain, and each character speaks in the idiom and uses the vocabulary appropriate to his circumstances in life. There is a wealth of slang, puns, colloquialisms of all kinds, grammatical solecisms and individual peculiarities of speech. Fortunately, however, the conversation of less serious-minded students, like the type of joke they find amusing, seems to change very little from age to age and from country to country, and Madame Vauquer's non-residential boarders speak quite naturally, I think, in English.

Balzac can follow and intermingle passages of such dialogue with utterances in his own voice full of profound reflections, and what he might call 'sublime sentiments', without the reader being conscious of the slightest jar or incongruity of style. This is because everything he says has the tone and force of spontaneous speech; and I have done my best, however inadequately, to preserve that effect of spontaneity and vigour in the English version. Difficulty in dealing with Balzac's style arises, in the case of this novel, not from verbosity, for which critics have sometimes blamed him, but from the fact, which is notorious, that his long sentences are packed with meaning, crammed with metaphor and allusion, and require to be disentangled and unwound into even longer English sentences.

The translator of Balzac need not mourn the loss of French lucidity and grace of style, for whereas force is of the essence of his writing, lucidity is often a minor consideration and grace of little importance to him. A translator, however, must be clear, and there are places where translation of Balzac becomes more than ordinarily a matter of interpretation. The obscurities are usually matters of detail, and I have tried throughout the book to be faithful to Balzac's meaning while translating his idiom into the idiom of modern English – a word for word translation of Balzac would be even more incomprehensible than most word for word translations.

I am very conscious that these brief notes do a great deal less than justice to Balzac's unique achievement. I can only say to the reader, 'Here's richness!' and leave him to explore it, assuring him, if he has not yet read any novels of the *Comédie humaine*, that *Old Goriot* is one of the most delightful to begin with. *La Comédie humaine* – a whole universe of breathing human beings working out their destinies amid the circumstances of their day – is sad and sordid at times, like life itself. The novels are often depressing and occasionally disgusting but no one who cares for literature, or life, can afford to miss them. I hope this translation may introduce new readers to one of the world's greatest novelists, or induce others who have found that a lack of ability to read French rapidly spoils their appreciation of Balzac, to take him up again. In that case I shall be in the happy position of being a public benefactor, while myself deriving the utmost pleasure and interest from what was truly a fascinating task.

M. A. C.

January 1950

To the Great and Illustrious

GEOFFROY-SAINT-HILAIRE

*as a testimony of admiration
for his labours and
his genius*

DE BALZAC

Old Goriot

FOR the last forty years the elderly Madame Vauquer, *née* de Conflans, has kept a family boarding-house in the Rue Neuve-Sainte-Geneviève between the Latin Quarter and the Faubourg Saint-Marcel. This boarding-house, known as the Maison Vauquer, is open to men and women, young and old, and its respectability has never been questioned by anyone. All the same, no young woman has been seen there for forty years, and if a young man stays there it is only because his family do not allow him much money. Yet in 1819, the time when this drama begins, an almost penniless girl was living there.

However discredited the word 'drama' may be because of the way it has been overworked and strained and twisted in these days of doleful literature, it must be used here; not that this story is dramatic in the real sense of the word, but perhaps some tears may be shed over it in the reading – *intra muros et extra*.

Will it be understood outside Paris? One may doubt it. Only between the heights of Montmartre and Montrouge are there people who can appreciate how exactly, with what close observation, it is drawn from life.

They live in a valley of crumbling stucco and gutters black with mud, a valley full of real suffering and often deceptive joys, and they are so used to sensation that it takes something outrageous to produce a lasting impression. Yet now and then in some overwhelming tragedy evil and good are so strangely mixed that these selfish and self-centred people are forced to pause in their restless pursuit of their own affairs, and their hearts are momentarily touched; but the impression made on them is fleeting, it vanishes as quickly as a delicious fruit melts in the mouth. The chariot of civilization, like the chariot of Juggernaut, is scarcely halted by a heart less easily crushed than the others in its path. It soon breaks this hindrance to its wheel and continues its triumphant course.

And you will show the same insensibility, as you hold this book in your white hand, lying back in a softly-cushioned arm-chair, and saying to yourself, 'Perhaps this one is amusing.' When you have read of the secret sorrows of old Goriot you will dine with unimpaired appetite, blaming the author for your callousness, taxing him with exaggeration, accusing him of having given wings to his imagination. But you may be certain that this drama is neither fiction nor romance. *All is true*, so true that everyone can recognize the elements of the tragedy in his own household, in his own heart perhaps.

The lodging-house is Madame Vauquer's own property. It stands at the lower end of the Rue Neuve-Sainte-Geneviève where it slopes so abruptly towards the Rue de l'Arbalète that carriages rarely use it. The absence of wheeled traffic deepens the stillness which prevails in these streets cramped between the domes of the Val-de-Grâce and the Panthéon, two buildings that over-shadow them and darken the air with the leaden hue of their dull cupolas. In this district the pavements are dry, the gutters have neither mud nor water, grass grows along the walls. The most carefree passer-by feels depressed where even the sound of wheels is unusual, the houses are gloomy, the walls like a prison. A Parisian straying here would see nothing around him but lodging-houses or institutions, misery or lassitude, the old sinking into the grave or the cheerful young doomed to the tread-mill. It is the grimmest quarter of Paris and, it may be said, the least known. The Rue Neuve-Sainte-Geneviève especially is like a bronze frame, the only one suited to this story, for which the mind must be prepared by gloomy colours and heavy thoughts, as a traveller descending to the Catacombs sees the light of day grow dim and hears the sing-song of his guide grow hollow as he goes down step by step. It is a true comparison, for who can decide which is more horrifying, the sight of empty skulls or of withered hearts?

The front of the lodging-house gives on a little garden and it is placed at right-angles to the Rue Neuve-Sainte-Geneviève from which you see it, as it were, in section.

A cobbled channel a fathom wide separates house and garden, and beside it runs a gravel path bordered with geraniums, oleanders and pomegranate trees in big blue and white earthenware pots. The path is reached by a side gate with a sign-board above it reading in large letters MAISON VAUQUER, and below in rather smaller type *Lodgings for Ladies and Gentlemen, etc.*

As you pass in the daytime you can catch a glimpse through a wicket gate with a shrill bell attached to it, of a green marble arch painted by local talent on the wall facing the street at the end of the path. A statue representing the God of Love is placed in this imitation shrine and its chipped scaling surface makes it look like a patient for one of the nearby hospitals, and provides an allegory for those who are fond of symbols. Under the pedestal, the half-obliterated inscription betrays its date by its evidence of the enthusiasm felt for Voltaire on his return to Paris in 1777:

Whoe'er thou art, thy master see;
He is, he was, or he should be.

At nightfall the wicket gate is replaced by a solid door.

The garden, as wide as the house-front is long, is enclosed by the street wall and the party wall of the house next-door, which is covered from top to bottom and completely hidden by a mantle of ivy. People in the street look up at this ivy-clad wall as they pass, attracted by its picturesqueness, rare in a city like Paris. Each of the garden walls has a trellis of espalier fruit-trees and vines, whose pitted and dusty fruit is watched over anxiously by Madame Vauquer every year, and forms a topic of conversation with her lodgers. Along each wall runs a narrow path leading to a clump of lime-trees, which Madame Vauquer persists in calling *line-trees*;

although as a de Conflans she should know better, and although her guests comment on her mistake. Between the side paths the space is filled in by a bed of artichokes, flanked by fruit-trees trained in a conical shape, and edged with sorrel, lettuce and parsley. Under the lime-trees there is a round, green-painted table with some seats, where the lodgers who can afford coffee come to enjoy it in the dog days, even though it is hot enough to hatch out eggs there.

The house itself, three storeys high without counting the attics, is built of hewn stone and washed with that yellow shade which gives a mean look to nearly every house in Paris. The five windows at the front on each floor have small panes, and their blinds are all drawn up to different levels so that the lines are at sixes and sevens. At the side there are two windows, and those on the ground floor are barred with an iron grille. A yard about twenty feet square lies behind the building, inhabited by a happy family of pigs, hens and rabbits, and beyond that there is a shed for fire-wood. The meat-safe is hung up between this shed and the kitchen window, and the greasy water from the sink flows below it. The cook sweeps all the refuse of the house into the Rue Neuve-Sainte-Geneviève through a little door in the yard, and uses floods of water to clean it up for fear of an epidemic.

The ground-floor is well-designed for use as a middle-class boarding-house. The first room is lighted by the two windows facing the street, and may be entered by a French window. A door in this sitting-room leads to a dining-room, which is separated from the kitchen by the well of a staircase, whose wooden steps have coloured waxed tiles set in them.

Nothing could be more depressing than the sight of this sitting-room, with its various chairs upholstered in a haircloth of alternately dull and shiny stripes. In the middle there is a round table with a top of Saint-Anne marble, and on it a white china tea-service with its gilt decoration half worn away, the kind of tea-service that is inevitably found everywhere to-day.

The flooring of the room is uneven. Its walls are panelled to elbow level, and above that the rest of the wall is hung with a varnished paper on which the principal scenes from *Télémaque* are depicted, with the classical characters in colour. The wall-space between the barred windows displays to the boarders the feast given to the son of Ulysses by Calypso. For forty years this picture has excited the humorous comment of the younger boarders, who imagine that they show themselves superior to their circumstances when they scoff at the meal which their poverty forces them to accept.

The stone chimney-piece is adorned with two vases full of faded artificial flowers imprisoned under glass shades, set on either side of a bluish marble clock in the worst possible taste. The cleanness of the hearth makes it plain that except on great occasions no fire ever burns there.

This first room exhales an odour without a name in the language; it ought to be called *boarding-house smell*. The atmosphere has the stuffiness of rooms which are never ventilated, and a mouldy odour of decay. Its dampness chills you as you breathe it, and permeates your clothing. Smells of all the meals that have been eaten in the boarding-house linger in the air. The whole place stinks of the kitchen and the scullery, and it has in addition the reek characteristic of all refuges for the unfortunate. If some way were known to measure the nauseating elements breathed out by every lodger young or old into the air, which is infected by his catarrh or other ailment, it might then be possible to describe this smell adequately. Yet, in spite of these stale horrors, you would find this sitting-room as elegant and as perfumed as a boudoir if you compared it with the dining-room next door.

The panelled walls of that room were once painted in a colour unrecognizable to-day. This paint forms a background on which successive layers of dirt have traced fantastic figures. Sticky side-boards line the room and are covered with a collection of chipped, stained decanters, discs of metal with a silk-like sheen, piles of plates of thick blue-bordered earthenware, manufactured in Tournai. The food-stained or wine-spattered table-napkins of the boarders are kept in numbered pigeonholes in a box standing in a corner.

The indestructible furniture which every other household throws out finds its way to the lodging-house, for the same reason that the human wreckage of civilization drifts to hospitals for the incurable. In this room you would find a barometer with a monk who appears when it is wet, execrable engravings bad enough to spoil your appetite and all framed in varnished black wood with gilt beading, a clock with a tortoiseshell case inlaid with copper, a green stove, Argand lamps coated with dust and oil, a long table covered with oil-cloth so greasy that a facetious boarder can write his name on it with his finger-nail, broken-backed chairs, wretched little esparto grass mats unravelling endlessly without ever coming completely to pieces, and finally miserable foot-warmers, their orifices enlarged by decay, their hinges broken and their wood charred. This furniture is all old, cracked, decaying, shaky, worm-eaten, decrepit, rickety, ramshackle and on its last legs; but its state could not be described fully without breaking the thread of the story and putting too great a strain on the tolerance of impatient people who read it. The red tiles of the floor are full of hollows made by scouring or washing with stain. In short, poverty without glamour reigns here, a narrow, concentrated, threadbare poverty. Although actual filth may be absent, everything is dirty and stained; there are no rags and tatters, but everything is falling to pieces in decay.

This room is in all its glory at about seven in the morning when Madame Vauquer's cat appears downstairs, a sign that his mistress is on the way. He jumps on the sideboards and sniffs at the plates covering several bowls of milk and purrs his morning greeting to the world. Soon the widow makes her appearance, adorned with her tulle cap perched on top of a false front set crooked on her head, and shuffles about in creased slippers. Her ageing puffy face dominated by a nose like a parrot's beak, her dimpled little hands, her body as plump as a church rat's, her bunchy shapeless dress are in their proper setting in this room where misery oozes from the walls and hope, trodden down and stifled, has yielded to despair. Madame Vauquer is at home in its stuffy air, she can breathe without being sickened by it. Her face, fresh with the chill freshness of the first frosty autumn day, her wrinkled eyes, her expression, varying from the conventional set smile of the ballet-dancer to the sour frown of the discounter of bills, her whole person, in short, provides a clue to the boarding-house, just as the boarding-house implies the existence of such a person as she is. There is no prison without its warder; you cannot conceive of the one without the other. The unwholesome plumpness of this little woman is a product of the life she lives here, by the same process that breeds typhoid fever from the noxious vapours of a hospital. Her knitted woollen petticoat dipping below the refurbished old dress which forms her skirt, its wadding escaping from rents in the ripped material, expresses the essence of the sitting-room, the dining-room and the little garden, makes you realize what the kitchen must be like, and foreshadows the boarders. When she is there the picture is complete.

Madame Vauquer is about fifty years old, and she resembles all *women who have had a peck of troubles*. She has the glassy eye and innocent air of a procuress ready with a show of virtuous indignation to squeeze a client for some extra payment, and she is, in fact, ready to lend herself to any shift that may make her path in life smoother, to betray Georges or Pichegru, if those generals were still hiding from Napoleon and could be betrayed. All the same she is *a good woman at heart*. So say the lodgers who believe her to be badly off when they hear her cough and groan like one of themselves. What had Monsieur Vauquer been? She never entered into explanations about her late husband. How had he lost his money? 'Mishap and misfortune,' was her answer. He had treated her badly, had left her only her eyes to weep with, the house to live in, and the right to withhold her sympathy from anyone in trouble because, as she said, she knew what real trouble was, she had suffered all that a woman could.

Hearing her mistress bustling about, fat Sylvie, the cook,

hurried to serve breakfast for the boarders who lived in the house. Those who ate at the lodging-house but did not live there, the *externes*, usually came only to dinner, which cost thirty francs a month.

At the time when this story begins the lodgers numbered seven. The best rooms in the house were on the first floor. Madame Vauquer occupied the less important of the two sets of rooms there, and the other was let to Madame Couture, the widow of a Commissary-General in the service of the Republic. With her she had an adolescent girl named Victorine Taillefer, who was her ward. Board and lodging for these two ladies amounted to eighteen hundred francs.

Of the two sets of rooms on the second floor an old man called Poiret occupied one; the other was held by a man of about forty who wore a black wig, dyed his whiskers, declared himself to be a retired merchant, and was called Monsieur Vautrin.

Two of the four rooms on the third floor were also let, one to an elderly spinster named Mademoiselle Michonneau, and the other to a retired manufacturer of vermicelli, Italian pastes and starch, familiarly known, without protest, as 'Old Goriot'. The other two rooms were allotted to birds of passage, to impecunious students who, like old Goriot and Mademoiselle Michonneau, could not afford more than forty-five francs a month for food and lodging; but Madame Vauquer cared very little to have lodgers of that sort and took them only when she could not find anyone better: they ate too much bread.

At this time one of these rooms was rented by a young man who had come to Paris from the neighbourhood of Angoulême to study law. The other members of his family, which was a large one, were pinching and scraping in order to be able to send him twelve hundred francs a year. Eugène de Rastignac, as he was called, was one of those young men whose noses are set to the grindstone by poverty, who understand very early in life the hopes their parents place in them, and carefully lay the foundations of a great career. From the beginning they plan their studies as means to an end, adapting them in advance to the probable turn of events in the future, so that they may be the first to squeeze a profit from social changes. But for his observant curiosity, and the adroitness with which he contrived to introduce himself into the salons of Paris, this story would not possess the colour of reality. It undoubtedly owes its truth to his alert mind and to his desire to fathom the mysteries of an appalling state of affairs, which was being as carefully concealed by the victim as by those responsible for it.

Above the third floor was a loft for drying laundry, and two attic rooms where the boots, Christophe, and fat Sylvie, the cook, slept.

As well as the seven lodgers in the house Madame Vauquer had, year by year, some eight medical or law students and two or three regular guests who lived in the neighbourhood. These all came for dinner only.

The dining-room seated eighteen at dinner, and at a pinch could hold twenty, but in the morning only seven people gathered round the table, so that breakfast had the air of a family meal. Everyone came down in slippers, and tongues were loosed in the atmosphere of intimacy, and everyone felt free to voice his opinions boldly; confidential remarks were passed about the dress and appearance of the dinner guests and the happenings of the evening before. These seven boarders were Madame Vauquer's spoiled children, and she distributed her attentions and favours among them with an astronomer's precision according to the sum of money each paid.

Chance had brought these persons together, but one consideration influenced them all. The two tenants of the second floor paid only seventy-two francs a month. Only in the Faubourg Saint-Marcel, between La Bourbe and La Salpêtrière, are such prices to be found, and Madame Couture was the only one in Madame Vauquer's house who did not take advantage of them, which makes it clear that excepting her these boarders must be bearing the weight of a more or less manifest poverty. Moreover the depressing spectacle the interior of the house presented was matched by the clothing of its inmates, who were every bit as dilapidated. The men wore coats whose original colour was unimaginable, shoes like those left abandoned in the gutters in smart districts, frayed linen, clothes which were only the shadow of their former selves. The women had old-fashioned dresses, dyed and faded and redyed again, darned old lace, gloves shiny with long use, collars which were always discoloured and frills frayed at the edges. But although their clothes were of such a kind, they nearly all possessed solidly-built bodies, constitutions which had withstood the storms of life. Although their cold, hard faces were worn, like those on coins withdrawn from circulation, their withered mouths were armed with avid teeth. These lodgers made one feel the aura shed by dramas, dramas over and done with or still being acted; not the kind of drama played behind the footlights in front of painted canvas, but living dramas acted in silence, icy dramas which seared the heart, on which no curtain is rung down.

Over her tired eyes Mademoiselle Michonneau, the elderly gentlewoman, wore a dirty, green taffeta shade bound with iron wire, which would have frightened the angel of pity away. Her shawl with its scanty drooping fringe seemed to cover a skeleton, so angular was her body. What acid had consumed the feminine curves of this creature? She must once have been pretty and well-formed. Was it vice, grief, greed? Had she loved too well? Had she been a dealer in second-hand clothing or simply a courtesan? Was she expiating the triumphs of a flaunting youth when the world had run after her to offer pleasure, by an old age shunned by the passer-by? Her blank look chilled the blood, her shrunken face seemed a threat. Her voice had the thin shrill note of a grasshopper, chirping in its thicket at the approach of winter. She said that she had taken care of an old gentleman suffering from catarrh of the bladder, and neglected by his children who believed him to be penniless. This old man had left her a life annuity of a thousand francs. His heirs periodically disputed this legacy, and she had no defence against their slanders. Although the play of passions had ravaged her face, a certain fairness and fineness of texture allowed one to suppose that her body still retained some vestiges of beauty.

Monsieur Poiret was a kind of automaton. He was to be seen moving like a grey shadow along one of the pathways at the Jardin des Plantes, a limp old cap on his head, his stick with the yellow ivory knob barely held in his finger-tips. The crumpled skirts of his frockcoat floating wide revealed breeches much too big for his shrunken thighs, and blue-stockinged legs that wavered like a drunk man's; while above, his waistcoat showed dirty white, and a gap revealed itself between his shirt-frill of coarse, wrinkled muslin and the tie knotted round his turkey-cock's neck. At sight of him many people wondered if this out-landish apparition belonged to the bold race of the sons of Japheth who flutter in the sun on the Boulevard Italien. What toil could have shrivelled him so? What passion had darkened his bulbous face, which would have seemed too exaggerated to be credible in a caricature? What had he been? Perhaps he had been employed in the service of Justice, in the office to which public executioners send in their expense accounts, entering the cost of supplying black veils for parricides, sawdust for the guillotine baskets, cord for the knives. Perhaps he had been a receiver at the door of a slaughter-house, or a sub-inspector in a Sanitary Department. Whatever his occupation, this man appeared to have been one of the drudges of our great social treadmill, one of those Parisian catspaws who do not even know the names of those whose chestnuts they pull out of the fire, some cog in the machine of public business when that business was dirty or unpleasant, one of those men, in short, of whom we say, 'The work can't be done without them, after all.' Elegant Paris knows nothing of their faces, wan with mental or physical suffering. But Paris is an ocean. Throw in the plummet, you will never reach bottom. Survey it; describe it. However conscientious your survey and careful your chart, however numerous and concerned to learn the truth the explorers of this sea may be, there will always be a virgin realm, an unknown cavern, flowers, pearls, monsters, things undreamed of, overlooked by the literary divers. The Maison Vauquer is one of those strange monstrosities.

Two figures formed a striking contrast with the rest of the lodgers and guests of the boarding-house. Although Victorine Taillefer had the unhealthy pallor of young consumptives, and was a part of this picture with its background of common suffering by reason of a habitual sadness, a troubled face, a drooping and fragile air, yet her face and voice were young, her movements active. In her youthful misfortune she was like a young shrub with its leaves turning yellow, when newly transplanted to an adverse soil. Her features, her complexion of a delicate tint that went with the tawny lights in her fair hair, her too slender body, all expressed that charm which modern poets find in mediaeval statuettes. Her grey eyes flecked with black showed a Christian sweetness and resignation. Her simple, inexpensive clothes set off her young figure. She was pretty by contrast with those round her. If she had been happy she would have been enchanting; for happiness makes women's poetry, and style and fashion are just the powder on their skins. If the excitement of a ball had reflected its rosy tints in her pale face, if her slightly hollow cheeks had been rounded and coloured by the amenities of a pleasant mode of living, if love had lit up her sad eyes, Victorine could have borne comparison with the loveliest girls. She lacked what revitalizes a woman, pretty clothes and love-letters. Her story would have furnished matter for a book. Her father believed he had sufficient reason for not acknowledging her, refused to have her near him, allowed her only six hundred francs a year, and he had realized his property in order to disinherit her and leave his whole fortune to his son. Victorine's mother was a distant relative of Madame Couture's and had come to her to die of a broken heart, and since then that lady had looked after the motherless girl as if she had been her own child. Unfortunately the widow of the Commissary-General to the armies of the Republic possessed nothing in the world but her marriage settlement and her pension; some day she might leave this poor girl in poverty and without experience, at the mercy of the world. The good woman took Victorine to mass every Sunday and to confession every fortnight in order to give her at any rate the consolations of religion. In this she was perfectly justified. Religious feeling offered hope for the future to the disowned child, who loved her father and set out every year to bring him her mother's message of forgiveness. Every year she found the way barred, and the door of her father's house inexorably closed against her. Her brother, her only means of communication, had not come once in four years to see her, and sent her no assistance. She prayed to God to unseal her father's eyes and soften her brother's heart, and prayed for them without accusing them. Madame Couture and Madame Vauquer could not find enough words in the dictionary of abuse to qualify the millionaire's barbarous conduct. When they heaped execrations on this infamous father gentle words were heard from Victorine, which sounded like the moan of the wounded dove, whose cry of pain is still the voice of love.

Eugène de Rastignac had a typically southern face, a fair complexion, black hair and blue eyes. In his appearance, manners and habitual bearing it was easy to see the son of a noble family who had been educated first of all in the traditions of good taste. Though he practised economy in his dress and wore out the best clothes of one year on ordinary occasions the next, he was able nevertheless to go out sometimes dressed like an elegant young man. He usually wore an old coat, a shabby waistcoat, with breeches to correspond, the student's wretched, tired, black, badly-knotted tie, and boots that had been resoled.

Between these two persons and the others, Vautrin, the man of forty with the dyed whiskers, stood mid-way. He was the kind of man people call 'A jolly fellow!' He had broad shoulders, a well-developed chest, muscular arms and heavy square hands with a vigorous growth of fiery red hair on the fingers. His prematurely wrinkled face showed signs of a harshness which was contradicted by his affable easy manner. His bass voice was by no means un-pleasing, and his great jovial laugh seemed in keeping with it. He was obliging and genial. If a lock stuck he soon had it taken to pieces, mended, oiled, filed, and put together again, with the remark, 'It's all in my line.' Nothing seemed to be out of his province, moreover. He knew all about ships, the sea, France, foreign parts, business, men, events, the law, great houses and prisons. If anyone grumbled unduly he would immediately offer his services. He had several times lent money to Madame Vauquer and to some of the lodgers, but those he obliged would rather have died than failed to repay him, because of a certain look of his, penetrating and full of determination, which inspired fear in spite of his good-humoured air. The very way in which he spat showed an imperturbable sang-froid which proclaimed him to be a man who would not stick at committing a crime if it offered a way out of a dubious position. His eyes, like a stern judge's, seemed to pierce to the heart of all questions, to probe all con-sciences and examine all feelings.

He was in the habit of going out after breakfast, returning for dinner, disappearing for the whole evening, and letting himself in about midnight with a latch-key which Madame Vauquer had entrusted to him. He was the only lodger to enjoy this mark of favour, but he was on the best of terms with the widow, calling her 'Ma' and putting his arm round her waist. She did not fully appreciate this flattering attention. The good woman thought it was still an easy thing to do, while only Vautrin had arms long enough to encircle her unwieldy circumference. It was character-istic of him to pay extravagantly fifteen francs a month for the coffee with a dash of brandy which he took after dinner.

People less superficial than these young men caught up in the whirl of Parisian life, or these old men indifferent to everything which did not touch them directly, would not have stopped short at the doubtful impression which Vautrin made on them. He knew or guessed the affairs of those round him, while no one could penetrate his thoughts or discover his occupations. Although he had thrown his manifest good-nature, his constant willingness to oblige and his jocularity like a barrier between the others and himself, he often let them catch glimpses through it of the terrifying depths of his character. He often appeared to delight in scoffing at the law, in lashing society and proving its illogicality in an outburst of invective worthy of Juvenal, which seemed to show that he held some grudge against the state, and had in the background of his life a carefully buried secret.

Mademoiselle Taillefer divided her stolen glances and her secret thoughts between this man of forty and the young student, attracted, perhaps unconsciously, by the vigour of the one and the beauty of the other; but neither of them seemed to think of her, although any day chance might change her position and make her wealthy and a desirable match.

Not one of these people, moreover, took the trouble to find out if the tales of misfortune told by the others were true or fictitious. They all felt for each other an indifference mingled with suspicion which was the result of their position relative to one another. They knew themselves powerless to relieve their neighbours' troubles, and in talking them over they had all exhausted their capacity for sympathy. Like long-married couples they no longer had anything to say to each other. There remained no relation between them now other than that made by the superficial contacts of life, the friction of unoiled machinery. They would all walk straight past a blind man in the street without a glance, or listen unmoved to a tale of disaster, and would see in death only the solution of a problem of misery which in their own suffering made them callous to the most terrible sufferings of others.

The happiest of these desolate souls was Madame Vauquer, who reigned over this unofficial asylum. For her alone this little garden, which silence and cold, infertility and damp, made vast and featureless as a steppe, was a smiling grove. For her alone this dark, depressing house which smelt of the verdigris of the counting-house was full of delights. These prison cells belonged to her.

She fed these convicts, admitted for a life term of penal servitude, and exercised an authority over them which they respected. Where else in Paris would these poor creatures have found, at the price for which she offered them, such sufficiently plentiful, wholesome food and a room which they were free to make, if not elegant or comfortable, at any rate clean and healthy? If she had chosen to commit an act of flagrant injustice the victim would have borne it without complaint.

Such a gathering should contain a sample of all the elements that make up society, and this one did so. Among the eighteen guests there was one poor creature despised by all the others, who acted as their butt. There always is such a laughing-stock in every school and in the world itself. At the beginning of his second year in the boarding-house this person became for Eugène de Rastignac the most outstanding figure of all those among whom he was compelled to live for another two years. This long-suffering victim was the retired vermicelli-merchant, on whose head a painter, like the teller of this story, would have made all the light of his picture fall. By what chance had the oldest lodger drawn on him this half-spiteful contempt, this half-pitying persecution, this lack of respect for misfortune? Perhaps he had laid himself open to them by those vagaries and eccentricities which the world forgives less easily than vices? These questions go to the root of many social injustices. Perhaps it is a part of human nature to pile burdens on those who make no protest because of their true humility, their weakness, or their indifference. Do we not all like to prove our strength at the expense of another person or a thing? The puniest specimen of humanity, the brat in the street, knocks at all the doors when the streets are slippery with frost, or climbs up to scribble his name on a virgin monument.

Old Goriot, who was then about sixty-nine years old, had come to live at the Maison Vauquer in 1813, when he retired from business. He had first taken the rooms now occupied by Madame Couture, and paid twelve hundred francs rent for them with the air of a man to whom five louis more or less was a mere trifle.

Madame Vauquer had done up the three rooms for a sum which she had charged him in advance, and which was said to cover the entire cost of the trashy furniture, yellow calico curtains, chairs of varnished wood covered with Utrecht velvet, a few wretched coloured prints and wall-papers that even the suburban pot-houses rejected. Perhaps it was the careless generosity with which he let himself be swindled that made Madame Vauquer consider old Goriot, who at that time was respectfully called Monsieur Goriot, a fool who knew nothing about business.

Goriot came with a well-furnished wardrobe, the excellent outfit of the business-man who denies himself nothing when he comes to shut up shop. Madame Vauquer had opened her eyes at the sight of eighteen cambric shirts whose fineness, moreover, was set off by an ornament the vermicelli-maker was accustomed to wear on his shirt front, two diamond pins linked with a slender chain; the stone each pin was set with was a large one. He usually wore a coat of blue-bottle blue, and every day put on a clean, white piqué waistcoat, across whose broad expanse lay a heavy gold chain with dangling seals, which rose and fell to the movement of the pear-shaped bow-window beneath. His snuff-box, also of gold, contained a locket full of hair, which seemed to prove that he had made several conquests among the ladies. When his hostess accused him of being a breaker of hearts a happy smile hovered on his lips, the smile of the worthy citizen whose vanity is tickled by allusion to a weakness he cherishes.

His cupboards, which he called 'ormoires' like a working man, were full of his household silver. The widow's eyes gleamed when she obligingly helped him to unpack and arrange the soup-ladles, table-spoons, knives and forks, cruet-stands, sauce-boats, various dishes, silver-gilt breakfast services, the more or less handsome pieces weighing a considerable number of ounces which he did not want to part with. These were presents which recalled the festivals of his married life.

'This is the first present my wife ever gave me to celebrate our anniversary,' he said to Madame Vauquer as he put away a saucer and a little silver bowl with two doves billing and cooing on the lid. 'Poor dear! She spent all the money she had saved before our marriage on it. Do you know, Madame, I would rather scratch the earth for a living with my nails than part with it. Thank God I can take my coffee in this bowl every morning for the rest of my life! I am not to be pitied. I have enough to keep the wolf from the door for many a day.'

Moreover Madame Vauquer with her magpie's eye had seen some entries in black and white in the list of shareholders in the funds which at a rough estimate credited this excellent Goriot with an income of some eight to ten thousand francs. From that day Madame Vauquer, *née* de Conflans, who was then forty-eight years old and owned to thirty-nine of them, had certain ideas in her head. Although Goriot's tear-ducts were everted and swollen and drooping, and he was obliged to keep on wiping his eyes, she thought him a nice gentlemanly man. She deduced moral qualities which she appeared to prize, too, from his large, fleshy calf and his long square nose, and these indications of character were confirmed by the old fellow's moon-like and foolishly simple face. This must be a solidly-built animal with little intelligence, but with a capacity for whole-hearted affection. His hair, which the hairdresser from the École Polytechnique came to powder every morning, was brushed into 'pigeon's wings' and lay in five points on his low forehead, framing his face becomingly. Although a little uncouth he was so spick and span, he took his snuff so luxuriously, inhaled it with such an air of certainty of always having his snuffbox full of *macouba*, that Madame Vauquer went to her bed in the evening of the day that saw him installed in her house, roasting like a partridge under its bacon over the fire of desire to abandon Vauquer's shroud and be born again as a Goriot. She would marry again, sell her boarding-house, walk arm in arm with this fine flower of the bourgeoisie, become a lady of importance in the district, make collections for the poor, plan little parties on Sundays for excursions to Choisy, Soissy, Gentilly, have a box at the theatre and go there at her own sweet

44

will, without waiting for the complimentary tickets which her lodgers sometimes gave her in July; she dreamed all the Eldorado of the Parisian housewife condemned to petty economies. She had told nobody that she herself possessed forty thousand francs accumulated sou by sou. Certainly as far as money was concerned she was a fitting match for him. 'As for anything else, I'm as good as he is!' she said to herself, turning over in her bed as if to assure herself of the charms of the form whose impression fat Sylvie found every morning in humps and hollows among the feathers.

From that day forward for nearly three months the widow Vauquer made use of the services of Monsieur Goriot's hairdresser and expended some money on her personal adornment, an extravagance which she excused by the necessity of giving her establishment a proper appearance in keeping with the respectable people who patronized it. She sought every excuse for weeding out her boarders and proclaimed her intention of accepting from that time on only people who were very distinguished in every respect. If a stranger presented himself she boasted of the preference which Monsieur Goriot, one of the best-known and most respected merchants of Paris, had shown for her house. She distributed prospectuses headed MAISON VAUQUER in print of the largest size. It was, she said, a long-established family boarding-house, one of the oldest and most highly recommended in the Latin Quarter. It had an exquisite view commanding the Vallée des Gobelins (which could indeed be seen from the third floor), and a *delightful* garden at the far end of which there STRETCHED an *AVENUE* of lindens. Reference was made to the good air and the quiet situation.

This prospectus brought her Madame la Comtesse de l'Ambermesnil, a widow of thirty-six, who was waiting for the winding up of her husband's estate and the allocation to her of a pension which was her due as the wife of a general who had died 'on the field of battle.' Madame Vauquer now looked to her table, lighted a fire in the sitting-room daily for nearly six months, and gave so much substance to the promises of her prospectus as to make inroads in her purse. The Countess told her too, calling her 'my dear friend', that she would get two new boarders for her, the Baronne de Vaumerland and the widow of a colonel, le Comte Picquoiseau. These were two of her friends who were just about to leave a boarding-house in the Marais much more expensive than the Maison Vauquer. These ladies would be very comfortably off, moreover, when the War Office had finished its formalities. 'But,' as she said, 'Government Departments never do come to an end of their red tape.'

The two widows used to go together after dinner to Madame Vauquer's room and enjoy a cosy little chat as they drank currant wine and ate delicacies reserved for the pleasure of the mistress of the house. Madame de l'Ambermesnil cordially approved of her hostess's ideas about Goriot; she said the scheme was an excellent notion, and declared that for that matter she had guessed it from the very first day; in her opinion Goriot was a model man.

'Ah! my dear lady, such a well-preserved man, as sound as my eye,' said the widow, 'he's a man who could still make a wife very happy.'

The Countess was good enough to make some remarks to Madame Vauquer about her dress, which was not in keeping with her aspirations. 'We must put you on a war footing,' she told her.

After a good deal of serious consideration the two widows went together to the Palais-Royal where they bought a feathered hat and a cap in the Galeries de Bois. The Countess next took her friend to the shop of *La Petite Jeannette* where they chose a dress and a scarf. When these weapons were in use and the widow under arms she looked exactly like the prize animal on the signboard of the *Bœuf à la Mode* eating-house, yet in her own eyes she was so changed for the better that she felt she owed the Countess something and, although she was not by nature very open-handed, begged her to accept a hat costing twenty francs. The fact was that she intended asking the Countess for further services; the Countess must sound Goriot and sing Madame Vauquer's praises to him. Madame de l'Ambermesnil lent herself

46

very amiably to this plot. She laid siege to the old vermicelli-maker, and succeeded in obtaining an interview with him. But when she found that her overtures, prompted by her private desire to secure him for herself, were received with embarrassment, not to say repulsion, she left him, revolted by his coarseness.

'My angel,' she said to her dear friend, 'you will never make anything of that man! He is ridiculously suspicious. He's a mean old miser, a blockhead, an old fool. He will bring you nothing but vexation!'

Such things lay between Monsieur Goriot and Madame de l'Ambermesnil that the Countess could not bear to be under the same roof with him any longer. The next day she left, forgetting to pay six months' rent and leaving behind cast-off clothes worth five francs. Inquire as she might, however bitterly and persistently, Madame Vauquer could obtain no news in Paris of the Countess de l'Ambermesnil.

The widow often spoke of this deplorable affair, blaming herself for her unsuspicious nature, although she was more mistrustful than a cat; but she was like many people who are on their guard against those nearest to them and blindly confide in the first stranger that comes along. This is a queer phenomenon but one often met with, whose origin it is easy to discover in the human heart. Perhaps certain people have nothing more to hope for from those they live with; having shown their friends the emptiness of their hearts they feel themselves judged with a severity which they deserve; but they still feel an unconquerable need for respect and admiration, or it may be they are consumed by anxiety to appear to possess the qualities they are lacking in, and so they fix their hopes on capturing the liking and regard of strangers even at the risk of forfeiting them later. Again there are other individuals who are born mercenary, who will do no kindness to their friends or relatives because these people have a claim upon them, while if they render a service to strangers they gain in self-esteem: the closer their friends are to them the less they like them, and the wider the circle of their acquaintance the more obliging they are to the members on its remoter fringes. Madame Vauquer had no doubt something in common with both these types, both essentially mean, false and detestable.

'If I had been here then,' Vautrin used to say at the end of the story, 'that bother would never have happened! I would soon have torn the mask off that joker. I know those people by their phiz.'

Like all narrow-minded persons Madame Vauquer was un-accustomed to consider why events happen; she concentrated her attention on the events themselves. Also it was her way to throw the responsibility for her own mistakes on others. When she incurred this loss she regarded the honest vermicelli-maker as the cause and origin of her misfortune and began then, as she put it, to lose her illusions about him. When she realized the uselessness of her blandishments and that the money she had spent on her adornment had been thrown away, she was not slow to guess the reason. She realized then that her lodger had already, according to her expression, 'some other attraction.' In short, it was brought home to her that the hope so tenderly cherished was just an idle dream, and that she would never 'make anything of that man,' to use the forceful phrase of the Countess, who appeared to have been a judge of character. Of necessity she went further in aversion than she had gone in love, for her hatred was not in proportion to her love but to her disappointed hopes. Though the human heart may have to pause for rest when climbing the heights of affection it rarely stops on the slippery slope of hatred. But Monsieur Goriot was her lodger and so the widow was obliged to smother the explosions of her wounded pride, stifle the sighs which this disappointment cost her, and swallow her desire for revenge, like a monk plagued by his prior.

Petty minds find vent for their feelings, benevolent or the reverse, in innumerable petty deeds. The widow set her feminine malice to work to devise covert ways of persecuting her victim. She began by cutting off the additional delicacies she had introduced to her table.

'No more gherkins, no more anchovies; they're a regular take-in!' she said to Sylvie one morning, and she returned to her old bill of fare.

Monsieur Goriot was a frugal man. The parsimony which people who have to make their own way in the world are obliged to practise had become a habit with him. Soup, boiled beef, a dish of vegetables had been and would always be his chosen dinner, so it was very difficult for Madame Vauquer to vex her lodger when she could not cross his tastes in anything. Despairing of ever showing her hostility to this unassailable man she set herself to belittle and discredit him, and so induced her lodgers to share her aversion to Goriot and made them the instruments of her revenge, which they carried out unwittingly, by way of amusing themselves.

Towards the end of the first year the widow's distrust of Goriot had risen to such a pitch that she asked herself why this wealthy merchant, owning an income of seven or eight thousand livres, a magnificent collection of silver, and jewels as fine as those of a kept woman, should live in her house and pay her a rent so disproportionately small.

During the greater part of this first year Goriot had often dined out once or twice a week; then he began to do so less and less frequently until at last he had dinner in town not more often than twice a month. These little private outings of Goriot's suited Madame Vauquer's interests too well for her not to be annoyed by the more and more frequent presence of her lodger at meals in the boarding-house. The change in his habits was attributed by his hostess not so much to a gradual diminution of his income as to a desire to vex her, for it is one of the most detestable habits of Lilliputian minds to suppose that others are equally petty.

Unfortunately for his reputation, towards the end of the second year Monsieur Goriot gave some colour to the gossip about him by asking Madame Vauquer if he might move to the second floor, and so reduce his board and lodging to nine hundred francs. His need to economize was so pressing that he did without a fire all through the winter. The widow Vauquer demanded payment in advance, and Monsieur Goriot agreed to this. From that day she called him 'Old Goriot.'

It was for anyone to guess the causes of this decline and downfall, but it was difficult to investigate. As the sham Countess had said, old Goriot was a secretive old devil and kept his mouth shut. According to the logic of empty-headed people, who are all indiscreet because they have no thoughts worth keeping to themselves, those who do not talk about their business must have good, or rather bad, reasons for it; so the merchant formerly thought so distinguished was now called a scoundrel, the gallant beau was an old scamp. Opinion about him varied. Sometimes, according to Vautrin, who came to live in the boarding-house about this time, old Goriot was a man who went to the Stock Exchange and *stagged*, as they call it picturesquely in financial circles, having previously ruined himself by speculation. Sometimes he was held to be one of those minor gamblers who try their luck every evening in the hope of winning about ten francs. Sometimes they decided he was a spy employed by the Home Office, but Vautrin did not think him sharp enough to be 'one of that crew.' Other theories were that he was a miser who lent money for short terms at enormous rates, or a man who lived by selling lottery tickets. In their eyes he was the essence of the mysterious underworld, the product of vice and shame and weakness. Yet however disgraceful his life might be, the repulsion they felt was not so strong as to compel them to have him evicted: after all he paid his rent. Then he had his uses too, as someone to snap at if they felt irritable, or try their wit on if they were in a good temper.

The theory which seemed most likely and which was generally adopted was Madame Vauquer's. According to her this man whom she had thought so well-preserved, as sound as her eye, who might have made any woman happy as his wife, was a libertine with strange tastes. These are the facts upon which she based her slanders.

Some months before the departure of that catastrophic Countess who had been smart enough to live for six months at her expense, the widow had heard one morning on the stairs, while she was still in bed, the rustle of a silk dress and the light step of a young and active woman who was slipping into Goriot's room, whose door stood conspiratorially ajar. Fat Sylvie came at once to tell her mistress that a girl too pretty to be good, 'dressed as fine as a goddess', wearing laced prunella boots without a speck of mud on them, had slid like an eel out of the street into her kitchen and asked for Monsieur Goriot's room. Madame Vauquer and her cook set themselves to listen and overheard several words affectionately spoken during this visit, which lasted for a considerable time. When Monsieur Goriot came out with 'his lady', fat Sylvie immediately seized her basket and pretended she was going to market in order to follow the loving pair.

'Oh, Madame!' she said to her mistress when she returned, 'Monsieur Goriot must have the devil's own money-bags, all the same, to keep them in such style. Only fancy! there was a splendid carriage waiting at the corner of the Estrapade, and *she* got into it.'

During dinner that evening Madame Vauquer went to the window and drew a curtain for Goriot's benefit, as the sun was shining in his eyes.

'You are pursued by beauty, Monsieur Goriot; even the sun seeks you out,' she said, alluding to the visit he had received. 'Well, bless me, you have good taste, she was very pretty.'

'That was my daughter,' he said with a kind of pride into which the boarders read the fatuous desire of an old man to save his face.

A month after this visit Monsieur Goriot received another. His daughter who had come the first time in a morning dress, came this time after dinner and dressed to go out. The boarders who were sitting talking in the sitting-room could see that she was a pretty slender blonde, graceful and much too distinguished-looking to be the daughter of a man like old Goriot.

'That makes two of them!' said fat Sylvie, who did not recognize her.

Some days later another girl, a tall and shapely brunette with dark hair and a lively eye, asked to see Monsieur Goriot.

'That's three!' said Sylvie.

This second girl, who had also come to see her father in the morning the first time, came again a few days afterwards in a carriage, dressed for a ball.

'Four of them!' said Madame Vauquer and fat Sylvie, who found no trace of the simply-dressed girl they had seen before in this fine lady.

Goriot was still paying twelve hundred francs at this time, and Madame Vauquer thought it quite natural that a rich man should have four or five mistresses: she even thought him very clever to pass them off as his daughters. She did not take exception to his inviting them to the Maison Vauquer, but seeing that these visits explained her lodger's indifference to her, from the beginning of the second year she went so far as to speak of him as 'a disgusting old man'; and when at length Goriot was paying her no more than nine hundred francs she asked him very insolently one day, as she saw him show out one of these ladies, what he took her house to be. Old Goriot replied that the lady was his elder daughter.

'You've three dozen of these daughters, have you?' said Madame Vauquer disagreeably.

'I have only two,' her lodger answered with the meekness of a ruined man who has reached the point of submission to all the humiliations that poverty heaps on him.

Towards the end of the third year old Goriot reduced his expenses still further, moving to the third floor where he paid forty-five francs a month. He did without tobacco, dismissed his hair-dresser, and used no more powder on his hair. When Goriot appeared for the first time without powder his hostess let an exclamation of astonishment escape her when she saw the dingy greenish-grey colour of his hair. His face, which some hidden sorrow had gradually made sadder day by day, seemed the most woebegone of all those round the table.

There could no longer be any doubt about it then: old Goriot was an old rake, and only a doctor's skill had saved his sight from destruction by the drugs whose use was made necessary by his diseases: the disgusting colour of his hair was due to his excesses, and to drugs he had taken in order to be able to continue them. The poor old man's physical and mental state gave some grounds for supposing that these absurd stories might be true. When his stock of clothes was worn out he bought calico at fourteen sous per ell to replace his fine linen. His diamonds, gold snuffbox, his chain and personal ornaments disappeared one by one. He had left off his bright blue coat and his whole prosperous-looking outfit, and summer and winter wore an overcoat of coarse chestnut-coloured cloth, a mohair waistcoat, and thick, grey, closely-woven woollen breeches. He grew thinner and thinner; his calves were shrunken; his face, once round and beaming with the contentment of a prosperous tradesman, became unusually lined; his forehead grew wrinkled, his jaw prominent. In the fourth year of his life in the Rue Neuve-Sainte-Geneviève he was no longer the same man. The good vermicelli-maker who used to look only forty instead of sixty-two, the stout comfortable tradesman, whose face was almost comical in its unsophisticated freshness, whose sprightly bearing had amused and diverted strangers who chanced to meet him in the street, whose smile was still young, now seemed at least seventy, and stupid, dull and uncertain. His blue eyes, formerly so lively, seemed to have turned a sad leaden grey; they had faded and dried up and their red rims seemed to ooze blood. People either pitied him or were shocked by him. Young medical students noticing the drooping of his lower lip and the conformation of his facial angle, when they had teased him for some time without drawing any response, declared him to be declining into cretinism.

One day, after dinner, when Madame Vauquer said to him banteringly, implying doubt of his paternal relationship, 'Well, so those daughters of yours don't come to see you any more now?' Goriot winced as if she had pricked him with a sword-point.

'They come sometimes,' he replied in a shaking voice.

'Oh! Oh! Do you still see them sometimes?' cried the students. 'Bravo, Papa Goriot!'

But the old man did not hear the witticisms at his expense that his reply provoked; he had fallen back into a dreamy state that superficial observers took for a senile stupor, due to his lack of intelligence. If they had only known they would perhaps have been keenly interested in the problem his physical and moral situation presented, but this was extremely obscure. Although it would have been easy enough to find out if Goriot had really manufactured vermicelli and what the exact figure of his fortune was, the old people who were inquisitive about him never left the district and lived in the boarding-house like oysters on a rock. As for the others, when they turned the corner of the Rue Neuve-Sainte-Geneviève they were caught up in the peculiar vortex of Parisian life, and did not spare a thought for the poor old man who was their butt. To the narrow-minded older people as to the heedless young, old Goriot's dumb misery and his stupid apathy were incompatible with the possession of wealth or of any kind of intellectual capacity. As for the women that he called his daughters, everyone shared the views of Madame Vauquer, who said with that strict logic which elderly women who spend all their evenings gossiping acquire through their habit of always finding an answer to fit every question, 'If old Goriot had daughters as rich as all the ladies who came to see him appeared to be, he would not be in my house, on the third floor, paying forty-five francs a month, and he would not be going about dressed like a beggar.'

These conclusions could not be gainsaid. And so towards the end of November 1819, at the time when the curtain rose on this drama, everyone in the boarding-house had very clear ideas about the old man. He had never had either a daughter or a wife;

a life of excesses had made a slug of him, an anthropomorphous mollusc to be classified among the *clothcapifers*, so said an official of the Muséum, one of Madame Vauquer's daily guests with a pretty wit of his own. Poiret was an eagle, a gentleman compared with Goriot: Poiret could talk and use his reason and answer when spoken to. As a matter of fact he never contributed anything to the subject under discussion when he talked or used his reason or replied, for it was his habit to repeat what the others said in other words; but he joined in the conversation, he was alive, he appeared responsive to his surroundings, while Goriot, so said this official, was constantly at o degrees Réaumur.

Eugène de Rastignac had returned to Paris at this time, in a frame of mind common enough in young men conscious of abilities above the average, or stimulated by difficult circumstances to outstrip their fellows for a time.

So little work is required of law-students for their preliminary examinations that in his first year in Paris Eugène had been free to see the sights and taste the pleasures of the city. A student, indeed, has little time to spare if he wants to become acquainted with the entire repertoire of every theatre, map the windings of the Parisian labyrinth, become a citizen of the capital with a knowledge of its usages, its language and its peculiar pleasures, and explore its every nook and corner of good or bad repute, while following the courses of lectures that please him and taking stock of the treasures piled up in museums.

At this stage in his career a student is on fire with enthusiasm for moonshine which appears magnificent to him. He has his hero, his great man, a professor at the Collège de France paid to adapt himself to the mental level of his audience. He adjusts his cravat and poses for the benefit of the women in the first galleries at the Opéra-Comique. Passing through one initiation after another he gradually loses his greenness, life's horizons expand before his eyes; and in the end he achieves some perception of how human beings are packed in strata, layer above layer, in the framework of society. If he has begun by admiring the carriages parading the Champs-Élysées on a sunny afternoon, he soon starts to covet them.

Eugène had reached this stage in the unconscious apprenticeship he was serving, when he left Paris for the long vacation after taking his degrees as Bachelor of Arts and Bachelor of Law. His childish illusions, his provincial ideas, had gone. His increased knowledge, his kindled ambition, had opened his eyes, so that once he was back in the manor-house in the family circle he saw things clearly as they were. His father, mother, two sisters and two brothers, and an aunt whose whole fortune consisted of annuities, all lived on the little estate of Rastignac. The income, about three thousand francs, from this property varied according to the varying price offered for the vine-crop, yet every year twelve hundred francs had to be drawn from it for him. Eugène noted the constant worry about money, which his family had generously concealed from him. He could not help comparing his sisters, who had seemed so lovely to him in his childhood, with the women of Paris, who had realized the beauty he had dreamed of. He was conscious that the uncertain future of this large family depended upon him. He watched the parsimony with which every crumb was hoarded, and saw the family drink wine made from the lees of the wine-press. In sum, a multitude of circumstances it is unnecessary to detail here made him long to distinguish himself, and his ambition to succeed increased tenfold.

Like all great minds Eugène wished to owe his success to nothing but his own merit. But his temperament was preeminently southern; so that when he came to carry them out his resolutions were bound to be affected by the hesitations that seize young people when they find themselves on the open sea, anxious to exert their strength but not knowing in which direction to steer, nor how to trim their sail to catch the wind. If at first he wanted to throw himself heart and soul into work he was soon diverted from this purpose by the necessity of acquiring social connections. Then he realized how much influence women have in social life, and suddenly made up his mind to strike out into the world to win patronesses for himself. How could they fail an eager and idealistic young man, whose ardour and wit were set off by an elegant appearance and a kind of vigorous beauty by which women are very readily attracted? These ideas assailed him in the fields, during the walks which he had formerly taken so gaily with his sisters, who now found him greatly changed.

His aunt, Madame de Marcillac, had been presented at Court and had there become acquainted with the highest in the land. Suddenly the ambitious young man recognized in the reminiscences with which his aunt had so often lulled him to sleep in nursery days, the elements of several social successes at least as important as the success that was his goal at the School of Law. He questioned her about relatives whose acquaintance might be claimed again. When she had shaken the branches of the genealogical tree the old lady judged that of all the persons who might be of use to her nephew among the selfish tribe of rich relations, Madame la Vicomtesse de Beauséant would be the most amenable. She wrote a letter in the old style to this young woman and entrusted it to Eugène, telling him that if he had a success with the Viscountess she would introduce him to his other relatives. A few days after his return to Paris, Rastignac sent his aunt's letter to Madame de Beauséant. The Viscountess replied with an invitation to a ball on the following evening.

Such was the general situation in the boarding-house at the end of November 1819.

Some days later Eugène, having gone to Madame de Beauséant's ball, came in about two in the morning. As he danced, this stout-hearted student had promised himself to make up for the time he had lost by working until daylight. He was going to remain awake all night for the first time in that silent quarter, for the sight of the splendours of society had magically given him a burst of artificial energy. He had not dined at the boarding-house: the lodgers would probably think that he would walk back from the ball at daybreak as he had sometimes done after a fête at the Prado or a ball at the Odéon, getting his silk stockings muddy on the way, and ruining his pumps.

Before bolting the door Christophe had opened it to look out into the street. Rastignac happened to arrive at this moment and was able to go up to his room without making any noise, followed by Christophe who was making a great deal. Eugène undressed, put on his slippers and an old coat, lit his turf fire, and prepared himself for work so rapidly that the clatter of Christophe's big boots drowned the very slight noise of his preparations.

Eugène sat absorbed in thought for several minutes before plunging into his law books.

He had just become aware that Madame la Vicomtesse de Beauséant was one of the queens of fashionable Paris, and that her house was known as the pleasantest in the Faubourg Saint-Germain. She was, moreover, by reason of her name and her fortune, one of the outstanding persons of the aristocratic world. Thanks to his Aunt de Marcillac the poor student had been kindly received in this house, before he had realized what a favour this was. To be admitted to these gilded salons was equivalent to being awarded a patent of nobility. By his appearance in this most exclusive of circles he had gained the right of admission everywhere.

Eugène had been dazzled by the brilliant assembly, and had scarcely exchanged a few words with the Viscountess. He had contented himself with singling out from among the crowd of Parisian goddesses with which this rout was packed, one of those women at whose feet a young man must fall from the very first. The Countess Anastasie de Restaud was reputed to have the prettiest figure in Paris; she was tall and gracefully made. Imagine great dark eyes, a beautiful hand, a finely-modelled foot, and movements full of fire and spirit, a woman that the Marquis de Ronquerolles called 'a thoroughbred'. Her highly-strung temperament had no complementary defect; she was well-developed and rounded, without anyone being able to accuse her of being too plump. 'Thoroughbred', 'woman of breeding', these locutions were beginning to take the place of the 'heavenly angels', the Ossianic figures of speech, all the old erotic mythology which dandies no longer affect. But for Rastignac, Madame Anastasie de Restaud was the woman longed for. He had contrived to write his name twice in the list of partners on her fan, and managed to snatch a few words with her during the first quadrille.

'Where can I see you again, Madame?' he said abruptly, with the passionate insistence that women find so flattering.

'Oh, anywhere,' she answered, 'in the Bois, at the Bouffons, in my own house.'

And the adventurous Southerner had done all he could to put himself on a footing of intimacy with this enchanting Countess, so far as a young man can cultivate a woman's acquaintance during a square dance and a waltz. When he told her that he was a cousin of Madame de Beauséant's, this great lady, as he took her to be, was prepared to receive him, and he was invited to her house; and the parting smile she threw him made him think that to call on her was a social duty.

He had had the good fortune to light upon a man who did not laugh at his ignorance, an unpardonable crime to the gilded young coxcombs of the day, men like Maulincourt, Ronquerolles, Maxime de Trailles, de Marsay, Ajuda-Pinto, Vandenesse, who were there in all the glory and pride of their dandyism, mingling with the most elegant ladies of fashion – Lady Brandon, the Duchesse de Langeais, the Comtesse de Kergarouët, Madame de Sérizy, the Duchesse de Carigliano, the Comtesse Féraud, Madame de Lanty, the Marquise d'Aiglemont, Madame Firmiani, the Marquise de Listomère and the Marquise d'Espard, the Duchesse de Maufrigneuse and the Grandlieus. It was lucky for him, then, that the green student happened upon the Marquis de Montriveau, the Duchesse de Langeais' lover, a general as simple as a child, from whom he learned that the Comtesse de Restaud lived in the Rue du Helder.

What joy it was to be young, athirst for the world and on fire for a woman, and to see two great houses open their doors to him! To plant a foot in the Faubourg Saint-Germain in the house of the Vicomtesse de Beauséant, and fall on his knees before the Comtesse de Restaud in the Chaussée d'Antin! To see before him a vista of all the salons of Paris, and to believe himself a fine enough fellow to find aid and protection there in a woman's heart! To feel himself ambitious enough to spurn the tight-rope along which he must walk with the self-assurance of the acrobat who cannot fall, and to have found in a charming woman the best of balancing-poles! With such thoughts in his head and a vision of this woman rising magnificent beside a fire of peat, between the Law on one side and Poverty on the other, who would not, like Eugène, have thrown an eager glance into the future, and decked it with success? His wandering fancy was anticipating his future joys so fast that he was dreaming himself by Madame de Restaud's side, when a sigh like the grunt of an overtasked Saint Joseph disturbed the silence of the night, and echoed in the young man's heart with an anguish which made him take it for the groan of a dying man. He opened his door softly and in the passage saw a line of light under old Goriot's door.

Eugène was afraid his neighbour must be ill. He put his eye to the keyhole, looked into the room, and saw the old man engaged in work of so criminal a nature that it was obviously his duty to society to investigate what the so-called vermicelli-manufacturer was up to in the night. Old Goriot had attached a silver-gilt saucer and vessel like a soup-tureen to the cross-bar of a table turned upside-down before him, and was twisting a thick rope round the richly-chased metal with such terrific force that he was bending it, apparently into the shape of ingots.

'Heavens! What a man!' said Rastignac to himself, watching the old man's muscular arm as with the help of the rope he noiselessly kneaded the silver as if it had been dough. Was he a thief or a receiver, then, who was feigning helplessness and stupidity and living like a beggar in order to carry on his traffic more securely? The student raised his head for a moment as he asked himself this, and then applied his eye to the keyhole again. Old Goriot had unwound his rope and spread his counterpane on the table. Now he took the flattened mass of silver and rolled it on the table to shape it into a bar, an operation which he performed with astonishing ease.

'He must be as strong as Augustus, King of Poland!' Eugène said to himself when the bar was almost finished.

Old Goriot looked at his handiwork sadly, with tears running down his cheeks. He blew out the wax taper which had lighted him at his task, and Eugène heard him groan as he got into bed.

'He's mad,' thought the student.

'Poor child!' said old Goriot aloud.

When he heard this Rastignac judged it prudent to keep this incident dark, and not condemn his neighbour too hastily. He was about to return to his own room when he suddenly heard an indescribable sort of noise, as if men in list slippers were coming upstairs. Eugène strained his ears, and did in fact make out the sound of two men breathing. He had not heard the door squeak or any footsteps, yet all at once he saw a dim light glimmer on the second floor, in Monsieur Vautrin's room.

'Queer goings-on for a family boarding-house!' he said to himself.

He went down several steps and listened intently, and caught the clink of money. Soon the light was extinguished, breathing was audible once more, without the door having been heard to open. Then the sound died away as the two men went downstairs.

'Who's there?' cried Madame Vauquer, opening her bedroom window.

'It's me, coming in, Mamma Vauquer,' said Vautrin in his deep voice.

'That's odd. Christophe bolted the door,' said Eugène to himself, as he went back to his room. 'In Paris you need to keep your eyes open at night to know what's going on around you.'

Distracted from his ambitious lover's dreams by these events he set himself to work, but his thoughts strayed to suspicions about old Goriot, and still more persistently to Madame de Restaud's face, which kept rising before him as the herald of a brilliant destiny. In the end he went to bed and slept with clenched fists. Out of ten nights dedicated to work by young men, seven are spent in sleep. One has to be older than twenty to stay awake all night.

Next morning Paris was wrapped in one of the dense fogs that envelop it sometimes and make it so dark that the most precise and punctual people are led astray. Business appointments are missed. Everyone thinks it is about eight o'clock when midday is striking.

It was half-past nine, and Madame Vauquer had not yet stirred from her bed. Christophe and fat Sylvie, also later than usual, were tranquilly taking their coffee, made with the top layer skimmed from the milk meant for the lodgers, whose share Sylvie was boiling well so that Madame Vauquer should not notice that this illegal tithe had been abstracted.

'Sylvie,' said Christophe, dipping his first piece of toast into his coffee, 'Monsieur Vautrin had two people here to see him last night again. If Madame asks about it mind you say nothing to her. He really isn't a bad sort, you know.'

'Did he give you anything?'

'He gave me one hundred sous for the month, one way of saying, "Keep your mouth shut".'

'Him and Madame Couture are the only ones who don't look twice at every penny. The others would all like to take away with one hand what they give us with the other on New Year's Day,' said Sylvie.

'And what do they give us?' said Christophe. 'A beggarly hundred sous! Old Goriot has cleaned his shoes himself for the last two years. Poiret's a miserly curmudgeon who does without cleaning altogether, he would rather drink the blacking than put it on his down-at-heel old shoes. As for that whippersnapper of a student, he gives me forty sous. Forty sous doesn't pay for my brushes, and he sells his old clothes into the bargain. What a hole this place is!'

'Nonsense!' said Sylvie, sipping her coffee, 'we're not so badly off. We have the best places round here that I know of. But what about that big fellow Vautrin, Christophe? Did anyone say anything about him?'

'Yes. I met a gentleman in the street a few days ago who asked me about him. He said, "Haven't you got a tall gentleman who dyes his whiskers staying in your place?" I said, "No, sir, he doesn't dye them. A gay spark like him hasn't the time." And when I told Monsieur Vautrin about it he said, "You were quite right, my lad! That's the way to answer them. There's nothing more annoying than letting other people know your weak points. It can spoil your chances of a good match".'

'They tried to pump me too in the market. They wanted to know if I ever saw him put his shirt on. What tomfoolery! – Goodness,' she interrupted herself, 'that's a quarter to ten striking at the Val-de-Grâce and nobody stirring!'

'What does it matter? They've all gone out. Madame Couture and her young lady went to mass at Saint-Étienne at eight o'clock. Old Goriot started off somewhere with a parcel. The student won't be back until his lecture is over at ten o'clock. I saw them all go when I was doing my stairs, and old Goriot gave me a slap with what he was carrying, something hard like iron. What do you make of the old codger? The others can't let him alone, they treat him like he was their plaything, but he's a decent soul all the same and worth more than all the lot of them put together. He doesn't give much himself, but the ladies he sends me to sometimes are dressed very fine and hand out grand tips.'

'The ones he calls his daughters, do you mean? There's a dozen of them.'

'I have only been sent to two. The same ones who came here.'

'There is Madame moving; she's going to kick up a fine shindy. I'd better go. You watch the milk, Christophe; mind the cat.'

Sylvie went upstairs to her mistress.

'How's this, Sylvie! A quarter to ten! You have let me sleep on like a dormouse! I've never heard of such a thing!'

'It's because of the fog. It's that thick you could cut it with a knife.'

'But what about breakfast?'

'Bah! the devil is in your lodgers to-day; they all cleared out at cockerel-crow.'

'Speak properly, Sylvie,' scolded Madame Vauquer, 'you should say "cock-crow".'

'I'll say whatever you like, Madame, but the fact remains that you can have your breakfast at ten o'clock. The Michonnette and Poireau pair haven't budged. They are the only ones in the house, and they're sleeping like logs.'

'But Sylvie, you talk of them as a pair, as if – '

'As if what?' asked Sylvie, bursting out into a loud silly laugh, 'They're a well-matched couple.'

'It's queer, Sylvie, how did Monsieur Vautrin get in last night after Christophe had bolted the door?'

'Not in the least queer. He heard Monsieur Vautrin and went down to open the door for him. And here was you thinking – '

'Give me my bodice and run and look after the breakfast. Dish up what's left of the mutton with potatoes, and you can put the stewed pears on the table, those that cost a farthing each.'

A few minutes later Madame Vauquer came downstairs, just at the moment when the cat had tipped over the plate covering a bowl of milk and was lapping away at full speed.

'Mistigris!' she cried.

The cat fled, and then came back to rub itself against her legs.

'It's all very well to look as if butter wouldn't melt in your mouth, you old humbug. Sylvie! Sylvie!'

'What's the matter now, Madame?'

'Just look what the cat's done.'

'It's that stupid Christophe's fault. I told him to lay the table.

Where has he gone to? – Don't worry, Madame, we'll make old Goriot's coffee out of this. I'll put water in it. He'll never notice. He never notices nothing, not even what he's eating.'

'Where has the old heathen gone to, I wonder?' said Madame Vauquer as she set the plates round the table.

'Who knows? He's up to all sorts of devilment.'

'I have over-slept myself,' said Madame Vauquer.

'But Madame looks as fresh as a rose –'

At this moment they heard the bell ring, and Vautrin came into the room, singing in his loud voice:

> 'I've roamed the world for years around
> No matter what my luck might be –'

'Oh! hullo, Ma Vauquer! good morning!' he called out at the sight of his hostess, putting his arms gallantly around her.

'Now, now, that's enough –'

' "You naughty man!" Go on, say it. Wasn't that what you were going to say? Hold on a minute, I'll help you lay the table. Oh! what a nice man I am. Don't you think so?

> 'With dark and blonde, I've always found
> In love –

'I've just seen something very funny –

> ' – they're all alike to me.'

'What?' asked the widow.

'Old Goriot in the Rue Dauphine at half-past eight this morning, at a jeweller's where they buy old plate and gold lace. He sold them a piece of silver plate, a nice piece of work for someone not in the trade, and got a good sum of money for it.'

'Not really?'

'Yes indeed. I was coming back here after seeing off one of my friends who was going abroad by Royal Mail steamer. I waited for old Goriot, to see what would happen. It's a good joke. He came back to this part of the world, to the Rue des Grès, the house of a well-known money-lender called Gobseck, a bad egg, capable of making dominoes out of his father's bones, a Jew, an Arab, a Turk, a scalawag, whatever you like to call him. It would be a hard job to rob *him*; he puts his pennies in the Bank.'

'What in the world can old Goriot be doing?'

'Doing nothing,' said Vautrin, 'contriving his own undoing. He's a madman, fool enough to ruin himself for the sake of girls who –'

'Here he is!' said Sylvie.

'Christophe,' called old Goriot, 'come upstairs with me.'

Christophe followed old Goriot, and then reappeared almost immediately.

'Where are you going?' Madame Vauquer asked her servant.

'On an errand for Monsieur Goriot.'

'What have you got there?' said Vautrin, pouncing on a letter in Christophe's hand and reading aloud, ' "Madame la Comtesse Anastasie de Restaud." And where are you taking it?' he added as he gave the letter back.

'To the Rue du Helder. I have to give it to nobody but the Countess.'

'What's inside it?' said Vautrin, holding the letter up against the light. 'A bank-note?' He peered into the envelope. 'No, a receipted account. My word! he's a gallant man, the old dotard! You get along now, you rascal,' he said to Christophe, giving him a cuff on the head with his big hand that made him spin round. 'You are sure to be given a fine tip.'

By this time the table was laid. Sylvie was boiling the milk. Madame Vauquer lit the stove with some aid from Vautrin, who was still humming to himself:

> I've roamed the world for years around,
> No matter what my luck might be – '

When everything was ready Madame Couture and Mademoiselle Taillefer came in.

'Where have you been this morning, my dear lady?' asked Madame Vauquer, turning to Madame Couture.

'We have just been saying our prayers at Saint-Étienne-du-Mont, for you know it's to-day we are to go to Monsieur Taillefer. Poor little thing, she is trembling like a leaf,' said Madame Couture, sitting down in front of the stove and holding out her steaming shoes to it.

'Warm yourself, Victorine,' said Madame Vauquer.

'It's all very well to pray to God to soften your father's heart,' said Vautrin, pushing forward a chair for the girl, 'but that's not enough. You need a friend who will make it his business to tell the blackguard some home truths. He has three millions, so they say, and he's a barbarian if he grudges you a dowry. A pretty girl needs a dowry in these hard times.'

'Poor child!' said Madame Vauquer, 'Never mind, my pet. If your father behaves in this monstrous fashion his wickedness will only bring misfortune down upon his own head.'

When she heard these words Victorine's eyes filled with tears, and at a sign from Madame Couture the widow held her tongue.

'If we could only see him, if I could speak to him myself and give him his wife's last letter!' said the Commissary-General's widow. 'I have never dared take the risk of sending it by post; he knows my handwriting –'

' "O innocent, unhappy and persecuted women!" ' declaimed Vautrin, interrupting her. 'Have things come to this pass? In a few days' time I will look after your affairs myself and then all will be well!'

'Oh! sir,' said Victorine with an ardent look from eyes still full of tears at Vautrin, who did not appear to be in the least touched by it, 'if you know any way of approaching my father, please tell him that his affection and my mother's honour are more precious to me than all the money in the world. If you could induce him to relent towards me I would remember you in my prayers. You may be sure of my gratitude –'

' "I've roamed the world for years around," ' sang Vautrin sarcastically.

At this moment Goriot, Mademoiselle Michonneau and Poiret

all came downstairs together. Perhaps the smell of the sauce which Sylvie was making to serve with what was left of the mutton had drawn them to the dining-room. As the six guests and their hostess said good-morning to each other and sat down to table ten o'clock struck, and the student's step was heard outside.

'Well, Monsieur Eugène,' said Sylvie, 'you are going to have the company of all the others at breakfast to-day.'

The student greeted the other lodgers and sat down beside old Goriot.

'I've just had an odd adventure,' he said, helping himself generously to mutton and cutting a slice of bread which Madame Vauquer kept her eyes fixed on as she silently estimated its size.

'An adventure!' said Poiret.

'Well, what do you find surprising about that, old cock?' Vautrin asked Poiret. 'This gentleman is just the sort to have them.'

Mademoiselle Taillefer glanced shyly at the young student.

'Tell us your adventure,' ordered Madame Vauquer.

'Yesterday I was at a ball at the house of a cousin of mine, the Vicomtesse de Beauséant. She has a magnificent house, the rooms are hung with silk, and she entertained us sumptuously. I was as happy as a king –'

' – Fisher,' said Vautrin interrupting him abruptly.

'What do you mean, sir?' said Eugène sharply.

'I say "fisher" because kingfishers enjoy much more happiness than kings do.'

'That's true. I would much rather be a carefree little bird like that than a king, because –' began Poiret, always eager to echo another's thought.

'Anyhow,' the student went on, cutting him short, 'I danced with one of the loveliest women at the ball, an enchanting countess, the most delightful creature that I have ever seen. She had peach-blossom in her hair, and a beautiful cluster of flowers, real sweetly-scented flowers, on her dress – but oh! you should have seen her, it's impossible to describe a woman glowing with the joy of dancing. Well, this morning I met this divine countess, about nine o'clock, on foot, in the Rue des Grès. My heart started thumping. I guessed – '

'That she was coming here,' said Vautrin, throwing a searching look at the student. 'She was probably going to visit old Gobseck, a money-lender. If ever you explore the hearts of Parisian women you will find the money-lender there rather than the lover. Your countess is called Anastasie de Restaud and lives in the Rue du Helder.'

At the sound of this name the student stared at Vautrin. Old Goriot abruptly raised his head and gazed at the two speakers with a look so full of intelligence and anxiety that the lodgers were astonished.

'Then Christophe will be too late; she must have gone there!' he exclaimed in an agonized voice.

'I guessed right,' said Vautrin, leaning over to whisper in Madame Vauquer's ear.

Goriot went on eating mechanically without knowing what he ate. He had never seemed more stupid or more lost in his own thoughts than he did at that minute.

'Who the devil can have told you her name, Monsieur Vautrin?' demanded Eugène.

'Aha! I have you there!' replied Vautrin. 'Old Goriot knew all about it, so why shouldn't I know too?'

'Monsieur Goriot?' exclaimed the student.

'What is it?' said the poor old man. 'So she was very lovely yesterday evening, was she?'

'Who?'

'Madame de Restaud.'

'Look at the old wretch,' said Madame Vauquer to Vautrin. 'Just see how his eyes are shining!'

'Then he does really keep her?' said Mademoiselle Michonneau in a low voice to the student.

'Oh! yes, she was lovely beyond words,' Eugène went on, while old Goriot watched him avidly. 'If Madame de Beauséant had not been there she would have been queen of the ball; the men had eyes for nobody else. My name was the twelfth on her list, and she danced every quadrille. The other women were furious. If anyone was happy yesterday it was certainly she. There never was a truer saying than that the most beautiful things in the world are a frigate in full sail, a galloping horse, and a woman dancing.'

'Yesterday dancing at a Duchess's ball,' said Vautrin, 'this morning visiting a money-lender; from the highest arc of fortune's wheel to the bottom of the social ladder: behold the progress of Parisian women! If their husbands can't support their unbridled extravagance they sell themselves. If they can't do that they are ready to tear the living vitals from their mothers to get the cash to make them shine. There's nothing they won't do. I know their kind, and well.'

Old Goriot's face, which had shone like the sun on a fine day as he listened to the student, clouded over at this cruel speech of Vautrin's.

'Well,' said Madame Vauquer, 'what was the adventure? Did you speak to her? Did you ask her if she would like to learn law?'

'She didn't see me,' said Eugène; 'but was it not strange to meet one of the prettiest women in Paris in the Rue des Grès at nine o'clock, when she could not have come from the ball before two in the morning? It's only in Paris you meet with such adventures.'

'Bah! You may meet with much funnier things than that,' exclaimed Vautrin.

Mademoiselle Taillefer had hardly listened to all this, she was so much preoccupied with the attempt she was about to make. Madame Couture now signed to her that it was time to go and dress. When the two ladies went out old Goriot followed them.

'Well, did you see that?' said Madame Vauquer to Vautrin and her other lodgers. 'It's clear as day that he has ruined himself for the sake of those women.'

'Never will you make me believe that the beautiful Comtesse de Restaud belongs to old Goriot,' cried the student.

'But we don't care very much whether you believe it or not,' Vautrin interrupted him. 'You are too young yet to know Paris. Later on you will find out that there are what we call "men with a passion" here.'

At these words Mademoiselle Michonneau looked at Vautrin with an awakened air, as if she were pricking up her ears like a trooper's horse at the sound of the trumpet.

'Aha!' said Vautrin, interrupting himself to throw a searching look at her. 'Have we had our little passions too?'

The old maid lowered her eyes like a nun beholding a statue.

'Well,' he went on, 'these people get their teeth into one idea and you can't shake them loose from it. They are thirsty, but only for water taken from one particular well, and often stale; to get a drink of it they would sell their wives and their children, they would sell their very souls to the devil. For some men this well is gambling, speculation on the stock exchange, or it may be music or a collection of pictures or insects. For others it is a woman who knows how to cater for their tastes. If you offered all the women in the world to these last they would not care a straw, they only want the one who gratifies their passion. Often this woman does not love them at all and treats them like dogs. Their scraps of satisfaction cost them very dear; but no matter, these odd fish never tire of it, and they would pawn their last blanket to raise their last five-france piece for her. Old Goriot is one of these men. The Countess exploits him because he is discreet; and that's the way of the fashionable world! The poor beggar hasn't a thought in his head that isn't devoted to her. Apart from his passion, as you see, he is a brute beast, but just start him on that topic and his face sparkles like a diamond. It's not hard to guess that secret. This morning he took silver to the melting-pot and I saw him visit Papa Gobseck in the Rue des Grès. Note what follows! On his return he sends that noodle Christophe to the Comtesse de Restaud. Christophe showed us the address of the letter and there was a receipted bill inside. It's clear as daylight that if the Countess was also going to the old money-lender the affair was urgent. Old Goriot has gallantly paid her debt for her. You don't even need to put two and two together for that to be plain as a pikestaff. That proves to you, my young student, that while your Countess was laughing and dancing and showing off her tricks, waving her peach-blossom crown about with her dress gathered into her hand, she was on pins and needles, as they say, thinking of her dishonoured bills, or her lover's.'

'You make me mad to know the truth,' exclaimed Eugène, 'I shall go to Madame de Restaud's to-morrow.'

'Oh, yes,' said Poiret, 'You must visit Madame de Restaud to-morrow.'

'Perhaps you will find friend Goriot there, come to receive the reward for his gallant services.'

'But,' said Eugène with disgust, 'your Paris is nothing but a slough.'

'And a very queer slough too,' replied Vautrin. 'If you get splashed with its mud riding in a carriage you're an honest fellow, while you're a rogue if you get dirty on foot. If you have the bad luck to nab something from somebody you become a peepshow for the crowd at the Place du Palais de Justice, but you are pointed out in the salons as virtue itself if you steal a million: and what's more you pay thirty millions to the police force and the law-courts to maintain this system of morality. It's a pretty state of affairs!'

'What was that you said?' exclaimed Madame Vauquer. 'Has old Goriot taken his silver breakfast-service to be melted down?'

'Were there two doves on the lid?' asked Eugène.

'That's the very bowl.'

'He must have thought a great deal of it, he wept when he had broken up the bowl and saucer. I happened to see him,' said Eugène.

'It was as dear to him as life,' replied the widow.

'You see how infatuated the old chap is,' exclaimed Vautrin. 'This woman must know how to tickle his soul.'

The student went up to his room. Vautrin went out. A few minutes later Madame Couture and Victorine got into a cab which Sylvie had gone to fetch. Poiret offered his arm to Mademoiselle Michonneau and they set off together to enjoy the two fine hours of the day strolling in the Jardin des Plantes.

'There you see, they are practically a married couple,' said fat Sylvie. 'It's the first time they've gone out together. They are both so hard and dry that if they knock against each other they'll strike a spark like flint and steel.'

'Look out for Mademoiselle Michonneau's shawl!' said Madame Vauquer, laughing. 'It will go up in a blaze like tinder.'

When Goriot came in at four o'clock he saw by the light of two smoky lamps that Victorine's eyes were red. Madame Vauquer was listening to the tale of the fruitless visit paid that morning to Monsieur Taillefer. Taillefer was annoyed with his daughter and this old woman because of their attempts to see him, and had granted them an interview only in order to make his views clear.

'Fancy, my dear lady,' Madame Couture was saying to Madame Vauquer, 'he did not even make Victorine sit down, and she had to stand the whole time. To me, he said (he wasn't at all angry, only very cold) that we were to spare ourselves the trouble of coming to see him; that the young lady, he did not call her his daughter, lowered herself in his opinion by pestering him (once a year, the monster!); that as Victorine's mother had no fortune when he married her Victorine could have no claim to anything: altogether he said such cruel things that he made the poor little thing cry. Then she threw herself at her father's feet and very bravely said to him that it was only for her mother's sake that she had gone on trying to see him, that she would obey his wishes without a murmur, but she implored him to read the poor dead woman's last sworn words. She took the letter and offered it to him with the most beautiful words in the world, and expressing the finest

73

feelings too. I don't know where she got them from, God must have given them to her, for the poor child was so plainly inspired that as I listened to her I couldn't help crying like a fool. And do you know what that abominable man was doing while she was speaking? Cutting his nails! He took the letter that poor Madame Taillefer drowned in her tears and threw it on the mantelpiece and said, "Well, that's all right." He was going to help his daughter to her feet and she took his hands and would have kissed them, but he pulled them away. Isn't it scandalous? And his great booby of a son came in and took no notice of her.'

'They must be monsters!' said old Goriot.

'Then,' went on Madame Couture without paying any attention to the old fellow's exclamation, 'the father and son went out, but they bowed to me first and begged me to excuse them; they had urgent business to attend to. And that was our visit. At least he has seen his daughter. I don't know how he can disown her; they're as like as two drops of water.'

Now the resident and daily boarders dropped in one after another, exchanging greetings and the meaningless remarks that pass for wit among certain classes of Parisians. Silliness is their basic ingredient and their whole point consists in the way they are said or the gesture that accompanies them. This kind of slang is always changing. The catchword on which it is founded never lives longer than a month. A political event, a case being heard at the law-courts, a song of the streets or an actor's gag, anything and everything may provide material for this kind of drollery, whose principle consists in treating ideas and words as shuttlecocks, to be bandied from one person to another as if with battledores. The recent invention of the Diorama, which had carried optical illusion one stage further than the Panorama, had led in some studios to the pleasantry of 'talking 'rama', and a young painter who frequented the Maison Vauquer had inoculated the boarders there with the disease.

'Well, Monsieur-r-r Poiret,' said the Muséum official, 'how is your little healthorama?' Then without waiting for a reply,

'Ladies, is there something wrong?' he said to Madame Couture and Victorine.

'Are we going to have dinnair?' shouted Horace Bianchon, a medical student, and a friend of Rastignac's. 'My little tum-tum is sinking *usque ad talones*.'

'It's desperately chillyorama,' said Vautrin. 'Move over there, Pa Goriot. The devil take it! Your foot is blocking up the whole front of the stove.'

'Illustrious Monsieur Vautrin,' said Bianchon, 'why do you say "chillyorama"? That's wrong, it should be "chillyrama."'

'No,' said the Muséum official, 'it's "chillyorama" by the same rule that you say, "my feet are *chillyor* than yours".'

'Oh! Oh!'

'Here's His Excellency the Marquis de Rastignac, Doctor of Law and Lawks!' cried Bianchon, seizing Eugène by the neck and nearly throttling him. 'Hi! you others, come on!'

Mademoiselle Michonneau entered quietly, nodded to the boisterous companions without saying anything, and walked over to take her place near the three women.

'That old bat always makes me shiver,' said Bianchon in a low voice to Vautrin, with a gesture in Mademoiselle Michonneau's direction. 'A man studying Gall's phrenological system, as I am, sees that she has the bumps of Judas.'

'Oh, Monsieur has met her, has he?' said Vautrin.

'Who hasn't come across her?' returned Bianchon. 'Upon my word, that ghastly blanched old maid reminds me of those long worms you find in beams that go on gnawing until the whole beam is eaten away.'

'There you have it, young man,' said the man of forty, running his fingers through his whiskers.

> 'A rose; and she has lived a rose's span,
> Three morning hours.'

'Aha! here comes a fine souporama,' cried Poiret, as Christophe came in respectfully bearing the soup.

'Excuse me, sir,' Madame Vauquer corrected him, 'it's cabbage soup.'

All the young men burst into guffaws.

'You're dished, Poiret!'

'Poirrrrrette is dished!'

'Score two points to Mamma Vauquer,' said Vautrin.

'Did anyone notice the fog this morning?' asked the official.

'It was a frantic fog,' said Bianchon, 'an unparalleled fog, a mournful, melancholy, pea-green, breath-catching fog, a Goriot of a fog.'

'A Goriorama,' said the painter, 'because you could not make out anything in it.'

'Hey! Lord Gaöriotte, they be talking about yah-oo.'

Goriot was seated at the lower end of the table, near the door through which Christophe was bringing in the food, and with his head thrown back was sniffing at a piece of bread which had been placed under his napkin. This was an old business habit of his to which he sometimes reverted.

'Well!' screamed Madame Vauquer sharply, in a voice that rose above the clatter of spoons and plates and the din of people talking. 'Is the bread not good?'

'On the contrary, Madame, it is made from Étampes flour, best quality.'

'How can you tell that?' asked Eugène.

'By its whiteness, its flavour.'

'You mean its smell, since you are smelling it,' said Madame Vauquer. 'You're so thrifty nowadays that you won't be long finding a way of keeping alive on the nourishing smell from the kitchen.'

'Take out a patent for the process, then,' cried the Muséum official. 'You'll make a fortune.'

'Never mind him, he does that to persuade us that he has been a vermicelli-maker,' said the artist.

'Then is your nose a corn-taster?' inquired the official.

'Corn-what?' asked Bianchon.

'Corn-el.'

'Corn-et.'

'Corn-elian.'

'Corn-ice.'

'Corn-ucopia.'

'Corn-crake.'

'Corn-cockle.'

'Corn-orama.'

These eight answers shot from all sides of the room like a rain of bullets, and the laughter they excited among the merry companions was all the more uproarious because old Goriot was looking at them with a bewildered air, like a man trying to understand a foreign language.

'Corn – ?' he said to Vautrin, who sat near him.

'Corns on your toes, old boy!' said Vautrin, giving him a tap on the head that drove his hat down over his eyes.

The poor old man was dumbfounded at this sudden attack, and made no movement for a moment. Christophe took his plate away, thinking that he had finished his soup, so that when Goriot pulled up his hat and started to use his spoon he knocked it on the table. All the boarders burst out laughing.

'You are a mischievous clown, sir,' said the old man, 'and if you take a liberty like that with me again – '

'Well what then, Pa?' Vautrin interrupted him.

'Well, you'll pay dearly for it some day – '

'In hell, you mean?' said the painter, 'in the little black corner where they put bad boys!'

'Well, Mademoiselle,' Vautrin said to Victorine, 'you are eating nothing. Your father was stiff-necked, was he?'

'He was horrible!' said Madame Couture.

'We'll have to bring him to his senses,' said Vautrin.

'Mademoiselle Victorine could bring an action for alimony since she can't eat,' said Rastignac, who was sitting near Bianchon. 'But just look how old Goriot is staring at her!'

The old man was forgetting to eat as he watched the poor girl whose face bore the marks of unmistakable grief, the grief of a child disowned by the father she loves.

'We've made a mistake about old Goriot, my boy,' said Eugène in a low voice. 'He's neither an imbecile nor an unfeeling block. Apply your Gall's system to him, and tell me what you make of him. Last night I saw him crush a silver dish as if it had been wax, and the expression on his face just now showed extraordinary emotion. His life seems to me to be too mysterious not to be worth the trouble of looking into. No, Bianchon, you needn't laugh, I'm not joking.'

'The man is a pathological case,' observed Bianchon. 'I agree with you there. If he wants me to I will dissect him.'

'No; feel his bumps.'

'Oh! all right. Perhaps his idiocy is catching.'

Next day Eugène dressed himself in style, and set out at about three o'clock in the afternoon to call on Madame de Restaud, busily building on the way those madly extravagant castles in the air which give young people's lives such a rich emotional colouring. When engaged in this exercise they think nothing of obstacles or dangers; success crowns everything they undertake. The mere play of their imagination gilds their existence with romance, and the failure of enterprises that never had a life outside their fevered fancy can reduce them to sadness or discouragement. If they were not inexperienced and shy the social world would be impossible.

Eugène walked with a thousand precautions against splashing himself with mud, but with his mind wholly fixed on what he would say to Madame de Restaud. He laid in a stock of wit; he invented scintillating retorts to imaginary remarks; he prepared his polished lines, his phrases in the style of Talleyrand, for imaginary situations favourable to the declaration on which he was to found his future. And so he became spattered with mud after all, poor student, and was forced to have his shoes polished and his breeches brushed at the Palais-Royal.

'If I were rich,' he said to himself as he changed a five-franc piece that he had brought *in case of need*, 'I should have gone by cab, then I could have thought at my leisure.'

At last he reached the Rue du Helder and asked to see the Comtesse de Restaud. With the cold rage of a man sure of triumphing some day he faced the scornful glances of the lackeys, who had seen him crossing the court on foot and had not heard the sound of any carriage driving up. He was all the more sensitive to their stare because he had already felt a pang of inferiority when he entered the court and saw a splendid horse in rich harness pawing the ground, and one of those smart cabs which blazon the luxury of a spendthrift existence, and imply the possession of all that is desirable in Parisian life. The student all at once felt out of humour with himself. The open drawers of his brain which he was relying on finding full of wit, closed up: his mind became a blank. A footman went to announce the visitor's name to the Countess, and while he waited for her answer Eugène stood on one foot before the window of an ante-room, leaned an elbow against the window-latch and looked vacantly into the court. He found the minutes pass slowly, he would have gone away if he had not been endowed with that southern tenacity of purpose which works miracles when it sees its path straight before it.

'Sir,' said the servant, 'Madame is in her boudoir and very busy. She did not answer me. But if you will go into the drawing-room, sir, there is already someone there.'

Wondering at the terrible power possessed by servants, who with a single word can accuse or condemn their masters, Rastignac deliberately opened the door by which the footman had come in, thinking, no doubt, to impress these insolent lackeys by his familiarity with the house; but he blundered very clumsily into a small room full of lamps and dressers and pipes for warming bath-towels, which led to a dark passage and a back staircase. Stifled laughter behind him in the ante-room completed his discomfiture.

'This is the way to the drawing-room, sir,' said the footman with that insincere show of respect which seems an added mockery.

Eugène turned to retrace his steps with such precipitation that he stumbled against a bath-tub, but fortunately managed to hold on to his hat and saved it from immersion. At this moment a door opened at the end of the long passage, which was lighted by a little lamp. At the same time Eugène heard Madame de Restaud's voice, the voice of Goriot and the sound of a kiss. He returned to the dining-room, crossed it, following the footman, and entered a reception-room. There he went immediately to the window when he noticed that it looked out into the court, for he was anxious to see if this old Goriot was really *his* old Goriot. His heart beat strangely: he remembered Vautrin's appalling reflections. The footman was waiting for Eugène at the door of the great drawing-room; then, suddenly, an elegant young man sprang through it and said impatiently,

'I'm going, Maurice. Tell Madame la Comtesse that I waited more than half-an-hour for her.'

This insolent young man, who no doubt had the right to dispense with ceremony, was humming an Italian roulade as he walked towards the window where Eugène stood, in order to see the student's face as well as to look into the court.

'But Monsieur le Comte would be better advised to wait a moment longer; Madame has finished,' said Maurice as he withdrew to the ante-room.

Just then old Goriot appeared through the door that opened from the little staircase into the court, near the carriage entrance. The old fellow was carrying his umbrella and preparing to open it, not noticing that the great door had been opened to allow a tilbury driven by a young man wearing the ribbon of a decoration to enter. Old Goriot had barely time to throw himself backward to avoid being run over. The spread of silk had frightened the horse and it shied before dashing forward towards the steps. The young man turned his head angrily, looked at old Goriot, and before jumping out bowed to him with the constrained courtesy shown to money-lenders when their services are needed, or the conventional show of respect, to be blushed for later, exacted by a man with a tarnished reputation. Old Goriot replied with a good-natured wave of the hand, full of friendliness. These events followed one another at lightning speed, and Eugène was too absorbed in watching them to notice that he was not alone. Suddenly he heard the Countess's voice.

'Oh! Maxime, were you going away?' she said in a reproachful voice which had a note of resentment in it too.

The Countess had not noticed the arrival of the tilbury. Rastignac turned round abruptly and saw her. She was coquettishly dressed in a fine white woollen wrap with knots of rose-coloured ribbon. Her hair was carelessly done up as Parisian women wear it in the morning. Her perfume filled the air; she had probably just come from a bath and her beauty seemed, as it were, softer and more voluptuous; her eyes had a liquid brilliance. Young men's eyes see everything; their spirit reacts to the charm a woman radiates just as plants breathe in the substances they need from the air; so Eugène did not need to touch this woman's hands to feel their freshness. He saw the rosy hue of her skin gleaming through the thin stuff of her gown, and his eyes lingered on the folds which sometimes fell softly open to reveal her bare throat. The Countess had no need of the aid afforded by a corset, only the belt of her wrap defined her slender waist; her neck was an invitation to love; her feet were pretty in their slippers. When Maxime took her hand to kiss it Eugène's eyes fell on Maxime, and the Countess's on Eugène.

'Oh! it is you, Monsieur de Rastignac, I am delighted to see you,' she said with that air of one accustomed to command which men of perception obey.

Maxime looked from Eugène to the Countess in a way which clearly indicated his opinion that this intruder should take his departure without more ado. 'Now then, my dear, I hope you are going to do me the favour of sending this odd little creature about his business!' That was the plain and obvious meaning of this proud and insolent young man whom the Countess had called Maxime, and whose face she was now studying with the submissive expression on her own that tells all a woman's secrets without her suspecting it. Rastignac felt a violent hatred of this young man rise within him. To begin with, Maxime's trim, fair, well-curled hair showed him how horrible his was; then Maxime's boots were of fine leather and clean, while his, in spite of the care with which he had walked, were stained with faint marks of mud; and then Maxime wore an overcoat which fitted him exquisitely and made him look like a pretty woman, while at half-past two in the afternoon Eugène was wearing a black coat. The thin-skinned child of the Charente keenly felt the disadvantage at which he was placed beside this tall, slender dandy with the pale face and the clear eye, this obvious trifler with the affections of unprotected girls.

Without waiting for an answer from Eugène Madame de Restaud flitted rapidly into the other drawing-room, the skirts of her loose gown floating and fluttering behind her and making her look like a butterfly; and Maxime followed her. Eugène, furious, followed Maxime and the Countess; so that these three people found themselves together again beside the fireplace in the middle of the long drawing-room. The student was perfectly well aware that he was going to annoy the detestable Maxime, but, even at the risk of displeasing Madame de Restaud, that was what he wanted to do. Suddenly, as he remembered having seen this young man at Madame de Beauséant's ball, he guessed the relation in which Maxime stood to Madame de Restaud; and with that youthful audacity which if it does not blunder sensationally is sensationally successful, he said to himself,

'This man is my rival. I'll settle his hash!'

Reckless fellow! He did not know that it was Count Maxime de Trailles' habit to provoke an insult, draw first, and kill his man; nor had Eugène, clever sportsman and fine shot though he was, yet brought down twenty clay pigeons out of twenty-two.

The young Count threw himself into a low chair by the fireside, took up the tongs and poked the fire so violently and ill-temperedly that a vexed look crossed Anastasie's pretty face. The young woman turned to Eugène and gave him one of those coldly interrogative stares which say so clearly, 'Why don't you go?' that well-bred people immediately find themselves uttering those farewell phrases which ought to be called 'exit platitudes'.

Eugène assumed his pleasantest expression and said,

'Madame, I was anxious to see you as soon as possible to – ' He stopped short. A door opened. The gentleman who had driven the tilbury suddenly appeared, hatless. He refrained from greeting the Countess, looked attentively at Eugène, and held out his hand to Maxime, saying, 'How do you do?' in a cordial way that oddly surprised Eugène. Young men from the provinces know nothing of how pleasant life can be in a partnership of three.

'Monsieur de Restaud,' said the Countess to the student, with a wave of her hand towards her husband.

Eugène made a profound bow.

'This gentleman,' she went on, presenting Eugène to the Count de Restaud, 'is Monsieur de Rastignac; he is related to Madame la Vicomtesse de Beauséant through the Marcillacs; I had the pleasure of meeting him at Madame de Beauséant's last ball.'

Related to Madame la Vicomtesse de Beauséant through the Marcillacs! These words, on which the Countess laid the slightest possible emphasis with a hostess's pride in proving that she receives only people of distinction, had a magical effect. The Count's coldly formal manner relaxed, and he returned the student's bow.

'Delighted to have an opportunity of making your acquaintance,' he said.

Count Maxime de Trailles himself cast an uneasy glance at Eugène, and suddenly dropped his insolent attitude.

This transformation, in which a name had played the part of a magician's wand, unlocked thirty pigeon-holes in the Southerner's brain, and gave him back the wit he had stored inside them. A sudden light pierced the murky atmosphere of aristocratic

Parisian society and he could see, though still but dimly. The Maison Vauquer, old Goriot, were at that moment very far from his thoughts.

'I thought the Marcillacs were extinct?' said the Count de Restaud, addressing Eugène.

'They are,' answered the law-student. 'My great-uncle, the Chevalier de Rastignac, married the heiress of the Marcillac family. He had only one daughter, who married the Maréchal de Clarimbault, grandfather of Madame de Beauséant through her mother. We are the younger branch of the family, and even poorer than we should otherwise have been since my great-uncle, the Vice-Admiral, lost all he had in the King's service. The Government during the Revolution refused to admit our claims when the Compagnie des Indes was liquidated.'

'Didn't your great-uncle command the *Vengeur* before 1789?'
'He did.'

'Then he must have known my grandfather who was in command of the *Warwick*.'

Maxime slightly shrugged his shoulders and looked at Madame de Restaud with an expression which said plainer than words, 'If he begins to talk naval shop with that fellow, heaven help us!' Anastasie understood him. With a woman's admirable command of the situation she smilingly said,

'Come, Maxime, I have something to ask you. We will leave you two gentlemen to convoy each other in the *Warwick* and the *Vengeur*.'

She rose and made a mock-conspiratorial sign to Maxime, who followed her towards the boudoir. The *morganatic* couple, to use a convenient German word which has no exact equivalent in our language, had barely reached the door when the Count interrupted his conversation with Eugène.

'Anastasie! Stay here, my dear,' he called out peevishly, 'You know very well that – '

'Coming, coming,' she interrupted him, 'I need just a moment to tell Maxime what I want him to do for me.'

84

She returned very soon. All women obliged to study their husbands' character in order that they themselves may do as they like quickly learn just how far they may go without endangering a trust they prize, and they never cross their husbands in the little things of life. The Countess had seen by the Count's tone that it would not be safe to remain in the boudoir. Eugène was the cause of this unpleasantness, and the Countess expressed her feelings to Maxime with a glance at the student and a gesture of vexation. Maxime said very tersely to the other three,

'Well, you are busy, I won't bother you. Good-bye,' and he strode away.

'Wait, Maxime!' cried the Count.

'Come to dinner,' said the Countess, once more abandoning the Count and Eugène and following Maxime to the first drawing-room, where they remained together long enough to make it seem likely that in the interval the student had taken his leave.

Rastignac could hear them shouting with laughter, and talking, with intervals when they fell silent; but the student maliciously exerted himself to entertain Monsieur de Restaud, flattering him and drawing him into discussion, for he had made up his mind to see the Countess again and find out what the relationship was between her and old Goriot. This woman was a complete mystery to him: clearly in love with Maxime, she yet ruled her husband, and was tied by some secret bond to the old tradesman. He longed to penetrate the mystery and so, as he hoped, gain sovereign power over this typical Parisian.

'Anastasie,' called the Count again.

'Come, my poor dear Maxime,' she said to the young man, 'we must resign ourselves. This evening – '

'I hope, Nasie,' he whispered in her ear, 'that you will keep your door closed to this little fellow. His eyes glowed like coals when he looked at you just now. He will declare his passion for you, and compromise you, and you will force me to kill him.'

'Are you mad, Maxime?' said she. 'Don't you realize that these little students, far from being dangerous, are excellent lightning conductors? I'll make Restaud wildly jealous of him, believe me!'

Maxime burst out laughing and went out, followed by the Countess, who stood at the window to watch him as he jumped into his carriage and set the horse prancing with a flourish of his whip. She returned only when the great door closed behind him.

'Just listen to this, my dear,' called the Count when she came in. 'This gentleman's family estate is not far from Verteuil on the Charente. His great-uncle and my grandfather were acquainted.'

'Charmed to have acquaintances in common,' said the Countess absent-mindedly.

'More than you think,' said Eugène in a low voice.

'What do you mean?' she said quickly.

'Just now,' the student went on, 'I saw a gentleman leave your house who lives next door to me in the same boarding-house, old Goriot.'

At this name, embellished with the word 'old', the Count who was mending the fire threw the tongs into it as if they burnt his fingers, and stood up.

'Sir, you might have said Monsieur Goriot!' he exclaimed.

The Countess at first turned pale as she saw her husband's annoyance, then she blushed and showed obvious embarrassment. She replied in a voice she tried to make natural, with an assumption of rather unreal ease,

'You could not be acquainted with anyone we are fonder of –' She stopped short, looked at her piano as if some sudden whim had seized her, and said,

'Do you like music?'

'Very much,' replied Eugène, red-faced and abashed by the crass social blunder he confusedly felt he had somehow committed.

'Do you sing?' she cried, going to her piano and vigorously executing a run from one end to the other of the keyboard. R-r-r-ah!

86

'No, Madame.'

The Count de Restaud paced up and down the room.

'Ah, that's a pity. It deprives you of an easy means of making your way. — *Ca-a-ro, ca-a-ro, ca-a-a-a-ro, non du-bi-ta-re*,' sang the Countess.

In pronouncing old Goriot's name Eugène had waved a magic wand again, but the effect was quite different from that he had produced with the words, 'related to Madame de Beauséant'. He found himself in the plight of a man introduced as a favour into the house of a collector of curios, who clumsily blunders against a show-case full of statuettes and knocks off three or four badly-joined heads. He wished the earth would open and swallow him. Madame de Restaud's face looked reserved and cold and her indifferent glance avoided the eyes of the hapless student.

'Madame,' he said, 'you have things to discuss with Monsieur de Restaud, so with your permission I – '

'Any time you come,' said the Countess hastily, stopping Eugène with a gesture, 'you may be sure that Monsieur de Restaud and I shall be delighted to see you.'

Eugène made a profound bow to the Countess and the Count and went out, followed by Monsieur de Restaud who insisted, in spite of his protest, on accompanying him to the ante-room.

'Whenever that gentleman calls,' said the Count to Maurice, 'Madame is not at home, nor am I.'

As Eugène set foot on the steps he saw that it was raining.

'Well,' he said to himself, 'I've just made a mess of things and I don't know how, or how much damage I have done. And now I'm going to ruin my hat and coat into the bargain. What I should do is sit in a corner and swot up law, and not look to be anything better than a boorish country magistrate. How can I go into society when to do the thing decently you have to have stacks of cabs and polished boots and all sorts of things, gold chains, and white doeskin gloves that cost six francs in the morning, and yellow gloves every evening? To blazes with you, old Goriot, you old scamp!'

When he reached the street door the driver of a hackney coach, who had obviously just set down a newly-married couple and who asked nothing better than to pick up some illicit fares in his master's time, seeing Eugène without an umbrella, and dressed in black with white waistcoat, yellow gloves and polished boots, hailed the student. Eugène was in the grip of one of those blind rages that drive a young man to plunge deeper into the abyss he has entered as if to find a happy issue there. With less than twenty-three sous in his pocket he nodded assent to the driver and stepped into the carriage, where some orange-blossom petals and silver thread bore witness to its previous occupation by bride and groom.

'Where to, sir?' asked the driver, who had already taken off his white gloves.

'The devil take it,' said Eugène to himself, 'since I'm going the pace I must at least get value for my money! Drive to the Hôtel de Beauséant,' he added aloud.

'Which?' said the driver.

This lofty question shook Eugène's composure. The unfledged dandy was not aware that there were two Hôtels de Beauséant; he did not know how rich he was in relations who did not care two straws about him.

'The Vicomte de Beauséant, Rue – '

'De Grenelle,' interrupted the driver, nodding his head. 'You see,' he added as he pulled up the step, 'there's the Count's house and the Marquis's in the Rue Saint-Dominique.'

'Yes, of course,' replied Eugène drily. 'Must everybody jeer at me to-day?' he said to himself, throwing his hat on the cushions in front of him. 'Here's a game that's going to cost me a king's ransom. But at least I'll call on my so-called cousin in solidly aristocratic style. Old Goriot has already cost me at least ten francs, the old scoundrel! Upon my word I think I'll tell Madame de Beauséant my adventure, it may make her laugh. She is sure to know the secret of the scandalous bond between the tail-less old rat and that beautiful woman. It's better for me to make

88

myself agreeable to my cousin than to risk being rebuffed by that shameless woman, who strikes me anyhow as having very expensive tastes. If the mere name of the fair Viscountess is so powerful, what could she herself not do for me? We must fly high. When you challenge Heaven you must needs aim at God.'

These words briefly summarize the thousand and one thoughts which floated through his mind. He regained something of his coolness and self-confidence as he watched the rain falling. He told himself that though he was about to squander two of his last precious five-franc pieces, the money was well spent in protecting his coat, boots and hat. He could not help feeling exultant when he heard his coachman shouting, 'Gate, if you please!' A porter in red and gold made the great gate groan on its hinges, and it was with a sweet satisfaction that Eugène saw his carriage pass under the arch, turn round the court, and draw up under the porch before the steps. The coachman in his voluminous blue great-coat bordered with red came to let down the step.

As Eugène was getting out of the cab he heard smothered laughter from under the peristyle. Three or four lackeys had been cracking jokes at the expense of this plebeian bride's turn-out. A moment later the student knew in a flash what they were making merry over, as he compared his carriage with one of the most elegant broughams in Paris. Its high-spirited horses had roses at their ears; they champed the bit, and a powdered, well-cravatted coachman held them in check, as if they were ready to dash off if he did not. At the Chaussée-d'Antin Madame de Restaud had the smart cabriolet of a young man of six-and-twenty in her court. At the Faubourg Saint-Germain a carriage which thirty thousand francs could not have bought awaited the pleasure of a great nobleman.

'Who can be here?' Eugène wondered, realizing a little late in the day that there must be very few women to be met with in Paris whose affections were not already engaged, and that the conquest of one of these queens cost more than blue blood. 'Confound it all! My cousin probably has her Maxime too.'

He walked up the steps with death in his heart. As he approached, the glass door was opened and he saw a number of footmen all looking as grave as judges. The party he had attended had been held in the large reception-rooms on the ground floor of the Hôtel de Beauséant, and as he had not had time between the invitation and the ball to call on his cousin he had not yet visited Madame de Beauséant's own apartments; so he was now going to see for the first time the wonders of the exquisite surroundings through which a woman of distinction expresses her own individual elegance, which reveal her soul and reflect her mode of living. His scrutiny of them was even more curious than it otherwise would have been since Madame de Restaud's drawing-room furnished him with a standard of comparison.

At half-past four the Viscountess might be seen. Five minutes earlier she would not have received her cousin. Eugène, who knew nothing of the various nice points of Parisian etiquette, was ushered towards Madame de Beauséant's apartments along a red carpet, up a great white staircase with gilt banisters and decorations of massed flowers. He was completely ignorant of her story, one of those biographical tales which are related by one friend to another with additions and alterations every evening in all the drawing-rooms of Paris.

For the last three years the Viscountess had had a connection with one of the richest and most distinguished noblemen of Portugal, the Marquis d'Ajuda-Pinto. It was one of those innocent friendships which are so absorbing to the persons concerned that they cannot endure the presence of a third party. The Vicomte de Beauséant had accordingly himself set an example to the public by respecting, whether willingly or no, this morganatic union. In the early days of the friendship anyone who came to see the Viscountess at two o'clock found the Marquis d'Ajuda-Pinto there. Madame de Beauséant was obliged to receive these visitors as she could not very well shut her door against them, but she received them so coldly and sat studying the ceiling so earnestly that every visitor understood how much he bored her. When it became known in Paris that callers between two and four o'clock bored Madame de Beauséant, she found herself left in the most complete solitude for those two hours. She went to the Bouffons or to the Opéra escorted by both Monsieur de Beauséant and Monsieur d'Ajuda-Pinto, but as a well-bred man of the world Monsieur de Beauséant always left his wife and the Portuguese when he had installed them in their seats. Now Monsieur d'Ajuda thought it his duty to marry, and was preparing for his wedding with a Mademoiselle de Rochefide. In the whole fashionable world only one person still knew nothing of the projected marriage, and that was Madame de Beauséant. A few of her friends had spoken of it to her in vague terms; she had laughed at them, believing that her friends wished to cloud a happiness that they were envious of. The banns were about to be published, however.

Although the handsome Portuguese had come this afternoon with the express purpose of telling the Viscountess about the marriage, he had not dared to breathe a word of his treachery. His hesitation is easy to explain, for there is indeed nothing harder than to deliver such an *ultimatum* to a woman. Some men find themselves more at ease on the duelling-ground, faced by a man who holds a sword-point against their heart, than they are when a woman after a two-hour spell of lamentation swears she is dying and calls for smelling-salts. At this moment, then, Monsieur d'Ajuda-Pinto was on thorns and longed to take his leave, telling himself that Madame de Beauséant would hear the news, he would write to her, it would be better to deal this death-blow to her heart by letter than by word of mouth. When the lackey announced Monsieur Eugène de Rastignac, the Marquis d'Ajuda-Pinto gave a start of joy.

It is worthy of note that a woman in love raises doubts for herself with even more ingenuity than she uses in seeking fresh forms of happiness. When she is on the point of being forsaken she leaps to the meaning of a gesture with greater swiftness than Virgil's courser scents the distant traces which speak to him of his mate. And so, of course, Madame de Beauséant surprised that involuntary start, slight but terrifying in its unaffected frankness.

Eugène did not know that in Paris one should never present oneself at anyone's house without previously learning from friends of the family the whole history of husband, wife and children, in order to avoid committing one of the blunders in regard to which they say picturesquely in Poland, 'Yoke five oxen to your cart!' probably because you will need them to pull you out of the quagmire into which your false step has plunged you. If these conversational misadventures are still without a name in France, it must be that they are thought to be impossible there because of the enormous publicity given to scandals.

No one but Eugène, after having bogged himself in the drawing-room of Madame de Restaud, who had not even given him time to yoke the five oxen to his cart, could have continued his floundering course by appearing in Madame de Beauséant's drawing-room: but if Madame de Restaud and Monsieur de Trailles had found him horribly in the way, Monsieur d'Ajuda was very pleased to see him.

'Good-bye,' said the Portuguese, hurrying to the door, as Eugène entered a dainty little grey and pink drawing-room where luxury seemed another name for elegance.

'But just till this evening,' said Madame de Beauséant, turning her head and looking at the Marquis. 'We are going to the Bouffons, are we not?'

'I can't go,' he said, with his fingers on the door-handle.

Madame de Beauséant rose and called him to her, without paying the least attention to Eugène, who was standing dazzled by the splendour of his fairy-tale surroundings, half believing the stories of the Arabian Nights were true, and not knowing where to hide his head as he found himself in the presence of this woman who took no notice of him whatever. The Viscountess had beckoned the Marquis with a graceful gesture of her right hand and pointed to a seat in front of her. The movement expressed so imperiously the strong compulsion of passion that the Marquis let go the door-handle and came. Eugène watched him, not without envy.

'So that's the man with the brougham!' he said to himself. 'But do you have to have prancing horses, servants in livery and oceans of money to catch a glance from a Parisian woman?'

Desire to have the power to make an ostentatious show gnawed like a demon at his heart, greed burned in him like a fever, thirst for gold dried up his throat. He had a hundred and thirty francs to spend every quarter. His father, mother, brothers, sisters, aunt, did not spend more than two hundred francs a month among them. This rapid comparison between his present situation and the goal ambition set before him completed his confusion.

'And why can you not come to the Italiens?' said the Viscountess laughing, to the Portuguese.

'Business! I am dining with the English Ambassador.'

'Throw him over!'

When a man starts to deceive he is inevitably compelled to pile lie upon lie. Monsieur d'Ajuda therefore said, with a laugh,

'You command me?'

'I do indeed.'

'That was what I wanted to hear you say,' he replied with a fond look that would have reassured any other woman. He took the Viscountess's hand, kissed it, and went.

Eugène passed his hand over his hair and wriggled, preparing to bow, supposing that Madame de Beauséant was about to recognize his existence. Suddenly she sprang up, rushed to the gallery, ran to the window there and watched Monsieur d'Ajuda step into his carriage. She listened to the order, and heard the porter repeat to the coachman,

'To Monsieur de Rochefide's house.'

These words, and the way Monsieur d'Ajuda dived hurriedly into his carriage were like a thunderbolt and a flash of illumination to this woman, who turned back devoured by deadly apprehensions. The most horrible catastrophes are not worse than those in the world of fashion. The Viscountess went into her room, sat down and took some dainty note-paper.

'When you dine with the Rochefides instead of at the English Embassy you owe me an explanation, and I am waiting for it.' She corrected several letters of her handwriting, shaken by the trembling of her hand, signed 'C' for Claire de Bourgogne, and rang.

'Jacques,' she said to the servant who appeared at once, 'go at half-past seven to Monsieur de Rochefide's house, and ask for the Marquis d'Ajuda-Pinto. If the Marquis is there send in this letter without waiting for an answer; if he is not there bring the note back to me.'

'Madame la Vicomtesse has someone waiting in her drawing-room.'

'Oh! yes, of course,' she said opening the door.

Eugène was beginning to feel very uncomfortable, when at last he saw the Viscountess appear. She said to him in a tone whose pathos tugged at his heart-strings,

'I beg your pardon, Monsieur, I had to write a note. I am now entirely at your service.'

She hardly knew what she was saying, for as she spoke she was thinking,

'Ah! he means to marry Mademoiselle de Rochefide! But does he imagine he is free? This very evening that marriage shall be broken off or I – But there will be no more question of it to-morrow.'

'Cousin,' replied Eugène.

'What!' exclaimed the Viscountess, with a look whose haughtiness froze Eugène. He understood this 'what!' In the last three hours he had learned a great deal and he was on his guard.

'Madame,' he started again, blushing. He hesitated, and then continued,

'Forgive me; I need your favour so badly that a scrap of relationship would have done no harm.'

Madame de Beauséant smiled, but sadly: she felt misfortune in the air around her growling and rumbling like an approaching storm.

'If you knew the situation my family is placed in,' he went on, 'you would love to play the rôle of the fairy godmother who scatters the obstacles that lie in her god-child's path with pleasure.'

'Well, cousin,' she said, laughing, 'what can I do for you?'

'But I can't tell even that! To be connected with you, even by a tie of kinship so slight that it is lost in obscurity, is a whole fortune in itself. You have set my brain in a whirl, I don't know now what I was going to say to you. I know no one else but you in Paris. Ah! if I could only ask you to be my counsellor, beg you to accept me as a poor child who wants to tie himself to your apron-strings, and who would gladly die for you!'

'You would kill a man for me?'

'Two,' asserted Eugène.

'Child! Yes, you are a child,' she said, holding back her tears. 'You at least would love sincerely!'

'Oh!' he said, nodding his head.

The audacity of the student's answer had aroused the Viscountess's keen interest. The Southerner had begun for the first time to calculate the effect of his words. Between Madame de Restaud's blue boudoir and the pink drawing-room of Madame de Beauséant he had made three years' advance in that *Parisian Law* which is never mentioned, although it constitutes a higher social jurisprudence which, well learned and carefully practised, is a high road to success.

'Ah! this is what I was going to say,' said Eugène. 'I met Madame de Restaud at your ball. This morning I went to call on her.'

'You must have been very much in her way,' said Madame de Beauséant, smiling.

'Oh, yes, I am an ignoramus who will set everyone against him if you refuse your help. I imagine that in Paris it is very difficult to meet an unappropriated woman who is young, rich, beautiful and elegant, and I am in dire need of someone who will teach me what you women can expound so well – life. I shall find a Monsieur de Trailles everywhere. So I came to you to ask you for the answer to a riddle, to beg you to tell me what kind of blunder I made. I spoke of an old – '

'Madame la Duchesse de Langeais,' announced Jacques, breaking in on the student, who made a gesture of intense annoyance.

'If you wish to be successful,' said the Viscountess in a low voice, 'you must first learn not to show your feelings so unrestrainedly.'

'Good-afternoon, my dear,' she exclaimed, rising and going to meet the Duchess, and pressing her hands with the caressing effusiveness she might have shown to a sister. The Duchess responded to this with the most touching fondness.

'These are two good friends,' said Rastignac to himself. 'From now on I shall have two protectresses. These two women must feel a partiality for each other's friends, and this one will surely take an interest in me too.'

'What happy inspiration gives me the pleasure of seeing you, my dear Antoinette?' said Madame de Beauséant.

'Oh, I saw Monsieur d'Ajuda-Pinto going into Monsieur de Rochefide's house, so I thought I should find you alone.'

Madame de Beauséant did not compress her lips, did not blush; her steady gaze did not falter; her forehead seemed to grow smoother as the Duchess uttered these deadly words.

'If I had known that you were engaged – ' added the Duchess, turning to Eugène.

'This gentleman is Monsieur Eugène de Rastignac, one of my cousins,' said the Viscountess. 'Have you any news of General de Montriveau?' she asked. 'Sérisy told me yesterday that no one sees anything of him nowadays. Did he call on you to-day?'

The Duchess, who was said to have been forsaken by Monsieur de Montriveau with whom she was madly in love, was pierced to the heart by the barbed question, and she blushed as she replied,

'He was at the Élysée yesterday.'

'On duty?' asked Madame de Beauséant.

'Clara, I suppose you know,' said the Duchess, looking at her in bitter hatred, 'that the banns of Monsieur d'Ajuda-Pinto and Mademoiselle de Rochefide are to be published to-morrow?'

This blow was too violent. The Viscountess turned pale as she answered with a laugh,

'That's one of the rumours that foolish people waste their time over. Why should Monsieur d'Ajuda bestow one of the noblest names in Portugal on the Rochefides? The Rochefides are upstarts, ennobled yesterday.'

'But they say that Berthe will have two hundred thousand livres a year.'

'Monsieur d'Ajuda is too rich to be a fortune-hunter.'

'But, my dear, Mademoiselle de Rochefide is a charming girl.'

'Ah!'

'Anyhow, he is dining there to-day. The arrangements have been concluded. I'm very much surprised you should know so little about it.'

'What was the blunder you made, Monsieur?' said Madame de Beauséant. 'This poor child is so newly launched into the world, my dear Antoinette, that he doesn't understand in the least what we're talking about. Have mercy on him, and let us put off our discussion of this until to-morrow. To-morrow things will be official, I presume, and your information, that you have so kindly shared with me, confirmed.'

The Duchess turned on Eugène the kind of insolent stare that looks a man over from head to foot, flattens him out, and leaves him feeling like a worm.

'I have plunged a dagger unwittingly into Madame de Restaud's heart, Madame; unwittingly – that was my crime,' said the student whose keen wits had served him well enough: he had recognized the biting sarcasm concealed in these remarks, apparently so affectionate. 'You continue to receive, and perhaps you even fear, people who understand how much they are hurting you, while the person who wounds and does not know how deeply is looked on as a fool, a clumsy fellow who cannot use his opportunities, and everyone despises him.'

Madame de Beauséant bestowed a soft look on the student, one of those looks in which a great soul can combine gratitude with dignity. This look was balm to the wound in the student's self-esteem inflicted by the way in which the Duchess had summed him up, with the appraising stare of a bailiff's valuer.

'And would you believe that I had just captured the good-will of the Comte de Restaud? For I should tell you, Madame,' he said, turning to the Duchess with an air both humble and malicious, 'I am still only a poor devil of a student, very much alone, very poor –'

'Don't say that, Monsieur de Rastignac. We women never want a thing that no one else wants.'

'Bah!' said Eugène, 'I am only twenty-two. I have to put up with the disadvantages of my time of life. Moreover I'm at confession – and it would be impossible to kneel in a prettier confessional: it's a place for committing the sins one confesses elsewhere.'

The Duchess's expression grew chilly as she listened to this flippant speech, and she rebuked its bad taste by turning to the Viscountess, and beginning,

'This gentleman has only just come –'

Madame de Beauséant began to laugh unaffectedly at her cousin and the Duchess.

'He has only just come, my dear, and is looking for a teacher to give him lessons in good taste.'

'Madame la Duchesse,' said Eugène, 'is it not natural to desire to find out the secret of what charms us?' ('Come,' he said to himself, 'I'm sure these are very prettily-turned phrases.')

'But I believe Madame de Restaud is herself the pupil of Monsieur de Trailles,' said the Duchess.

'I knew nothing whatever about it, Madame,' said the student, 'and so I threw myself between them like a blind fool. However

I had reached a fairly good understanding with the husband, and found myself tolerated for a time at least by the wife, when I took it into my head to tell them that I knew a man whom I had just seen leaving by a back staircase, and who had kissed the Countess in the shadows of a passage.'

'Who was it?' said the women simultaneously.

'An old man who lives for two louis a month at the bottom of the Faubourg Saint-Marceau, as I, a poor student, do; a poor wretch whom everybody laughs at, and whom we call old Goriot.'

'But, child that you are,' cried the Viscountess, 'Madame de Restaud was a Mademoiselle Goriot.'

'The daughter of a vermicelli-maker,' added the Duchess, 'a little woman who was presented at Court the same day as a pastry-cook's daughter. Don't you remember, Clara? The King began to laugh and made a joke in Latin about flour. People – what was it? People –'

'*Ejusdem farinae*,' said Eugène.

'That was it,' said the Duchess.

'Oh, is he her father?' said the student, horror-stricken.

'Yes, indeed. The worthy man has two daughters whom he is half mad about, although they have both virtually cast him off.'

'Didn't the second marry a banker with a German name, a Baron de Nucingen?' said the Viscountess, looking at Madame de Langeais. 'Her name is Delphine, isn't it? She's a blonde and she owns a side-box at the Opéra and goes to the Bouffons too, and laughs very loudly in order to attract attention – isn't that the other daughter?'

The Duchess smiled, and said,

'Really, my dear, I wonder at you. Why should you concern yourself so much about people of that kind? One would have to be infatuated, as Restaud was, to have anything to do with Mademoiselle Anastasie and her flour-sacks. Oh! he won't gain much by that bargain! She is in the hands of Monsieur de Trailles, and he'll ruin her.'

'They have cast off their father,' Eugène repeated.

'Yes, indeed, their own father,' replied the Viscountess, 'the father, a father, a good father who, they say, gave each of them five or six hundred thousand francs to ensure their happiness by marrying them well, and kept only eight or ten thousand livres a year for himself, believing that his daughters would remain his daughters, that in their new lives he had created two new existences for himself, gained two houses where he would be made much of and adored. Within two years his sons-in-law had banished him from their company as if he were the lowest of social outcasts.'

Tears sprang to Eugène's eyes. He had recently been exposed to the pure and holy influence of family affection; he was still held by the spell of youthful beliefs; and this was only his first day on the battlefield of Parisian civilization. True emotion is so infectious that for a moment these three persons looked at one another in silence.

'Ah! yes, indeed,' said Madame de Langeais, 'it seems very terrible, and yet we see it every day. Isn't there a reason for that? Tell me, my dear, have you ever considered what a son-in-law is? A son-in-law is a man for whom we shall rear, you and I, a dear little creature to whom affection binds us with a thousand ties, who will be the joy of her family for seventeen years, its white soul as Lamartine would say, but is destined to become its torment. When this man takes her from us he will begin by using her love for him as an axe to cut out, root and branch, from the living heart of this angel all the feelings which bound her to her family. Yesterday our daughter was all ours, as we were all hers; to-morrow she has changed into an enemy. Do we not see this tragedy enacted every day? Here a daughter-in-law is unspeakably rude to her father-in-law, who has sacrificed everything for his son. There a son-in-law turns his wife's mother from his door. I hear people asking if anything dramatic ever happens in society nowadays; but the drama of the son-inlaw is appalling, to say nothing of our marriages which have become very sorry farces. I understand quite well what happened to the old vermicelli-maker. I believe I recollect that this Foriot – '

'Goriot, Madame.'

'Yes, this Moriot was President of his Section during the Revolution; he was in the know about the notorious famine, and laid the foundation of his fortune at that time by selling flour for ten times as much as it cost him. He had as much flour as he wanted. My grandmother's land-steward sold him enormous quantities. This Noriot no doubt shared the loot, as persons of his kind always did, with the Committee for Public Welfare. I remember that the land-steward told my grandmother that she could remain in perfect safety at Grandvilliers, because her grain was an excellent certificate of civic merit. Well, this Loriot who sold corn to the cut-throats had only one passion, so they say: he adored his daughters. He gave the elder a roosting-place under the de Restaud roof, and grafted the other on the Baron de Nucingen: a rich banker who sets up for a Royalist. You can quite understand that so long as Buonaparte was Emperor the two sons-in-law did not much mind having the old '93 man in their houses: but when the Bourbons were restored it was a different story; the old fellow was in Monsieur de Restaud's way, and even more tiresomely in the banker's. The daughters, who were still perhaps fond of their father, wanted to save both the goat and the cabbage, to run with the hare and the hounds, to please both father and husband. They saw the Goriot when they had no other visitor, and invented pretexts for doing this which made it seem due only to affection. "Papa, come at such-and-such a time. It will be nicer then because we shall be alone together!" and so forth. But I believe for my part, my dear, that real feeling has eyes and intelligence: the heart of our poor '93 must have bled. He saw that his daughters were ashamed of him; that if they loved their husbands he made trouble between them and his sons-in-law. He was bound to sacrifice himself then. He did sacrifice himself, being a father: he made himself an exile from their homes. When he saw his daughters happy he knew that he had done well. Father and children were accomplices in this little crime. You see the same sort of thing everywhere. What could this old Goriot have been but a grease-stain in his daughters' drawing-rooms? He would have felt awkward and he would have been bored. What has happened to this father with his daughters might happen to the prettiest woman in Paris with the man she loves best: if she tires him with her love he will fly from her; he will commit the meanest actions to escape her. It's the same with all our feelings. Our heart is a treasury; if you spend all its wealth at once you are ruined. We find it as difficult to forgive a person for displaying his feeling in all its nakedness as we do to forgive a man for being penniless. This father had given everything. Throughout twenty years he had given his love, his whole heart; he gave his fortune in one day. When the lemon was well squeezed his daughters left the rind in the gutter.'

'The world is vile,' said the Viscountess, her fingers playing with the fringe of her shawl and her eyes downcast, for she was touched to the quick by the words which Madame de Langeais had aimed at her in telling this story.

'Vile? No.' answered the Duchess. 'It goes its way, that's all. If I talk like this about it, it's only to show you that I am not taken in by the world. I think as you do,' she said, pressing the Viscountess's hand, 'the world is a slough, so let us try to stay on higher ground.'

She rose and kissed Madame de Beauséant on the forehead. Then she said,

'You are very lovely, just now, my dear, I have never seen you with a prettier colour in your cheeks.'

With a slight bow to the cousin she took her leave.

'Old Goriot is sublime!' said Eugène as he remembered how he had watched his neighbour crushing his silver plate during the night.

Madame de Beauséant did not hear, she was lost in her own

thoughts. Some moments passed in silence, and the poor student in a sort of paralysis of embarrassment dared neither go nor stay nor speak.

'The world is vile and malicious,' said the Viscountess at last. 'As soon as misfortune overtakes you there is always a friend ready to come and announce it, and probe your heart with a dagger while bidding you admire the hilt. Sarcasm and mockery already! Ah! but I shall defend myself.'

She raised her head like the great lady she was, and lightning flashed from her proud eyes.

'Ah!' she said, catching sight of Eugène. 'You are here!'

'Yes, still,' he said, piteously.

'Well, Monsieur de Rastignac, treat this world as it deserves. You want to succeed and I will help you. You shall sound the depths of feminine corruption, and measure the immensity of the miserable vanity of men. Although I am well-read in the book of the world there were pages I had not turned. Now, I know it all. The more cold-bloodedly you calculate the farther you will go. Strike ruthlessly and you will be feared. Regard men and women only as you do post-horses that you will leave worn out at every stage, and so you shall arrive at the goal of your desires. Keep in mind that you will be no one here unless you have a woman to interest herself in you. She must be young, rich, fashionable. But if you have any real feeling, hide it like a treasure; never let it be suspected or you will be lost. You would no longer be the executioner then but the victim. If you ever fall in love, guard your secret well! Do not yield it up unless you are very sure you know to whom you are opening your heart. To preserve your love while it is still unborn, learn to distrust this world. Listen to me, Miguel' (she called him by this name quite naturally, without noticing her mistake), 'the desertion of the father by the two daughters who wish he were dead is hideous enough, but there is something still more hideous, the rivalry of the two sisters among themselves. Restaud is of good birth, his wife has been accepted by fashionable society, she has been presented at court;

but her sister, her rich sister, the beautiful Madame Delphine de Nucingen, the wife of a man of wealth, is ready to die of chagrin; jealousy devours her, she and her sister are a hundred leagues asunder; her sister is her sister no longer; they have cast off each other as they cast off their father. And so Madame de Nucingen would lap up all the mud between the Rue Saint-Lazare and the Rue de Grenelle if it enabled her to enter my drawing-room. She fancied that de Marsay would help her to attain her end, and she has made herself de Marsay's slave, she plagues de Marsay. De Marsay cares very little about her. If you present her to me you will be her Benjamin, she will adore you. Love her if you can after that, if not, then make use of her. I will have her as a guest once or twice, at a large party when there is a mob, but I will never receive her here in the morning. I will bow to her when we meet; that is enough. You have closed the Countess's door against you by uttering old Goriot's name. Yes, my friend, you may go twenty times to call on Madame de Restaud and twenty times you will find her "not at home". You will not be admitted there. Well, then, let old Goriot gain you entrance to Madame Delphine de Nucingen's house. The beautiful Madame de Nucingen shall be a banner for you: she shall make you known. If you are the man she favours, other women will dote on you. Her rivals, her friends, her best friends will want to steal you from her. There are women who love a man because he has been chosen by another, just as there are poor middle-class women who copy our hats and think by doing so to acquire our manners too. You will have a success. In Paris social success is everything, it is the key of power. If the women think that you have wit and talent the men will believe it if you don't undeceive them. You can then set your ambitions as high as you like, you will have the entry everywhere. You will find out then what the world is, an assembly of fools and knaves. Take care that you do not belong to either class. I give you my name as an Ariadne's clue to help you thread this labyrinth. Do not compromise it,' she said, raising her chin as she spoke and casting a queenly glance at the student, 'give it back to me, untarnished. Go now, and leave me. We women have our own battles to fight.'

'If you should need a man who would gladly set off a mine for you?' said Eugène, interrupting her.

'Well?' she said.

He struck his heart, smiled in answer to his cousin's smile, and went out.

It was five o'clock. Eugène was hungry and he was afraid he would be late for dinner. This made him feel the comfort and convenience of being carried quickly across Paris; but the purely physical pleasure left his mind free to struggle with the thoughts that assailed it. Contemptuous treatment flicks a young man of that age on the raw; he flies into a rage and shakes his fist at society in general; he is determined to avenge himself, yet his self-confidence is shaken. Rastignac now could think of nothing but the words, 'You have shut the Countess's door against you.'

'I shall call on her!' he said to himself, 'and if Madame de Beauséant is right, if I am refused admittance – I – Madame de Restaud shall meet me in every drawing-room she enters. I will learn to fence and practise pistol-shooting. I will kill her Maxime for her!'

'And what about money?' cried his conscience. 'Where will you get that from?'

At once there shone before his eyes the wealth displayed at the Comtesse de Restaud's mansion. He had seen there the luxury which a Mademoiselle Goriot was bound to love, the gilding, the expensive objects prominently displayed, the undiscriminating splendour of the newly rich, the senseless extravagance of the courtesan. This fascinating picture was eclipsed by a sudden vision of the imposing Hôtel de Beauséant. As his imagination soared among the giddy heights of Parisian society a thousand dark thoughts stirred in his heart, his views grew broader and his conscience slacker. He saw the world as it is; saw how laws and moral judgements are without power among the rich, and found in success the *ultima ratio mundi*.

'Vautrin is right, success is virtue!' he told himself.

When he reached the Maison Vauquer he ran upstairs to get ten francs to give the coachman; and then went into the nauseating dining-room, where he found the eighteen guests feeding like animals at a trough. This lamentable room with its poverty-stricken inmates was hateful to him. The transition was too abrupt, the contrast too complete, not to act as a powerful stimulant, to force the growth of his ambition beyond measure. On the one hand fresh and charming pictures of social life at its most civilized presented themselves, young and lively people, faces full of poetry and passion, in a setting provided by the marvellous creations of art and luxury: on the other there were gloomy canvases set in grime, and faces from which the passions had fled, leaving only their mechanism and the strings that worked the puppets. The precepts that anger had wrung from Madame de Beauséant when she found herself a woman forsaken, and her fair-seeming offers, returned to his memory; and poverty underlined them. Rastignac resolved to open two parallel lines of attack on Fortune, to lean on Knowledge and on Love, to be a learned doctor of law and a man of the world. He was still very much a child! Those two lines are asymptotes, and can never meet.

'You are very serious, my lord Marquis,' said Vautrin, throwing him one of the penetrating looks with which this man seemed to read the innermost secrets of the heart.

'I'm not in the humour to put up with facetiousness from people who call me "my lord Marquis",' replied Eugène. 'To be really a marquis here you would need a hundred thousand livres a year, and a man who lives in the Maison Vauquer is not exactly Fortune's darling.'

Vautrin looked at Rastignac with a half-fatherly, half-sneering air, as if he were saying, 'Young cub! I could make just one mouthful of you!' Then he replied,

'You are miffed perhaps because you haven't been successful with the beautiful Comtesse de Restaud?'

'She has shut her door against me because I said her father ate at our table,' cried Rastignac.

The guests looked at one another. Old Goriot lowered his eyes and turning away began to wipe them.

'You threw some snuff in my eye,' he said to his neighbour.

'Anyone who annoys old Goriot shall answer for it to me from now on,' said Eugène, looking at the old vermicelli-maker's neighbour. 'He's worth more than all of us put together – I'm not speaking of the ladies,' he added, turning towards Mademoiselle Taillefer.

These remarks dumbfounded everyone. Eugène had uttered them in a way which reduced the guests to silence. Only Vautrin said jeeringly,

'If you are taking old Goriot on your shoulders and making yourself his keeper, you'll need to learn how to use a sword and make yourself a first-rate shot.'

'I intend to do so,' said Eugène.

'So you are setting out for the wars to-day?'

'Perhaps I am,' replied Rastignac, 'but that's my own business and I don't need to give an account of it to anyone, especially as I don't poke my nose into what other people are doing after dark.'

Vautrin cast a sinister sidelong glance at him.

'If you don't want to be taken in by puppets, my son, you must go behind the scenes and not peep through holes in the curtain. That's enough,' he added as he saw Eugène on the verge of flaring up. 'We shall have a few things to say to one another at whatever time you like.'

A general feeling of depression and gloom settled down on the dinner-table. Old Goriot was sunk in the abyss of grief into which the student's exclamation had plunged him, and did not understand that the popular attitude towards him had changed, and that a young man capable of imposing silence on his persecutors had taken up the cudgels on his behalf.

'Do you mean to tell us here and now that Monsieur Goriot is the father of a Countess?' said Madame Vauquer in a low voice.

'And of a Baroness, too,' replied Rastignac.

'That's about all he could be,' said Bianchon to Rastignac. 'I've had a look at his head: there's only one bump on it – the bump of paternity; he will be an *Eternal Father*.'

Eugène had too much on his mind to laugh at Bianchon's joke. He was anxious to put Madame de Beauséant's advice to good use, and was considering where and how he could get hold of some money. As he saw the savannahs of the world spread out before him, profitless to him now but full of possibilities, he lost himself in anxious calculation. The others finished their meal and went out one after another, leaving him still sitting there, alone except for old Goriot.

'Then you have seen my daughter?' said Goriot in a voice shaken with emotion.

Eugène, roused from his daydream, took the old man's hand in his, and regarding him with some tenderness said,

'You are a good and noble man. We will talk about your daughters by and by.'

He got up without waiting to hear what old Goriot had to say, and went to his room, where he wrote the following letter to his mother:

My dear Mother,

See if you have not a fresh source of maternal bounty to tap for me. I am in a position to make my fortune immediately, but I need twelve hundred francs, and I must have them at all costs. Say nothing of this to my father, he might raise objections and if I do not get this money I shall be overwhelmed by such dreadful despair as may lead me to blow my brains out. I will explain everything as soon as I see you, for I should need to write volumes to make you understand my present situation. I have not been gambling, dear Mother, I have no debts; but if you wish to preserve the life you gave me you must find this sum of money. As a matter of fact I am going to visit the Vicomtesse de Beauséant, who has taken me under her wing. I have to go into fashionable society, and have not a penny to buy clean gloves. I can learn to eat dry bread and drink nothing but water, I can fast if need be; but I cannot do without the tools they cultivate the vine with in this country. I have to make up my mind to dig out my path or stick in the mud for ever. I know all the hopes that you have placed in me and long to fulfil them quickly. My kind Mother, sell some of your old jewels, I will soon replace them. I know our family circumstances well enough to appreciate what such a sacrifice means, and you must believe that I do not ask you to make it lightly, I should be a monster if I did. You must see that my appeal is the cry of an over-riding necessity. Our whole future depends on this subsidy which I need to open my campaign, for life in Paris is a perpetual battle. If my Aunt's lace has to be sold to make up the sum tell her that I will send her some much more beautiful before long.

The letter continued in the same strain.

He wrote to both his sisters asking for their savings. To prevent any mention in the family circle of the sacrifice which he knew they would gladly make, he enlisted their delicacy, touching the chords of honour which are strung so tautly and resound so strongly in young hearts. Nevertheless when he had written the letters he felt an involuntary tremor, his heart beat fast and he trembled. Although the pressure of his young ambition urged him on, he knew the spotless nobility of the souls which had grown, apart from the world, in solitude; he knew what shifts he would put his sisters to, and also how great their joy would be, with what pleasure they would talk to each other in secret, at the bottom of the garden, of their beloved brother. His conscience rose like a shining light and showed them to him counting over their little treasure in secret: he saw them using the malicious talent young girls have for teasing mystery, to send him this money unknown to their parents, essaying their first deceit for a sublimely unselfish end. 'A sister's heart is a diamond in purity, a well of tenderness!' he said to himself. He was ashamed of the letters he had written.

How passionate their prayers for him would be, how pure the impulse of their hearts towards heaven! What delight would they not take in their sacrifice for him! What grief would strike his mother's heart if she could not send the whole sum he asked for! This noble affection, these costly sacrifices, were to serve him as a ladder to reach Delphine de Nucingen. A few tears, the last grains of incense thrown on the sacred altar of the family, fell from his eyes. He strode up and down his room in an agitation mingled with despair.

Old Goriot, seeing him in this state through the half-open door, came in and inquired,

'What's the matter, Monsieur?'

'Ah! my good neighbour, it's just that I am as much a son and a brother as you are a father. You have good reason to fear for Countess Anastasie; she is in the power of a certain Monsieur Maxime de Trailles who will be her ruin.'

Old Goriot withdrew, stammering something incomprehensible to Eugène.

Next day Rastignac went to the post with his letters. He hesitated until the last moment, but finally threw them into the box, saying, 'I shall succeed!' These are the words of the gambler, of the great soldier, fateful words which have been the salvation of a few, but the ruin of many.

Some days later Eugène called on Madame de Restaud; she was not at home. Three times he returned and three times he found the door closed against him, although he presented himself at an hour when Count Maxime de Trailles was not there. The Viscountess had been right.

The student studied no longer. He went to his lectures to answer to his name and, having attested his presence, made off. He had persuaded himself, as most students do, that he should postpone his studies until it was time to sit for his examinations; he would let his second and third year's work pile up, and then apply himself to learning law seriously in one last spurt at the last moment. This left him free for fifteen months to sail the Parisian ocean and devote all his energies to fishing fortune from it, or to the chase and capture of a prize, a woman who would act as his patroness.

He saw Madame de Beauséant twice during this week, calling on her only when he had seen the Marquis d'Ajuda's carriage drive away. For a few days longer this distinguished woman, the most romantic figure of the Faubourg Saint-Germain, grasped at victory and staved off the marriage of Mademoiselle de Rochefide with the Marquis d'Ajuda-Pinto. But these last days, which the fear of losing her happiness made the most rapturous of all, could only bring the catastrophe nearer. The Marquis d'Ajuda agreed with the Rochefides in regarding this quarrel and its patching up as favourable to his plans; they hoped that Madame de Beauséant would grow accustomed to the idea of the marriage, and in the end would sacrifice her meetings with d'Ajuda for what she must see to be a natural step in a man's career. So that in spite of the most solemn promises, daily renewed, Monsieur d'Ajuda was playing a part, and the Viscountess willingly let the wool be pulled over her eyes.

'Instead of heroically jumping from the window she lets herself be pushed downstairs,' said her best friend, the Duchesse de Langeais.

These last gleams of happiness, however, shone long enough to keep the Viscountess in Paris and serve the interests of her young relative, for whom she had a slightly superstitious affection. Eugène had shown himself full of devotion to her and sensibility in a situation where women see no pity, no real desire to console in anyone's look, where if a man says something flattering to them it is with some motive of self-interest.

As Rastignac was anxious to take his bearings before attempting to board the Maison de Nucingen he made up his mind to find out all he could about old Goriot's previous history, and he gathered reliable information which may be summed up thus:

Before the Revolution Jean-Joachim Goriot was an ordinary workman employed by a vermicelli-maker. He was a skilful and thrifty man, and enterprising enough to buy his employer's business when by chance the latter fell a victim to the first upheaval in 1789. He established himself in the Rue de la Jussienne, near the Corn Exchange, and had the great good sense to accept the Presidency of his Section so that his business might have the protection of the most influential persons of those dangerous times. This judicious action laid the foundation of his fortune, which he started to build up in the days of the famine, real or artificial, during which the price of grain soared to dizzy heights in Paris. Many people fought to the death for bread at the bakers' doors, while others went quietly without any fuss to the grocers, to get hold of Italian paste foods. During this year Citizen Goriot amassed the capital which later enabled him to carry on his business with all the advantage which a solid backing of money gives to its possessor. He had the luck of all men who have only average ability: his mediocrity was his salvation. Moreover as his success became known only when it was no longer dangerous to be rich, he excited no one's envy. His dealings in grain seemed to have absorbed all his intelligence. In considering corn or flour or tailings, recognizing their quality and their source, attending to their storage, foreseeing their market price, prophesying the harvest yield, procuring cereals cheaply, laying in a store of them in Sicily or the Ukraine, nobody could touch Goriot. Anyone who watched him carry on his business or explain the laws regulating the export and import of grain, elucidating the principles involved, seizing on the weak points, would have judged him capable of filling a Minister's shoes. Patient, active, energetic, unvarying, prompt in despatch, he had an eagle's eye, anticipated everything, foresaw everything, knew all, hid all; he had a diplomat's power of understanding a situation, the capacity of a soldier on the march for patiently, tirelessly, slogging on. Take him from his speciality, from his humble obscure counting-house, – on whose step he used to linger in his hours of leisure, his shoulder against the door-post – and he became once more the uncouth, slow-witted workman, incapable of following an argument, insensible to all the pleasures of the mind, a man who fell asleep at the play, a Parisian Doliban, outstanding only in stupidity. Natures such as his are almost all alike; at the heart of almost all of them you find a noble passion. Two engrossing passions had filled the vermicelli-maker's heart, had absorbed all his tenderness as the grain business had absorbed all his intelligence. His wife, the only daughter of a rich farmer of La Brie, was first the object of his worshipping admiration, his unbounded love. In her Goriot had found a delicate yet strong personality, a fine and sensitive nature, which contrasted strikingly with his own. If there is one feeling innate in the heart of man, surely it is pride in extending constant protection to a defenceless being throughout life. To this pride add love, the lively gratitude felt by all unspoiled natures for the prime source of their pleasures, and you will understand a host of oddities in human nature. After seven years of cloudless happiness Goriot lost his wife in an evil hour. She was by that time beginning to influence him, outside the sphere of domestic affection. Perhaps she might have cultivated this heavy clod-like nature, perhaps awakened him to an apprehension of the world outside his business, and of life; but as things were, paternal feeling developed to the point of mania in Goriot: the wealth of affection which death had frustrated was transferred to his two daughters, and at first they fully satisfied all his emotional needs. However brilliant the proposals made to him by merchants or farmers anxious to give him their daughters, he remained a determined widower. On this point his father-in-law, the only man for whom he had some friendship, professed to know that Goriot had sworn not to be unfaithful to his wife, even though she was dead. The men of the Corn Exchange were incapable of understanding this sublime piece of folly; they made jokes about it and gave some ridiculous nickname to Goriot. The first of them who, fresh from sealing a bargain with wine, took it into his head to call him by it received a blow on the shoulder that sent him flying head first into a Rue Oblin gutter. Goriot's unreflecting devotion and touchy, easily alarmed, protective love for his daughters was so well known that one day one of his competitors, who wanted to make him leave the Exchange in order to have the field to himself, told him that Delphine had just been knocked down by a cab. The vermicelli-maker, his face ghastly pale, left the Exchange at once. He was ill for several days as a result of the shock of this false alarm and the reaction from it. If he did not make this man feel the weight of his murderous fist he yet drove him from the

Corn Exchange, forcing him into bankruptcy at a crisis in his affairs.

Naturally his two daughters were spoiled: their education was not subject to the dictates of common sense. Goriot was worth more than sixty thousand francs a year and spent barely twelve hundred on himself; his sole pleasure was to gratify his daughters' whims. The best masters were engaged to endow them with the accomplishments which are the hallmark of a good education; they had a chaperon — luckily for them she was a woman of intelligence and good taste; they rode; they kept their carriage; they lived like the mistresses of a rich old lord; they had only to express a wish for something, however costly, to see their father rush to give it to them, and he asked nothing in return but a kiss. Goriot raised his daughters to the rank of angels, and so of necessity above himself. Poor man! He even loved them for the pain they caused him.

When the two girls were of an age to marry they were free to choose their husbands according to their taste: each was to have as dowry the half of her father's fortune. Anastasie, who was courted for her beauty by the Comte de Restaud, had aristocratic aspirations which led her to leave her father's house for an exalted social sphere. Delphine loved money: she married Nucingen, a banker of German origin who became a Baron of the Holy Roman Empire. Goriot remained a vermicelli-maker.

It soon became a shocking thing to Goriot's sons-in-law and daughters that he should continue in business, although this business was his whole life. He stood out against their entreaties for five years, and then consented to retire on the money raised by the sale of his business and the profits of those last years. It was this capital which Madame Vauquer, when he first came to live in her house, had estimated to bring in eight to ten thousand francs a year. Goriot had buried himself in the boarding-house in despair when his daughters were forced by their husbands to refuse not only to have him staying under their roof, but also to allow him to call on them, except in private.

This was all the information that could be obtained about old Goriot from a Monsieur Muret who had bought his business. The suppositions that Rastignac had heard the Duchesse de Langeais make were thus confirmed. So ends the prologue of this obscure but terrible Parisian tragedy.

Towards the end of the first week in December Rastignac received two letters, one from his mother, the other from his elder sister. The familiar handwriting made his heart leap with joy, and yet he felt a thrill of apprehension. These two fragile sheets of paper pronounced a sentence of life or death on his hopes. He entertained some misgivings when he remembered his parents' poverty, yet he had had too much experience of their fondness for him not to fear that they had shed the last drops of their life-blood. His mother's letter ran as follows:

My dear Child,

I am sending you what you asked me for. Make good use of this money: if it were to save your life I could not find so large a sum again without telling your father of it, and it would make trouble here. We should be obliged to mortgage our land to obtain it. It is impossible for me to judge the merits of plans I do not know; but of what kind can they be that make you afraid to confide in me about them? An explanation did not need volumes, a word is enough for a mother, and it would have spared me the anguish of uncertainty. I cannot conceal from you the painful impression your letter made on me. My dear son, what feeling forced you to strike such dismay into my heart? You must have suffered greatly in writing to make me suffer so greatly in reading what you wrote. On what enterprise are you embarking? Are your life, your happiness to be pledged to make you appear what you are not, to let you see a world into which you could not go without an expenditure of money which you cannot sustain, without a loss of time precious for your studies? My good Eugène, believe your mother's heart, devious paths never lead to anything great. Patience and resignation must be the virtues of young men in your position. I am not scolding you, I do not want to tinge our gift with bitterness. I speak as a mother as full of trust in you as she is watchful for you. If you know to what you are committed, I know too how pure your heart is and how excellent your intentions. And so I can say to you without fear, 'Go ahead, my darling!' I tremble because I am a mother; but every step you make will be with our good wishes and our blessings. Be careful, dear child. You must use a man's wisdom, the destinies of five persons dear to you lie on your shoulders. Yes, all our fortune is bound up in you, and your success is ours. We all pray to God to help you in everything you do. Your Aunt Marcillac has been of unheard-of goodness in this matter: she knew at once how things must be, even to what you tell me about your gloves. 'But I have a weakness for the eldest child!' she said to me gaily. Eugène, you must love your Aunt dearly, I shall not tell you what she has done for you until you have succeeded; otherwise her money would burn your fingers. You children do not know what it means to sacrifice the things that are a part of one's memories! But what would we not sacrifice for you? She charges me to send you a kiss on your forehead from her, and would like the kiss to bring you plenty of good fortune. The dear kind woman would have written to you herself, but she has gout in her fingers. Your father is well. The 1819 harvest is better than we expected. Goodbye, dear child. I shall not say anything about your sisters: Laure is writing to you, and I shall let her have the pleasure of gossiping about the little family happenings. Heaven send you success! Oh! yes, you must succeed, Eugène, you have made me know a pain too poignant for me to bear again: I have known what it is to be poor and want wealth to give my child. Well, now, goodbye. Do not leave us without news. And now take the kiss your mother sends you.

When Eugène had finished this letter he was in tears. He thought of old Goriot breaking up his silver plate and selling it to pay his daughter's bill of exchange.

'Your mother has broken up her jewels!' he said to himself. 'Your aunt must have wept as she sold some of her keepsakes! What right have you to condemn Anastasie? You have just done selfishly for your own future what she did for her lover! Which is the better, she or you?'

The student felt himself gnawed within by a sensation of intolerable heat. He wanted to renounce the world, he wanted to refuse the money. He experienced that noble-spirited secret remorse whose merit is rarely appreciated by men when they judge their fellows, which often makes the angels in Heaven absolve the criminal condemned by earthly justice. He opened his sister's letter, and its innocence and sweetness fell like balm upon his heart.

Your letter came at just the right moment, dear brother, for Agathe and I wanted to lay out our money so many different ways that we could not make up our minds how to spend it. You have done what the King of Spain's servant did when he dropped his master's watches; you have made us agree. Really and truly, Eugène, we were squabbling all the time about what we should buy first, and we couldn't find a way to do all the things we both wanted. Agathe jumped for joy. Indeed we were like two mad creatures all day, 'to such a fantastic degree', to use Aunt's expression, that Mother said to us in her severest manner, 'What *is* the matter with you, young ladies?' If we had been scolded a little we should have been still better pleased, I believe. A woman must find great satisfaction in suffering for the person she loves! But I was vexed and sorrowful in the midst of my joy. I shall certainly make a bad wife, I am a dreadful spendthrift. I bought myself two sashes and a pretty stiletto to pierce the eyelets of my bodices, silly odds and ends I didn't want, so that I had less money than that great Agathe who is thrifty and hoards her pennies like a magpie. She had two hundred francs! And I, my poor boy, have only a hundred and fifty. I am well punished for it, I should like to throw my sash down the well, I shall always hate wearing it because it has robbed you. Agathe was a dear about it. She said, 'Let's send the three hundred and fifty francs from us both!' But I couldn't help telling you just how things happened.

Do you know how we set about obeying your commands? We took our lovely money, we went out for a walk together and as soon as we had reached the main road ran hotfoot to Ruffec, where we just handed the money over to Monsieur Grimbert of the Messageries Royales. We were as light as swallows coming back. 'Does happiness give us wings?' Agathe asked me. We told each other a thousand things which I shall not repeat to you, Monsieur le Parisien, for they were all about you. Oh! dear brother, we love you dearly, that is the whole thing in a nutshell. As for keeping the secret, according to Aunt little monkeys like us are capable of anything, even of holding our tongues.

Mother has gone on a mysterious errand to Angoulême with Aunt, and they both kept silent about the high politics of their journey, which was not embarked on without long conferences beforehand, from which we were shut out, and Monsieur le Baron too.

Great schemes are afoot in the State of Rastignac. The muslin dress sprigged with openwork flowers which the Infantas are embroidering for Her Majesty the Queen progresses in the profoundest secrecy: there are only two more breadths to do. It has been decided not to build a wall along by Verteuil, there is to be a hedge instead. Our people will lose fruit and espaliers by it, but strangers will gain a fine view. If the heir-presumptive needs handkerchiefs he is hereby given notice that the Dowager de Marcillac rummaging through her treasures and her trunks, known as Herculaneum and Pompeii, discovered a piece of cambric which she didn't know she had.

The Princesses Agathe and Laure put at his command their thread, needles and hands which, alas! are always a little too red. The two young princes Don Henri and Don Gabriel are still sadly in the habit of gorging themselves with grape jam, plaguing their sisters, not wanting to learn anything, amusing themselves robbing birds' nests, kicking up a rumpus, and cutting osiers in defiance of the State Laws, to make themselves switches. The Papal Nuncio, commonly called Monsieur le Curé, threatens to excommunicate them if they continue to neglect the sacred canons of grammar for the martial cannons of the hollow elder-tree.

Goodbye, dear brother, never did a letter carry so many good wishes for your success, or so much happily satisfied love. You will have lots of things to tell us when you come home! You must tell me everything because I'm the eldest. Aunt gave us grounds for suspecting that you had had some social successes.

'They speak of a lady, and then they are mute – '

Of course they are, in this family! By the way, Eugène, if you like, instead of handkerchiefs we could make you some shirts. Give me an answer soon about this. If you need good shirts well made at once we ought to set to work without delay; and if there are fashions in Paris which we don't know you should send us a pattern, especially for the cuffs.

Goodbye, goodbye! I send you a kiss for your forehead, on the left side, on the temple which belongs exclusively to me. I am leaving the other side of the page for Agathe and she has promised not to read what I have written, but to make quite sure of it I am going to stay beside her while she writes.– Your loving sister,

LAURE DE RASTIGNAC

'Oh! yes,' said Eugène to himself, 'whatever it costs I must succeed now! A treasury of gold could not repay devotion such as this. I wish I could heap every kind of happiness on them. Fifteen hundred and fifty francs!' he went on, after a pause. 'I must make every penny tell. Laure is right, trust a woman! I have no fine shirts. Where someone else's welfare is concerned a girl is as wide-awake as a card-sharper. Guileless in what concerns herself and full of foresight for me, she is like the angel in heaven who pardons earthly faults with no comprehension of them.'

The world was his! Already his tailor had been summoned, sounded and subjugated. One glance at Monsieur de Trailles had made Rastignac realize the influence that tailors exercise in young men's lives. No mean exists, alas! between the two extremes: a tailor by the mere fact of his business relation becomes either a mortal enemy or a devoted friend. In his tailor Eugène met a man who understood the paternal obligations of his office, and considered himself as a connecting link between a young man's present and his future: and Rastignac in gratitude made the fortune of this man by one of the epigrams in which he later in life excelled.

'I know two pairs of his trousers,' he said, 'which have made matches worth twenty thousand livres a year.'

Fifteen hundred francs and clothes *ad lib.*! At that moment the poor son of the South no longer had any doubts about anything, and went down to breakfast with that indefinable air which possession of any sum of money gives a young man. Immediately money slides into a student's pocket he feels, in fancy, a pillar rise within him to give him moral support. He strides out more manfully than before; he feels he has found a place to stand from which he can apply his lever to the world; he looks you straight in the face and his movements are vigorous and determined. Yesterday he was shy and self-effacing, ready to take rough treatment from anybody; to-day he would stand up to a prime minister. Amazing changes take place within him: nothing is beyond his ambition, and nothing beyond his reach; he sets his fancy on this or that at random; he is gay, generous and expansive. In short, the fledgeling bird has found he can use his wings.

A penniless student snatches a crumb of pleasure like a dog snapping up a bone amid a host of dangers, who crunches it as he flies from the pursuit, sucks the marrow and runs on again: but the young man who can jingle a few fleeting gold coins in his pocket savours the full flavour of his pleasures, tastes them drop by drop and turns them on his tongue; he floats above the earth, the word 'poverty' for him no longer holds a meaning, the whole of Paris is his.

Those are the days when the whole world is radiant with delight, when everything sparkles and flames. Days of joyous energy which no man, nor woman either, can harness for gain!

Days of debts and lively apprehensions which give a ten times sharper edge to all the pleasures! The man who does not know the left bank of the Seine, between the Rue Saint-Jacques and the Rue des Saints-Pères, knows nothing of life.

'Ah! if the women of Paris only knew!' Eugène told himself, as he ate the stewed pears at a farthing each served by Madame Vauquer, 'they would come here to find a lover.'

Just then the wicket-gate bell rang, and a messenger from the Messageries Royales appeared at the dining-room door. He asked for Monsieur Eugène de Rastignac, and handed him two bags and a receipt to sign. Thereupon Eugène was searched by an unfathomable look from Vautrin, which stung him like a lash.

'Now you can pay for fencing lessons and shooting practice,' the man said.

'Your ship has come home,' said Madame Vauquer, eyeing the bags.

Mademoiselle Michonneau did not dare glance at the money for fear of showing her greed in her eyes.

'You have a good mother,' said Madame Couture.

'You have a good mother, sir,' echoed Poiret.

'Yes, Mamma has been bled white,' said Vautrin, 'so now you can sow your wild oats, go out into society and fish for heiresses, and dance with Countesses with peach-blossom in their hair; but take my advice, young man, practise shooting.' And Vautrin aimed an imaginary gun at an adversary.

Rastignac wanted to tip the messenger but found his pockets empty. Vautrin fumbled in his and threw a franc to the man.

'Your credit is good,' he said, looking at the student.

Rastignac was forced to thank him, although since the sharp words they had exchanged at dinner on the day he had visited Madame de Beauséant he could not endure this man. For a week Eugène and Vautrin had been silent when both were present, and had closely observed each other. The student asked himself why in vain.

Unquestionably, ideas are projected with a force in direct

proportion to the force with which they are conceived, and fly straight to the mark at which the brain aims them, by a mathematical law as exact as that which directs the course of shells projected from a mortar. The effects produced are various. There are tender natures in which they lodge with devastating results, and there are strongly-fortified natures, brazen-fronted skulls, against which the wills of others flatten themselves and fall like bullets against a wall; then there are doughy, yielding brains in which other men's ideas are spent, as shot is killed in the soft earth of redoubts. Rastignac's was a head stuffed with gunpowder, ready to explode at the slightest shock. He was too young and quick not to be vulnerable to that projection of ideas, that influence of others' feelings, whose results strike us as so strange and startling when we are ignorant of their cause. His mental vision had the clearness and range of his physical eyes, which were as keen as a lynx's. All his mental powers of perception, corresponding to his physical powers had the mysterious extension, the power of flexible thrust and recovery, which makes us marvel at men of superior intellect, who are like fencers skilled in finding the chink in any armour.

During the last month, moreover, Eugène's good qualities and his weaknesses had developed rapidly. Contact with the world and the attempt to satisfy his growing desires had been a forcing-frame for his weaknesses. His good qualities included that Southern impetuosity which drives headlong at a difficulty, and which allows no man from beyond the Loire to remain long in any uncertainty whatsoever. Northerners call this quality a weakness, and they point out that if Murat made his fortune by it he also came by his death. From this we may conclude that when a Southerner can add the guile of the North to the dash and daring of the South side of the Loire he is a man complete and, like Bernadotte, may win and keep the crown of Sweden.

And so Rastignac could not long remain under fire from Vautrin's batteries without knowing if this man was his enemy or his friend. It seemed to him that this strange being examined his feelings every moment and read his inmost heart, while Vautrin himself was so closely sealed that he seemed to possess the still depths of a sphinx, who knows all, sees all, and keeps silent. With the self-confidence bred of full pockets Eugène was ready to rebel.

'Be so good as to wait a moment,' he said to Vautrin, who was rising to go out after enjoying his last mouthfuls of coffee.

'What for?' replied the older man, putting on his wide-brimmed hat, and taking up the sword-cane which he was accustomed to flourish like a man defying attack from four thieves at once.

'I want to repay you,' said Rastignac, promptly undoing one of his bags and counting out a hundred and forty francs for Madame Vauquer. 'Short reckonings make good friends,' he said, turning to the widow. 'That clears our accounts until Saint-Sylvestre. Can you give me change for this five-franc piece?'

'Good friends make short reckonings,' repeated Poiret, looking at Vautrin.

'Here is a franc,' said Rastignac, holding out a coin to the sphinx in the black wig.

'Anyone would think you were afraid to owe me a trifle,' exclaimed Vautrin, his eyes probing the young man's very soul, and on his lips one of those cynical jeering smiles which had provoked Eugène a hundred times to the point of fury.

'Well – yes, so I am,' rejoined the student, who was grasping his two bags and had risen to go to his room.

Vautrin went out by the door to the drawing-room, and the student prepared to leave by the other, leading to the staircase.

'Do you know, Monsieur le Marquis de Rastignacorama, that what you are saying to me is not exactly polite?' said Vautrin then, flicking the drawing-room door shut and striding up to the student, who stared at him coldly. Rastignac closed the dining-room door and drew Vautrin with him to the foot of the staircase. As they stood there in the passage between the dining-room and the kitchen, below the iron-barred glass panel over the door which led to the garden, Sylvie appeared from her kitchen.

'*Mister* Vautrin, I am not a Marquis and my name is not Rastignacorama,' the student said.

'They are going to fight,' said Mademoiselle Michonneau indifferently.

'Fight!' echoed Poiret.

'Oh no, not at all,' replied Madame Vauquer, stroking her heap of coins lovingly.

'But there they are going under the trees,' cried Mademoiselle Victorine, rising to look out into the garden; 'the poor young man is in the right, all the same.'

'Come upstairs, my dear child,' said Madame Couture; 'these things are no business of ours.'

But as Madame Couture and Victorine rose, fat Sylvie appeared in the doorway and blocked their way.

'Whatever are they up to?' she said. 'Monsieur Vautrin said to Monsieur Eugène, "Let's lay our cards on the table!" he said. Then he took him by the arm and now they're tramping about among our artichokes!'

As she was speaking Vautrin came in.

'Don't be frightened, Ma Vauquer,' he said, smiling. 'I'm going to try my pistols under the lime-trees.'

'Oh! sir,' said Victorine, clasping her hands, 'why do you want to kill Monsieur Eugène?'

Vautrin took two steps backwards and stared at Victorine. 'Aha! here's something new!' he exclaimed in a mocking voice that made the poor girl blush. 'That's a nice young fellow out there, don't you think? You've put a notion in my head,' he went on. 'I'll make you both happy, my fair maid.'

Madame Couture took her ward's arm and hurried her off, saying in her ear as they went,

'Really, Victorine, I'm amazed at you this morning!'

'I don't want anyone firing shots in my garden,' said Madame Vauquer. 'Do you want to frighten all the neighbours, and bring the police about our ears at this time of day?'

'Come, come, don't upset yourself, Ma,' replied Vauquer.

'There, there, make your mind easy; we'll go to the shooting-gallery.'

He rejoined Rastignac, and took him familiarly by the elbow.

'If I proved to you that at thirty-five paces I can put my bullet through the pip on the ace of spades five times in succession, even that wouldn't damp your ardour, I suppose. You strike me as being rather a hot-headed young man, and you would get yourself killed like an idiot,' he said.

'You're backing out,' said Eugène.

'Don't get my dander up,' replied Vautrin. 'It isn't cold this morning, we'll go and sit over there,' and he pointed to the green-painted seats; 'no one will overhear us there. I have a few things to say to you. You are a good little young man and I don't wish you ill. As sure as my name is Cheat – (good God!) – Vautrin, I have a liking for you. Why I like you you shall hear. Meantime I can tell you that I know you as well as if I had made you myself, and I am going to prove it to you. Put your bags down there,' he went on, pointing to the round table.

Rastignac put his money on the table and sat down with the liveliest expectation. He was consumed with curiosity, which had been raised to the highest pitch by the change in the manner of this man, who had first talked of killing him, and was now posing as his protector.

'You would very much like to know who I am, what my past history is, and what I am doing now,' went on Vautrin. 'You are too curious, little man. Come, keep cool. You are going to hear more surprising things than that! I have had my misfortunes. Listen to me first and then you can talk afterwards. Here is my past life in three words. Who am I? Vautrin. What am I doing? What I please. So much for that. Would you like to know my nature? I am good to those who are good to me, or whose heart speaks to mine. Those people can treat me as they like, they may kick me on the shins and I won't even say, "Take care!" But, by heaven! I'm as vicious as the devil with people if they annoy me, or if I don't take to them, and it is just as well that you should know that killing a man means as little to me as that!' and he spat. 'But I make a point of killing him decently, and only when it's absolutely necessary. I am what you might call an artist. Such as you see me. I have read the *Memoirs* of Benvenuto Cellini, and in Italian too! He was a rare sportsman, and he taught me to follow the example set by Providence who kills us right and left haphazard, and also to love beauty wherever it is to be found. Isn't it a fine game to play, after all, to be alone against mankind and to have luck on your side? I have thought a great deal about the present constitution of your social disorder. My dear little fellow, duelling is a game for children, it's downright folly. When of two living men one must leave the stage it's lunatic to leave it to chance. A duel is a toss-up, that's all. See here! I can put five successive shots through the middle of an ace of spades, one on top of the other, and at thirty-five paces too! When a chap has that little trick up his sleeve he may feel sure of killing his man. Well, I shot at a man at twenty paces and I missed him. The fellow had never handled a pistol in his life. Look at this!' said the extraordinary man, undoing his waistcoat and displaying a chest as shaggy as a bear's back. The reddish, coarse hair aroused a sort of horror, mixed with disgust, in Eugène. 'That greenhorn singed my fur,' he went on, guiding Rastignac's finger to a deep scar in his breast, 'but I was a child then, I was your age, twenty-one. I still had some beliefs left — in a woman's love, a pack of nonsense that you'll get mixed up with soon enough. You would have fought me, wouldn't you? You might have managed to kill me. Suppose me buried, and where would you be then? You would have to clear out, go to Switzerland, squander Papa's money, although he has little enough for himself. I am going to open your eyes, to show you your position as it is, and I am going to do it as a man who can see clearer than you can, who has examined things here below and seen that there are only two courses to follow: stupid obedience or revolt. I obey in nothing, is that clear? Do you know how much you'll need in the direction you are going? A million and at once; without it we might as well go and cool our hot little head in the drag-nets at Saint-Cloud to find out if there's a God. I will give you that million.'

He paused, and looked at Eugène.

'Aha! you look more kindly now on your little Papa Vautrin. When you hear that you're like a girl to whom someone has said, "I'll see you this evening," and who licks her lips like a cat lapping milk as she prinks herself before her mirror. Well and good! Now we can get down to brass tacks, you and I. Here is your balance-sheet. We have yonder Papa, Mamma, Great-Aunt, two sisters (eighteen and seventeen years old), two little brothers (fifteen and ten), that's the muster-roll of the crew. The aunt brings up your sisters. The curé comes to teach the two brothers Latin. The family eats more chestnut soup than white bread. Papa takes care not to wear out his trousers; if Mamma has a fresh dress for the summer, and one for the winter, that's about all she has; our sisters make do as best they can. I know all about it, I have lived in the South. That's how things are at home if they send you twelve hundred francs a year and your little estate brings in only three thousand. We have a cook and a man-servant, for Papa is a Baron and we must keep up appearances.

'As for us, we are ambitious; we are connected with the Beauséants, and we go on foot; we want to be rich and haven't got a halfpenny; we eat Ma Vauquer's messes and have a taste for the fine dinners of the Faubourg Saint-Germain; we sleep on a pallet and long for a mansion! I don't blame you for wanting these things. To have ambition, my bright lad, is not given to everyone. Ask women what kind of men they run after – "ambitious men" is the answer. The backs of the ambitious are stronger, their blood more rich in iron, their hearts warmer than those of other men. And a woman knows herself so happy and so lovely in the hours when she is strong, that she prefers above all men the man whose strength is enormous, even though it may mean her destruction.

126

'I'm listing your ambitions to put the question that faces you before you squarely; and here is the question. We're as hungry as a wolf, our little teeth are sharp, how shall we set about providing for the pot? We have the Code to swallow first; it's not amusing, it teaches us nothing, but it has to be done. So far so good. We make ourselves a lawyer with a view to becoming President of an Assize Court, in order to send poor devils who are better men than we are to the galleys with T.F. branded on their shoulders, so that the rich may be shown that they can sleep in peace. It's not amusing, and then it takes a long time. First, two years' drudgery in Paris, looking at the goodies we're greedy for but never laying hands on them. It's tiresome to keep on wanting things and never having them. If you were an anaemic, slug-like creature there would be nothing to fear, but we have the feverish blood of lions in our veins and an appetite for twenty foolhardy acts a day. So you will succumb to this torture, the ghastliest form of torture we know of in God's hell. But suppose you are a good boy, and bemoan your troubles over a glass of milk; then, gallant fellow that you are, after plenty of troubles and hardships enough to drive a dog mad, you will have to begin by becoming deputy to some rascal in a hole of a town where the Government will fling you a thousand francs a year, like scraps to a butcher's dog. Bark after thieves, plead the cause of the rich, send high-spirited folk to the guillotine. Thanks a lot! If you have no influence you will rot in your provincial court. At the age of thirty you will be a Justice at twelve hundred francs a year, if you haven't thrown your gown to the nettles before then. When you reach forty you will marry some miller's daughter, worth about six thousand livres a year. Thanks again! With the help of influence you will be Public Prosecutor at thirty with a salary of three thousand francs, and will marry the mayor's daughter. If you stoop to a few petty political dirty tricks, such as reading Villèle for Manuel on a bulletin (the names rhyme and that sets one's conscience at rest) at forty you'll probably be an Attorney-General, and may be made a Deputy.

Note, my dear young friend, that we shall have rubbed a certain amount of bloom off our little conscience, that we shall have had twenty years of tiresome worries and secret wretchedness, and that our sisters will be old maids. I have the honour to point out to you, moreover, that there are only twenty Attorney-Generals in France, and that you aspirants to that rank are twenty thousand strong, among whom are rascals who would sell their families to climb one rung.

'If that sort of thing disgusts you let's look at something else. Does the Baron de Rastignac think of becoming an advocate? Oh, excellent! He must slave for ten years, live at the rate of a thousand francs a month, have a library and chambers, go into society, go down on his knees before a solicitor for briefs, sweep the floor of the Palais de Justice with his tongue. If this led to anything good I should not say no; but show me five advocates in Paris who earn more than fifty thousand francs a year at fifty! Bah! Sooner than shrivel my soul like that I would turn pirate. Moreover, where would you find the cash? That question is no joke. We have one resource in a wife's dowry. Do you feel like marrying? That will put a millstone round your neck; and then if you marry for money what becomes of our notions of honour, our fine feelings? You might as well begin your revolt against human convictions to-day. It would be nothing to grovel like a snake before a wife, to lick her mother's feet, commit vile acts that would disgust a sow, ugh! if you at least found happiness, but you would be as wretched as the stones of a gutter with a wife whom you married on those terms. It's a much better thing to fight men than to bicker with one's wife.

'There are the crossroads of life, young man; choose! In fact you have already chosen: you went to your cousin de Beauséant's house and sniffed the sweet odour of luxury there; you went to Madame de Restaud, old Goriot's daughter, and there became conscious of the Parisian woman. That day you came back with one word written on your forehead and I knew well how to read it – it was *Success!* success at any price. "Bravo!" I said. "Here's a fine fellow who suits me well." You needed money. Where were you to get it? You bled your sisters. All brothers sponge on their sisters more or less. Your fifteen hundred francs, squeezed out God knows how! in a country where chestnuts are more plentiful than five-franc pieces, will slip away like soldiers on a raid. And then what will you do? Will you work? Work, or what you understand by work at this moment, leads in old age to a room in Mamma Vauquer's boarding-house, for men of Poiret's calibre. Fifty thousand young men at this very moment are in your position and are racking their brains to find a quick road to success. There are as many of you as that. You may judge of the efforts you must make and the bitterness of the struggle. You must devour each other like spiders in a pot, seeing there are not fifty thousand good positions for you. Do you know how a man makes his way here? By the brilliance of genius or the cunning use of corruption. You must cut a path through this mass of men like a cannon-ball, or creep among them like a pestilence. Honesty is of no avail. Men give way before the power of genius, they hate it and try to blow upon it because it takes without sharing the plunder, but they give way if it persists; in short, they worship it on their knees when they have failed in their efforts to bury it under the mud. Corruption is powerful in the world: talent is scarce. So corruption is the instrument of swarming mediocrity, and you will feel its point everywhere. You will see wives whose husbands have six thousand francs a year, all told, spend more than ten thousand francs on dress. You will see officials with a salary of twelve hundred francs buy estates. You will see women sell themselves to enter the carriage of the son of a peer of France who can spin to Longchamps on the middle carriageway. You have seen that poor simpleton, old Goriot, obliged to meet the bill of exchange endorsed by his daughter, whose husband has an income of fifty thousand francs a year. I defy you to walk two steps in Paris without encountering hellishly underhand dealings. I would bet my head against a head of that salad that you'll stir up a wasps' nest in the first woman you admire, be she rich, beautiful and young. They are all law-dodgers, all at logger-heads with their husbands about everything. I should go on for ever if I had to describe the deals that are made for lovers, finery, children, housekeeping, or for vanity, rarely for the sake of virtue, you may be sure. So the honest man is the common enemy.

'But who do you think the honest man may be? In Paris the honest man is the man who holds his tongue and refuses to share his loot. I'm not speaking of those poor helots who do the work everywhere without any reward for their toil, whom I call the brotherhood of God's almighty duffers. Certainly virtue is there in the full flower of its stupidity, but so is poverty. I can see the sour faces of those honest folk if God played us the ill-mannered trick of being absent on the Last Judgement day.

'Well then, if you want to make a fortune quickly you must already be rich, or appear to be so. It's a matter here of playing for high stakes; if you don't you're trifling, you cut no ice, and goodbye to you! If in the scores of professions you might follow ten men rise to the top quickly the public calls them thieves. Draw your own conclusions. That is life in its true colours. It's not much more attractive than the kitchen, it's just as smelly and you have to dirty your hands if you want to live well. The only thing that matters is to know how to get them clean again; in that art lies the whole morality of our times.

'If I talk to you like this about the world it's because it has given me reason to do so, I know it well. Do you think I blame it? Not at all. It has always been like this. Moralists will never change it. Man is no angel. He is sometimes more of a hypocrite and sometimes less, and then fools say that he has or has not principles. I don't think the rich are any worse than the masses: men are much the same at the top, the bottom, and in the middle of the social scale. In a million of this herd of human cattle there are ten sharp fellows to be found who climb above everything, even above laws; I am one of them. You, if you're above the common herd, go straight forward with your head high. But you will have to fight against envy, slander, mediocrity, against the whole world. Napoleon came up against a Minister of War called Aubry who just failed to send him to the Colonies. Sound yourself! See if you will be able to get up every morning with a will more determined than it was the night before. In that case I am going to make you an offer that nobody would refuse. Mind what I say.

'You see I have a fancy. My notion is to go and live the patriarchal life on a great estate, say a hundred thousand acres, in the United States of America, in the deep South. I intend to be a planter, to have slaves, earn a few nice little millions selling my cattle, my tobacco, my timber, living like a monarch, doing as I like, leading a life unimaginable by people here where we live crouched in a burrow made of stone and plaster. I am a great poet. My poems are not written: they are expressed in action and in feeling. I possess at this moment fifty thousand francs, which would give me scarcely forty niggers. I need two hundred thousand francs, for I want two hundred niggers to carry out my idea of the patriarchal life properly. Negroes, you see, are children ready-made that you can do what you like with, without a nosy Public Prosecutor coming to ask you questions about them. With this black capital, in ten years I shall have three or four millions. If I succeed no one will say to me, "Who are you?" I shall be Mr Four-Millions, American citizen. I shall be fifty years of age, not yet rotten; I shall enjoy myself in my own fashion.

'In one word, if I find you an heiress worth a million will you give me two hundred thousand francs? Twenty per cent commission; well, is that too much? You will make your little wife love you. Once married you will make a show of uneasiness and remorse, you will go about with a long face for a couple of weeks. Then one night after some tomfoolery you will confess to your wife between two kisses that you have debts amounting to two hundred thousand francs, and call her "Darling!" This farce is played every day by young fellows of the highest rank. A young woman does not refuse her purse to the man who captures her heart. Do you think that you will be a loser by it? Not you. You will find a way to make up your two hundred thousand francs again by a stroke of business. With your capital and your sharp wits you will pile up a fortune as large as your heart could wish. *Ergo* in six months you will have made us all happy, yourself, a sweet wife, and your old Papa Vautrin, not to speak of your family, blowing on their fingers in the winter-time for want of fire-wood. Don't let my offer, or what I ask for either, startle you. Out of sixty fashionable marriages taking place in Paris forty-seven are made on similar terms. The Chamber of Notaries forced Monsieur – '

'What must I do?' said Rastignac, eagerly interrupting him.

'Practically nothing,' Vautrin replied, with an involuntary movement of delight like the suppressed exclamation of an angler feeling a bite at the end of his line. 'Mark this well. The heart of a poor unfortunate and unhappy girl is the thirstiest of sponges to soak up love, a parched sponge which expands as soon as a drop of tenderness falls on it. To court a young woman you meet in circumstances of loneliness, despair and poverty, when she has no suspicion of the wealth in store for her; by Heaven! it's like having a sequence of five and a quatorze at piquet, it's knowing the numbers in the lottery beforehand, it's playing the stock market with secret information. On a solid foundation you are building an indestructible marriage. When the girl comes into millions she will throw them at your feet like pebbles. "Take them, my dearest Adolphe!" she will say, or "Take them, my dearest Alfred!" or "Eugène", or anyone who has had the wit to sacrifice himself for her. By "sacrifice" I mean selling your old coat in order to eat mushrooms on toast with her at the Cadran-Bleu and go on afterwards to the Ambigu-Comique in the evening, or pawning your watch to give her a shawl. I needn't say anything to you about scribbling love-letters to her, or the sentimental monkey-tricks that go down so well with women, such as sprinkling drops of water on your writing-paper like tears when you are separated from her: you seem to me to be perfectly well acquainted with the lingo of the heart.

'Paris, you see, is like a forest in the New World where a score of savage tribes, the Illinois, the Hurons, struggle for existence: each different social class lives on what it can get by hunting. You are a hunter of millions; to capture them you employ snares, limed twigs, decoys. There are many ways of hunting. Some hunt heiresses, others catch their prey by shady financial transactions; some fish for souls, others sell their clients bound hand and foot. The man who comes back with his game-bag well lined is welcomed, fêted, received into good society. Let us be just to this hospitable place, here you have to do with the most accommodating city in the world. If the proud aristocracies of all the capitals of Europe refuse to give a blackguard millionaire admittance to their ranks, Paris holds out her arms to him, runs to his parties, eats his dinners and clinks glasses with his infamy.'

'But where should I find such a girl?' said Eugène.

'She is there, before your eyes, and yours already!'

'Mademoiselle Victorine?'

'Precisely.'

'Say that again!'

'She loves you already, your little Baroness de Rastignac!'

'She hasn't got a sou,' said Eugène in astonishment.

'Ah! now we're coming to it. Another word or two and everything will be clear. Father Taillefer is an old scoundrel who is credited with having murdered one of his friends during the Revolution: he is one of my brave boys who are independent in their views. He is a banker, senior partner in the firm of Frédéric Taillefer and Company. He has only one son and means to leave all he possesses to him, to the prejudice of Victorine. Such injustices don't please me. I'm like Don Quixote, I like to defend the weak against the strong. If it were the will of Heaven to take his son from him Taillefer would acknowledge his daughter.

He would want to have someone or other to leave his money to, it's a weakness of human nature, and he's not likely to have any more children, I know. Victorine is gentle and sweet, she will soon twist her father round her little finger, and make him veer like a weathercock in the wind of sentiment! She will appreciate your devotion too much to forget you and you will marry her. For my part I will take the rôle of Providence upon myself: I'll persuade the will of Heaven to act in the right way. I have a friend I've done some very good turns to, a colonel in the Army of the Loire who has just been transferred into the Garde Royale. He's a man who listens to my advice and he turned ultra-royalist: he isn't one of those idiots who stick to their opinions. If I have one more piece of advice to give you, my sweet lad, it is this – don't stick any more firmly to your opinions than to your word. When you are asked for them, sell them. A man who boasts of never changing his opinions is a man who forces himself to move always in a straight line, a simpleton who believes he is infallible. There are no such things as principles, there are only events; there are no laws, there are only circumstances: the man who is wiser than his fellows accepts events and circumstances in order to turn them to his own ends. If there were fixed principles and laws nations would not change them as easily as we change our shirts. The individual is not expected to be more scrupulous than the nation. The man who has rendered least service to France is the uncompromising La Fayette, yet he is a fetish, venerated because he has always seen everything in bright colours; at best he's good enough to be put in the Conservatoire among the machines, and labelled like the rest of the exhibits: while Talleyrand, the tortuous Talleyrand, the prince at whom everyone has a stone to fling, who has sufficient contempt for humanity to spit as many vows as it asks for in its face, was the man who saved France from being torn to pieces at the Congress of Vienna – they fling mud at him and they owe him laurel wreaths. Oh! I know what's going on in the world. I hold the key to many men's secrets! That's enough. I shall hold an unalterable opinion when I find three minds agreed on the application of a principle, and I shall wait a long time! There are not three judges in the law-courts with the same opinion about a point of law.

'Well, to return to my man, – he would put Christ back on the cross if I told him to. At a single word from his Papa Vautrin he will pick a quarrel with that scamp who doesn't send so much as a five-franc piece to his sister, and' – Vautrin rose to his feet, took up a defensive posture like a fencing-master, and then lunged. ' – and underground!' he added.

'Oh, horrible!' said Eugène. 'You're joking, Monsieur Vautrin, aren't you? You must be!'

'Now, now, keep cool!' said the man. 'Don't behave like a child. Still, if it amuses you, you can stamp your foot and fly into a rage. You can call me a scoundrel, a scalawag, a rapscallion, a ruffian, only don't call me a blackleg or a spy. Go ahead, fire your broadside. I forgive you, it's so natural at your age. I was like that myself once. Only, consider: you will do worse some day. You will go and flirt with some pretty woman, and you will take her money. The thought has entered your mind, of course,' said Vautrin, 'for how are you to get on if your love-making doesn't bring you money? Virtue, my dear student, is indivisible: it either is, or it is not. They tell us to do penance for our sins: that's a fine system which rids you of a crime by an act of contrition! You seduce a woman in order to set your foot on some rung of the social ladder, you stir up dissension among the children of a family, you stoop to all the shameful practices that are employed, under the rose or openly, for the sake of pleasure or personal advantage: do you believe those are works of faith, hope and charity? Why should the toff who robs a boy of half his fortune in a night get off with two months in prison, while the poor devil who steals a hundred-franc note with aggravating circumstances is sent to penal servitude? Those are your laws. There isn't a clause in them which doesn't touch absurdity. The honey-tongued man in yellow gloves has committed many a murder, he sheds no blood, but his victim sweats blood for him all the same; the other rascal opened a door with a jemmy: dark deeds both of them! Between what I propose and what you will one day do there's no difference, bar the bloodshed. And you believe in absolute standards in that world! Despise men then, and look for the holes you can slip through in the Law's net. The secret of great fortunes with no apparent source is a forgotten crime, forgotten because it was properly carried out.'

'Oh, don't say any more! I don't want to listen to you, you make me doubt myself. At this moment I only know what I feel.'

'As you please, my fine fellow. I thought you were tougher,' said Vautrin. 'I won't say any more. Just one thing though.' He stared hard at the student. 'You know my secret,' he said.

'A young man who refuses you will know he must forget it.'

'That's well said. I'm pleased with you. Anyone else, you know, will be less scrupulous. Bear in mind what I want to do for you. I'll give you a fortnight to decide about my offer. You can take it or leave it.'

'What a will of iron that man has!' said Rastignac to himself as he watched Vautrin walk unconcernedly away, his stick under his arm. 'Yet he only told me bluntly what Madame de Beauséant dressed up in polished phrases. He tore my heart with claws of steel. Why do I intend to visit Madame de Nucingen? He guessed my motives before I knew them myself. In fact that outlaw told me more about virtue than I've ever learned before from men or books. If virtue admits of no compromise have I robbed my sisters, then?' he said, throwing the bag on the table. He sat down again, his brain in a whirl, and went on pondering. 'Must I be faithful to virtue, a heroic martyr? Bah! Everyone believes in virtue, but who practises it? Every nation worships liberty, but where on the face of the earth can you find a free nation? My youth is still like a blue, unclouded sky. Does wishing to be great or rich mean that I must make up my mind to lie, give way, cringe and spring up again, flatter and dissemble? Does it mean making myself the lackey of other men who have lied, yielded and cringed? I must be their servant before I can be their accomplice. Well, then, no! I mean to work honourably and uprightly; I will work day and night, and owe my fortune to nothing but my own exertions. It will be the slowest of roads to fortune, but every night I shall lay my head on my pillow, untroubled by evil thoughts. What can be finer than to look back on your life and find it as free from stain as a lily? Life and I are like a young man and his sweetheart. Vautrin has let me see what happens after ten years of married life. Hell! my head is swimming. I don't want to think about anything at all, the heart is a sure guide.'

Fat Sylvie's voice roused Eugène from his musings. She announced that his tailor had come, and Eugène went to interview the tailor with his money-bags in his hand, and was not at all displeased to be appearing thus. Having tried on his dress clothes he put his new morning costume on, and was transformed completely by it.

'I'm every bit as good as Monsieur de Trailles now,' he said to himself. 'That is to say, I look like a gentleman!'

Old Goriot came to the student's door. 'You asked me, sir, if I knew the houses Madame de Nucingen visits,' he said.

'Yes.'

'Well, she is going to the Maréchal Carigliano's ball on Monday. If you can manage to be there you will let me know how my two girls enjoyed themselves, and what they wore and all about it, won't you?'

'How did you find that out, my good Goriot?' asked Eugène, giving his visitor a chair by the fire.

'Her maid told me. I hear about everything they do from Thérèse and Constance,' he added gleefully. The old man was like a lover who is still young enough to be delighted by a stratagem which gives him a point of contact with his mistress without her knowledge. '*You* will see them both!' he went on, naïvely betraying his pang of jealousy.

'I don't know,' Eugène replied. 'I'll call on Madame de Beauséant and ask if she can present me to the Marshal's wife.'

Eugène felt a thrill of secret joy as he thought of appearing before the Viscountess dressed as he would be from that day forward. What moralists call 'the abysses of the human heart' are only the treacherous thoughts, the involuntary impulses, of self-interest. Those strayings from the course marked out, which are so often inveighed against, those sudden changes of direction, are moves prompted by the hope of pleasure. Rastignac, seeing himself well-dressed, with the correct gloves and boots, forgot his virtuous resolutions. Youth, moreover, when it turns to wrong-doing dares not look at itself in the mirror of conscience, while maturity has seen itself there: the whole difference between these two phases of life lies in that.

In the last few days Eugène and his neighbour, old Goriot, had become good friends. This growing secret friendliness had the same psychological causes as the antipathy which the student was beginning to feel to Vautrin. The bold philosopher who sets out to establish the effects produced in the physical world by our emotions will undoubtedly find more than one proof of their influence on matter in the means of communication they set up between us and the lower animals. What physiognomist is quicker to apprehend a character than a dog is at knowing whether a stranger likes him or not? 'Atoms', 'affinities', familiar words in common use, are facts whose names have survived in modern languages to the confusion of those fatuous philosophers who like to winnow the chaff from the fundamental words of the language. We *feel* that we are loved. Feeling affects everything, and can cross space. A letter is a living soul, it is so faithful an echo of the voice which speaks in it that sensitive spirits count it among love's richest treasures. Old Goriot's devotion, a matter of feeling not of mind, had given him the sublime sensitivity of the canine world, and he had intuitively perceived the compassion for him, the kindly admiration, the youthful sympathy, which had stirred in the student's heart.

This dawning friendship, however, had not yet led to any confidences. If Eugène had made his desire to see Madame de Nucingen clear, it was not because he was relying on the old man to introduce him to her house; but he hoped that an indiscretion might serve him well. Old Goriot had only spoken of his daughters to him in reference to what Eugène had said so frankly in public about them, on the day of his two afternoon calls.

'My dear sir,' he had said to him next day, 'how could you have thought that Madame de Restaud was cross with you for mentioning my name? My two girls are very fond of me. I am a happy father; but my sons-in-law have behaved badly. I did not want my darlings to suffer because of my differences with their husbands, and so I prefer to see them in secret. My clandestine glimpses of them give me far more pleasure than other fathers enjoy who can see their daughters whenever they like. I can't do that, you understand, and so when it is fine I go to the Champs-Élysées, after finding out from the maids if my daughters are going out. I wait for them to pass; my heart beats fast when their carriages come; I admire them in their fine dresses; they throw me a little smile as they pass and then the sun seems to come out and gild all nature for me. I wait, for they will come back the same way, and I see them again! The air has done them good, their cheeks are rosy. I hear someone near me say, "That's a beautiful woman!" That makes my heart rejoice. Are they not my flesh and blood? I love the horses that draw them, and envy the little dog on their lap. I live in their pleasure. Every man loves in his own fashion; mine does no harm to anyone, so why should people trouble themselves about me? I am happy in my own way. Is there any law against my going to see my daughters in the evening, when they are leaving to go to a ball? What a disappointment it is if I get there too late and they say, "Madame has gone out." Once I waited till three in the morning to see Nasie, when I had not seen her for two days. I nearly died of joy! Please don't speak of me unless you want to say how good my girls are. They would like to spoil me with all sorts of presents, but I don't let them. "Keep your money," I tell them. "What should I do with it? I don't want anything." For what, my dear sir, am I after all? A wretched old carcase whose soul is wherever my daughters are. When you have seen Madame de Nucingen you must tell me which you think most of,' the old fellow added after a moment, as he watched Eugène preparing to go out. He meant to pass the time walking in the Tuileries gardens until he could venture to present himself in Madame de Beauséant's drawing-room.

That walk was fatal to the student's good intentions. Several women noticed him: he was so handsome, so young, dressed with such elegance, in such good taste! When he saw himself the centre of an almost admiring attention he thought no more about his plundered sisters and aunt, nor of his virtuous qualms. He had seen passing over his head that fiend whom it is so easy to take for an angel, the Devil with the iridescent wings who scatters rubies, and shoots his golden arrows against palaces, who clothes women in splendour and gilds thrones, so simple in their original function, with a senseless magnificence; he had listened to the flashy allurements of that Vanity whose crackling tinsel seems to us a symbol of power. Cynical as Vautrin's words were they had effected a lodgement in the student's heart, as the sordid profile of an old crone hawking rags dwells in the memory of the girl for whom she has predicted 'oceans of love and money'.

Eugène idly strolled along until about five o'clock, and then called at Madame de Beauséant's. There he received one of the terrible blows against which young hearts are defenceless. Up to that moment the Viscountess had always shown him the polished courtesy, the bland graciousness of manner, which are the gift of an aristocratic training but are perfect only when they come from the heart. Now when he came in Madame de Beauséant made a sharp gesture, and said curtly,

'Monsieur de Rastignac, I can't possibly see you, at least not now; I'm busy – '

To an observer, and Rastignac had rapidly become one, these words and the gesture, her glance, the inflexion of her voice, told the whole story of the character and usages of her caste. He perceived the iron hand under the velvet glove, the selfishness, the egotism, under the good breeding, the wood beneath the varnish. He understood at last the edict WE THE KING which issues from under the plumes above the royal throne and is still heard under the crest of the simplest nobleman.

Eugène had trusted a woman too whole-heartedly; he could not believe in her haughtiness. Like all the unfortunate he had signed in good faith the liberal pact which should bind the benefactor to the beneficiary, and whose first article demands complete equality between two generous hearts. The charity which binds two souls together and makes them one is a divine passion as little understood and as rare as true love is: both are the generous gift of noble natures.

But Rastignac was set on going to the Duchesse de Carigliano's ball, so he swallowed this rebuff.

'Madame,' he said in a faltering voice, 'I should not have come to trouble you if it were not a matter of importance; be so kind as to allow me to see you later, I can wait.'

'Very well, then, come and dine with me,' she said, a little embarrassed by the harshness with which she had spoken; for this woman was truly as kind in nature as she was noble in rank.

Although Eugène was touched by this sudden change of tone he said to himself as he went away,

'You must crawl, put up with anything. What can the others be like if one of the kindest of women cancels all her promises of friendship in a moment, and casts you off like an old shoe? Is it every man for himself, then? It is true that her house is not a shop, and I put myself in the wrong by needing her. As Vautrin said, you should smash your way like a cannon-ball.'

But the bitterness of his reflections soon disappeared in the pleasure of looking forward to dinner with the Viscountess.

Thus by a sort of fatality the slightest accidents of the student's life conspired to push him into an arena where, according to the observations of the terrifying sphinx of the Maison Vauquer, he must kill to avoid being killed, as if on a battlefield, betray to avoid being betrayed; where he must leave his conscience and his heart at the gate, put on a mask, use men ruthlessly like pawns, and, as in ancient Sparta, seize the prize without being seen, to deserve the crown.

On his return he found the Viscountess as gracious and kind as she had always been to him. They entered a dining-room where the Viscount was waiting for his wife near a table furnished with the sumptuousness which, as is well known, was carried to extremes in the time of the Restoration. Like many wearying men of the world, Monsieur de Beauséant had few pleasures left other than those afforded by good food; in fact he was a gourmand of the school of Louis XVIII and the Duc d'Escars. His table, then, offered a double luxury: delicious food was served in splendid vessels. This was the first time Eugène had dined in one of the houses where traditions of magnificence are hereditary, and his eyes were dazzled by a spectacle the like of which he had never seen before. A change of fashion had done away with the supper with which balls formerly ended, a custom made necessary in the time of the Empire because the officers who were present must be fortified before departing for the combats awaiting them, which might be very near at hand; and so far Eugène had only been invited to balls. The self-possession which distinguished him so pre-eminently later in life came to his aid even then and prevented him from gaping boorishly; but as he noticed the beautifully fashioned silver plate, and the many elegant appointments of a sumptuous table, and for the first time in his life admired a noiseless service, it was difficult for a man of his ardent imagination not to prefer this refined and cultured way of living to the life of hardship he had chosen that morning. For a moment he called before his mind a picture of the boarding-house, and was seized with such deep loathing of it that he vowed to himself that in January he would leave it, desiring as much to be in tolerable surroundings as to shake off Vautrin, whose great hand he seemed to feel on his shoulder.

When one begins to think of the innumerable forms, clamorous or mute, which corruption takes in Paris, any man of common sense may inquire by what aberration the State founds schools there, and assembles young people; he wonders how pretty women can be respected there, and why the coins displayed by money-changers do not take wings to themselves and fly away out of the wooden bowls. But if one goes on to consider that there are few cases of crime, or even of misdeeds committed by young men, what respect one must feel for those patient Tantaluses who wrestle with themselves and are almost always victorious! Depicted exactly as he is in his struggle with Paris, the poor student would furnish one of the most dramatic subjects of our modern civilization.

Madame de Beauséant kept looking at Eugène as if to invite him to talk, but in vain; there was nothing he wished to say in the presence of the Viscount.

'Are you taking me to the Italiens this evening?' the Viscountess asked her husband.

'You cannot doubt the pleasure it would give me to obey you,' he replied with a mocking gallantry which the student accepted at its face value, 'but I have to meet someone at the Variétés.'

'His mistress,' she told herself.

'Is d'Ajuda not coming for you this evening, then?' the Viscount asked.

'No,' she answered shortly.

'Well, if you positively must have someone's arm, take Monsieur de Rastignac's.'

The Viscountess turned to Eugène with a smile.

'That would be very compromising for you,' she said.

' "The Frenchman loves danger, because in danger he finds glory," to use Monsieur de Chateaubriand's words,' replied Rastignac, with a bow.

A few moments later, seated by Madame de Beauséant's side in her brougham, he was being swiftly borne through Paris to the fashionable theatre, and imagined himself to be under some magic spell as he entered a box facing the stage and saw all the lorgnettes levelled at the Viscountess in her charming toilet, and at himself. He passed from enchantment to enchantment.

'You must talk to me, you know,' said Madame de Beauséant. 'Ah! look, there is Madame de Nucingen three boxes away. Her sister and Monsieur de Trailles are on the other side.'

As she spoke the Viscountess was looking at the box where Mademoiselle de Rochefide should be, and as she saw that Monsieur d'Ajuda was not there her face grew radiant.

'She's bewitching,' said Eugène, when he had gazed at Madame de Nucingen.

'She has white eyelashes.'

'Yes, but what a pretty slender figure!'

'And her hands are large.'

'But her eyes are lovely.'

'How long her face is!'

'The long shape has distinction.'

'That's fortunate for her, then. Look how she fidgets with her opera-glasses. Her Goriot ancestors show in every movement she makes,' said the Vicountess, much to Eugène's astonishment, for Madame de Beauséant was scanning the whole assembly through her glasses and apparently paying no attention to Madame de Nucingen, yet nothing she did escaped her. All the loveliest women in Paris were there, so that Delphine de Nucingen was not a little flattered to be engaging the exclusive attention of Madame de Beauséant's young, handsome and fashionably-dressed cousin; he had eyes only for her.

'If you go on devouring her with your eyes, you'll give rise to scandal, Monsieur de Rastignac. You'll never succeed if you throw yourself at a person's head like that.'

'My dear cousin,' said Eugène, 'you have already shown great kindness to me; if you care to complete your work I only ask a favour which will cost you little trouble and be of great service to me. I have lost my heart.'

'Already?'

'Yes.'

'And to that woman?'

'Would my aspirations elsewhere be listened to?' he said with a searching look at his cousin. He paused a moment, and then went on, 'Madame la Duchesse de Carigliano is a friend of the Duchesse de Berry, you are sure to see her. Will you be so kind as to present me to her and take me with you to the ball which she is giving on Monday? I shall meet Madame de Nucingen there and engage in my first skirmish.'

'Willingly,' she answered, 'if you have taken a liking for her already your love-affairs are getting along very well. Look, that is de Marsay in the Princesse Galathionne's box. Madame de Nucingen is on the rack, she is disconsolate. There is no better time for approaching a woman, especially if she's a banker's wife. Those ladies of the Chaussée d'Antin all love revenge.'

'What would you do, then, in the same circumstances?'

'I? I would suffer in silence.'

At this point the Marquis d'Ajuda presented himself in Madame de Beauséant's box.

'I'm playing the deuce with my affairs to come and join you,' he said. 'I'm telling you so that it may not be a sacrifice.'

The radiance of the Viscountess's face taught Eugène to recognize the expression of a genuine love; from that time forward he could not confound it with the affectations of Parisian coquetry. He looked at his cousin with admiration, fell silent, and sighing yielded his place to Monsieur d'Ajuda.

'How noble, how sublime a woman is when she loves so deeply!' he said to himself. 'And this man would forsake her for a doll. Oh! how could anyone forsake her?'

He felt a boy's rage fill his heart. He wanted to fling himself at Madame de Beauséant's feet; he longed for the power of demons to carry her off to the stronghold of his heart, as an eagle snatches a white suckling kid from the plain and carries it off to his eyrie. He felt humiliated at being alone in this great Gallery of Beauty, without his picture, without a mistress of his own.

'To have a mistress, and a place in this almost royal caste,' he said to himself, ' – that is the badge of power.' And he looked at Madame de Nucingen as a man insulted looks at his adversary.

The Viscountess turned towards him and with her eyes expressed a thousand thanks for his discretion. Just then the first act came to an end.

'Do you know Madame de Nucingen well enough to present Monsieur de Rastignac to her?' she asked the Marquis d'Ajuda.

'She will be delighted to see Monsieur de Rastignac,' said the Marquis.

The handsome Portuguese rose and took the student's arm, and in a twinkling Eugène found himself before Madame de Nucingen.

'Madame,' said the Marquis, 'I have the honour to present to you the Chevalier Eugène de Rastignac, a cousin of Madame de Beauséant's. You have made such a profound impression on him that I felt I should complete his happiness by bringing him nearer his idol.'

These words were said with a certain note of good-humoured mockery which made it possible to overlook their slightly disrespectful meaning. Such flattery as they implied, if it is presented with propriety, is never displeasing to a woman. Madame de Nucingen smiled, and offered Eugène the place her husband had just left.

'I don't venture to suggest that you should stay with me, Monsieur,' she said, 'a man who is fortunate enough to be Madame de Beauséant's escort does not like to leave her for long.'

'But it seems to me, Madame,' said Eugène in a low voice, 'that I should please my cousin best by staying with you. Before Monsieur le Marquis arrived we were talking of you and remarking on your extremely distinguished appearance,' he added aloud.

Monsieur d'Ajuda withdrew.

'You are really going to stay?' said the Baroness. 'Then we shall get to know one another. Madame de Restaud has already made me very anxious to meet you.'

'She is very insincere, then, for she has given orders not to have me admitted to her house.'

'How can that be?'

'I will be frank and tell you the reason, Madame, but I claim all your indulgence when I confide such a secret. I am a neighbour of your father's. I had no idea that Madame de Restaud was his daughter and I was rash enough to talk about him, in all innocence, and I vexed your sister and her husband. You cannot think what a bad impression this unfilial disloyalty made on the Duchesse de Langeais and my cousin; they thought it in very bad taste. When I described the scene to them they laughed till they cried. Then Madame de Beauséant made some reference to the difference between you and your sister and spoke of you in the most favourable terms. She told me how very fond you are of my neighbour, Monsieur Goriot. How, indeed, could you help loving him? He adores you so passionately that I am quite jealous of him. We talked about you this morning for two hours. Then this evening I was dining with my cousin, and I was so full of what your father had told me that I said to her that you could not possibly be as beautiful as you were affectionate. It was no doubt because she realized how warm my admiration was, and wished to gratify it, that Madame de Beauséant brought me with her to-night; she said in her usual gracious way that I should see you here.'

'So, Monsieur, I owe you a debt of gratitude already, do I?' said the banker's wife. 'In no time we shall be old friends.'

'Although friendship with you must be an exceptional pleasure,' said Rastignac, 'I should never wish to be your friend.'

These imbecilities are stereotyped for the use of beginners making their first social encounters, but they always appear charming to women, and are banal only when read in cold blood. The gesture, the tone, the look of a young man give them amazing eloquence. Madame de Nucingen thought Rastignac was fascinating. Then, like any woman, unable to reply to the student's frankly challenging admiration she answered something quite different.

'Yes, my sister does herself no good by the way she behaves to my poor father, who has really been an angel to us. It was only when Monsieur de Nucingen absolutely forbade me to see him except in the morning that I yielded the point, and I have been very unhappy about it for a long time; I shed many tears over it. This cruel decree, coming as it did on top of my husband's brutal treatment, is one of the things that have made my marriage so unhappy. In the world's eyes I am certainly the most enviable woman in Paris, but the most to be pitied in reality. You will think I must have gone out of my mind to talk to you like this, but you know my father, and so I cannot think of you as a stranger.'

'You can never have encountered anyone,' said Eugène, 'more intensely anxious to be your devoted servant. What do all women seek? Is it happiness?' he went on, in soul-stirring tones. 'If happiness for a woman consists in being loved, adored, in having a friend to whom she can confide her desires and her fancies, her sorrows and her joys, to whom she can lay bare her soul with all its engaging faults and noble virtues and have no fear of being betrayed, believe me you can only find an unfailingly devoted ardent heart in a man whose youthful ideals are still untarnished, who would go to his death at a sign from you, who knows nothing yet of the world, and desires to know nothing, because you will be all the world to him. When I tell you about myself you will laugh at my simplicity. I came straight from the depths of the country, completely raw and green, having known only true and loving hearts; and I expected to live without love. It so happened that I met my cousin, who let me read her heart from very near, and through her I caught a glimpse of the infinite treasures of passion. Now, like Chérubin, I am the lover of all women until the day when I can devote myself to one alone. As soon as I saw you when I came in this evening I felt myself borne towards you as if by a tide of the sea. I had already thought so much about you! But I had not dreamed that you would be so beautiful. Madame de Beauséant ordered me not to stare at you so much. She does not know how fascinating it is to see your pretty red lips, your milky

148

skin, your eyes that are so soft. Now I suppose you think *I* am out of *my* mind, but let me babble still – '

Nothing pleases women better than to hear such soft nothings addressed to them: the most inflexible puritan listens even when she may not respond. Rastignac, having once begun, went on telling his tale in an intimate undertone, and Madame de Nucingen encouraged him with smiles, yet glanced from time to time at de Marsay who continued to sit in the Princesse Galathionne's box.

Rastignac did not leave Madame de Nucingen until her husband came to take her home.

'I shall have the pleasure of calling on you, Madame,' said Eugène, 'before the Duchesse de Carigliano's ball.'

'As Matame infites you,' said the Baron, a heavy Alsatian whose round face wore an expression of sinister cunning, 'you are cerdain of a fery goot velcome.'

'Things look promising for me, for she did not resent it when I said, "Can you love me?" The bit is in the horse's mouth, now it only remains to mount and take control,' Eugène told himself, as he went to pay his respects to Madame de Beauséant, who had risen and was about to leave with d'Ajuda. He did not know, poor student, that the Baroness's thoughts were far from him; she was expecting a letter from de Marsay, one of those fateful letters that lacerate the heart. Happy in his delusion, Eugène accompanied the Viscountess to the peristyle, where people wait for their carriages.

'Your cousin looks like a different man,' said the Portuguese, laughing, to the Viscountess, when Rastignac had left them. 'He's going to break the bank! He's as supple as an eel, and I think he will go far. No one but you could have picked a woman out of the dovecote for him at the very moment when she needed a consoler.'

'But,' said Madame de Beauséant, 'we don't know whether she still loves the man who is forsaking her.'

The student walked back from the Théâtre-Italien to the Rue Neuve-Sainte-Geneviève, revolving as he went the most delightful schemes. He had not failed to notice the close scrutiny Madame de Restaud had favoured him with when he entered the Viscountess's box and sat later in Madame de Nucingen's, and concluded that the Countess's door would not be closed in future. He had now four important allies, for he counted on impressing the Marshal's wife favourably, in the innermost circle of Parisian society. He was aware by now that in the complicated play of forces set up in this world by the action and reaction of various interests, he must attach himself to part of the machinery if he wanted to rise to the top of the machine; and, without defining the means he must use too clearly, he felt himself strong enough to grasp at it and make it bear his weight.

'If Madame de Nucingen takes an interest in me I will teach her to manage her husband. The husband deals in the money-market, and with his help I might pick up a fortune in one stroke of business.'

He did not state this baldly to himself in so many words, he had not the subtlety yet to sum up a situation, estimate its possibilities and calculate its chances; these ideas floated on the horizon of his mind in the form of hazy clouds, and although they had not the barbarity of Vautrin's reflections they would have yielded nothing very pure if tested in the crucible of conscience.

So men lapse, by a succession of compromises with evil of that kind, into the lax moral state which is characteristic of this epoch. To-day one meets more rarely than in any previous age with those firmly-based unyielding men who stand four-square against temptation, to whom the slightest deviation from the straight line of rectitude amounts to crime, such magnificent figures of integrity as have inspired two masterpieces, Molière's *Alceste* and, in our own day, Jeanie Deans and her father in Walter Scott's novel. Perhaps a work of the converse kind depicting the devious paths into which a man of the world, a man of ambition, forces his conscience, as he tries to sail close to the wind to reach his end while keeping up appearances, would be not less fine, nor less dramatic.

Rastignac arrived at his lodgings in a state of admiration of

Madame de Nucingen's charms. He remembered how slender she was, as clean-lined and graceful as a swallow. The intoxicating sweetness of her eyes, the delicate silky texture of her skin under which it seemed to him he could perceive the flow of the blood, the enchantment of her voice, her fair hair, he recalled them one by one; and perhaps the exercise of walking by quickening his blood enhanced her fascinations. He knocked impetuously at Goriot's door.

'I have seen Madame Delphine,' he said.

'Where?'

'At the Italiens.'

'Was she enjoying herself? Come in – ' and the old fellow got out of bed, opened the door and promptly returned to bed again.

Eugène who had never been in old Goriot's room before, could not repress a start of astonishment, when, coming straight from the theatre where he had admired the daughter's finery, he saw the wretched hole which was the father's living-place. The window was curtainless. In several places damp had made the paper peel away from the walls and curl up, revealing the smoke-darkened plaster. The old fellow lay on a miserable bed with but one thin blanket and a wadded quilt made from the less worn pieces of Madame Vauquer's old dresses. The floor was damp and dirty. Opposite the window stood a chest of drawers made of rosewood, one of the old-fashioned kind with a bulging front and brass handles representing twisted vine stems bearing leaves or flowers. On an ancient piece of furniture topped with a wooden shelf stood a ewer and wash-basin, and all the things required for shaving. Shoes lay in one corner; a table by the bedside lacked both door and marble top; by the empty grate, which showed no trace of fire, stood the square walnut table whose cross-bar Goriot had made use of to crush his silver tureen. A ramshackle writing-desk on which lay the old man's hat, an armchair stuffed with straw, and two chairs, completed the pitiful furniture. From the canopy of the bed, which was secured to the ceiling by a tatter, hung a ragged strip of cheap red-and-white checked material. The humblest errand-boy could not have been worse lodged in his attic than old Goriot was in Madame Vauquer's boarding-house. Just to look at this room made you shudder and feel oppressed, it was like a prison's most dismal cell. Fortunately Goriot did not see the expression on Eugène's face as the student put down his candle on the bedside table. The old man turned on his side and lay with the bedclothes drawn up to his chin.

'Well,' he said, 'which do you like the best, Madame de Restaud or Madame de Nucingen?'

'I like Madame Delphine the best,' replied the student, 'because she loves you the most.'

When he heard these words, which were warmly spoken, the old fellow thrust an arm out from under the bedclothes and grasped Eugène's hand.

'Thank you, thank you,' he said gratefully. 'What did she say about me?'

The student repeated the Baroness's words, with some embellishments of his own, and the old man listened as if he were hearing Holy Writ.

'Dear child!' he said. 'Yes, yes, indeed she is very fond of me. But don't believe what she said about Anastasie. The two sisters are jealous of each other, don't you see? It's one more proof of their affection. Madame de Restaud is very fond of me too, I'm sure of it. A father with his children is like God with all of us, he sounds the depths of the heart and judges the intentions. One is as loving as the other. Oh! if I had had good sons-in-law I should have been too happy. No happiness here below can be complete, I suppose. If I had lived with them my heart would have danced with joy just at hearing their voices and knowing that they were there, and seeing them go out and come in as I used to when I had them with me at home. Were they nicely dressed?'

'Yes,' said Eugène. 'But, Monsieur Goriot, when your daughters have such splendid houses how can you live in a hole like this?'

'Heavens,' he said with seeming casualness, 'why should I want a better lodging? I can hardly explain how things are; I'm not very good at stringing words together. It's all there,' he added, tapping his heart. 'My life is lived through my two girls. If they are enjoying themselves, if they are happy and finely dressed and have carpets to walk on, what does it matter what sort of cloth covers me or what sort of place I sleep in? I don't feel cold if they are warm, and I'm never dull if they are laughing. The only troubles I have are their troubles. You will know what it's like when you are a father, when you say to yourself as you listen to your children's prattle, "They take their life from me!"; when you feel that you are bound to these little creatures by every drop of blood in your veins, of which they are the creation and the fine flower, for that's how it is! You will feel as if their skin covered your own body and as if you went with them in every step they took. I hear their voice answer me everywhere. A sad glance from them makes my blood run cold. Some day you will know that a father is much happier in his children's happiness than in his own. I cannot explain it to you: it is a feeling in your body that spreads gladness through you. In short, I live three times over. Shall I tell you something strange? Well, when I became a father I understood God. He is there complete in everything because creation sprang from Him. It is just like that with me and my daughters. Only I love my daughters more than God loves the world, for the world is not as beautiful as God is, and my daughters are more beautiful than I. They dwell so closely in my soul that I had a feeling somehow that you would see them this evening. By Heaven! I would be the devoted slave of a man who would make my little Delphine as happy as a woman is when she is adored; I would black his boots and run his errands for him. I knew from what her maid told me that that little Monsieur de Marsay was a miserable cur: I have longed at times to wring his neck. What! he does not love a jewel of a woman with a nightingale's voice, and made like a model! Had she no eyes when she married that great log of an Alsatian? They should both have had nice handsome young men whom they could have loved. Ah, well, they followed their fancy.'

Old Goriot was sublime. Eugène had never before had the chance of seeing him ablaze with the fires of paternal love. The power of animation strong feeling possesses is worthy of remark. However, heavy the clay of which a man is made, as soon as he gives utterance to a deep and true affection there flows from him an ethereal fluid which modifies the aspect of his face, gives life to his gesture and colour to his voice. Impelled by passion, the most stupid human being often achieves the highest eloquence of ideas, if not of words, and seems to move in a world irradiated. Just then the voice and gesture of the simple old man had that power of winning an instant responsive sympathy which distinguishes the great actor. But are not our deep affections the poetry created by the mind?

'Well,' said Eugène, 'perhaps you will not be sorry to hear that she is likely to break with de Marsay soon. That fine fellow has left her to pursue the Princesse Galathionne. For my part, I fell in love with Madame Delphine this evening.'

'Nonsense!' said old Goriot.

'I did indeed, and I found some favour in her eyes. We talked love for a whole hour, and I am to go and see her the day after to-morrow, Saturday.'

'Oh! my dear sir, how I should love you if she grew fond of you! You are kind, you would never cause her pain. If you did forsake her I would cut your throat at once. A woman does not love twice, you know. But, heavens, I'm talking rubbish, Monsieur Eugène! It's cold here, you should not stay. And so you really heard her speak? What message did she give you for me?'

'None at all,' said Eugène to himself. 'She told me,' he replied, aloud, 'to say that your daughter sent you a loving kiss.'

'Good night, my neighbour! Sleep well, and pleasant dreams! After your message I've no need to dream. God grant you all you wish! You have come in this evening like a good angel, and brought a sweet breath from my daughter.'

'Poor man,' said Eugène as he went to bed, 'it's enough to touch a heart of stone. His daughter no more thought of him than she did of the Grand Turk.'

This conversation made old Goriot perceive that his neighbour was an unlooked-for confidant and friend. They were joined together by the only bond with which this old man could be attached to another man. The passions never make mistakes. Old Goriot felt himself a little closer to his daughter Delphine, he thought that he would be more welcome if Eugène were dear to her. Moreover he had confided one of the things that troubled him to Eugène. Madame de Nucingen, whose happiness he prayed for a thousand times a day, had never known the sweetness of love. Most certainly Eugène was, to use his own expression, one of the nicest young men he had ever seen, and he seemed to feel prophetically that she would find in Eugène all the joy that she had missed. Thus a friendship began between the old man and his neighbour which went on growing. But for this friendship it would almost certainly have been impossible to learn how this story ended.

Next morning at breakfast old Goriot looked affectionately at Eugène when he came in, and took a seat beside the student. The other lodgers watched him in surprise as they heard him address a few remarks to his neighbour, and noticed the change in his face, which as a rule had as little expression as a plaster cast. Vautrin stared at the student as if he would read his soul: this was the first time he had seen him since their talk. Before falling asleep the night before Eugène had surveyed the vast field of opportunity that lay before him, and now as he thought of Vautrin's plan he was inevitably reminded of Mademoiselle Taillefer's dowry, and he could not help looking at Victorine as the most virtuous young man may look at a wealthy heiress. She chanced to glance at him and their eyes met. The glance which they exchanged was sufficiently expressive to leave Rastignac in no doubt that she felt for him that vague emotion that stirs in the hearts of all young girls, and finds its object in the nearest attractive human being.

'Eight hundred thousand francs!' a voice cried in his ear, but he hastily summoned up his memories of the evening before, and told himself that his made-to-order passion for Madame de Nucingen was his safeguard, and a refuge from evil thoughts that pursued him against his will.

'They were doing Rossini's *Barber of Seville* at the Italiens yesterday,' he said. 'I never heard such delightful music. People with a box at the Italiens have heaven's own luck!'

Goriot hung on his lips, and watched his face like a dog ready to jump up at his master's first movement.

'You men live in clover,' said Madame Vauquer, 'you do just what you like.'

'How did you get back?' Vautrin asked.

'I walked,' replied Eugène.

'You're not like me,' rejoined the tempter, 'I don't care to do things by halves. I should like to go to the theatre in my carriage, sit in my box, and come back comfortably. All or nothing! That's my motto.'

'And a good one too,' said Madame Vauquer.

'Perhaps you will see Madame de Nucingen to-day,' said Eugène in a low voice to Goriot. 'She is sure to receive you with open arms; she will want to ask you lots of little things about me. I have heard that she would do anything in the world to be received at my cousin's, Madame de Beauséant's. Don't forget to tell her that I love her too much not to have thought of trying to give her that pleasure.'

Rastignac went off to the École de Droit at once; he did not want to stay longer than he had to in that hateful house. Afterwards he spent nearly the whole day idly loafing, a prey to the fever in the brain well known to young men afflicted with too lively expectations. Vautrin's arguments gave him food for thought, and he was lost in meditation upon the social order when he chanced to meet his friend Bianchon in the Jardin du Luxembourg.

'Where did you get that solemn face?' said the medical student, putting an arm through his, and walking on with him towards the Palais.

'Temptations give me no peace.'

'What kind of temptations? Temptations can be got rid of.'

'How?'

'By yielding to them.'

'You may laugh, but you don't know what you're laughing at. Have you read Rousseau?'

'Yes.'

'Do you remember the passage where he asks the reader what he would do if he could make a fortune by killing an old mandarin in China by simply exerting his will, without stirring from Paris?'

'Yes.'

'Well?'

'Bah! I'm at my thirty-third mandarin.'

'Don't play the fool. Look here, if it were proved to you that the thing was possible and you only needed to nod your head, would you do it?'

'Is your mandarin well-stricken in years? But, bless you, young or old, paralytic or healthy, upon my word – The devil take it! Well, no.'

'You're a good chap, Bianchon. But suppose you loved a woman madly enough to turn your conscience inside out for her, and she needed money, a lot of money, for her clothes, her carriage, all her whims in fact?'

'You turn my head, and then ask me to use it!'

'Oh! Bianchon, I'm out of my mind, see if you can cure me. I have two sisters who are angels of beauty and innocence, and I want them to be happy. Where am I to get two hundred thousand francs for their dowry within five years? That's the question that confronts me. There are circumstances in life, you see, when you have to play for big stakes and it's no use wasting your luck picking up pennies.'

'But you're simply stating the problem that everybody entering on life is faced with, and you want to cut the Gordian knot with a sword! If you act like that, my dear fellow, you must be Alexander, otherwise you go to prison. I'm quite content, myself, with my humble fortune, to live the quiet country life I mean to fashion for myself, and step into my father's shoes in due course like any stick-in-the-mud. A man's affections are just as fully satisfied within the smallest circle as in a vast circumference. Even Napoleon could only dine once, and could have no more mistresses than a medical student takes when he's living in at the Capucins. Happiness, my dear fellow, will always lie in what's between the soles of our feet and the crown of our head; and whether it costs a million a year or only a hundred louis our appreciation of it is the same in essence, and rests entirely with us. I come to the conclusion that the Chinaman should be allowed to live.'

'Thanks, Bianchon, you have done me good. We will always be cronies, you and I.'

'Look here,' remarked the medical student, 'just now as I was coming from Cuvier's lecture at the Jardin des Plantes I saw that Michonneau woman and Poiret sitting on a bench, talking to a gentleman I saw in the disturbances last year, hanging about the Chambre des Députés. It struck me then that he was a tool of the police disguised as an honest retired tradesman. We had better keep an eye on that pair, I'll tell you why later. Goodbye; I must go to answer to my name at four o'clock.'

When Eugène returned to the boarding-house he found old Goriot waiting for him.

'Look,' said the old man, 'here's a letter from her. Isn't the handwriting pretty?'

Eugène broke open the seal and read as follows:

'My father has told me, Monsieur, that you like Italian music. I shall be delighted if you will do me the pleasure of accepting a seat in my box. We are to hear Fodor and Pellegrini on Saturday, so I am sure that you will not refuse me. Monsieur de Nucingen joins me in requesting you to dine with us informally. If you accept you will please him by making it unnecessary for him to escort me, a husband's duty which he finds irksome. Do not answer, simply come. –

Yours sincerely,

D. DE N.

'Let me see it,' said the old fellow, when Eugène had read the letter. 'You will go, won't you?' he added, holding the writing-paper against his face. 'How nice it smells! Her fingers have touched that, it's easy to see.'

'A woman doesn't throw herself at a man's head like that,' the student was thinking. 'She wants to use me to bring de Marsay back. Only pique could make a person act in this way.'

'Well,' said old Goriot, 'what are you thinking about?'

Eugène was not aware of the mad vanity which possessed some women at that time: he did not know that to open a door in the Faubourg Saint-Germain a banker's wife would stick at nothing. Those who were admitted to the company of the Faubourg Saint-Germain clique were regarded by the fashion of the day as queens among women. They were known as 'Dames du Petit-Château', and in this set Madame de Beauséant, her friend the Duchesse de Langeais, and the Duchesse de Maufrigneuse were brilliant stars. Rastignac was alone in his ignorance of the feverish efforts made by the women of the Chaussée d'Antin to climb to those lofty spheres where the brightest constellations of their sex shone. But his distrustful disposition served him well; it gave him coolness of judgement, and the not altogether pleasurable power of imposing conditions instead of submitting to them.

'Yes, I will go,' he answered Goriot.

So curiosity led him to Madame de Nucingen, yet if she had treated him with disdain he might well have been brought to her by passion. Nevertheless it was not without a certain amount of impatience that he waited for the next day to come, and the hour when he should go to her. A first intrigue has perhaps as much charm for a young man as a first love-affair. The certainty of success is a source of great happiness, although no man ever acknowledges this, and it is in this that all the charm of certain women lies. The desire to conquer is as quickly aroused by the easiness of a triumph as by its difficulty: these two incentives excite or sustain every human passion and divide love's empire between them. Perhaps this division is one of the consequences of the great question of temperaments which, whatever people may say about it, is a dominant force in society. Though melancholic men may need the stimulation of flirtatious rebuff, the nervous or sanguine may be put to rout if resistance lasts too long. In other words, the paean of victory is as essential to the choleric temperament as the mournful, pleading, elegiac strain is to the lymphatic.

As he got ready Eugène took all the pleasure in the details of his toilet that young men usually enjoy, because such dandyism tickles their vanity, although they dare not breathe a word of it for fear of being laughed at. He thought as he arranged his hair how a pretty woman's glance would steal over the dark curls. He indulged in as much childish prinking as a young girl dressing for a ball. As he smoothed out the creases in his coat he looked complacently at his slim figure, and said to himself,

'There are certainly worse-looking people in the world!'

Then he came downstairs when all the boarding-house guests were seated at the dinner-table, and received with a gay good-humour the uproarious burst of silly witticisms which his elegant dress excited. The boorish amazement with which a well-groomed appearance is regarded is characteristic of boarding-house manners. No one can wear a new coat but everyone must make his comment.

'Tck, tck, tck, tck,' said Bianchon, clicking his tongue against the roof of his mouth as if to encourage a horse.

'As smart as a duke or a belted earl!' cried Madame Vauquer.

'Is the gentleman going courting?' inquired Mademoiselle Michonneau.

'Cock-a-doodle-doo!' crowed the artist.

'My compliments to your lady spouse!' This came from the Muséum official.

'Have you a spouse?' asked Poiret.

'Yes, a spouse with compartments, watertight and buoyant, fast colour guaranteed, prices from twenty-five to forty, checked patterns in the latest fashion, washes well, looks pretty, half-linen, half-cotton, half-woollen, cures toothache and other com-

plaints approved by the Royal College of Physicians! Excellent
for children as well! Better still as a remedy for headaches, feelings
of fullness and other maladies of the oesophagus, eyes and ears!'
cried Vautrin, with the comic volubility and patter of a quack at a
fair. 'And how much shall we say for this marvel, gentlemen?
Two sous! No. It's just giving it away. All that is left of stock
supplied to the Great Mogul; and all the crowned heads of Europe,
including the Gr-r-r-r-rand Duke of Baden wished to see it!
Walk up! Walk up! Straight in front of you, and pay at the desk.
Strike up the band! Brooum, la, la, trinn! la, la, boum! boum!
You there, sir, playing the clarinet, you're out of tune,' he went
on hoarsely, 'I'll rap your knuckles for you.'

'Goodness! what an amusing man he is!' said Madame Vauquer
to Madame Couture. 'I should never know a dull moment with
him in the house.'

Under cover of the outburst of laughter and joking provoked
by this comical oration Eugène caught Mademoiselle Taillefer's
surreptitious glance, as she bent over Madame Couture and
whispered a few words in her ear.

'The cab's here,' Sylvie announced.

'But where is he going to dine?' asked Bianchon.

'At the Baroness de Nucingen's.'

'Monsieur Goriot's daughter,' the student added.

At this all eyes were turned to the old vermicelli-maker, who
was gazing at Eugène with some envy.

When he reached the Rue Saint-Lazare Rastignac found that
his destination was one of those airy houses with slender pillars
and a mean portico that Parisians call 'pretty'. It was a true
banker's house, full of costly showiness, with stucco-work on
the walls, and landings of marble mosaic. He found Madame de
Nucingen in a little drawing-room hung with paintings in the
Italian style and decorated like a restaurant. The Baroness seemed
in low spirits. The efforts she made to hide her sadness excited
all the more interest in Eugène because they were entirely without guile. He had expected to delight a woman by his presence

O.G.   161   G and found her despondent. This disappointment piqued his vanity.

'I have very little right to claim your confidence, Madame,' he said, after rallying her on her preoccupation, 'but if I am in the way, I count on your good faith, please tell me so frankly.'

'No, stay with me,' she said. 'I should be all alone if you went away. Nucingen is dining in town, and I do not want to be alone, I need distraction.'

'But what is wrong?'

'You are the last person I should tell,' she exclaimed.

'I should like to know. I must be concerned in some way in this secret.'

'Perhaps! But no,' she went on, 'it's one of those family quarrels that ought to be buried in the depths of one's heart. Did I not tell you something about it the day before yesterday? I am not at all happy. Chains of gold are the heaviest chains to bear.'

When a woman tells a young man that she is very unhappy, if this young man is intelligent and well-dressed and has fifteen hundred francs lying idle in his pocket he is bound to think what Eugène thought, and grows a little conceited.

'What can you have to wish for?' he replied. 'You are young, beautiful, rich, adored.'

'Don't let's talk about me,' she said, with a dismal shake of her head. 'We will dine alone together, and go to hear the most enchanting music afterwards. Do I look all right?' she went on, rising and displaying her dress, which was of white cashmere with decorative Persian designs of the most exquisite richness.

'I wish you were all mine,' said Eugène. 'You are charming.'

'You would have a sorry piece of property,' she said, smiling bitterly. 'Nothing here speaks of misfortune, and yet in spite of all appearances I am in despair. I can't sleep because of my troubles, I shall be quite ugly soon.'

'Oh! that's impossible,' said the student; 'but I am curious to know what troubles these are that cannot be smoothed out by devoted love.'

'Ah! if I told you about them you would fly from me,' she said. 'You love me only by a gallant convention which is a sort of good manners in men; but if you really loved me you would be plunged into dreadful despair. You see that I must hold my peace. For pity's sake let's speak of something else. Come and see my rooms.'

'No, let's stay here,' replied Eugène, sitting down on a sofa before the fire, near Madame de Nucingen, and boldly taking her hand.

She let him take it, and even pressed the young man's fingers in a vehement grasp that betrayed intense emotion.

'Listen,' said Rastignac, 'if you have troubles you must tell me about them. I want to prove to you that I love you for your own sake. Either you will talk to me frankly and tell me your sorrows so that I can put an end to them, even if it entails killing half-a-dozen men, or I shall go and never come back again.'

'Very well,' she cried, striking her forehead in an agony of despair, 'I'll put you to the test this very moment. Yes,' she added to herself, 'there's no longer any other way.' She rang the bell.

'Is your master's carriage ready?' she asked the footman.

'Yes, Madame.'

'Then I shall take it. You must give him mine, with my horses. Do not serve dinner until seven o'clock.'

'Come with me,' she said to Eugène, who thought, when he found himself in the banker's carriage beside Madame de Nucingen, that he must surely be dreaming.

'To the Palais-Royal,' she said to the coachman; 'near the Théâtre-Français.'

On the way she appeared troubled and excited, and gave no answer to the innumerable questions put to her by Eugène, who did not know what to make of this obstinate silence, this mute resistance.

'In another moment she'll slip through my fingers,' he said to himself.

When the carriage stopped the Baroness looked at the student in a way which arrested the wild rush of words on his lips, for his feelings had been wrought to breaking point.

'You do really love me?' she said.

'Yes,' he replied, hiding the uneasiness which filled him.

'You will not think ill of me, whatever I may ask you to do?'

'No.'

'You are ready to obey me?'

'Blindly.'

'Have you ever been to a gambling-house?' she said in a voice that shook.

'Never.'

'Ah! I can breathe again. You will have luck. Here is my purse. Take it!' she said. 'There are a hundred francs in it, all that such a fortunate woman possesses. Go to a gambling-house; I don't know where they are, but I know that there are some near the Palais-Royal. Stake the hundred francs in a game they call roulette, and either lose it all or bring me back six thousand francs. I will tell you my troubles when you come back.'

'The devil fly away with me if I understand in the least what I'm going to do, but I will obey you,' he said, with exultation as he thought, 'She has committed herself too deeply to draw back; she can refuse me nothing now.'

Eugène took the pretty purse and hurried to number nine, the nearest gambling-house, pointed out to him by an old-clothes dealer. He went upstairs, gave up his hat, and asked the way to the roulette-table. An attendant took him, much to the astonishment of the regular clients, to a long table. In spite of the stares of all the spectators Eugène demanded without any false shame to be told where he should put his stake.

'If you put a louis on any one of the thirty-six numbers and it comes up you will win thirty-six louis,' said a respectable-looking elderly man with white hair.

Eugène threw the hundred francs on the number of his age,

twenty-one. Before he had time to collect his thoughts there was a cry of surprise. He had won without knowing what he did.

'Take off your money,' said the elderly gentleman; 'one doesn't win twice by that system.'

Eugène took the rake the man handed to him, drew in his three thousand six hundred francs and, still knowing nothing of the game, staked again on the red. The bystanders watched him enviously as he continued to play. The wheel turned, he won again, and the banker threw him three thousand six hundred francs once more.

'That's seven thousand six hundred francs you have now,' said the elderly man in his ear; 'take my advice and go; the red has turned up eight times. If you are charitable you will acknowledge this good counsel by relieving the distress of an old prefect of Napoleon's who is down on his luck.'

Rastignac in a daze saw the white-haired man pocket ten louis, and went out with his seven thousand francs, as ignorant of the game as ever but dumbfounded by his luck.

'So that's that! And now where will you take me?' he said, showing the seven thousand francs to Madame de Nucingen as soon as the carriage door had closed behind him.

Delphine flung her arms wildly round him and kissed him fervently, but without passion.

'You've saved me!' she cried, and tears of joy streamed down her cheeks. 'I'm going to tell you everything, my friend. You will be my friend, won't you? You think I am rich, very rich. I want for nothing, or so it appears. Let me tell you that Monsieur de Nucingen does not let me have control of one sou: he pays for everything, all the household expenses, and my carriages and box at the theatre. He gives me an allowance, but it is not enough to pay for my dress; he reduces me to secret poverty by cold-blooded design. I should be the vilest of creatures if I bought his money at the price he wants me to pay! Are you wondering how I could ever have let myself be stripped of every penny when I had a fortune of seven hundred thousand francs of my own?

Through pride, through indignation. We are so young, so simple, when we begin married life. When I ought to have asked my husband for money the words stuck in my throat, I could not utter them. I spent the money I had saved and what my poor father gave me, then I ran into debt. Marriage for me is a horrible mockery, I cannot talk to you about it; let it suffice to say that I would throw myself out of the window if I had to live with Nucingen in any other way than as we do now, in separate rooms. When I had to confess my debts to him, debts that every young woman runs up, for jewellery and trifles of various kinds (my poor father indulged us so much that we had grown accustomed to refuse ourselves nothing), I suffered tortures; but in the end I found the courage to declare them, for after all, had I not a fortune of my own? Nucingen flew into a rage, he said that I would ruin him and all kinds of brutal things. I longed for the earth to open and bury me a hundred feet under! As he had taken my dowry, he paid; but he stipulated that I should keep to a fixed allowance for my personal expenses from that day on, and I gave way for the sake of peace. And then,' she went on, 'I wanted to do what suited the self-esteem of someone whom you know. Even if he has deceived me I should be wrong not to say that he was magnanimous: but after all, in the end he left me shamefully. If a person has heaped money on a woman in an hour of need he should never forsake her; he should love her for ever! A high-principled man like you, the soul of honour, twenty-one years old, with all the innocence of youth, will ask me how a woman could take money from a man. Oh God! is it not natural to share everything with the being to whom we owe our happiness? When one has given oneself completely, who could worry about a fraction of that whole? Money counts for something only when feeling is dead. Has one not bound oneself for life? Which of us foresees a separation when she believes herself dearly loved? You swear eternal love to us, how then can we have interests apart?

'You do not know what I suffered to-day when Nucingen

166

absolutely refused to give me six thousand francs, a sum he gives every month to his mistress, an opera dancer. I thought of killing myself. The maddest thoughts came into my head. There were moments when I envied a servant's lot, the lot of my own maid. How should I look to my father for help? That would be senseless. Anastasie and I between us have bled him white. My poor father would have sold himself if his body could have fetched six thousand francs; I should only have driven him to despair, to no purpose. You have saved me from shame and death, I was beside myself with anguish. Ah! Monsieur, I owed you this explanation: I treated you in a preposterously unreasonable way. When you left me just now, and I couldn't see you any longer, I wanted to run away – where, I do not know. Half the women in Paris live a life like mine, with luxury on the surface and cruel cares in the heart. I know of poor creatures even more unhappy than I. Indeed there are women who are driven to ask their tradesmen to present false accounts, and others rob their husbands. Some men believe that a cashmere shawl worth a hundred louis is given away for five hundred francs, and other husbands that a five hundred franc shawl is worth a hundred louis. Poor women exist who let their children go hungry, and scrimp and save to get a dress, because they have no money. At least I am innocent of those mean shifts. This is my last affliction. If some women sell themselves to their husbands in order to dominate them, I, at any rate, am free! I could have gold heaped on me by Nucingen if I chose, but I prefer to weep with my head on the heart of a man I can respect. Ah! to-night Monsieur de Marsay will no longer have the right to look on me as a woman he has paid.'

She covered her face with her hands to hide her tears from Eugène, but he drew her hands away and looked at her. She seemed to him sublime at that moment.

'To mix money with love! Isn't it horrible? You could not love me now,' she said.

Eugène was overwhelmed by this revelation of the ideas of

honour which make women so great, combined so strangely as it was with the disclosure of the transgressions which society, as it is at present constituted, forces on them. He murmured gentle consoling words, and marvelled at the beautiful woman beside him, so artlessly indiscreet in her cry of grief.

'You will not use this as a weapon against me, will you?' she said; 'promise me.'

'Ah! Madame, I could not,' he answered.

She took his hand and placed it on her heart in a gesture full of gratitude and sweetness.

'Thanks to you I'm free again and happy. I was living as if I were squeezed in an iron hand. I mean to live simply now, without spending a penny. You will like me just as well, won't you, my friend? Keep this one,' she added, as she took only six of the bank-notes. 'In conscience I owe you three thousand francs, for I really should go halves with you.' Eugène protested as fiercely as a maiden defending her honour, but when the Baroness said, 'I must look on you as my enemy if you are not my confederate,' he took the money.

'It shall be a stake held in reserve, in case of misfortune,' he said.

'That's what I was afraid of hearing,' she exclaimed, turning pale. 'If you want me to count for anything in your life, swear to me that you will never enter a gambling-house again. By heaven! if I should corrupt you I should die of sorrow.'

By this time they had arrived at the Rue Saint-Lazare. Eugène was stunned by the contrast between the magnificence of the house and the wretched state of its mistress, and Vautrin's sinister words began to echo in his ears.

'Sit down there,' said the Baroness, pointing to a low chair near the fire in her room. 'I have a very difficult letter to write. Give me your advice.'

'Don't write anything,' said Eugène; 'put the bank-notes in an envelope, address it, and send them by your maid.'

'You're a darling,' she said. 'Ah! now we see what it is to

have been well brought up! That's pure de Beauséant,' she added, laughing.

'She is charming,' Eugène said to himself, falling deeper in love every moment.

He looked round the room, which betrayed a certain vulgarity of taste in its voluptuous luxury.

'Do you like it?' she asked, as she rang for her maid.

'Thérèse, take this to Monsieur de Marsay yourself, and give it into his own hands. If he is not at home bring the letter back to me.'

Thérèse took the letter, and threw a malicious glance at Eugène as she left the room.

Dinner was announced. Rastignac gave his arm to Madame de Nucingen, and they walked to an exquisite dining-room where he saw a display as sumptuous as that which had excited his wonder at his cousin's.

'You must come to dinner on opera days,' she said, 'and escort me to the Italiens afterwards.'

'I should soon grow accustomed to this pleasant life if it were to last; but I am a poor student with my way to make.'

'Don't worry, you will prosper,' she said, laughing; 'you see, everything turns out well. I did not expect to be so happy.'

It is part of women's nature to prove the impossible by the possible, and upset facts by their intuition. When Madame de Nucingen and Rastignac took their seats in her box at the Bouffons, her face wore a look of happiness which made her so beautiful that defamatory remarks rose unchecked to everyone's lips. Against such aspersions women have no defence, and they often cause gratuitously invented slanders to be accepted as the truth. People who know Paris never believe a word of what is said, and say nothing of what is done, there.

Eugène took the Baroness's hand, and they shared the pleasure the music gave them with each other by the light touch or closer clasping of their fingers. For both of them it was an evening of intoxicating joy, and when they left together Madame de

Nucingen insisted on taking Eugène in her carriage as far as the Pont-Neuf, refusing him by the way one of the kisses she had so warmly lavished on him at the Palais-Royal. Eugène reproached her with this inconsistency.

'Ah! it was gratitude, then, for devotion I had not hoped for,' she replied, 'but now it would be a promise.'

'And you don't want to make me any promise, ungrateful woman!' he said huffily. With one of those quick impetuous gestures that delight a lover she held out her hand for his kiss, and he took it with a sulkiness she found enchanting.

'I shall see you on Monday, at the ball,' she said.

Walking home under the calm clear light of the moon, Eugène fell into serious thought. He was both happy and regretful: happy in an adventure whose probable outcome would give him his desire, one of the prettiest and most elegant women in Paris; regretful at seeing his plans to gain a fortune brought to nothing; and it was then that the thoughts that had passed vaguely through his mind two days before took definite shape. Disappointment always shows us how strong our hopes were. The more Eugène enjoyed of the pleasures of life in Paris, the less he wanted to remain obscure and poor. He crumpled the thousand-franc note in his pocket, and thought of dozens of plausible arguments for keeping it for himself.

At last he reached the Rue Neuve-Sainte-Geneviève, and at the top of the stairs saw a light burning. Old Goriot had left his door open and his candle alight to prevent the student from forgetting to 'tell him all about his daughter', to use his own expression. Eugène told him the whole story.

'What!' cried Goriot in frantic jealousy and grief. 'They think I'm ruined, do they, and I still have an income of thirteen hundred livres a year! Good heavens, the poor little thing, why didn't she come to me? I would have sold some of my stocks and shares; we could have used some of the principal and bought a life-annuity for me with what was left. My good neighbour, you should have come and told me about her difficulty. How could you have the heart to risk her poor little hundred francs on a turn of the wheel? It's enough to break one's heart. So that's what sons-in-law are! Oh! if I could only lay hands on them I would wring their necks! My God! did you say she was crying?'

'With her head on my waistcoat,' said Eugène.

'Oh! give it to me,' said Goriot. 'What! my daughter's tears have fallen on this – my darling Delphine who never cried when she was a little girl! I'll buy you another one, don't wear this again, leave it with me. By the terms of her marriage settlement she should enjoy the use of her own property. Ah! I'll get hold of Derville to-morrow, he's a lawyer. I'll see that her money is invested in her own name. I know the law. I am an old wolf. I mean to show my teeth.'

'Take this, Papa, it is a thousand francs which she wanted to give me out of our winnings. Keep it for her in the waistcoat pocket.'

Goriot looked at him, and on his hand, as the old man reached out and grasped it, the student felt a tear fall.

'You will succeed in life,' said the old man. 'God is just, you understand. I know an honest man when I see one, and I can tell you there are very few men like you. So you wish to be my dear child too? Go and sleep. You can sleep, for you are not a father yet. She was crying, you tell me, and I was calmly eating my dinner like an idiot while she was suffering – I who would sell the Father, Son and Holy Ghost to save either of them a tear!'

'Upon my word,' said Eugène to himself, as he went to bed, 'I think I'll be an honest man all my life. It gives you such a pleasant feeling to do as conscience bids you.'

It is perhaps only those who believe in God who do good secretly, and Eugène believed in God.

Next day at the appointed time Rastignac called on Madame de Beauséant, and she took him with her to the Duchesse de Carigliano's ball. He was most graciously received by the Marshal's wife, and in her drawing-room he saw Madame de Nucingen. Delphine had put all her best finery on in the hope of winning general admiration, and so appearing still more attract-ive to Eugène. She was waiting impatiently for a glance from him, and thought no one saw how impatient she was. For a man who can see into a woman's heart such a moment is delicious. Who has not taken pleasure in withholding his approval and tantalizingly hiding his delight, in causing disquiet for the sake of extorting a confession of affection, and enjoying the fears he will presently dissipate with a smile?

In the course of the evening the student suddenly saw what his position was; he realized that he had some status in this world, as the acknowledged cousin of Madame de Beauséant. The con-quest of the Baroness de Nucingen, which he was already credited with, made him a conspicuous figure, and the envious glances of all the other young men gave him his first taste of the pleasures of the fop. Passing from one reception room to another, and moving through the throng of guests, he overheard people talking about his luck. The women all foretold success for him. Delphine, fearing she might lose him, promised not to refuse him that evening the kiss she had been so obdurate in denying him the evening before.

Rastignac received several invitations during the evening. His cousin presented him to other women, all of whom could claim to be persons of fashion, and whose houses were con-sidered pleasant; he felt that he was fairly launched into the smartest and most brilliant social world in Paris. So this evening had all the charm of a brilliantly successful first appearance in society, and he was to remember it to the end of his days, as a woman remembers the ball where she had her girlish triumphs.

The next morning at breakfast he told the tale of his success to old Goriot and the other boarders. Vautrin began to smile diabolically, and applied his savage logic to the situation.

'And do you really believe,' he exclaimed, 'that a young man of fashion can live in the Rue Neuve-Sainte-Geneviève, in the Maison Vauquer, an exceedingly respectable boarding house, certainly, in every respect, but something less than fashionable?

It is solid and substantial, it is blessed in the warmth of its over-flowing hospitality, it is proud to be the temporary mansion-house of a Rastignac; but still it is in the Rue Neuve-Sainte-Geneviève, it has nothing to do with luxury, it is purely *patri-archalorama*. If you want to cut a dash in Paris, my young friend,' Vautrin went on, in a paternally bantering way, 'you must have three horses, a tilbury for the morning and a brougham for the evening, nine thousand francs in all for your conveyance. You would be unworthy of your fate if you spent less than three thousand francs with your tailor, six hundred for perfumery, a hundred crowns at your bootmaker's, a hundred crowns for hats. As for your laundress, she will relieve you of another thousand francs – young men of fashion must not fail to be extremely fastidious about their linen: how many people look beyond a nice clean shirt? Love and the Church need fine cloths on their altars. That's fourteen thousand francs. I'm saying nothing about what you will pay out for losses at cards, bets, presents; you can't budget for less than two thousand francs for pocket-money. I've led that sort of life and I know what it takes. All those things are absolutely necessary. Add three hundred louis for your grub and a thousand francs for a roosting-place. Well, my lad, we have to fork out our little twenty-five thousand francs a year or we find ourselves in the gutter in the mud, and people are laughing at us, and it's goodbye to our career, our success and our mistress! I'm forgetting your valet and your groom! Is Christophe to carry your love-letters? Will you write them on the paper you use now? It would be suicidal. Believe the word of an old fellow who has had plenty of experience,' he added, his bass voice deepening and increasing in volume, 'you must either betake yourself virtuously to a garret, and wed your-self to your work, or choose another way.'

And Vautrin winked at Eugène, with a leer at Mademoiselle Taillefer which recalled and recapitulated all the seductive argu-ments, all the seed he had planted in the student's mind for its corruption.

Several days went by, and Rastignac spent them in a gay round of pleasures. He dined nearly every evening with Madame de Nucingen, and escorted her wherever she went. He came back to the boarding-house at three or four in the morning, and rose at noon to put on his fine clothes and go for a walk in the Bois with Delphine if the sun was shining, squandering his time without a thought of its value, with a greedy thirst for all the seductions of luxury, and a mind as wide open to absorb all it could teach him as the flowers of the date-palm to receive the fertilizing pollen. He played for high stakes, won or lost large sums of money and ended by taking the extravagant life of a young man about town as a matter of course. Out of his first winnings he had repaid fifteen hundred francs to his mother and sisters, and sent handsome presents with the money. Although he had announced his intention of leaving the Maison Vauquer, the end of January found him still there, and still without plans for departure.

Young men are nearly all subject to a law which is inexplicable on the face of it, but is actually due to their very youth and the ardour with which they throw themselves into the pursuit of pleasure. Rich or poor, they never have any money for the necessaries of life, but they can always find it to gratify their fancies. They are wasteful of anything obtainable on credit, but thrifty if they have to pay cash down; and if they cannot get everything they want, they seem to take their revenge by scattering all they can get to the winds. For example, to put it plainly, a student takes much more care of his hat than he does of his coat. A tailor makes a large profit and so is prepared to wait for his money; while the total cost of a hat is so small that a hatter is not ready to be accommodating about it, and in fact is one of the most difficult of the whole tribe with whom the student is forced to come to terms. The young man in the balcony of a theatre may display a resplendent waistcoat to the opera-glasses of the pretty women, but it is doubtful if he has any socks; the hosier is another of the weevils eating holes in his purse.

Rastignac was no exception to the general rule. His purse was always empty of rent for Madame Vauquer and always full when vanity demanded it: the index of the state of his finances fluctuated madly with a series of reverses and successes, yet he was never left with sufficient funds for the most ordinary payments. If he wanted to leave the mean, malodorous boarding-house which constantly humbled his pride, he must first pay his landlady a month's board and lodging, and then buy furniture for the rooms he must take, in keeping with his pretensions as a young man of fashion. He could never afford it. To have money in hand for gambling Rastignac would buy watches and gold chains at an exorbitant price at his jeweller's out of his winnings, and then when his luck was out take them to the pawnbroker, that melancholy but discreet friend of youth; but invention and dash both deserted him when it was a question of paying for board and lodging, or of buying the things he needed to make the most of the fashionable life. Vulgar necessity, debts contracted for needs which were past and done with, held no inspiration now. Like most people who live from hand to mouth, he waited till the last moment to pay off those debts that steady respectable people regard as sacred engagements; he was like Mirabeau, who never paid his baker's bill until it presented itself in the formidable form of a bill of exchange.

About this time, when Rastignac had been unlucky and had run into debt, it came home to him that he could not possibly continue this existence without some fixed source of income. But even as he groaned in the thorny discomfort of his precarious situation he felt he could not bear to sacrifice the pleasures of this extravagant way of living, and determined to continue it at all costs. The castles in the air he had built when reckoning the chances of fortune favouring his pursuit of wealth became more and more chimerical, and the real obstacles grew. His initiation into the secrets of the Nucingen household had shown him clearly that if he were to use love as a stepping-stone to success he must lose all sense of shame, and renounce the generous ideas that redeem the sins of youth. This life, outwardly so splendid but gnawed by all the worms of remorse within, whose fleeting pleasures were dearly paid for by enduring pain, had become his way of life, he had embraced it, he wallowed in it, making himself a bed, like *Le Distrait* of La Bruyère, in the muddy ditch; but like *Le Distrait* he had as yet soiled only his clothing.

'So we've killed the mandarin, have we?' Bianchon said to him one day as they rose from table.

'Not yet,' he replied, 'but he's at his last gasp.'

The medical student took this for a joke, but it was not meant for one. Eugène had looked thoughtful during the meal, which was the first dinner he had taken at the boarding-house for a long time. Instead of going out when dessert was on the table he had remained in the dining-room, sitting near Mademoiselle Taillefer, and giving her an expressive glance from time to time. A few boarders still sat there too, eating nuts; others were walking up and down, continuing a discussion they had begun at table. The boarders usually lingered after the meal for a longer or shorter period determined by their interest or lack of interest in the conversation, and the more or less sluggish frame of mind engendered by the processes of digestion, and went out one by one when they felt like it. In winter the last one rarely left the dining-room before eight o'clock, and then the four women had it to themselves, and made up for the silence which they were obliged by their sex to keep when the room was full of men.

Vautrin had been struck by Eugène's preoccupation, and he remained in the dining-room, although he had at first seemed to be in a hurry to leave. He placed himself in such a position as not to be observed by Eugène, who must have thought he had gone; then, instead of leaving with the boarders who went out last, he took up a post of observation surreptitiously in the drawing-room. He had read the student's mind and suspected that a crisis was at hand.

Rastignac, indeed, found himself in a perplexing situation of a kind that many young men must have experienced. Whether Madame de Nucingen really loved him or was merely playing with him, she had made Rastignac suffer all the pains of a genuine passion, and had availed herself for his benefit of every subterfuge in the art of feminine evasiveness as practised in Paris. Although she had compromised herself by appearing in public with Madame de Beauséant's cousin, and so bound him to her, she hesitated to give him the lover's privileges everyone thought he enjoyed. For the last month she had so worked upon his feelings as to affect his heart. If the student had thought himself the master in the early days of his attachment, Madame de Nucingen had since gained the upper hand by her diplomatic treatment, the effect of which had been to rouse up in Eugène every instinct, good and bad, of the two or three men that make up a young Parisian. Was it a calculated stroke of policy on her part? Not so. Women are always true even when their actions appear most equivocal, because they are yielding to some natural impulse. Perhaps it was because she had let this young man gain an ascendancy over her so quickly and had shown him so much affection, that Delphine later appeared to change her mind about her concessions, or took pleasure in delaying them, in an impulse to reassert her injured dignity.

It is so natural to a Parisian woman to hesitate when she is on the verge of being carried away by passion, to try the heart of the man to whom she is about to commit her future! All Madame de Nucingen's hopes had been betrayed once, and her fidelity to a selfish young egotist had been treated with contempt. She had good reason to be distrustful. Perhaps she had perceived a certain lack of respect in Eugène's manner towards her, for the oddness of their situation had affected him, and his head had been turned by his rapid success. He was so young she probably wanted to impress him, to appear as a person of consequence in his eyes, after having counted for so little in the eyes of the man who had deserted her. She did not wish Eugène to believe her an easy conquest just because he knew that she had belonged to de

Marsay. And then, after suffering the degradation of submitting to a heartless and inhuman young rake, she found it so sweet to wander in the flower-strewn realm of true love that she must have wanted to linger long in dreamy enjoyment of its every aspect, to listen to the murmur of its streams and let its pure soft breezes caress her cheek. The true lover was paying for the sins of the false one. Such feminine inconsistency will unfortunately continue to be met with, so long as men do not know how many flowers are mown down in a young woman's heart by the first sharp blasts of treachery.

Whatever her reasons, Delphine was playing with Rastignac, and took pleasure in playing with him, no doubt because she knew that he loved her, and was sure she could put an end to his troubles as soon as it suited her woman's royal good pleasure. For the sake of his self-respect Eugène was not willing to let his first engagement with love end in defeat, and he persisted in his attack, like a sportsman who will let nothing stop him from bringing down a partridge in celebration of his first Feast of Saint Hubert. His anxiety, his wounded vanity, his despair, however groundless it may have been, bound him more and more closely to this woman. All Paris credited him with the conquest of Madame de Nucingen, and yet he was as far from achieving it as he had been on the day that he first met her. He had yet to learn that the fascination of a woman's coquetry is sometimes more delightful than the pleasure of secure possession of her love, and he fell into blind rages.

If at this time, while she fought a bout with love, Eugène enjoyed the early fruits of love's springtime, these were becoming as expensive as they were green, tart yet delicious to the taste. Sometimes, seeing himself without a penny and without any prospects for the future, he thought in spite of his conscience of the chance of wealth which Vautrin had shown him to be possible, in a marriage with Mademoiselle Taillefer. And now an hour had come when his poverty spoke with so eloquent a tongue that he yielded almost involuntarily to the wiles of the terrible sphinx whose stare had so often held him in a spell.

When Poiret and Mademoiselle Michonneau went upstairs to their rooms Rastignac believed that he was alone with Mademoiselle Taillefer, except for Madame Vauquer and Madame Couture, who was knitting woollen sleeves for herself and dozing over the stove, and he looked so tenderly at her that she lowered her eyes.

'Perhaps something is worrying you, Monsieur Eugène?' she said, after a pause.

'Hasn't every man got something to worry about?' answered Rastignac. 'If we men were sure of being loved, truly loved, with a devotion which would make up for the sacrifices which we are always ready to make, then perhaps we shouldn't have any worries.'

Victorine only gave him a look in answer, but its meaning could not be mistaken.

'You, Mademoiselle, for instance, think you are sure of your heart to-day; but could you answer for its never changing?'

A smile quivered on the poor girl's lips; it was as if a ray of light had leapt from her soul, and it made her face so radiant that Eugène was startled at the outburst of feeling he had provoked.

'Ah! but suppose you became rich and happy to-morrow, suppose an immense fortune fell from the clouds for you, would you still love the poor young man who found favour in your eyes in your days of poverty?'

She nodded her head sweetly.

'A very unhappy young man!'

She nodded again.

'What nonsense are you talking there?' exclaimed Madame Vauquer.

'Never mind,' replied Eugène, 'we understand each other.'

'So Monsieur le Chevalier Eugène de Rastignac is to be betrothed to Mademoiselle Victorine Taillefer?' said a deep voice, and Vautrin appeared suddenly at the dining-room door.

'Oh! how you startled me!' cried Madame Couture and Madame Vauquer together.

'I might choose worse,' said Eugène, laughing. He had never in his life felt such a cruel pang as that which shot through him at the sound of Vautrin's voice.

'No bad jokes, gentlemen,' said Madame Couture. 'Let us go upstairs, my dear.'

Madame Vauquer followed her two boarders, intending to spend the evening with them, and so save candlelight and fire. Eugène was left face to face with Vautrin.

'I knew very well you would come round to it,' Vautrin said with his usual imperturbable coolness, 'but look here! I have as much delicacy as the next man. Don't make up your mind just now, you're not as chirpy as usual, you have debts. I want your calm good sense to bring you round to my way of thinking, not passion or desperation. Perhaps you need a thousand crowns or so? Here they are, if you want them.'

And that fiend in human form took out a pocket-book and extracted three bank-notes, which he fluttered before the student's eyes. Eugène was in a cruel fix. He had debts of honour, he owed a hundred louis to both the Marquis d'Ajuda and the Comte de Trailles. He had not got the money, and because of this had not dared to go to spend the evening at Madame de Restaud's, where he was expected. It was to be one of those informal parties, at which the guests drink tea and eat little cakes, but at which it is possible to lose six thousand francs, playing whist.

'After what you have told me, Monsieur,' said Eugène, trying to hide the convulsive tremor which shook him, 'you must see that I cannot possibly lay myself under an obligation to you.'

'Oh, well, I should have been disappointed if you had said anything else,' replied his tempter. 'You are a fine, high-principled young man, as proud as a lion, and as tender as a girl. You would be a fine haul for the devil's bag. I like youngsters to have such stuff in them. When you have worked your way through a few more conscientious scruples you will see the world as it is. A man who knows what he's about acts a virtuous part in a few scenes and then he can do exactly what he likes amid great applause from the idiots in the gallery. In a very few days you will be with us. Ah! if you would only let me be your tutor I would make you achieve the summit of ambition. You would only have to form a wish to have it instantly gratified, whatever you might wish for – honours, riches, women. The whole civilized world would flow with milk and honey for you. You would be our spoiled child, our Benjamin, we would all put ourselves out of the way for your sake with pleasure. Any obstacle in your path would be razed to the ground. Do you cherish scruples still? So you take me for a scoundrel, do you? Well, Monsieur de Turenne, a man of quite as much integrity as you possess, or rather think you still possess, put through some little deals with brigands, and did not consider that that had tarnished his honour. You don't choose to be under an obligation to me, eh? Don't let that stand in your way,' Vautrin went on, not troubling to hide a smile. 'Take these scraps of paper, and write down on this,' he pulled out a piece of stamped paper, '*Accepted the sum of three thousand five hundred francs payable in twelve months' time.* Date it! The interest is stiff enough to relieve you of all scruples; you can call me a Jew, and need feel no gratitude. I don't mind your despising me now because I'm sure that you'll feel differently later on. You will find unfathomable depths in my nature, vast concentrated forces that fools call vices; but you will never find me mean-spirited or ungrateful. In short, I am neither a pawn nor a bishop, but a castle, my young friend.'

'What manner of man are you?' Eugène exclaimed. 'Were you born to torment me?'

'Certainly not. I am a good-natured fellow who is willing to soil his own hands so that you may keep yours clean and be raised out of the slough for the rest of your days. Do you wonder why I should show you such devotion? Well, I'll tell you one of these days, I'll whisper a word in your ear. I startled you at first when I gave you a glimpse of the mechanism of the social machine, and put you up to the ropes; but your first fright will pass off like a conscript's on the battlefield, you will get used to regarding men as soldiers who have made up their minds to die, in the service of those who are crowned kings by their own hands. Times are changed indeed. Once you said to a rascal, "Here are a hundred crowns, kill Monsieur So-and-so for me," and you ate your supper in peace after giving a man his quietus for a mere fleabite. But now I propose to help you to a handsome fortune at a nod from you which compromises you not at all, and you shilly-shally. This age has no backbone.'

Eugène signed the draft, and handed it over in exchange for the bank-notes.

'Now then, let's talk sense,' Vautrin went on. 'I mean to leave this country in a few months for America, to go and plant my tobacco. I will send you the cigars of friendship. If I make money, I will help you. If I have no children (which is likely to be the case: I am not anxious to plant scions of my own stock here), I will leave you my fortune. Well, what do you think of that? Is that acting like a friend? But I am fond of you, and sacrificing myself for someone else is my passion. I have done it before. You see, my lad, I live in a sphere raised above that of other men. I consider actions as means to an end, and the end is all I see. What is a man's life to me? Not that!' and he snapped his thumbnail against his teeth. 'A man is everything to me, or nothing at all. He is less than nothing if he is a Poiret: you can crush him like a bug, he is flat and smelly. But a man is a god when he is like you; he is no longer a piece of mechanism covered with skin, but a theatre where the finest sentiments find play, and I live only for sentiments – fine thoughts and noble feelings. What is a sentiment but the whole world in a thought? Look at old Goriot: his two daughters are the whole universe to him, they are the clue by which he finds his way through creation. Well, for me, and I have turned life inside out, only one real sentiment exists – friendship between man and man. Pierre and Jaffier, such a bond as theirs is what I care for most. I know *Venice Preserved* by heart. Have you seen many fellows staunch enough when a comrade says, "Come and bury a corpse," to go without batting an eyelid or bothering him with a sermon? I have done it. I wouldn't talk like this to everyone, but you're not like an ordinary man, I can tell you everything because you can understand it. You will not mess about much longer in these swamps with the bloated pigmies that surround us here. Well, I need say no more. You will marry. We may both carry our point – mine is cold steel, and I never yield it, ha! ha!'

Vautrin went out quickly to avoid hearing the student's protest, so that he might not embarrass him. He seemed to understand the resistance that men still offer when almost defeated, the shadow-boxing they indulge in, which serves to bolster their self-respect and justify their blameworthy actions in their own eyes.

'He may do as he likes, I will certainly not marry Mademoiselle Taillefer!' said Eugène to himself.

Though this man appalled him, the very cynicism of his ideas and the audacity with which he used society to serve his own ends made him loom larger in the student's eyes; but the thought of a compact with him threw Eugène into a fever. When he felt a little calmer he dressed, called for a cab and went to Madame de Restaud's.

For some days the Countess had been increasingly attentive to him, as she saw that the young man's every step was a triumphal advance into the fashionable world, and foresaw that he might some day possess formidable power. He paid Messieurs de Trailles and d'Ajuda, played whist for part of the evening, and won back all that he had lost. Like most men who have their way to make and are more or less fatalistic, Eugène was superstitious, and it pleased him to regard his luck as a reward from heaven for his perseverance in the right path. Next morning he lost no time before asking Vautrin if he still held the bill he had given him, and when Vautrin replied in the affirmative Eugène paid back the three thousand francs with a not unnatural satisfaction.

'Everything is going well,' Vautrin said to him.

'But I am not your accomplice,' said Eugène.

'I know, I know,' Vautrin broke in. 'You're still behaving like a child. You let a painted devil bar your way!'

Two days later Poiret and Mademoiselle Michonneau were to be found seated on a bench in the sun, by a lonely pathway in the Jardin des Plantes, talking to the gentleman who had aroused the medical student's suspicions, not unjustifiably.

'I cannot see any reason for your scruples, Mademoiselle,' this Monsieur Gondureau was saying. 'His Excellency Monseigneur the Minister for Police –'

'Ah! His Excellency Monseigneur the Minister for Police –' echoed Poiret.

'Yes, His Excellency is taking an interest in the matter,' said Gondureau.

It is not easy for anyone to believe that Poiret, a retired clerk, and no doubt a man of middle-class virtues although lacking in intelligence, continued to listen to the so-called gentleman of means from the Rue Buffon once that gentleman had uttered the word 'police', and let the face of a detective from the Rue de Jérusalem peer from the mask of a decent man. Nothing, however, was more natural. If one considers what has already been noted by certain observers, although nothing has been published on the subject yet, one may understand better the particular species Poiret belonged to in the great family of fools.

There is a race of quill-drivers only found in the columns of the budget between the first degree of latitude, which includes salaries of twelve hundred francs, a kind of administrative Greenland, and the third degree, where salaries begin to warm up from three thousand to six thousand francs, a temperate region where bonuses acclimatize themselves and flourish in spite of the difficulties of cultivation. A marked characteristic of this hireling race, and one which best reveals the feebleness and narrow limits of its mental capacity, is a kind of involuntary, automatic, instinctive respect for the Grand Lama of every Ministry, who is known to the rank and file only by an illegible signature, and by his title – HIS EXCELLENCY MONSEIGNEUR LE MINISTRE, five words which produce as much effect as the *Il Bondo Cani* of the *Calife de Bagdad*, and which in the eyes of this spiritless tribe represent a sacred power from which there is no appeal. As the Pope is infallible in the eyes of Catholics, so His Excellency is administratively infallible in the eyes of the petty official. His acts, his words, and those done or uttered in his name, are all invested with his peculiar lustre; his cloak covers everything, and legalizes whatever is done by his order; his very title 'Excellency' attests the purity of his intentions and the righteousness of his wishes, and serves as a passport for ideas that otherwise would not be entertained for a minute. Acts that these poor people would not do for their own interests are done eagerly if the words 'His Excellency' are uttered. Government Departments, like the Army, have their system of passive obedience, a system which stifles the conscience, destroys the individual utterly, and ends, in time, by making a man nothing more than a screw or a nut in the administrative machine. And so Monsieur Gondureau, who seemed to be able to size men up, recognizing Poiret at once as one of these bureaucratic fools, brought out the *Deus ex machina*, the magic words 'His Excellency', at the proper moment when he was unmasking his batteries and needed to dazzle the man. He took Poiret to be the male equivalent of the Michonneau woman, and Mademoiselle Michonneau seemed to him the female form of Poiret.

'If His Excellency himself, His Excellency the Minister – Ah! that makes a great difference,' said Poiret.

'You hear what this gentleman says, and I think you trust his judgement,' said the sham man of means, addressing Mademoiselle Michonneau. 'Well, now, His Excellency is absolutely certain at this very moment that the so-called Vautrin, lodging in the

Maison Vauquer, is a convict escaped from the Toulon convict-prison, where he was known by the name of *Cheat-Death*.'

'Oh! Cheat-Death!' said Poiret. 'He is a very lucky man if he has earned that nickname.'

'Well, yes,' replied the detective, 'he owes the nickname to his luck in saving his skin in all the extremely risky schemes he has carried out. The man is dangerous, you must understand. He has qualities which raise him above the ruck. The very thing he was sentenced for brought him no end of honour in his own gang.'

'What, he's a man of honour, is he?' cried Poiret.

'In a way, according to his own ideas. He agreed to take the responsibility for another man's crime. It was a forgery committed by a very fine young man whom he had taken a fancy to, a young Italian, a bit of a gambler, who has since gone into the Army where he has behaved himself and done very well.'

'But if His Excellency the Minister for Police is sure that Monsieur Vautrin is this Cheat-Death, why should he need my help?' said Mademoiselle Michonneau.

'Ah! yes indeed,' said Poiret, 'if the Minister, as you have done us the honour of telling us, has any kind of certainty –'

'Certainty is not the word; he only suspects it. You will soon understand how the land lies. Jacques Collin, alias Cheat-Death, is implicitly trusted by every convict in three prisons and they have appointed him to be their agent and banker. He makes a good thing out of this business; of course it takes a man of mark –'

'Ha! ha! do you see the pun, Mademoiselle?' said Poiret. 'The gentleman calls him a man of *mark*, because he is *marked* – branded, you know.'

'The so-called Vautrin,' the detective continued, 'receives the convicts' money, invests it for the gentlemen, looks after it and holds it at their disposal if they escape, or gives it to their families if they leave a will, or to their mistresses when they draw on him for them.'

'Their mistresses! You surely mean their wives,' remarked Poiret.

'No, sir; criminals don't usually marry their sweethearts. We call these illegitimate connections concubines.'

'Then they all live in a state of concubinage?'

'That follows.'

'Oh, dear me!' said Poiret. 'That's a scandal His Excellency ought not to tolerate. As you have the honour of seeing His Excellency it's up to you, since you seem to have philanthropic ideas, to let him know about the immoral behaviour of these people: they set a very bad example to the rest of society.'

'But the Government does not hold them up as models of all the virtues, my dear sir.'

'That's true. All the same, sir, allow me –'

'Just let the gentleman say what he wants to tell us, dearie,' said Mademoiselle Michonneau.

'You see it's like this, Mademoiselle,' went on Gondureau, 'the Government may have a considerable interest in getting hold of an illicit hoard of money: they say it amounts to a pretty penny. Cheat-Death rakes in large quantities of cash not only from his convict friends, but from the Society of the Ten Thousand as well –'

'Ten Thousand Thieves!' exclaimed Poiret in alarm.

'No, the Society of the Ten Thousand is an association of high-class sharks, men who go for big money and won't touch a piece of business unless there is ten thousand francs in it for them. The pick of our customers who are sent straight to the Assize Courts when they come up for trial belong to this society. They know the Code and never risk making themselves liable to the death penalty if they are nabbed. Collin is their confidential agent, their legal adviser. His immense resources have made it possible for him to build up a sort of counter-detective system of his own, with very extensive ramifications which it is quite impossible to unearth. Although we have kept him under close observation for a year, with spies all round him, we have not yet been able to drag his little game into the light of day. And so his hoard of money and his brains are always at the service of vice, supply the funds for crime, and maintain a standing army of scamps who wage incessant war against society. If we can catch Cheat-Death and seize his money-bags we shall strike at the root of this evil; and that's why this scheme has become a State affair, a highly important piece of official business likely to bring great kudos to those who lend a hand and help to carry it out. Why, you yourself, sir, might very well be asked to work for the Government again, they might make you secretary to a Commissary of Police, and that need not prevent you from still drawing your retiring pension.'

'But,' interposed Mademoiselle Michonneau, 'why does Cheat-Death not make off with the money?'

'Oh!' said the detective, 'if he robbed the convicts he would be followed wherever he went by a man told off to kill him. Besides it's not so easy to carry off a chest of money as it is to run away with a nice young lady. Collin is not the sort of chap who could do a thing like that, in any case; he would think himself disgraced.'

'Monsieur,' said Poiret, 'you are right, he would be utterly disgraced.'

'All this does not explain why you don't simply come and take him,' observed Mademoiselle Michonneau.

'Well, Mademoiselle, I'll tell you – but keep your gentleman friend from interrupting me,' he added in a whisper, 'or we shall never have done: the old boy should pay people well if he wants them to listen to him. Cheat-Death when he came here got into the skin of an honest man, he made himself into a good Parisian citizen, lodging in an unpretentious boarding-house; he's no fool, believe me! you won't catch him with chaff. Then Monsieur Vautrin is a generally respected man, and he does a good deal of business.'

'Naturally,' said Poiret to himself.

'If the Minister were to make a mistake and arrest a real

Vautrin public opinion would be against him, and he would fall foul of every business-man in Paris. Monsieur le Préfet de Police is in a ticklish position. He has enemies, and if a blunder were made they would take advantage of the outcry and clamour the Opposition would be sure to set up, to have him sent packing, and then the people who want his position themselves would be happy. We must handle this business just as we did the Cogniard affair, the sham Comte de Sainte-Hélène; if he had been a real Comte de Sainte-Hélène we should have blotted our copy-book. And so we must make quite sure we know what we're doing.'

'Yes, but what you need is a pretty woman,' said Mademoiselle Michonneau briskly.

'Cheat-Death would not let a woman come near him. Let me tell you a secret – he doesn't like women.'

'Still, I fail to see what use I should be in verifying his identity, supposing I did consent to do it for two thousand francs.'

'Nothing easier,' said the stranger. 'I will give you a little bottle containing a dose of a liquid which induces a fit, like an apoplectic fit, but quite harmless. You can put the drug into wine or coffee, it doesn't matter which. You carry your man to a bed at once, and undress him to find out if he's dying. As soon as you are alone you give him a clap on the shoulder, and lo and behold! you see the branded letters appear.'

'But that's no trouble at all,' said Poiret.

'Well, will you do it?' Gondureau asked the old maid.

'But, my dear sir,' said Mademoiselle Michonneau, 'supposing there are no letters, should I have the two thousand francs all the same?'

'No.'

'How much would you give me for my trouble, then?'

'Five hundred francs.'

'You want me to do a thing like that for so little! Whatever the result may be it will lie just as heavy on my conscience, and I must consider my conscience, Monsieur.'

'I assure you,' said Poiret, 'that this lady has a great deal of conscience, besides which she is a very amiable person and very clever.'

'Well,' Mademoiselle Michonneau went on, 'give me three thousand francs if he is Cheat-Death, and nothing at all if he's an ordinary man.'

'Done!' said Gondureau, 'but on condition that the thing is carried out to-morrow.'

'I can't settle that now, my dear sir. I must consult my confessor.'

'You're as slippery as an eel,' said the detective as he rose to go. 'I'll see you to-morrow, then. And if you should want to see me in a hurry, go to the Petite Rue Sainte-Anne, at the end of the Cour de la Sainte-Chapelle. There is only one door under the archway. Ask for Monsieur Gondureau.'

The sufficiently striking name 'Cheat-Death' caught Bianchon's ear as he was returning from Cuvier's lecture, and he overheard the famous Chief of the Sûreté say, 'Done!'

'Why did you not close with him? It would be three hundred francs a year,' Poiret said to Mademoiselle Michonneau.

'Why didn't I?' returned the old maid. 'It needs thinking over. If Monsieur Vautrin is this Cheat-Death we might make a better bargain if we came to some arrangement with him. Still, if he was asked for money the alarm would be sounded and he is just the sort of man to make off without paying a penny, and that would be an abominable sell.'

'Suppose you did warn him,' said Poiret, 'didn't that gentleman tell us that he was watched? You would lose everything.'

'Anyhow,' thought Mademoiselle Michonneau, 'I don't like the man at all! He can't speak to me without saying something disagreeable.'

'But you can do better than that,' Poiret continued. 'As that gentleman said, and he seemed to be a very proper sort of man besides being very tidily dressed, as he said, it is an act of obedience to the laws to rid society of a criminal, however virtuous he may be. Once a thief, always a thief. What if he should take it into his head to murder us all? Why, bless my soul! we should be responsible for those murders, without taking into account that we should be the first victims of them.'

Mademoiselle Michonneau was absorbed in thought and did not give much heed to the remarks falling one after another from Poiret's mouth, like drops of water dripping from a leaky tap. Once he had started on his string of utterances, since Mademoiselle Michonneau did not intervene to stop him, the old fellow kept on talking as if he had been wound up. The first subject he broached led him by way of one parenthesis after another to others entirely different, and he went on and on without putting a period to any topic on the way. By the time they reached the Maison Vauquer a chain of examples, quotations and incidental allusions had brought him to an account of the evidence he had given in the case of the Sieur Ragoulleau *versus* Dame Morin, when he had appeared as a witness for the defence.

It did not escape his companion's eye when they went in that Eugène de Rastignac was engaged in an intimate conversation with Mademoiselle Taillefer, which was of such thrilling interest that neither of them had any attention to spare for the two older boarders as they passed through the dining-room.

'It was bound to end like that,' Mademoiselle Michonneau remarked to Poiret. 'They've been making eyes at each other for a week past in a way that would hale the heart from your body.'

'Yes,' he answered. 'So she was found guilty.'

'Who was?'

'Madame Morin.'

'I am talking about Mademoiselle Victorine,' said the woman, entering Poiret's room without appearing to notice what she was doing, 'and you answer "Madame Morin". Who may she be?'

'What can Mademoiselle Victorine be guilty of?'

'She's guilty of falling in love with Monsieur Eugène de Rastignac, and she's going ahead full tilt, not knowing where she is going, poor innocent!'

That morning Madame de Nucingen had driven Eugène to despair. In his own mind he had surrendered completely to Vautrin, shutting his eyes to the motives that extraordinary man might have for professing friendship for him, and refusing to consider what the outcome of such an alliance might be. Only a miracle could save him now from the abyss into which he had slipped an hour before, when he had given the sweetest promises of love to Mademoiselle Taillefer and received hers in exchange.

Victorine thought she was hearing an angel's voice, the heavens opened to let her in, the Maison Vauquer took on the bright, unreal colouring stage decorators give to palaces: she loved, and she was loved; or at least she believed so! And what woman would not have believed as she did after seeing Rastignac and listening to his voice in that hour stolen away from the Argus eyes of the boarding-house? Rastignac, struggling against his conscience, knowing he was doing wrong and forcing himself to do it with the whole strength of his will, told himself that he would atone for this venial sin by ensuring a woman's happiness. Desperation lent new beauty to his face, it shone with the splendid light of the fires of hell within his heart.

Luckily for him the miracle happened. Vautrin came in, in high spirits, and at once read the soul of these two young people whom he had united by the contrivance of his diabolic genius. But now his deep, mocking voice broke in upon their bliss, singing:

'My dear Fanchette is charming
  In her simplicity – '

Victorine fled, with a happiness in her heart that completely made up for all the sorrow which life had so far brought her. Poor girl! Rastignac's hand holding hers, his hair brushing her cheek, his words spoken so close to her ear that she had felt his warm lips, a trembling arm round her waist, a stolen kiss on her neck, these were her solemn betrothal rites, and the nearness of fat Sylvie, who might intrude into this now radiant dining-room at any moment, made them more ardent, more intense, more entrancing than any fine tokens of devotion the most famous love-stories could boast of. These *sweet posies*, to use a pretty expression of our forefathers, seemed almost crimes to a devout young girl who went to confession every fortnight. In that hour she had poured out more of the treasure of her heart's deepest feelings, than she would have given in later days of wealth and happiness, in surrendering herself completely.

'The thing is done,' said Vautrin to Eugène. 'Our two dandies have fallen out. It all came about in proper form – a difference of opinion – our pigeon insulted my falcon – to-morrow in the redoubt at Clignancourt. At half-past eight Mademoiselle Taillefer will become sole heiress to her father's fortune and affection, while she is calmly sitting here dipping her sippets of bread and butter in her coffee. Isn't it comic to be able to foretell that? The Taillefer youth is very clever with the sword and he's as cock-sure as if he had a fistful of aces; but he'll be let blood by a thrust I have invented, a way of raising the sword and pinking your man in the face. I must show you the thrust, it's uncommonly useful.'

Rastignac listened in stupid dumbness, unable to utter a word. Just then old Goriot, Bianchon and a few other boarders came in.

'Now you're in just the frame of mind I wanted to see you in,' Vautrin said. 'You know what you're about. All right, my little eaglet! You shall be a ruler among men; you are strong, you stand on your own feet, you've got spunk; I think the world of you!'

He made a movement as if to take Eugène's hand, but Rastignac brusquely withdrew it and fell into a chair, the colour ebbing from his face. He seemed to see a pool of blood spread before his eyes.

'Ah! so a few tattered swaddling clothes still cling about us, the stained rags of our virtue still hang together!' said Vautrin in a low voice. 'But Papa d'Oliban has three millions, I know what his pile is. The dowry will wash you as white as a wedding-dress, even in your own eyes.'

Rastignac hesitated no longer. He made up his mind that he would go that evening and warn both the Taillefers, father and son. Vautrin left the room, and Goriot came over to him and said in his ear,

'You look down in the mouth, my boy; I'll cheer you up. Come with me.'

The old vermicelli-maker was lighting his taper at one of the lamps as he spoke, and Eugène followed him upstairs with considerable curiosity.

'Let's go into your room,' said the good-natured old fellow; he had asked Sylvie for the student's key. 'You thought this morning that she didn't love you, didn't you now? She sent you away with a flea in your ear, and you went feeling cross and miserable. Silly boy! she was waiting for me, don't you see? We were to go and finish arranging about a set of rooms, a regular jewel of a place, which you will move into three days from now. Don't give me away; she wants it to be a surprise, but I don't care to keep you in the dark any longer. You will be in the Rue d'Artois, only a step or two from the Rue Saint-Lazare. You'll be as comfortable as a prince there! The furniture we've got for you is good enough for a bride! We've done a lot of things in the last month, without a word to you. My lawyer has begun the battle, my daughter is to have thirty-six thousand francs a year, the interest on her money, and I am going to insist on having her eight hundred thousand francs invested in good solid land.'

Eugène was dumb. He paced up and down, with his arms folded, from end to end of his wretched, untidy room. Old Goriot seized the occasion, when the student had his back to him, to put on the mantelpiece a red morocco box with the Rastignac arms stamped on the leather in gold.

'My dear child,' said the kind old fellow, 'I've been in this business up to the neck, but you see there was plenty of selfishness in my concern with it; I am an interested party in your change of abode. You won't refuse me, will you, if I ask something of you?'

'What is it?'

'Above your rooms there's a room on the fifth floor which is to let with them, that's where I shall live; don't you agree? I am growing old and I'm too far from my girls. I shall not trouble you at all, I'll just be there, that's all. You will come and talk to me about her every evening. That won't be tiresome for you, will it? When you come in after I have gone to bed I shall hear you and say to myself, "He has just seen my little Delphine. He has been to a ball with her. She is happy, thanks to him." If I were sick it would do my heart good just to hear you coming in or going out, or moving about. There'll be so much of my daughter in you! It's only a step to the Champs-Élysées where they go every day, I shall never get there too late to see them, as I sometimes do now. And perhaps she will come to your rooms! I shall hear her, and see her trotting about in her morning quilted gown, picking her steps daintily like a little cat. In the last month she has become my little girl again, as gay and frisky as she was before. Her heart is growing well again, and she owes her happiness to you. Oh! I would fetch the moon out of the sky for you. Just now when we were coming back she said to me, "Papa, I am so happy!" It chills me when they call me "Father" stiffly; but when they call me "Papa" I seem to see them as little children again, they bring back all my memories. I am more truly their father then. I forget that they are not still mine and no one else's.' The poor man wiped his eyes, he was in tears.

'It was a long time since I had heard her call me that, a long time since she last put her arm in mine. Ah! yes, it is all of ten years since I last walked arm-in-arm with one of my daughters. How sweet it is to suit my step to hers, to feel the light touch of her dress and the warmth of her arm! I took Delphine everywhere this morning. I went into the shops with her, and brought her back home again. Oh! you must let me live near you. Sometimes you'll need someone to do a service for you, and I shall be there to do it. Oh! if only that great block of an Alsatian would die, if his gout had the sense to attack his stomach, how happy my poor girl would be! You would be my son-in-law then, you would be her husband openly. Bah! she has never known what it is to be happy, as this world counts happiness, and that excuses everything in my opinion. God, who is good, must surely be on the side of fathers who love their children. She cares for you quite enough, and more than enough,' he said, nodding his head, after a moment's silence. 'As we went along she was chattering about you to me, "He is good-looking, Father, isn't he? He has a kind heart! Does he talk to you about me?" Bah! between the Rue d'Artois and the Passage des Panoramas she said enough about you to fill a library of books. Yes, yes, she poured out her heart to me. For the whole of this fine morning I was an old man no longer; I felt so light, I did not weigh an ounce. I told her that you had passed on the thousand franc note to me — she was moved to tears, poor darling. But what's that you have there on your mantelpiece?' said old Goriot at last; he was dying of impatience as he saw Rastignac standing there without a sign.

Eugène was standing looking at his neighbour in a bemused way. He was completely dumbfounded. This news of the realization of his dearest hopes contrasted so violently with Vautrin's announcement of the duel arranged for next day, that he experienced all the sensations of a nightmare. He turned to the mantelpiece, saw the little square box, opened it and found inside a watch made by Breguet, wrapped in paper. On the paper these words were written:

I want you to think of me every hour, *because* –
DELPHINE

The last word referred, no doubt, to some scene that had taken place between them; it touched Eugène's heart. His arms were enamelled inside the gold watch-case. He had long coveted just such a trinket: the chain, the key, the workmanship, the design were all he could have wished. Old Goriot's face was beaming. He must have promised his daughter that he would tell her every little detail of the effect her present produced, and of Eugène's surprise; he was a sharer in the young people's feelings of anticipation and excitement, and seemed to be not the least happy of the three. He loved Rastignac already, both for his daughter's sake and for his own.

'You must go and see her this evening, she expects you. That great lump of an Alsatian is having supper with his dancer. Aha! he looked pretty silly when my lawyer told him where he stood. And he professes to love my daughter this side idolatry, does he? Just let him lay a finger on her and I'll kill him! The very thought that Delphine is his' (he heaved a sigh) 'it's reason enough for me to make away with him, and you couldn't call it manslaughter – he has a pig's body and a calf's brains. You will take me with you, won't you?'

'Yes, dear Father Goriot, you know very well that I am fond of you – '

'Yes, indeed, I can see that you are; you are not ashamed of me! Let me embrace you,' and he held the student closely in his arms.

'You will make her really happy, promise me that! You will go this evening, won't you?'

'Oh! yes. I have to go out on business I can't put off.'

'Can I be of any use to you?'

'Well, yes, you could. Will you go to old Taillefer while I visit Madame de Nucingen, and ask him to see me some time this evening? I want to speak to him about a matter of the utmost importance.'

'Can it be true then, young man,' exclaimed Goriot, his face suddenly darkening; 'are you really courting his daughter, as those imbeciles down below say? By God! you don't know what a rap from Goriot can mean. If I found that you were throwing dust in our eyes, one blow from my fist would soon settle your business – Oh! no, the thing's not possible!'

'I swear to you that I love only one woman in the world,' said the student, 'though it's only in these last few minutes that I've realized it.'

'Oh! what happiness!' cried Goriot.

'But Taillefer's son is fighting a duel to-morrow,' the student went on, 'and I have heard that he is to be killed.'

'What is that to you?'

'But he must be told to prevent his son from going – ' cried Eugène.

Vautrin's voice interrupted him; the man was standing at the threshold of his door and singing,

> 'O Richard! O my king!
> All the world abandons thee –

Broum! broum! broum! broum! broum!

> I've roamed the world for years around
> No matter what –

Tra la, la, la, la.'

'Gentlemen,' shouted Christophe, 'the soup is waiting for you, and they're all at table.'

'Here,' called Vautrin, 'come and take down a bottle of my Bordeaux.'

'Do you think your watch is pretty?' asked Goriot. 'She has good taste, eh?'

Vautrin, old Goriot and Rastignac went down together, and because they were late found themselves obliged to sit together at table. Eugène was as distant and cold in his manner to Vautrin during the meal as he could be, but Vautrin, so charming a man in Madame Vauquer's eyes, had never shown himself more gay and light-hearted. He fairly sparkled with wit, and his sallies set the whole table in a roar. His assurance and coolness filled Eugène with dismay.

'What's come over you to-day?' Madame Vauquer asked him. 'You're as merry as a grig.'

'I'm always happy when I've made a good bargain.'

'Bargain?' said Eugène.

'Yes, why not? I have just delivered a consignment of goods, and I shall be paid a handsome commission for it. Don't you like my face, Mademoiselle Michonneau?' he went on, turning to the old maid, as he noticed that she was watching him closely. 'Is there something wrong with it that you goggle at it like that? If so, you must tell me and I'll have it changed, just to please you. We shan't fall out about it, Poiret, eh?' he added, leering at the retired clerk.

'By Jupiter! you'd make a wonderful model for Hercules out on a spree,' the young artist said to him.

'All right, I'll be your model, if Mademoiselle Michonneau will pose for the Venus of Père-Lachaise,' replied Vautrin.

'And what about Poiret?'

'Oh! Poiret shall pose as Poiret. He'll be a garden god!' cried Vautrin. 'His name means a pear – '

'A sleepy pear!' Bianchon broke in. 'You would be served between the pear and the cheese then.'

'What nonsense you're talking!' said Madame Vauquer. 'You would do better to pour us some Bordeaux from that bottle I see poking its nose up yonder! That will do our hearts good, besides being very *stomachical*.'

'Gentlemen,' said Vautrin, 'Madame President calls us to order. Madame Couture and Mademoiselle Victorine will not take your jokes amiss; but respect the innocent ears of aged Goriot. I propose a little bottleorama of the wine of Bordeaux, rendered doubly illustrious by the name of Laffitte, no political allusion intended. Come on, you heathen idol!' he added, staring at Christophe who was standing like a post. 'Here, Christophe! Do you not know your own name? Trot out the booze, heathen!'

'There you are, sir,' said Christophe, holding out the bottle.

Vautrin filled Eugène's glass and Goriot's and then slowly poured a few drops into his own, and merely tasted the wine while his two neighbours drank. Suddenly he made a grimace.

'The devil! It's corked. You can have the rest of this yourself, Christophe, and get some more for us. Take the bottles from the right-hand side, you know, don't you? There are sixteen of us; bring eight bottles.'

'As you're turning your pockets inside out for us,' said the artist, 'I'll stand us a hundred chestnuts.'

'Oh! Oh!'

'Booououh!'

'Prrrr!'

Exclamations shot from all corners of the table, like squibs from a firework.

'Come on, now, Ma Vauquer, a couple of bottles of champagne!' cried Vautrin.

'What's that you say? Is that all you want? Why not ask for the whole house when you're at it? Two bottles of champagne! That would cost twelve francs. I haven't enough money coming in to be able to afford all that, no indeed! But if Monsieur Eugène has a mind to pay it, I'll provide currant wine.'

'I know that currant wine, it's as good as a black draught,' muttered the medical student.

'Shut up, Bianchon,' cried Rastignac. 'I can't bear to hear anyone talking of black draughts! It makes me – Yes, champagne by all means. I'll pay for it,' he added.

'Sylvie,' said Madame Vauquer, 'get out the biscuits and the little cakes.'

'Your little cakes have grown up,' said Vautrin; 'they've got beards. But bring forward the biscuits.'

Soon the Bordeaux circulated, the guests grew livelier, the fun waxed faster and more furious. Wild guffaws were interrupted by imitations of various animal cries. When the Muséum official took it into his head to mimic a Paris street cry which had some resemblance to the caterwauling of an amorous tomcat, eight voices at once struck up:

'Knives to grind!'

'Birdseed for little birdies!'

'Cream cornets, ladies, cream cornets!'

'Mend your crockery, mend your crocks!'

'All aboard! All aboard! For a sail on the sea!'

'Your wives beaten! Your clothes beaten!'

'Old clothes, old lace, old hats for sale!'

'Cherries! Sweet cherries!'

But Bianchon was awarded the palm for the way he whined through his nose, 'Umbrella ma-a-a-n!'

In a few seconds an ear-splitting din filled the room, a volley of wild absurdities, a real cat's concert which Vautrin directed as if he were conducting an orchestra, while at the same time he kept an eye on Eugène and old Goriot, who seemed to be fuddled already. They were leaning back in their chairs, drinking little, and contemplating the scene before them in all its unwonted confusion with an air of gravity. They were both preoccupied with the thought of what they had to do that evening, and yet they felt that it was impossible to get up and go. Vautrin was watching the change that came over their faces, and chose the moment when their eyelids fluttered and seemed about to close, to bend over Rastignac and say in his ear –

'We're not fly enough, my little lad, to match ourselves against our Papa Vautrin, and he's too fond of you to let you make a fool of yourself. When I have made up my mind to do a thing only Heaven itself is strong enough to stand in my way. Oh! so we thought we would go and warn old Taillefer, did we? – tell tales out of school like a child! The oven is hot, the dough kneaded, the bread on the baker's peel; to-morrow we'll eat it and make the crumbs fly; and would we prevent the loaf from being put into the oven? – No, no, it's going to be baked! If we have a few little conscientious scruples they'll all be digested with the bread. While we take our little nap Colonel Count Franchessini's sword-point will clear the way to Michel Taillefer's inheritance for us. As her brother's successor Victorine will have a snug fifteen thousand francs a year. I have already made inquiries, and I know that her mother's estate amounts to more than three hundred thousand – '

Eugène heard these words but had no power of replying: he felt his tongue immovably glued to the roof of his mouth and found himself overtaken by an irresistible drowsiness; already the table and the faces of the guests swam in his field of vision through a luminous fog. Presently the noise subsided; the boarders left, one after another. Then when there remained only Madame Vauquer, Madame Couture, Mademoiselle Victorine, Vautrin and old Goriot, Rastignac saw, as if in a dream, Madame Vauquer busily engaged in filling up some bottles with the dregs of all the others.

'Ah! how lively they are! What it is to be young!' said the widow.

These words were the last that reached Eugène's mind.

'There's no one like what Monsieur Vautrin is for livening things up,' said Sylvie. 'Well, just take a look at Christophe, he's snoring like a humming-top.'

'Goodbye, Ma,' said Vautrin. 'I'm off to a theatre on the boulevard to see M. Marty in *Le Mont Sauvage*, a grand play taken from *Le Solitaire*. I will take you with me if you care to go, and these ladies too.'

'Thank you, I must refuse,' said Madame Couture.

'What, my good lady!' cried Madame Vauquer. 'You refuse to go and see a play made from *Le Solitaire*, a work by Atala de Chateaubriand which we enjoyed reading so much, and which was so affecting that we wept like Magdalenes over it under the *line-trees* last summer? And then it's a moralizing work which might be very edifying for your young lady!'

'We are forbidden to go to the play,' answered Victorine.

'Just look, these two have left us,' said Vautrin, shaking the heads of old Goriot and Eugène in a comical way. He settled the student more comfortably with his head against the back of the chair, kissed him warmly on the forehead, and began to sing:

> 'Sleep on, my sweet angels!
> I'll watch while you're sleeping!'

'I am afraid he may be ill,' said Victorine.

'Stay and look after him, then,' answered Vautrin. 'That's what you should do as a dutiful wife,' he whispered in her ear. 'The young man adores you, and you will be his little wife —

there's your fortune for you. In short,' he added aloud, 'they were esteemed throughout the land, lived happily ever after and had lots of children. That's how all the romances end. Come on, Ma,' he went on, turning to Madame Vauquer and giving her a hug, 'put on your hat, your fine flowered dress and the Countess's scarf. I'm going out to fetch a cab for you, all on my own.'

And he departed, singing:

> 'Sun, O Sun, whose gorgeous rays
> Make the pumpkins' faces blaze – '

'Goodness me! God bless my soul! I can tell you, Madame Couture, I could live happily with that man on the house-tops. Look at this,' she said, turning to look at the vermicelli-maker, 'here's old Goriot tight. It never once entered *his* head to take me *emmywhere*, the old miser. But, heavens above! he's going to tumble down on the floor. It's downright indecent for a man of his years to fuddle his wits like that. You'll be telling me that he can't fuddle what he hasn't got. Sylvie, get him up to his own room.'

Sylvie supported the old fellow under his arms, walked him upstairs, and threw him just as he was across the bed, like a parcel.

'Poor young man,' said Madame Couture, drawing back a lock of Eugène's hair which had fallen over his eyes, 'he's like a girl, he doesn't know what dissipation is.'

'I can tell you this,' said Madame Vauquer, 'thirty-one years I have kept my boarding-house, and no end of young fellows have passed through my hands, as the saying is, but I've never seen as nice a one as Monsieur Eugène, nor one as noble-looking either. Doesn't he look handsome sleeping? Just let his head lean on your shoulder, Madame Couture. There! he's sliding over towards Mademoiselle Victorine's. There's a providence looks after young things. A little more and he would have split his head against the knob of the chair. They'd make a very pretty couple, those two.'

'Hush, my dear neighbour!' cried Madame Couture. 'What a thing to say! – '

'Bah!' said Madame Vauquer, 'he doesn't hear. Come on, Sylvie, come and help me dress. I am going to put on my best stays.'

'What! your big stays, after dinner, Madame?' said Sylvie. 'No, find someone else to lace you up, I'm not going to be your murderer. It's terrible foolishness and you could easily get your death by it.'

'I don't care. I must do credit to Monsieur Vautrin.'

'Are you as fond of your heirs as all that?'

'Come, Sylvie, don't answer back,' said the widow, as she left the room.

'At her age, too!' said the cook to Victorine, with a jerk of her thumb in the direction of her departing mistress.

Madame Couture and her ward were left alone in the dining-room with Eugène, who still slept on Victorine's shoulder. Christophe's snores echoing through the silent house made Eugène's quiet slumber seem still more peaceful by contrast; the student slept as engagingly as a child does. Victorine was happy in being free to do one of those loving-kindnesses in which a woman's overflowing heart finds its expression, and one which brought the young man so innocently close to her that she could feel the beating of his heart. Her face revealed a maternal protectiveness and pride which gave her dignity. Amid the countless thoughts that thronged in her young pure heart, she was conscious of a quick flutter of her pulses at the warmth of the young body that lay so artlessly against hers.

'Poor dear child,' said Madame Couture, squeezing her hand.

The old lady looked at the girl's open face, with its look of suffering endured, on which happiness now shed a soft radiance, as if a halo encircled her head. Victorine was like one of the naïve paintings of the Middle Ages in which all accessories are neglected, and the artist reserves the magic of his brush for the painting of the calm, proud face, whose pallor seems to catch a golden reflection from Heaven.

'But he only took two glasses, after all, Mamma,' said Victorine, passing her fingers through Eugène's hair.

'If he were a dissipated young man, child, he would have carried his wine like all the others. The fact that he was overcome by it speaks in his favour.'

They heard the sound of wheels outside in the street.

'Mamma,' said the girl, 'here comes Monsieur Vautrin. You take Monsieur Eugène. I would rather not let that man see me like this; he says things which leave a stain in your mind, and his looks make you feel as if you had nothing on.'

'Oh, no, you are mistaken,' said Madame Couture, 'he is a fine man, a little like my late husband, Monsieur Couture; rather abrupt in his manner but with a kind heart; his bark is much worse than his bite.'

As she spoke Vautrin came in without a sound, and looked at the picture the two young things made in the lamplight, which seemed to caress them with its soft beams.

'Well, now,' he said, folding his arms, 'here's a scene which would have inspired good Bernardin de Saint-Pierre who wrote *Paul et Virginie* to write some pretty pages. Youth is a lovely thing indeed, Madame Couture! Poor child, sleep on,' he added, with his eyes on Eugène. 'Luck sometimes comes while we are sleeping. There's something touching and attractive to me in this young man, Madame. It's because I know his nature is as noble as his face. Look, is he not like a cherub leaning on an angel's shoulder? He is a man worth loving. If I were a woman I would die (no, nothing so stupid), live for him. As I see them together like this, Madame,' he went on in an undertone, bending to speak in the widow's ear, 'I cannot help thinking that God made them for one another. God works in a mysterious way, He searches the heart and the reins,' he declaimed aloud. 'When I see you together, my children, united by the innocence of both, and by all the affections of the human heart, I say to myself that it is impossible that you should ever be parted in the future. God is just. – But it seems to me,' he said to the girl, 'I have seen the line of prosperity marked in your hand. Let me see it, Mademoiselle Victorine; I know something about palmistry, I have often told fortunes. Come now, don't be afraid. Ah! what's this I see? Upon my word, before very long you will be one of the richest heiresses in Paris. You will heap happiness upon the man who loves you. Your father calls you to his side. You marry a handsome young man with a title, who adores you.'

The heavy footsteps of the flirtatious widow coming downstairs interrupted Vautrin's fortune-telling at this point.

'Ah! here comes Ma Vauquerre, fair as a star-r-r, decked like a Christmas tree. – Do we not feel just a shade too tight, Ma?' he asked, laying a hand on the lady at the place where her corset took most strain. 'Our little front is well squeezed in. If we get worked up there will be an explosion; but I will gather up the fragments with an antiquary's care.'

'There's a man who can speak the language of French gallantry!' said the widow, bending to speak in Madame Couture's ear.

'Goodbye, my children!' Vautrin went on, turning to Eugène and Victorine. 'My blessing on you,' he said, laying his hands on their heads. – 'Believe me, Mademoiselle, the prayers of a righteous man count for something, they are bound to bring good fortune, God hears them.'

'Goodbye, dear friend,' said Madame Vauquer to her boarder. 'Do you think,' she added in a whisper, 'that Monsieur Vautrin has intentions with regard to me?'

'Mercy on us!'

'Oh! Mamma dear,' said Victorine with a sigh, examining her hands, when the two women were left alone, 'suppose what that kind Monsieur Vautrin said came true!'

'Well, there's only one thing needed to make it happen,' replied the old lady. 'If your monster of a brother just fell off his horse – '

'Oh! Mamma!'

'Goodness! perhaps it's a sin to wish ill to your enemy,' the widow continued. 'Oh, well, I will do penance for it. Still it's no lie to say that I would carry flowers to his grave with pleasure. Black-hearted creature that he is! He's too much of a coward to speak up for his own mother, and he cheats you out of your share of what she left by his artful dodges. My cousin had a handsome fortune. Unfortunately for you, the personal property she brought with her has never been so much as mentioned.'

'I could hardly bear my good luck if it cost someone's life,' said Victorine. 'And if my brother had to die to make me happy, I would rather stay here always.'

'Heaven knows it's just as that good Monsieur Vautrin says; and you can see he is very religious,' said Madame Couture. 'I was very pleased to find that he is not an unbeliever like the rest of them, who speak of God with less respect than they give to the Devil. Ah, well, as he says, who can tell by what ways it may please Providence to lead us?'

Helped by Sylvie, the two women finally carried Eugène to his room and laid him on his bed, and the cook loosened his clothes to make him more comfortable. Before they left him, when her guardian's back was turned, Victorine kissed Eugène's forehead with all the bliss that this very criminal act could bring her. Then she looked round his room, gathering together, as it were, into a single thought, all the thousand and one delights of that day; and after long contemplation of the picture she had made of her memories, she fell asleep, the happiest creature in Paris.

The merrymaking that evening, under cover of which Vautrin had made Eugène and old Goriot drink drugged wine, was a decisive factor in the man's ruin. Bianchon, half tipsy, forgot to question Mademoiselle Michonneau about Cheat-Death. The very mention of this name would certainly have put Vautrin on his guard, or rather Jacques Collin, to give him his real name, for he was in fact the famous convict. Then the joke about the Venus of Père-Lachaise made Mademoiselle Michonneau make up her mind to betray the criminal, although she had noted Collin's generosity and had been wondering a moment before whether she might not make a better bargain for herself by warning him and helping him to escape during the night. She had gone out, escorted by Poiret, to look for the famous chief detective in the Petite Rue Sainte-Anne, still thinking that she was dealing with a senior official named Gondureau. The great man received her politely. They talked for a time, arranging exactly how Mademoiselle Michonneau was to confirm that Vautrin's shoulder bore the fatal brand, and then she asked for the draught she was to use. The great man turned to look for the little phial in a drawer of his desk with a gesture of such satisfaction that she began to suspect that there was something more important involved in this capture than the mere arrest of a runaway convict. She racked her brains to find what it might be, and guessed that traitors in the prison had given information, and that in consequence of this the police were hoping to arrive in time to lay hands on a considerable sum of money. When she voiced her suspicions the old fox of the Petite Rue Sainte-Anne began to smile, and he tried to put her off the scent.

'You are mistaken,' he replied. 'Collin's is the most dangerous *sorbonne* ever known among the criminal classes, that's all. The rascals know it well; he is the flag they rally round, their support and stay, their Napoleon in short; they are all devoted to him. That joker will never leave his *tronche* in the Place de Grève.'

As Mademoiselle Michonneau seemed rather bewildered, Gondureau explained the two slang words he had used. *Sorbonne* and *tronche* are forcible expressions from the lingo used by thieves, invented to satisfy the need, which they were the first to feel, to consider the human head under two aspects. The *sorbonne* is the head of the living man, his brain, his power of advising and directing. *Tronche* is a contemptuous word designed to express the uselessness of a head parted from its body by the executioner.

'Collin makes a fool of us,' he went on. 'When we meet men like him who are like a bar of tempered English steel, there's one thing we can do, we can make shift to kill them if they take it into their heads to offer the slightest resistance when we're arresting them. We are counting on finding several pretexts for killing Collin to-morrow morning. It saves a trial, and society is rid of him without having to pay for guarding and feeding him. It costs much more than the three thousand francs which you are going to get, to proceed with the case, summon witnesses and compensate them, carry out the sentence and so on, all the red-tape necessary to rid us legally of one of these rapscallions. We save time too. With a good bayonet-thrust in Cheat-Death's bread-basket we prevent a hundred crimes and avoid the corruption of fifty scamps who will very prudently take the hint and stay outside the law-courts. That is good police work. Real philanthropists will tell you that we prevent crime by going to work that way.'

'And it's serving our country,' said Poiret.

'Bless me!' replied the chief detective. 'You're talking sense this evening. Yes, of course, we are serving our country; and people in general are very unjust in the way they think of us. We render society very great services which go unrecognized. Well, it's the duty of a superior man to rise above and be indifferent to prejudice, and a Christian must resign himself to enduring the wrongs that doing right entails, when it is not done in accordance with conventional notions. Paris is Paris, you see! That explains my life. I have the honour to wish you good evening, Mademoiselle. I shall be at the Jardin-du-Roi to-morrow with my men. Send Christophe to the Rue de Buffon to the house I was staying in, and tell him to ask for Monsieur Gondureau. Monsieur, I am obliged to you. If you ever have anything stolen from you, come to me and I'll do what I can to have it found. I am at your service, sir.'

'Well,' said Poiret to Mademoiselle Michonneau, 'to think that there are idiots who are all of a tremble at the very name of the police! That was a most agreeable gentleman, and what he wants you to do is as easy as A.B.C.'

The next day was to take its place in the annals of the Maison Vauquer as one of the most extraordinary it had ever known. Until then the most startling event in its peaceful existence had been the meteoric apparition and departure of the false Comtesse de l'Ambermesnil. But everything was to pale before the catastrophes of this great day, which was destined to furnish matter for conversation to Madame Vauquer to the end of her days.

To begin with, Goriot and Eugène de Rastignac slept till eleven o'clock. Madame Vauquer, who had returned from the Gaîté at midnight, lay in bed till half-past ten. The household work was in arrears because Christophe, who had finished the bottle of wine Vautrin had given him, was sleeping off the effects. Poiret and Mademoiselle Michonneau had no complaint to make about the delay in serving breakfast. Victorine and Madame Couture, too, slept late. Vautrin went out before eight o'clock and came back just as breakfast was served. Nobody grumbled at the lateness of the hour, therefore, when Sylvie and Christophe knocked at all the doors at a quarter past eleven and announced that breakfast was waiting.

Mademoiselle Michonneau came down first. While Sylvie and the man-servant were out of the room she emptied the potion into the silver cup belonging to Vautrin, in which the cream for his coffee was heating in a bain-marie, with the other cups. The old maid had reckoned on this particular custom of the boarding-house for the carrying-out of her plot.

At last the seven boarders were gathered in the dining-room, not without some difficulty. As Eugène was coming down last of all, stretching himself and yawning as he came, a messenger handed him a letter from Madame de Nucingen, which ran thus:

Where you are concerned, my friend, I feel neither false pride nor anger. I waited for you till two o'clock in the morning, waited for a person I love! That is such torture that no one who has known it can ever inflict it on another. It is easy to see that you have never loved before. What can have happened? I am devoured by anxiety. If I had not been afraid of betraying my heart's secrets I would have come to find out what good fortune or calamity had befallen you; but how could I walk or drive out at that hour, would it not have been ruin? I have been feeling how wretched it is to be a woman. Send me some reassuring word, explain why you did not come after what my father told you. I shall be angry with you, but I will forgive you. Are you ill? Oh! why do you live so far away? Send me just one word, for pity's sake. You will come soon, won't you? If you are busy a word will be enough. Say, 'I'm on my way,' or 'I'm ill.' But if you were ill my father would have come to tell me! What can have happened? —

'Yes! what has happened?' cried Eugène, crumpling the letter in his hand without reading any more, and bursting into the dining-room. 'What time is it?'

'Half-past eleven,' said Vautrin, as he added sugar to his coffee.

The escaped convict cast a basilisk glance at Eugène, the blood-congealing, mesmeric look that certain men of outstanding magnetic power possess the secret of, with which it is said they can quell raving madmen in the madhouses. Eugène shook in every limb. Outside, the noise of a cab became audible, and a second later a servant in Monsieur Taillefer's livery, instantly recognized by Madame Couture, with a scared face, rushed into the room.

'Mademoiselle,' he exclaimed, 'your father is asking for you. A dreadful thing has happened. Monsieur Frédéric has been fighting a duel and has a sword-thrust in the forehead. The doctors have given up hope of saving him: you will scarcely be in time to say goodbye to him, he has lost consciousness!'

'Poor young man!' cried Vautrin. 'How can a man engage in brawls when he has a solid thirty thousand livres a year? There's no doubt at all the young people of to-day don't know how to behave themselves.'

'Sir!' shouted Eugène.

'Well, what's the matter, my big baby?' said Vautrin, calmly drinking all his coffee at one draught, an operation which Mademoiselle Michonneau was watching too closely for her to have any excitement to spare for the extraordinary event that had struck everyone else dumb with amazement. 'Aren't there duels every morning in Paris?'

'I will go with you, Victorine,' said Madame Couture. The two women hurried off without waiting to put on either hat or shawl. Before she went Victorine, with tears in her eyes, gave Eugène a glance that said, 'I did not think our happiness would bring me tears!'

'My word! you must be a prophet, Monsieur Vautrin!' said Madame Vauquer.

'I am all sorts of things,' said Jacques Collin.

'How strange it is!' Madame Vauquer went on, improving the occasion with a string of platitudes. 'Death takes us off without warning. The young people often go before the old. We women are lucky not to have to fight duels, but we have other troubles that men don't suffer from. We bear children, and a mother's pains last a long time. What a stroke of luck for Victorine! Her father will be forced to acknowledge her now.'

'There, you see,' said Vautrin, looking at Eugène, 'yesterday she hadn't a penny, to-day she's worth several millions.'

'Well, now, Monsieur Eugène,' exclaimed Madame Vauquer, 'you've done pretty well for yourself.'

When he heard this old Goriot looked at the student, and saw the crumpled letter in his hand.

'You didn't read it all! What does this mean? Can you be like all the others?' he asked.

'Madame, I shall never marry Mademoiselle Victorine,' said Eugène, turning to Madame Vauquer. The horror and loathing in his tone astonished his hearers.

Old Goriot seized the student's hand and grasped it warmly. He could have kissed it.

'Oho!' said Vautrin. 'The Italians have a good saying – *col tempo!*'

'Is there an answer?' said Madame de Nucingen's messenger to Eugène.

'Say I will come.'

The man left. In Eugène's violently excited state he could not think of prudence.

'What should I do?' he cried aloud. 'There is no proof!'

Vautrin began to smile, though the draught had been absorbed by his system and was beginning to take effect. The convict was so strong that he was able to rise to his feet, stare at Rastignac, and say in a hollow voice,

'Young man, luck comes while we are sleeping.'

Then he fell stiffly, as if he were struck dead.

'So there is justice in Heaven!' said Eugène.

'Oh! my goodness! what's come over him? Poor dear Monsieur Vautrin!'

'A stroke!' cried Mademoiselle Michonneau.

'Sylvie, quick, girl, run and fetch the doctor,' said the widow. 'Ah! Monsieur Rastignac, fly to Monsieur Bianchon's; Sylvie may not catch our doctor, Monsieur Grimpel.'

Rastignac rushed out of the room, glad to have an excuse for leaving that den of horrors.

'Hurry, Christophe, run along to the chemist's and ask for something that's good for a stroke.'

Christophe also departed.

'Now, Father Goriot, can't you give us a hand to get him upstairs to his own room?'

Vautrin was lifted, carried with some difficulty up the staircase, and laid on his bed.

'I'm not any use to you here, I'm going to see my daughter,' said Monsieur Goriot.

'Selfish old brute!' screamed Madame Vauquer. 'Be off with you. I only hope you will die like a dog.'

'See if you can find some ether, Madame Vauquer,' said Mademoiselle Michonneau. With some help from Poiret she had unfastened Vautrin's clothes.

Madame Vauquer went downstairs to her room, leaving Mademoiselle Michonneau mistress of the field.

'Come on, take off his shirt and turn him over, quick! Spare my modesty, and show yourself good for something, do, instead of standing there like a statue,' she said to Poiret.

When Vautrin had been turned over Mademoiselle Michonneau slapped his shoulder smartly, and the two fatal letters appeared, standing out white on the reddened patch of skin.

'My word, it hasn't taken you long to earn your three thousand francs reward,' exclaimed Poiret, holding Vautrin up, while Mademoiselle Michonneau slipped his shirt over his head. 'Ouf! he's heavy,' he added, as he laid him down.

'Hush! Now, suppose there's a strong-box here?' said the old maid eagerly. As she spoke she was scrutinizing everything in the room, down to the smallest articles of furniture, with such greedy intensity that her eyes seemed to pierce the walls. 'Suppose we opened that writing-desk on some pretext or other?'

'Perhaps it wouldn't be right,' replied Poiret.

'Why not?' said she. 'It's money stolen from here, there and everywhere. It doesn't belong to anyone now. But there's no time. I hear that Vauquer woman coming.'

'Here's some ether,' said Madame Vauquer. 'Bless my soul! we've a chapter of accidents to-day indeed. Goodness! that man can't have had a stroke, he's as white as a chicken.'

'As a chicken?' repeated Poiret.

'His heart-beat is regular,' said the widow, with her hand on his breast.

'Regular?' said Poiret, in an astonished voice.

'He's well enough.'

'You think so?' asked Poiret.

'Upon my word, he looks as if he were sleeping. Sylvie's gone to find a doctor. Look, Mademoiselle Michonneau, he's sniffing at the ether. Bah! it's only a *spassum*. His pulse is steady. He's as strong as a Turk. Just look, Mademoiselle Michonneau, what a mat of hair he has on his chest! He'll live to be a hundred, that's the sort of man he is! His wig holds on well, in spite of everything. Gracious, it's glued on! His own hair is red, that's

214

why he wears a wig. They say that redheads are all either angels or devils; he would be one of the good ones, I suppose, wouldn't he?'

'Good for hanging,' said Poiret.

'You mean on a pretty woman's neck,' exclaimed Mademoiselle Michonneau hastily. 'Take yourself off now, Monsieur Poiret, it's women's business to look after you men when you're ill. Besides, for all the use you are to us you might as well go about your own affairs,' she added. 'Madame Vauquer and I will take good care of dear Monsieur Vautrin.'

Poiret went off meekly, without a murmur, like a dog kicked out by his master.

Rastignac had gone out to walk, to breathe in the open air, for he felt suffocated. The evening before he had made up his mind to prevent this crime, which nevertheless had been committed at the appointed hour. What had happened? What ought he to do now? He trembled at the thought that he might be held to have some complicity in it. Vautrin's coolness made the whole thing still more appalling.

'Yet what if Vautrin were to die without saying anything?' Rastignac asked himself.

He hurried along the walks of the Luxembourg as if a pack of hounds were closing in on him and he already heard them baying at his heels.

'Well,' Bianchon hailed him, 'have you seen the *Pilote*?'

The *Pilote* was a Radical sheet, edited by Monsieur Tissot, which issued an edition for the provinces, with the day's news, several hours later than the morning papers; and so brought news of the morning's events into country districts twenty-four hours earlier than the other local papers.

'There's a grand story in it,' the medical student went on. 'Young Taillefer fought a duel with Count Franchessini of the Old Guard, and got two inches of cold steel in his forehead. Here's little Victorine one of the richest matches in Paris! Ah! if we had only known that! What a lottery death is – you draw a ticket or you don't! Is it true that Victorine cast a favouring eye on you, my lad?'

'Oh, don't talk about it, Bianchon, I shall never marry her. I'm in love with a charming woman, and she loves me. I – '

'You say that as though it took a great deal out of you to remain faithful to her. Just show me the woman worth sacrificing old Taillefer's fortune for!'

'Are all the devils in Hell after me?' cried Rastignac.

'What in the world is bothering you? Are you mad?' said Bianchon. 'Here, give me your hand and let me feel your pulse. You're feverish!'

'Just go to Ma Vauquer's if you want a patient,' said Eugène. 'That scoundrel Vautrin dropped like a dead man a short time ago.'

'Ah!' said Bianchon. 'You confirm my suspicions. I must go and make certain for myself.' And he left Eugène alone with his thoughts.

The law student walked for a long time, soberly reflecting and considering. He laid his conscience, as it were, before the tribunal of his own mind, and prosecuted a searching inquiry into every hole and corner of it; but although he took a drubbing, suffered pangs of doubt and self-distrust, at least his integrity emerged scatheless from that sharp and terrible trial like a steel bar that has been tried and has stood the test.

He remembered the confidences old Goriot had made to him the evening before; he thought again of the rooms chosen for him near Delphine in the Rue d'Artois; he took the letter from his pocket, read it again, and kissed it.

'A love like this is my sheet anchor,' he said to himself. 'The poor old man must have suffered dreadfully in his heart. He says nothing about what he has endured, but anyone can guess it. Well, I will look after him as though I were his son; I will fill his life with happiness. If she loves me she will often come to spend the day near him in my rooms. That grand Comtesse de Restaud is a heartless wretch, she would make a lackey of her father. Dear Delphine! she is kinder to the old fellow, she is worthy of being loved. Ah! how happy I shall be this evening!'

He pulled out the watch, and admired it.

'Everything has turned out happily for me! When people love each other for always it is permissible for them to help one another, and I can accept this. Besides, I shall succeed; of course I shall, and I'll be able to repay it all a hundredfold. There's no crime in this liaison, nor anything which could bring a frown to the most austerely virtuous face. How many respectable people contract similar unions! We are deceiving no one; and it is deceit which is degrading. If you lie you lose your self-respect, surely? She has lived apart from her husband for a long time. Moreover, I will tell that Alsatian myself that as he doesn't know how to make his wife happy he must give her up to me.'

Rastignac's battle with himself lasted a long time, and in the end victory inevitably lay with the virtues of youth. Nevertheless, an irresistible curiosity drew him back to the Maison Vauquer, about four o'clock, as it was getting dark; though as he went he swore to himself that he would leave it for ever. He wanted to know if Vautrin was dead.

It had occurred to Bianchon to administer an emetic to Vautrin, and he had had the vomited matter taken to his hospital for a chemical analysis. His suspicions were strengthened by Mademoiselle Michonneau's insistence that this matter should be got rid of. Moreover, Vautrin had recovered so quickly that Bianchon could not help suspecting that there had been some plot against the jolly fellow who was the life and soul of the boarding-house.

When Rastignac came back Vautrin was standing near the stove in the dining-room. The news of the younger Taillefer's duel had brought the boarders in earlier than usual, full of curiosity and anxious to hear all the details of the affair, and what changes it had wrought in Victorine's destiny; they were all there, except old Goriot, and all busily discussing it. When Eugène came into the room he saw Vautrin standing there as imperturbably as ever; his eyes met Vautrin's, and he shuddered as he felt that piercing gaze strike home to the depths of his heart, and stir to life its darkest impulses.

'Well, my dear boy,' said the escaped convict, 'there's life in the old dog yet, and will be for a long time to come. Death won't put me in the bag so easily. According to these ladies, I've pulled through a stroke that might have killed an ox.'

'Or you might even say a bull!' cried the widow.

'Is it possible you are sorry to see me alive?' said Vautrin in a whisper to Eugène, believing he read his thoughts. 'You must be confoundedly sure of your own strength!'

'Mademoiselle Michonneau was talking the day before yesterday,' said Bianchon, 'of a gentleman called "Cheat-Death". Upon my word, that name would suit you very well.'

This remark seemed to strike Vautrin like a thunderbolt: he turned pale and staggered; his magnetic glance fell like a ray of bright light on Mademoiselle Michonneau, and the old maid's legs seemed to crumple under her as she felt the impact of the man's strong will. She collapsed into a chair. Vautrin's expression was so ferocious that Poiret hastily stepped between them, understanding that the old maid was in danger. The genial mask that had disguised the convict's real nature had gone. The other boarders, still entirely in the dark as to the meaning of this dramatic scene, were staring in blank amazement. At this moment of tension the tramp of marching soldiers was heard approaching outside, followed by the ring of several rifles grounded on the pavement of the street. As Collin automatically scanned walls and windows for a way of escape, four men, headed by the chief detective, appeared at the drawing-room door.

'In the name of the Law and the King!' said one of them, but his words were almost drowned by a murmur of astonishment.

Then silence fell on the room. The boarders stood aside to let three of the men pass; each man kept one hand in his pocket, grasping a cocked pistol. Two policemen followed the detectives and guarded the entrance to the drawing-room, while two others appeared at the doorway opening on the staircase. Outside in the garden footsteps crunched in the gravel of the pathway that ran along the front of the house, and the rattle of the rifles of several soldiers was heard again under the windows. All way of escape for Cheat-Death was thus blocked, and to him every eye was irresistibly drawn. The chief walked straight up to him and began operations by striking him so violently on the head that the wig flew off, and the convict's terrifying head was revealed without disguise. The short, brick-red hair lent a shocking suggestion of strength combined with cunning to the face; the whole head gave an impression of power in harmony with the powerful chest and shoulders, and at that moment the soul and spirit of the man were apparent in his face, as if he stood in a lurid glare thrown by the flames of Hell. Everyone present instantly understood the manner of man Vautrin was, his past, present and future, his pitiless doctrines, his religion of his own good pleasure, the royal power given him by his contemptuous appraisal of other men and his cynical treatment of them, and by the strength of an organization that was prepared for anything, and stopped at nothing.

The blood rose to his face, his eyes glittered like a wildcat's. He gathered himself for a spring with such infuriated strength, he roared so savagely that his ferocity wrung cries of terror from the boarders. When they saw him thus crouch like a lion for the attack the detectives, taking advantage of the general uproar to achieve their purpose, drew their pistols. Collin at once realized his danger when he saw the raised fire-arms shine, and instantly gave proof of his possession of a power of the highest order. The transformation in his face was both impressive and horrifying; it seemed like a phenomenon of nature only comparable to that presented by a boiler full of steam with power enough to heave a mountain up, when a drop of cold water dissipates its force in the twinkling of an eye. The drop of water that cooled his fury was a reflection that flashed across his brain like lightning. He broke into a smile, and looked down at his wig.

'To-day isn't one of your politest days,' he said to the chief detective, and he held out his hands to the policemen, and motioned them forward with a jerk of his head.

'You gentlemen put on the bracelets or the manacles,' he said. 'I call all here to witness that I make no resistance.'

A murmur of admiration ran through the room, forced from the onlookers by the vehemence with which the lava and the flames poured from this human volcano, and the rapidity with which they were brought under control.

'That takes the wind out of your sails, my hopeful blade!' the convict added, looking at the famous detective.

'Come on, strip!' was the contemptuous answer of the man from the Petite Rue Sainte-Anne.

'Why?' said Collin. 'There are ladies present. I deny nothing, and I give myself up.'

He paused and looked round like an orator about to astonish his audience.

'Write it all down, Papa Lachapelle,' he said to a little old man with white hair who had sat down at the end of the table, with a form for the official report of the arrest, which he had taken from a pocket-book. 'I acknowledge myself to be Jacques Collin, otherwise known as Cheat-Death, sentenced to twenty years' imprisonment; and I have just proved my title to the nick-name. If I had so much as raised my hand,' he said to the boarders, 'I should have been raspberry jam spattered all over Ma Vauquer's sacred hearth. Those three fine fellows there make it their job to arrange little traps!'

When she heard this Madame Vauquer felt rather ill.

'Good gracious!' she said to Sylvie, 'it gives me quite a turn; and me at the Gaîté with him only last night!'

'Hold on to your philosophy, Ma,' retorted Collin. 'Did it do you any harm to sit in my box at the Gaîté yesterday? And, after all, are you any better than us?' he exclaimed. 'We bear the mark of shame on our shoulders, but there's a deeper mark in your hearts, you flabby members of a rotting society: the best man among you could not stand up to me.'

His eyes rested on Rastignac, and he smiled at him, a pleasant smile that looked strange on his harsh, forbidding face.

'Our little bargain still holds good, my dear, sweet, innocent lad; that is when you accept it! You know?

> My dear Fanchette is charming
> In her simplicity.'

he sang.

'Don't worry about anything,' he added. 'I have my ways and means of getting my money in. People find me much too formidable a chap to try to diddle me!'

The life that this speech suddenly laid bare was life as it is lived in jail, with its own peculiar manners and language, its sudden sharp transitions from the genial to the horrifying, its appalling power and importance, its complete lack of respect for anyone or anything, its baseness; and the speaker no longer seemed a mere individual but was the mouthpiece and the type of a whole degenerate people, a barbarous and brutal, supple, yet calmly logical and clear-headed race. As he spoke, Collin became a poet, a poet of Hell, expressing all impulses and passions that move the human soul, save one – repentance. He looked about him like the fallen archangel whose only wish was for eternal enmity. Rastignac lowered his eyes, acknowledging, in expiation of his secret evil thoughts, the kinship with him that the criminal claimed.

'Who betrayed me?' said Collin, and his terrible eyes raked the company. They came to rest on Mademoiselle Michonneau.

'It was you, you old money-grubber,' he said. 'That faked stroke of apoplexy was your work, nosy-parker! I have only to say two words to have your neck wrung within a week. But I forgive you, I am a Christian. Besides, it wasn't you who sold me. But who was it? – Aha! are you rummaging up there?' he exclaimed, as he heard the police officers opening his cupboards and taking possession of his effects. 'The birds are flown; they left the nest yesterday, and you will learn nothing there. My business books are here,' and he tapped his forehead. 'Now I know who sold me, it must have been that blackguard Fil-de-Soie. That's who it was, isn't it, old catch-'em-alive-o?' he said, turning to the chief. 'It was timed so neatly to trap our little bank-notes while they stayed upstairs. All gone, my little sleuth-hounds, nothing left! As for Fil-de-Soie, he'll be pushing up the daisies in a fortnight; you couldn't save him if you called out the entire police-force for his protection. – What did you give this Michonnette woman?' he asked the policemen. 'Three thousand francs! Oh, you Ninon in decay, you ragged Pompadour, you Venus of the Père-Lachaise, I was worth more than that! If you had warned me you should have had six thousand francs. Ah! you didn't imagine that, did you, you old dealer in human flesh, or I should have had the preference. Yes, I would have given that to avoid a journey that interferes with my plans and makes me lose some money,' he said, as they put the handcuffs on his wrists. 'These people will get some fun out of making me cool my heels till the end of time, just to plague me and give me the blues. If they sent me to prison straight away, I should soon be back at work again, in spite of our sweet simpletons at the Quai des Orfèvres. In there they'll all move heaven and earth to get their general, good old Cheat-Death, out of the coop! Is there one of you who can say, as I can, that he owns ten thousand brothers all ready to do absolutely anything for him?' he asked proudly. 'There's some good in there,' he said, tapping his heart; 'no one has ever been betrayed by me! Look here, muck-worm, do you see?' he said to the old maid; 'they're all afraid of me, but their gorge rises at the sight of *you*. Pick up the pelf you've won.'

He paused a moment, and gazed at the boarders' faces.

'What blockheads you all are! Have you never seen a convict before? A convict of the stamp of Collin, who stands before you, is a man less lily-livered than the rest, who dares to raise his voice against the colossal fraud of the Social Contract. That's what Jean-Jacques Rousseau called it, and I glory in being his pupil. In short, I stand alone against organized authority with its mass of law-courts and police and revenues to back it up, and I beat it hollow.'

'Christ!' said the painter. 'What a marvellous subject!'

'Tell me, hangman's minion,' he added, turning to the chief detective, 'lord of the Widow' (a nickname full of dreadful poetry that convicts give the guillotine), 'be a good lad and tell me if it was Fil-de-Soie who sold me. I don't want him to suffer for somebody else, it wouldn't be fair.'

But just then the men who had been upstairs examining and making an inventory of everything belonging to Collin came in again, and said a few words in a low voice to the chief. The official preliminaries were complete.

'Gentlemen,' said Collin, turning to the boarders again, 'they are going to carry me off directly. You have all been very pleasant during my stay among you, and I shall remember that. Accept my farewell good wishes. You will permit me to send you some figs from Provence.'

He started to move away, and then turned round to look at Rastignac.

'Goodbye, Eugène,' he said with a sad gentleness in striking contrast to the rough, blunt tone of his previous speeches. 'If you should get into difficulties I've left you a devoted friend.' In spite of his handcuffs he managed to assume a defensive posture, called 'One, two!' like a fencing-master, and lunged. 'If something goes wrong, apply there. Man and money, they're both at your service.'

This strange being played the buffoon successfully enough to ensure that no one but Rastignac understood that his last words held a serious meaning.

When the house was clear of police, soldiers and detectives, Sylvie, who was rubbing her mistress's temples with vinegar, looked at the dumbfounded boarders.

'Well!' she said, 'all the same, he was a man, he was.'

Her words broke the spell which had held them all speechless and motionless while the torrent of diverse emotions the scene produced overwhelmed them. Now all the boarders looked at one another, and then as one man turned their eyes on Mademoiselle Michonneau crouching near the stove, a lank, bloodless, dried-up figure like a mummy, her eyes downcast as if she were afraid that the shadow of her eyeshade was not deep enough to hide the expression in her eyes. The causes that had produced the appearance of that face, and the antipathy they had felt to it for so long, were suddenly made plain. A low murmur arose as all the boarders' voices chimed together to express unanimous disgust. Mademoiselle Michonneau heard it, and made no movement. Bianchon took the lead; he bent over his neighbour and said in an undertone,

'If that creature is going to stay here and have dinner with us, I'm off.'

In a twinkling it was clear that everyone except Poiret was of the student's mind, and, fortified by the general approval, he bore down upon that elderly gentleman.

'As you are Mademoiselle Michonneau's special friend, you must speak to her,' he said. 'Make her understand that she must go at once.'

'At once?' repeated Poiret, in astonishment.

He went over to the figure by the stove, and said something to her in a whisper.

'But I've paid my quarter's rent, I've as much right to be here as anyone else,' she said, with a malignant look at the boarders.

'Never mind that,' said Rastignac, 'we'll all club together and pay it back to you.'

'This gentleman sides with Collin,' she said, scrutinizing the student, with an expression of venomous inquiry on her face. 'It's not difficult to understand why.'

Eugène sprang forward as if to throw himself upon the old maid and strangle her. The treacherous intention of her look was obvious, and it had let a flood of hideous light into his mind.

'Let her alone!' cried the boarders.

He folded his arms, and said nothing.

'Let's have done with Mademoiselle Judas,' said the painter. 'Unless you send that woman packing, Madame Vauquer, we'll all clear out, every one of us, and we'll tell everybody that the place is full of spies and convicts. If you do turn her out, though, we'll hold our tongues about the business, for after all it might happen in the best society, until they take to branding convicts on the forehead, and prevent them dressing themselves up as decent citizens of Paris, and carrying on like the set of silly jokers they all are.'

When Madame Vauquer heard this she immediately recovered, as if by a miracle. She sat up, folded her arms, and opened a pair of sharp eyes that showed no trace of tears.

'My dear sir, do you want to ruin my boarding-house completely? There's Monsieur Vautrin – Oh! goodness me,' she interrupted herself, 'I can't help calling him by the name he went under as an honest man! That's one room empty,' she went on, 'and you want to give me two more to let, at this time of year when everyone is suited!'

'Gentlemen, we'll take our hats, and go and have our dinner at Flicoteaux's in the Place Sorbonne,' said Bianchon.

With a single flicker of her eyelids Madame Vauquer calculated which course would be most advantageous to her interests, and waddled over to Mademoiselle Michonneau.

'Come, now, my dear kind soul, you don't want to bring my establishment to rack and ruin altogether, do you? You see the proper fix these gentlemen have put me in; just go up to your own room for this evening.'

'No! no!' shouted the boarders. 'She must go at once, this very minute!'

'But she hasn't had any dinner, poor lady,' said Poiret piteously.

'She can go and get it wherever she likes!' cried several voices. 'Chuck her out, the spy!'

'Chuck both the spies out!'

'Gentlemen,' cried Poiret, suddenly swollen with the courage love lends even to male sheep, 'respect the weaker sex!'

'Spies don't have any sex,' said the painter.

'A fine sexorama!'

'Out into the streetorama!'

'Gentlemen, this behaviour is not proper. When you turn people out of the house you ought to do it politely, and show good manners. We have paid our money, and we're staying here,' said Poiret, putting on his cap and settling himself in a chair beside Mademoiselle Michonneau, who was being harangued by Madame Vauquer.

'Naughty boy!' said the painter drolly. 'Run along now, naughty little boy!'

'Well, if you aren't going, we are,' said Bianchon, and the boarders moved in a body towards the drawing-room door.

'Mademoiselle, what do you expect me to do now?' screamed Madame Vauquer. 'I'm a ruined woman. You can't stay here. They are running wild and there'll be violence done before they stop.'

Mademoiselle Michonneau rose to her feet.

Shouts of 'She's going!' 'She's not going!' 'She is!' 'She isn't!' broke out on all sides, and were repeated in a clamour of assertion and contradiction, together with various suggestions, made with a growing hostility, as to how she should be treated; and Mademoiselle Michonneau found herself obliged to take her departure, though not before she had made some stipulations in a low voice to her hostess.

'I'm going to Madame Buneaud's,' she said, with a threatening look.

'Go where you like, Mademoiselle,' retorted Madame Vauquer, who regarded it as a murderous stab in the back that she should choose an establishment that was a rival of Madame Vauquer's, and which she naturally detested. 'By all means go to the Buneaud's; you'll get wine fit to make a goat dance there, and food bought from hawkers at the back door.'

The boarders stood in two rows to let her pass between them, in complete silence. Poiret looked so wistfully after Mademoiselle Michonneau, he showed himself so artlessly undecided whether to follow her or stay, that the boarders, full of relief at getting rid of Mademoiselle Michonneau, began to look at one another and laugh.

'Tchick, tchick, tchick, Poiret,' the painter urged him on. 'Go on, gee-hup, gee-hup!'

The official from the Muséum started to sing with a comical air the beginning of the well-known ballad:

> 'Leaving for Syria,
>   The handsome young Dunois –'

'Go on, Poiret, you're dying to go, *trahit sua quemque voluptas*,' said Bianchon.

'Everyone follows his own fancy – free translation of Virgil,' said the tutor.

Mademoiselle Michonneau glanced at Poiret, and made a movement as if to take his arm; he could not resist such an appeal and stepped forward to give the old maid his support, and there was a burst of applause, followed by an explosion of laughter.

'Bravo, Poiret!'

'Good old Poiret!'

'Poiret Apollo!'

'Poiret Mars!'

'Poiret the brave!'

Just then a messenger came in with a letter for Madame Vauquer, and when she had read it she sank back on her chair.

'The house will be burnt down next, that's all that's left to happen. It's just one thunderbolt after another. Young Taillefer died at three o'clock. That's what I get for wishing well to those ladies at that poor young man's expense! Madame Couture and Victorine want me to send them their things, they are going to live with her father. Victorine's father is allowing her to keep the widow Couture with her as a lady companion. Four rooms to let! Five lodgers gone!'

She sat up, and seemed on the point of bursting into tears.

'A curse has come upon my house!' she cried.

They suddenly heard the rumbling of a carriage drawing up outside.

'Here's another windfall for somebody,' said Sylvie.

But it was Goriot's flushed face that suddenly appeared at the door. He was beaming with happiness, and looked as if he had taken a new lease of life.

'Goriot in a cab!' said the lodgers. 'It's the end of the world!'

The old fellow went straight to Eugène, who was standing pensively in a corner, and took him by the arm.

'Come on,' he said exultantly.

'You haven't heard the news, then?' said Eugène. 'Vautrin was a convict and he has just been arrested, and young Taillefer is dead.'

'Well, what matter? That's nothing to do with us,' replied old Goriot. 'I am going to dine with my daughter, at your house, do you understand? She is waiting for you. Come on!'

He tugged so vehemently at Rastignac's arm that he had no choice but to go with him, and Goriot hurried him away like a lover carrying off his sweetheart.

'Let's have dinner,' cried the painter, and everyone then took his chair and sat down at the table.

'Well, I do declare,' said fat Sylvie, 'everything's gone wrong for us to-day, here's my haricot mutton has gone and stuck to the saucepan. Bah! it can't be helped, you'll have to eat it burnt.'

Madame Vauquer was too dispirited to say a word as she saw ten persons, where there should have been eighteen gathered round her table, but everyone tried to console her and cheer her up. Although the guests talked at first about Vautrin and the events of the day, the conversation soon drifted by devious paths to discussion of such topics as duels, jails, justice, prison-life and laws which ought to be altered; and before long Jacques Collin, Victorine, and her brother, were very far from their thoughts. Although there were only ten of them they made noise enough for twenty; indeed there seemed to be more of them than usual, and that was the only thing that made that dinner different from dinner the day before. To-morrow this selfish crew would find another prey to devour, another tit-bit to chew over, in the day's events in Paris, and now their usual careless indifference to the fate of others resumed its accustomed sway. Madame Vauquer, too, let herself be soothed by the voice of Hope, speaking in the accents of fat Sylvie.

Throughout that long day persons and scenes had passed before Eugène's dazed eyes like a phantasmagoria, and the day was not ended yet. In spite of his strong will and clear head he did not know how to disentangle his ideas from the confusion that had overtaken them when he found himself sitting in the cab beside old Goriot, listening to his conversation, which expressed an extraordinary elation, but which sounded to Eugène, stupefied by so much emotion, like words heard in a dream.

'It was finished this morning. The three of us are dining together, together! do you understand? It's four years since I last dined with Delphine, my own little Delphine. I'm going to have her for a whole evening. We've been at your rooms since morning. I've been working with my coat off like a porter. I helped carry in the furniture. Oh! you don't know how sweet she is at table, she'll pet me and look after me. "Here, Papa, have some of this, it's nice," she'll say, and after that I can't eat anything. Ah! it's a long, long time since I've had such a peaceful happy time with her as we shall have now.'

'Is the whole world standing on its head to-day?' said Eugène.

'On its head?' said Goriot. 'The world has never been so sane and normal and cheerful before. I see only smiling faces in the streets, people shaking hands and embracing each other, looking as happy as if they were all going to dine with their daughters and tuck in at a nice little dinner I heard her order with my own ears from the chef at the Café des Anglais. But, there! gall and wormwood would be as sweet as honey in her company.'

'I feel as if I were coming back to life,' said Eugène.

'Hurry up, driver!' called old Goriot, opening the window in front. 'Go a bit faster. I'll give you five francs extra if you get me you know where in ten minutes.'

When he heard this promise the driver whipped up his horse and drove through Paris like lightning.

'This fellow's crawling,' said old Goriot.

'But where in the world are you taking me?' Eugène asked him.

'To your own house,' said Goriot.

The cab stopped in the Rue d'Artois. The old fellow got out first, and threw ten francs to the driver with the reckless generosity of a man who has no wife to curb his extravagance, and who is far too happy to worry about trifles.

'Come along, upstairs,' he said to Rastignac, leading him across a courtyard and up to the third floor at the back of a house which was newly built, and of good appearance. The door was opened before Goriot could ring, by Thérèse, Madame de Nucingen's maid, and Eugene found himself in a delightful set of bachelor's rooms, with an ante-room, a little sitting-room, a bed-room and a study, looking on a garden. In the little drawing-room, whose furniture and decoration could sustain comparison with the prettiest and most charming rooms in Paris, he saw Delphine in the candle-light. She rose from a low chair by the fireside, put her screen down on the mantelpiece, and said to him in a voice full of tenderness,

'So we had to go and fetch you, sir! Now do you understand?'

Thérèse left the room. The student took Delphine in his arms, hugged her tightly, and shed tears of joy. So much strain and excitement had taxed his heart and brain in that day full of trouble, that now the contrast between what lay before his eyes and the scenes he had come through proved the last straw, and his over-wrought nerves gave way.

'I knew very well myself that he loved you,' said old Goriot in a low voice to his daughter, while Eugène, completely over-come, lay back on the sofa, unable to utter a word or make sense yet of the way in which the magic wand had been waved again for this final transformation scene.

'But come and see,' said Madame de Nucingen, taking his hand and leading him into a room whose carpet, furniture and even the most trifling ornaments, were like those of her own room, on a smaller scale.

'There's no bed,' said Rastignac.

'No, sir,' she said, blushing and holding his hand more tightly.

Eugène looked at her, and, young as he still was, understood what true modesty lives in the heart of a woman in love.

'You are one of those beings a man must adore for ever,' he said in her ear. 'Yes, I can dare to tell you so since we understand each other so completely: the more intense and sincere love is, the more veiled and mysterious it should be. We must not share our secret with anyone.'

'Oh! what about me? I'm not anyone, I suppose,' grumbled old Goriot.

'You know quite well that "we" means you.'

'Ah, that's what I wanted to hear you say. You won't give any heed to me, will you? I shall go and come like a good fairy who is felt to be everywhere but remains unseen. Well, Delphinette, Ninette, Dedel! wasn't I right when I said to you, "There are some fine rooms in the Rue d'Artois, let's furnish them for him!" You didn't want to. Ah! it was I who gave you your happiness as I gave you your life. To be happy, fathers must always be giving; it is ceaselessly giving that makes you really a father.'

'Was that how it came about?' said Eugène.

'Yes, she wouldn't hear of it; she was afraid that people would say stupid things about her, as if what people say mattered as much as her happiness! But all women dream of doing what she has done – '

Old Goriot was talking to himself, for Madame de Nucingen had led Rastignac into the study, and he heard the sound of a kiss, gently though it was taken.

The study was in keeping with the elegance of the whole suite, in which, indeed, no fault could be found.

'Did we guess well what you wanted?' she asked, as they came back to the sitting-room for dinner.

'Yes,' he said, 'only too well, alas! These rooms are the realization of some fine castles in Spain, they are so well-appointed and luxurious, they are all that a young man's fancy could paint as a setting for a life of elegance, I appreciate them too much not to feel that they ought to be mine; but I cannot accept them from you, and I am still too poor to – '

'Oh, so you are resisting me already?' she said with a teasing little air of authority, screwing up her face in a charming pout as women do when they want to laugh some scruple out of existence: but Eugène could not yield to this coaxing and deny his sense of what was right. His heart-searchings of that morning were still fresh in his mind, and Vautrin's arrest, by revealing the depth of the pit he had narrowly escaped, had shown him only too clearly that the path pointed out to him by delicacy and his better impulses was the right one. A profound sadness took possession of him.

'What!' said Madame de Nucingen, 'would you really refuse? Do you know what such a refusal means? That you are doubtful of the future, that you do not dare bind yourself to me! Are you afraid of betraying my affection then? If you love me, if I – love you, why do you shrink from accepting such a trifling obligation? If you only knew how much I have enjoyed seeing to all the arrangements for this bachelor establishment you would not hesitate any longer, and you would beg my pardon for hesitating so long. I had money of yours and I have spent it well, that's all. You think you are being noble, and it is very petty of you. You are asking for much more – ' (she drew a deep breath as she caught a passionate look from Eugène) 'and you make a fuss about silly trifles. If you don't love me at all, oh! then you are right to refuse. My fate hangs on one word from you, what have you to say? – Father, make him see reason,' she added after a pause, turning to Goriot. 'Does he really believe that I am less sensitive than he about our honour?'

Old Goriot was looking on and listening to this pretty lovers' quarrel with the fixed smile of a man in a trance.

'You are a child!' she began again, seizing Eugène's hand. 'You are on the threshold of life; you find a barrier before you that many people find insurmountable; a woman's hand opens the way for you, and you draw back! But you are bound to succeed, you will carve a brilliant career for yourself, success is written on that noble forehead of yours; and can't you repay me then anything I lend you now? Long ago didn't ladies give armour to their knights, swords, helmets, coats of mail, horses, so that a knight could go to fight in the tournaments in his lady's name? Well, Eugène, the things I offer you are the weapons of the times, tools needed by a man who wants to make himself someone of consequence. That attic you live in must be a pretty place if it's like Papa's room! Come, are we never to sit down to dinner to-day? Do you want to make me miserable? Do answer!' she said, catching hold of his hand and shaking it. 'My Heavens, Papa, make him make up his mind, or I will go away and never see him again.'

'I am going to settle the matter for you,' said old Goriot, coming out of his rapturous trance. 'My dear Monsieur Eugène, you are going to borrow money from the Jews, aren't you?'

'There's nothing else for it,' said Eugène.

'Good! you're my customer then,' said the good old man, drawing out a cheap pocket-book of shabby well-worn leather. 'I've turned Jew myself, I've paid all the bills, here they are. You don't owe a farthing for anything here. It doesn't amount to very much – five thousand francs at most, and I'll lend it to you. You won't refuse me, I'm not a woman. You can write me a receipt on a scrap of paper, and pay it back later.'

Eugène and Delphine looked at each other in surprise, and tears suddenly filled their eyes. Rastignac held out his hand to Goriot, and grasped his hand warmly.

'Well, what's all this about? Are you not my children?' said Goriot.

'But, my poor Father,' said Madame de Nucingen, 'how did you manage to do it?'

'Ah! that's soon told,' he replied. 'When I had persuaded you that you should move him nearer you, and I saw you buying things as if you were furnishing rooms for a bride, I said to myself, "She's going to find herself in difficulties!" The lawyer says that the proceedings against your husband to make him disgorge your fortune will take at least six months. Well and good. I have sold the investments that brought me in thirteen hundred and fifty livres a year, and bought myself a well-secured annuity of twelve hundred francs a year for fifteen thousand francs, and I paid your tradesmen with the rest of the capital, children. As for me, I have a room up above there at one hundred and fifty francs a year, I can live like a prince on two francs a day, and still have something left over. I never wear anything out so I don't need much money to buy new clothes. For the last fortnight I've been laughing up my sleeve and saying to myself, "How happy they're going to be!" and, well now, aren't you happy?'

'Oh! Papa, Papa!' cried Madame de Nucingen, throwing herself into the arms of her father, who took her on his knee. She covered him with kisses, her fair hair caressed his cheeks, her tears fell on his beaming radiant old face.

'Dear Father, you are a father indeed! There's not another like you in the whole world. Eugène loved you dearly already, what must he feel for you now?'

'Oh, children!' cried old Goriot, who for ten years had not felt his daughter's heart beating against his. 'Oh, Delphinette! do you want to make me die of joy? My poor heart will break. Come, Monsieur Eugène, your debt is paid already!' And the old man strained his daughter to him with such wild and passionate force that she cried out,

'Ah! you're hurting me.'

'I'm hurting you!' he repeated, turning pale. He looked at her with an expression of grief of more than human poignancy on his face. The faces the princes of the palette have depicted in their masterpieces, recording their vision of the agony suffered by the Saviour of men for the sake of mankind, alone show a grief that could compare with the grief that transfigured the face of this Christ-like father. He very gently kissed the waist that his fingers had grasped too roughly.

'No, no, I didn't hurt you, did I? 'he said, smiling questioningly. 'It was I who was hurt by that cry of yours. The things cost rather more than that,' he whispered in her ear, kissing her cautiously, 'but I had to throw a little dust in his eyes or he would have been vexed.'

Eugène was dumbfounded by the man's inexhaustible devotion, and gazed at him with that ingenuous admiration that the young feel with almost religious fervour.

'I will be worthy of it all!' he exclaimed.

'O my Eugène, that is nobly said.' And Madame de Nucingen kissed the student's forehead.

'He turned down Mademoiselle Taillefer and her millions for you,' said old Goriot. 'Yes, the little one was in love with you; and there she is now, with her brother dead, as rich as Croesus.'

'Oh! why say anything about it?' exclaimed Rastignac.

'Eugène,' said Delphine in his ear, 'now I have one regret this evening. Ah! I will love you with all my heart, and for ever.'

'This is the happiest day I have known since you and your sister were married!' exclaimed Goriot. 'Now God may send me as much suffering as He thinks good, provided it is not through you I suffer, and I shall only say, "In February this year, in one short month, I had more happiness than other men can achieve in their whole lifetime." Look at me, Fifine!' he said to his daughter. 'She is very lovely, isn't she? Tell me, have you come across many women with her pretty colour and that little dimple of hers? Not many, now, have you? And to think that it was I who made this darling woman! And now her happiness in you will make her a thousand times lovelier. Now I could go to Hell gladly, my neighbour; if you need my share of Heaven I give it to you willingly. Come, let's eat, let's eat,' he added, scarcely knowing what he was saying, 'everything is ours.'

'Poor, dear Father!'

'If you only knew, child,' he said, rising and going to her, taking her head in his hands, and setting a kiss among the plaits of hair, 'if you only knew how easily you can make me happy! Come and see me sometimes; I shall be up there, above you; you won't have more than a step to go. Promise me that you will!'

'Yes, Father dear.'

'Say it again.'

'Yes, dear, kind Father.'

'That's enough. I should make you say it a hundred times over if I listened to my own heart. Let's have dinner.'

They all behaved like children that evening, and old Goriot was not the least giddy of the three. He lay at his daughter's feet and kissed them, he gazed long into her eyes, he rubbed his head against her dress; in short, no young lover could have been more foolish or more tender.

'You see!' said Delphine to Eugène. 'When my father is with us I must give him all my attention. It will be very tiresome sometimes.'

Eugène, who had already felt several twinges of jealousy, was not disposed to quarrel with this sentiment, although the remark contained the seed of all ingratitude.

'And when will the rooms be finished?' he asked, looking round him. 'We shall all have to leave them this evening, I suppose?'

'Yes; but to-morrow you will come to dinner with me,' she said slyly. 'To-morrow is the day we go to the Italiens.'

'I shall go to the pit,' said Goriot.

It was midnight. Madame de Nucingen's carriage was waiting for her. Old Goriot and the student walked back to the Maison Vauquer together, talking of Delphine as they went with an enthusiasm that grew more and more heated, and led to a curious rivalry between the two violent passions, as each man strove to outdo the other in expressions of love and admiration. Eugène could not help seeing that the father's love, which was completely unselfish, surpassed his own in its unchanging constancy and all-embracing generosity. To the father his idol was always pure and lovely, and his adoration drew its strength from the whole past, as well as from his anticipation of the future.

They found Madame Vauquer sitting by her stove, alone but for Sylvie and Christophe. The old landlady sat there like Marius among the ruins of Carthage, waiting for the two lodgers that still remained to her, and bemoaning her troubles to Sylvie. Although the lamentations Lord Byron has put into Tasso's mouth are eloquent enough, they fall far short of the heartfelt sincerity of Madame Vauquer's jeremiad.

'Only three cups of coffee to make to-morrow morning, Sylvie. Oh, dear, dear, to think of my house being deserted like this, isn't it heart-breaking? What is life without my boarders? Nothing! Nothing at all! It's like taking the furniture out of a house; what is a house without its furniture, and what is a boarding-house without its men? What wrong have I done against Heaven to draw all these disasters down on me? And beans and potatoes laid in for twenty persons! Police in my house! We'll have to live on potatoes now, and I shall send Christophe away!'

The Savoyard, who was fast asleep, woke up suddenly and said, 'Madame?'

'Poor lad! he's just like a great big dog,' said Sylvie.

'And in the slack season too! Everyone is suited. Are boarders likely to drop from the sky? It will drive me out of my mind. And that old witch of a Michonneau carrying Poiret off with her! What did she do to that man to make him stick to her and follow her about like a pet poodle?'

'Ah! bless us, yes,' said Sylvie, shaking her head. 'These old maids! They're up to all the dodges.'

'That poor Monsieur Vautrin they made a convict out of!' the widow went on. 'It's no use, Sylvie, it's too much for me, I just can't swallow it. A lively man like that, who took brandy in his coffee at fifteen francs a month, and paid his money down on the nail!'

'And wasn't he free with his money, just!' Christophe chimed in.

'There must be some mistake,' said Sylvie.

'No, no, it's quite true, he said so himself,' replied Madame Vauquer. 'To think that all these things should happen in my house, in a district where there's never a cat stirring! Upon my word as an honest woman I must be dreaming! For it's true we've seen Louis XVI have his accident, we've seen the Emperor fall, we've seen him come back and fall again; but that's all in the natural order of things, those are things that can easily happen, you see, whereas middle-class boarding-houses are firmly settled, unchanging things, they don't have upsets like that: you can do without a king but you can't do without your dinner; and when a respectable woman, a de Conflans by birth, provides a good meal with everything any one could ask for, well then, nothing short of the end of the world – but there, that's just what it is, it is the end of the world!'

'And just fancy, Mademoiselle Michonneau who did you all these ill turns is to have three thousand francs a year for it, so they say!' cried Sylvie.

'Don't mention her name to me, she's a wicked woman,' said Madame Vauquer, 'and to add insult to injury she's going to that Buneaud! But she's capable of anything, she must have committed all sorts of dreadful atrocities, she has killed and stolen in her day, I'll be bound. She ought to have gone to jail instead of that poor dear man – '

At this point Eugène and old Goriot rang the bell.

'Ah! here come my two faithful ones,' said the widow with a sigh.

But the two faithful ones, who had only the haziest recollection of the boarding-house disasters, announced offhandedly to their landlady that they were going to live in the Chaussée d'Antin.

'Ah! Sylvie, that finishes me,' said the widow. 'You have been the death of me, gentlemen. That struck me in the *stomachial* regions, I have a stroke there. This day has put ten years upon my head. It'll drive me crazy, upon my soul, it will! And what's to be done with the beans? – Ah, well, if I'm to be left alone here you may pack your bag to-morrow, Christophe. Good night, gentlemen.'

'What on earth is the matter with her?' Eugène asked Sylvie.

'Well, bless me! here's all the boarders gone for one reason or another. That's given her a bit of a turn and made her cranky. There, I hear her crying. It won't do her any harm to snivel a bit. That's the first time she's had a good cry since I've been with her.'

By the morning Madame Vauquer had 'talked herself round to putting a bold face on it', to use her own expression. She still appeared as afflicted as a woman must be who has lost all her lodgers, and whose life has been turned upside down; but she had all her wits about her, and it was plain what her real trouble was – the deep grief caused by an attack on her purse and a break in her routine. Certainly no farewell look a departing lover casts at the house that enshrines his mistress could have been more disconsolate than Madame Vauquer's glance at the empty places round her table. Eugène tried to cheer her by telling her that Bianchon, whose term of residence in hospital was due to end in a few days, would probably take his room in the Maison Vauquer, that the Muséum official had often expressed a wish to have Madame Couture's rooms, and that in a very few days she would have her establishment full again.

'Please Heaven you're right, my dear Monsieur Eugène! but ill-luck is among us. There will be a death in the house before ten days are out, you mark my words,' and she threw a lugubrious look round the dining-room. 'Who will be taken, I wonder?'

'I'm glad we're moving out of here,' said Eugène quietly to old Goriot.

'Madame,' said Sylvie, running in with consternation on her

face, 'there hasn't been sight nor sign of Mistigris for three days past.'

'Ah well, if my cat is dead, if he has left us, I – '

The poor widow could not finish, she wrung her hands and buried her face against the back of her chair, quite overcome by this terrible foreboding.

About noon, the time when postmen reach the Panthéon district, Eugène received a letter in a dainty envelope, sealed with the Beauséant arms. It contained an invitation, addressed to Monsieur and Madame de Nucingen, to the Viscountess's great ball, which all Paris had been looking forward to for a month. A little note for Eugène was enclosed with the card. It ran:

I thought, sir, that you would be pleased to undertake the task of conveying my sentiments to Madame de Nucingen, and so I send you the invitation you asked me for. I shall be delighted to make the acquaintance of Madame de Restaud's sister. Bring your charming friend to see me, but see to it that she does not capture the whole of your affection – a great deal of it is due to me in return for the affection I feel for you.

VICOMTESSE DE BEAUSÉANT

'Well,' said Eugène to himself, as he read the note again, 'Madame de Beauséant makes it pretty clear that she does not want the Baron de Nucingen.'

He went to call on Delphine at once, delighted at having procured a pleasure for her for which he would no doubt receive his reward. Madame de Nucingen was in her bath. Rastignac waited in her boudoir with the impatience natural to an ardent young man, in a hurry to take possession of a prize he has longed for in vain for a whole year. Young men do not feel such emotions as his twice in a lifetime. The first woman to whom a man is drawn, if she is really a woman, if she presents herself to him in the splendour of the setting required of a member of Parisian society, can never have a rival. Love in Paris has no resemblance to love elsewhere. In Paris neither men nor women are taken in by the gay, showy wrapping of conventional disinterested devotion, with which people cover their more or less selfish motives for the sake of decorum. In that world it is not enough for a woman merely to satisfy the senses and the heart; she knows perfectly well that she has greater obligations to fulfil, to satisfy the demands of the vanity that enters in a thousand and one ways into every aspect of life. Above all, love is there essentially a boastful, insolent, spendthrift, ostentatious charlatan. When there was not a woman at the Court of Louis XIV who did not envy Mademoiselle de la Vallière the reckless impetuosity of passion which drove the great monarch to forget that the ruffles at his wrists had cost six thousand francs, and tear them, for the sake of helping the Duc de Vermandois enter this world, what then can one expect of the rest of humanity? You must be young, rich and titled, or better off still if you can; the more incense you bring to burn at the altar of your idol, the more favour will be shown you. Love is a religion, and its cult must needs cost more than those of all other gods. Love passes swiftly and is gone, but the path he has taken is marked, like a wanton urchin's, by a trail of devastation. Extravagant display in love is the poetry of those who live in city garrets; without such riches what would become of love there?

If there are exceptions to these laws of the Parisian code, rigorous as the laws of Draco the Athenian, they are found in solitary places, in choice spirits who have not allowed themselves to be led astray by the doctrines of society, who live remote, beside some clear spring of living waters, fleeting yet perennial. Content in their green shades, happy to listen to the voice of the Infinite, which echoes for them in everything around them, and is heard in their own hearts, they patiently await their flight to Heaven, and pity those of earth.

But Rastignac, like most young men who have tasted grandeur early, meant to present himself in full armour in the lists of the world. He had been caught up into the feverish struggle, and perhaps he felt within himself the strength to conquer; but he did not know what means he should use or what his ultimate goal was. If a man has no pure and sacred love to fill his life, this thirst for power may take its place and become an entirely noble thing; it can strip a man of all selfish desires, and make him seek not his own greatness but the greatness of a whole nation. But the student had not yet reached that stage in his development when he could stand aside from the current of life, and consider it with detachment. So far he had not even entirely shaken off the charm of the influences that surround the youth of a child brought up in the country, as if with the sweet-smelling freshness of green leaves. He had hesitated on the brink of the Parisian Rubicon. In spite of his impelling urge to plunge headlong into life he had cast some lingering glances over his shoulder at the serene happiness of the existence of the true nobleman in his château. His last doubts had vanished, however, the evening before, at the sight of his new rooms. When he enjoyed the material advantages of wealth, as he had long enjoyed the distinction conferred by birth, he cast his provincial slough and slipped easily and effortlessly into a position which opened a fair prospect before him.

And so, waiting for Delphine, lounging in the pretty boudoir where he felt he had some right to be, he saw himself as so remote from the Rastignac who had come to Paris a year before, that, scrutinizing that Rastignac through a kind of mental telescope, he wondered if he was indeed the same person as that young man.

Thérèse's voice broke in upon his reflections and made him start.

'Madame is in her room,' she said.

He found Delphine leaning back in her low chair by the fire, looking tranquil and fresh. The picture she presented, reclining amid billows of muslin, irresistibly suggested one of those beautiful Indian trees on which the fruit appears before the flowers have shed their petals.

'Well, here you are,' she said, in a voice that shook.

'Guess what I've brought you,' said Eugène, sitting down beside her and taking possession of her arm to raise her fingers to his lips.

Madame de Nucingen made a gesture of delight as she read the

242

invitation. She looked at Eugène with her eyes glistening with tears; then threw her arms round his neck and drew him to her in a transport of gratified vanity.

'And it's you – (darling!' she said in his ear, 'but Thérèse is in my dressing-room, and we must be circumspect) – you I owe this happiness to! Yes, I may call it happiness, for when you get it for me it is surely something more than a triumph for my vanity? No one was willing to introduce me into that social set. Now you will think me as petty, frivolous and giddy as any woman in Paris; but remember, my dear, that I am ready to give up everything for you, and if I long to be admitted to the Faubourg Saint-Germain more ardently than ever before, it's because I shall meet you there.'

'Don't you think,' said Eugène, 'that Madame de Beauséant tells us very plainly that she is not expecting to see the Baron de Nucingen at her ball?'

'Yes, indeed,' said the Baroness, returning the letter to Eugène. 'Those women have a talent for insolence. But no matter, I shall go. My sister is bound to be there, I know she is getting a beautiful dress made. Eugène,' she went on, lowering her voice, 'she's going to the ball to avoid giving people grounds for talking about her: they suspect her of appalling things. You don't know the rumours that are flying! Nucingen came to tell me only this morning that they were talking about her yesterday at the club and they didn't mince matters. On what, ye gods! does a woman's reputation and a family's honour rest? I felt myself struck at and wounded through my poor sister. According to what some people say Monsieur de Trailles has put his name to bills amounting to a hundred thousand francs. They are nearly all over-due and he is going to be sued for the money. To meet this desperate situation my sister is said to have sold her diamonds to a Jew, those beautiful diamonds that you may have seen her wearing, that belonged to Monsieur de Restaud's mother. For the last two days it has been on everyone's tongue, nothing else has been talked about but that. I fancy, then, that Anastasie is having a gold lamé dress made for herself because she wants to draw all eyes at Madame de Beau-séant's ball, when she appears in all her glory, wearing her diamonds. But I don't want to be cast into the shade by her. She has always tried to outshine me, she has never shown any kind-ness to me, and I did so much for her, and always had money for her when she had none. But let's forget about other people; to-day I mean to be completely happy.'

Rastignac was still with Madame de Nucingen at one o'clock in the morning. As they said goodbye with lovers' extravagance, a lovers' sweet goodbye full of promises of joys to come, she said, looking at him sadly, 'I'm so uneasy, so superstitious, call my presentiments what you like, I'm quaking for fear I shall have to pay for my happiness through some dreadful catastrophe.'

'Silly child!' said Eugène.

'Oh! so I'm the child this evening!' she said laughing.

Eugène returned to the Maison Vauquer completely certain that he would be leaving it next day, and he gave himself up along the way to those enchanting dreams all young men indulge in, when the taste of happiness still lingers on their lips.

'Well?' old Goriot called out, as Eugène passed his door.

'Well,' replied Eugène, 'I'll tell you everything to-morrow.'

'Everything, from beginning to end, isn't that so?' cried the good old man. 'Go to bed. Our happy life begins to-morrow.'

Next day Goriot and Rastignac were ready to leave the boarding-house, and were only waiting for the good offices of a porter. About midday, however, the wheels of an approaching carriage woke the echoes of the Rue Neuve-Sainte-Geneviève, and the vehicle stopped at the Maison Vauquer door. Madame de Nucingen alighted, and asked if her father was still in the boarding-house, and when Sylvie said that he was she went hastily upstairs.

Eugène was in his own room, although it so happened that his neighbour was not aware of it. At breakfast he had asked old Goriot to see to the removal of his luggage, saying that they would meet at four o'clock in the Rue d'Artois. But while the good-natured old man was out fetching porters, Eugène, who had speedily paid his duty visit to the École de Droit to answer to his name at roll-call, returned, unnoticed by anyone, to settle Madame Vauquer's bill. He did not wish to leave this task to Goriot, for the old man in his fanatical affection would probably have insisted on paying for him. The landlady, however, had gone out. Eugène went up to his room again to make sure that he had not forgotten anything, and he congratulated himself on having done this when he found the blank bill signed by Vautrin in a drawer of his table, where he had carelessly thrown it the day he had repaid the money. He was about to tear it up, as he had no fire, when he heard Delphine's voice and, not wishing to make a noise, he stopped and listened, thinking that she could have no secrets from him. Then from the very first words he found the conversation between father and daughter so interesting that he could not interrupt it.

'Ah! Father,' she said, 'Heaven send I am not utterly ruined, that the thought of demanding an account of my money did not occur to you too late! Is it safe to talk?'

'Yes, there's no one in the house,' said old Goriot, in a faltering voice.

'What's the matter?' asked Madame de Nucingen.

'You have just struck me a staggering blow,' replied the old man. 'God forgive you, child! You do not know how much I love you, or you would not blurt out such news as that without any warning, especially if things are not desperate. What can have happened that is so urgent that you had to come to look for me here about it? In a few minutes we should all have been in the Rue d'Artois.'

'Oh! Father, can you control your first impulse in a catastrophe? I'm at my wit's end! Your lawyer has brought to light a little earlier a state of things that will no doubt become public property later on. We're going to need your long business experience, and I rushed to get hold of you as instinctively as a drowning man clutches a branch. When Monsieur Derville saw that Nucingen was throwing endless difficulties in his way, he threatened him with a lawsuit, and told him that it would not be hard to obtain a warrant from the President of the Tribunal. Nucingen came to me this morning to ask if I was anxious to ruin him and myself too. I replied that I knew nothing whatever about that; I had a fortune, I ought to be in possession of my fortune; that the whole business was in my lawyer's hands, I knew absolutely nothing about it and it was impossible for me to discuss it with him. Isn't that what you told me to tell him?'

'Yes. You were quite right.'

'Well, then,' Delphine went on, 'he told me how his affairs stood. He has thrown all his capital and mine into ventures which are barely begun and require large sums for their development. If I force him to hand over my dowry he will be obliged to go bankrupt; while if I will only wait a year he pledges his honour to give me a fortune twice or three times as great, by an investment in building-land which in the end will make me mistress of the whole property. My dear Father, he was sincere, he frightened me. He begged my pardon for his conduct, he gave me my liberty, set me free to act as I liked in my personal affairs if I would leave him entirely free to manage the financial business in my name. To prove his good faith he said he would call in Monsieur Derville any time I pleased to make sure that the title-deeds to the land were properly drawn up in my name. In short he threw himself upon my mercy, bound hand and foot. He wants the household arrangements to go on as before for two more years, and he begged me not to spend more money for my personal expenses than he sets aside for me. He made it clear that it is as much as he can do to keep up appearances; he has sent his opera dancer away, and he will be obliged to practise the strictest economy as unobtrusively as possible, if he is to hold on till his investments bear fruit without damaging his credit. I rated him, I queried everything he told me, so as to drive him to distraction and find out more: he showed me his books, and in the end he wept. I never saw a man in such a state: he lost his head completely and raved; he talked of killing himself. I felt sorry for him.'

'And you really believe this gammon?' cried old Goriot. 'He's just playing upon you. I have come across Germans in business: they are nearly all honest, straightforward people; but when their show of frankness and good fellowship is bogus they are the worst sharks and humbugs of all. Your husband is throwing dust in your eyes. He feels himself hard pressed and he shams dead. He's trying to place himself more firmly in the saddle under your name than he is under his own. He's going to take advantage of this situation to screen himself against his business risks. He's as cunning as he is treacherous; he's a bad lot. No, no, I'm not going to lie down and go to the Père-Lachaise, and leave my girls stripped of every farthing! I still know a thing or two about business. He has, so he says, sunk his capital in various undertakings. Well, if that is so, his interests in them are represented by securities, receipts, agreements! Let him produce them, and come to some arrangement with you. We will choose the most promising speculations, and take our chance of their turning out badly; and we will have the certificates transferred to your name, Delphine Goriot, and kept quite separate from the estate of the Baron de Nucingen. Does the man take us for idiots? Does he imagine that I could stand the idea of leaving you without a penny, without a crust of bread, for two days? I will not stand it one day, nor one night, nor two hours! If this cock-and-bull story had any foundation of fact I should not survive it. What! work forty years of my life, carry sacks on my back, lard the earth with my sweat, and pinch and save my whole life long for you, my darlings, who made all work easy for me and every burden light, only to see my fortune, my life, go up in smoke! If that were so I should go raving mad, and die. By all that's holiest in Heaven and earth we're going to drag this business into the light of day: we'll go through the books, find out what capital is invested, and look into the companies! I will not sleep, I will not rest nor eat, until I have made sure that your fortune is there, and is complete. Thank God your money is settled on you! and you will have Maître Derville, an honest man fortunately, as your lawyer. By God's daylight! you shall keep your nice little million, your fifty thousand francs a year, till the end of your days, or I'll know the reason why, never fear! I would appeal to the Chambers if the Tribunals let us down. The knowledge that you had a mind at ease and happy as far as money goes used to lighten all my troubles, and soothe my unhappiness. Money is life itself, it's the mainspring of everything. What yarn is that great dolt of an Alsatian spinning us? Delphine, don't concede a quarter of a farthing to that great brute, who chained you up and made you miserable. If he needs you we shall have the whip-hand of him, and we will make him behave himself. God! my head's on fire, there's red-hot torture in my skull. My Delphine in the gutter! Oh! my Fifine, you? Ye stars in heaven! Where are my gloves? Come on, let's go. I'll go and see everything, books, cash, correspondence, everything, straight away. I shall have no peace of mind until I've seen it all with my own eyes, and satisfied myself that your fortune is secure.'

'Oh, Father, dear, do be careful, mind what you do. If you betray the slightest hint of a desire for vengeance, if you show yourself openly hostile, it will be all up with me. He knows you, he found it quite natural that, prompted by you, I should show some uneasiness about my money; but I swear to you, he holds it in his hands, and meant to hold on to it. He is just the man to make off with the whole capital and leave us stranded, the scoundrel! He knows very well that I will not dishonour the name that I bear by taking legal proceedings against him. He's in a strong position, and yet at the same time he needs me. I have looked into everything thoroughly. If we drive him to extremities I am lost.'

'Is the man nothing but a swindler, then?'

'Well, yes, Father,' she said, throwing herself into a chair and bursting into tears, 'that's what he is! I wanted to keep it from you. I wanted to spare you the mortification of knowing you had married me to a man of that sort. His private morals are just as bad as his business ones: his conscience, soul and body are all of a piece! It's dreadful, I hate and despise him. Yes, after all that vile man has told me I haven't a grain of respect for him left. A man capable of being involved in the shady dealings he has spoken of to me must be utterly unscrupulous, and it's because I read what's in his heart so plainly that I'm afraid. He, my own husband, bluntly proposed to me that I should be free – if you know what that means? – if I would be a tool in his hands, and let him use my name to protect himself, if things went wrong.'

'But there are such things as laws!' exclaimed old Goriot. 'There's a Place de Grève for that sort of son-in-law! I would guillotine him myself if there were no public executioner to do it for me!'

'No, no, Father, the law can't touch him. Listen to this, it's what he says in plain terms, stripped of his fancy phrases: "Unless you let me carry my undertakings through, everything is lost, you will be completely ruined, you won't have a farthing; for I can have no other accomplice in this business but you." Do you see? He still depends on me. He is confident that he can trust his wife; he knows that I will leave him his money, and be content to have my own. I am forced to enter into a compact with him, a wicked, dishonest, crooked compact, if I don't want to be ruined. He buys my conscience, and pays for it by setting me free to be anything I choose to Eugène. "I'll turn a blind eye to your misdeeds, provided you don't interfere with my crimes, and let me get on with the job of swindling poor people out of their money." Is that explicit enough? Do you know what he calls doing a good stroke of business? He buys undeveloped land in his own name, then has houses built on it, acting through men of straw. These men draw up the contracts for the buildings with all the contractors, and pay them by long-dated bills. They hand over possession of the houses to my husband for a small sum, and slide out of their debt to the duped contractors by going bankrupt. It was plain to me that the name of the firm of Nucingen was used to dazzle the poor contractors. I noticed, too, that to prove the firm had paid enormous sums, in case proof should be needed,

Nucingen has sent bills for considerable amounts abroad, to Amsterdam, London, Naples and Vienna. How could we get hold of those bills?'

Eugène heard a dull thud on the floor next door, as if old Goriot had fallen on his knees.

'God! what have I done to you? My daughter at the mercy of that scoundrel! He will wring every penny from her as he pleases. Forgive me, child!' cried the old man.

'Yes, if I am in the depths of despair, it's perhaps partly your fault,' said Delphine. 'We have so little sense when we get married. What do we know of the world, or business, or men, or life? Fathers ought to think for us. Dear Father, I'm not blaming you at all, forgive me for saying that. This is all my own fault. No, don't cry, Papa,' she said, kissing her father's forehead.

'Don't you cry either, little Delphine. Show me your eyes, and let me kiss the tears away. There! I'm going to put my thinking cap on and I'll find the loose end in this ravelled skein your husband has tangled for us.'

'No, let me do it; I'll know how to manage him. He has some affection for me. Well and good. I'll use my influence over him to induce him to invest some of my money in landed property for me. Perhaps I could persuade him to buy back Nucingen in Alsace in my name, he is fond of the place. All the same you should come to-morrow and go through his books and look into the transactions. Monsieur Derville knows nothing about business. No, not to-morrow. I don't want to be upset. Madame de Beauséant's ball is the day after, and I must take care of myself if I'm to look serene and at my best, and do honour to my dear Eugène! Let's go now and see what his room is like.'

At that moment a carriage drew up in the Rue Neuve-Sainte-Geneviève, and Madame de Restaud's voice was heard outside. She was on her way upstairs, and was saying to Sylvie, 'Is my father in?'

This interruption came in the nick of time for Eugène, whose only plan had been to throw himself on his bed and pretend to be asleep.

'Oh, Father, have you heard about Anastasie?' said Delphine, when she recognized her sister's voice. 'It seems that very queer things are happening in her household too.'

'What next?' said Goriot. 'This will be the death of me. My poor head will not stand another calamity like this.'

'Good morning, Father,' said the Countess as she came in. 'Ah! you here, Delphine.'

Madame de Restaud seemed rather taken aback at finding her sister there.

'Good morning, Nasie,' said the Baroness. 'Do you really find it strange that I should be with my father? *I* see him every day.'

'Since when?'

'If you came here yourself you would know.'

'Don't tease, Delphine,' said the Countess in a woeful voice. 'I am very unhappy, I am ruined, my poor Father! Oh, completely done for this time!'

'What is it, Nasie?' cried Goriot. 'Tell us all about it, child. How pale she is! Come, Delphine, do something to help her, be kind and affectionate to her, and I will love you even more, if that's possible.'

'Poor Nasie,' said Madame de Nucingen, gently pushing her sister into a chair; 'tell us everything. We are the two persons in the world who will always love you well enough to forgive you anything. You know, family affection is the most loyal.'

She gave her smelling-salts to inhale, and the Countess soon felt better.

'This will kill me!' said Goriot. 'Come, now,' he went on, poking his peat fire, 'come nearer both of you. I'm cold. What is wrong, Nasie? Tell me quick, I'm dying of – '

'Well,' said the poor woman, 'my husband knows everything. Think of it, Father! Do you remember that bill of Maxime's some time ago? Well, it wasn't the first; I had paid several before.

251

About the beginning of January Monsieur de Trailles seemed to be very depressed. He said nothing to me, but it is so easy to read the hearts of those you love, a trifle is enough; then you feel things intuitively. And then he was more loving, more tender than I had ever known him; I felt happier in his affection every day. Poor Maxime! in his thoughts he was saying goodbye to me, so he has told me since; he had made up his mind to blow his brains out. In the end I worried him so much, begged so hard, I knelt by his knees for two hours one day – and he told me that he owed a hundred thousand francs! Oh, Papa, a hundred thousand francs! I was out of my mind. You hadn't got so much money. I had swallowed up everything you had – '

'No,' said Goriot, 'I could not have found so much money, short of going and stealing it. But I would have done that, Nasie. I will do it yet.'

When he said this mournfully, expressing all the agony of a father's powerlessness to help his children in a voice that sounded hoarsely like the death-rattle of a dying man, the two sisters fell silent and there was a pause. What selfish heart could have remained unmoved at this cry of despair echoing hollowly like a stone flung into an abyss, revealing depths of suffering?

'I raised the money by selling what was not mine to sell, Father,' said the Countess, bursting into tears.

Delphine was touched and wept too, resting her head on her sister's shoulder.

'It's all true then,' she said.

Anastasie hung her head. Madame de Nucingen put her arms round her waist and kissed her tenderly, and said, holding her against her heart,

'Here you will always be loved, and no one will ever judge you.'

'My darlings,' said Goriot feebly, 'why must it be disaster that brings you together?'

'To save Maxime's life, to save all my own happiness,' the Countess went on, cheered by these demonstrations of a warm and living affection, 'I went to that money-lender you know, Monsieur

Gobseck, a man created in Hell with a heart nothing could ever soften, and I took him the family diamonds Monsieur de Restaud thinks so much of, his and mine, I sold them all. Sold them! Do you understand? He was saved, but I am done for. Restaud found out everything.'

'How did he find out? Who told him? Tell me and I'll kill him!' cried Goriot.

'Yesterday he called me to his room, and when I went – "Anastasie," he said, in such a voice – (oh! his tone was enough, I guessed it all), "where are your diamonds?" "In my room." "No," he said, looking at me; "there they are on my chest of drawers." And he showed me the jewel-box which he had hidden under his handkerchief. "You know where they come from?" he said. I fell at his feet – I wept, I asked him what death he wished to see me die.'

'You asked him that!' shouted Goriot. 'By God's sacred name, whoever harms either of you, as long as I'm alive, may be sure that I will roast him over a slow fire! Yes, I will slash him into strips like – '

He stopped, the words died in his throat.

'And then, dear, he asked me to do something harder than dying. May heaven preserve all women from hearing what I heard him say.'

'I will murder that man,' said Goriot calmly. 'But he has only one life and he owes me two. Well, go on, what then?' he added, looking at Anastasie.

'Well,' continued the Countess, 'after a pause he looked at me: "Anastasie," he said, "I will bury this in silence; we will not separate, there are the children; I will not kill Monsieur de Trailles, I might miss him in a duel, and to get rid of him in a different way might bring me into collision with the law, if I killed him in your arms it would bring disgrace upon those children. But if you are not to see your children perish, nor their father, nor me, you must submit to two conditions. Answer me this: have I one child which is my own?" I said "Yes." "Which?"

"Ernest, our eldest." "Very well," he said. "Now swear to obey me from this time forward on one point." I swore. "You will sign an agreement for the sale of your property when I ask you to do so." '

'No! No! Do not sign,' cried old Goriot. 'Never sign that away. Ah! Monsieur de Restaud, you do not know how to set about making a wife happy, she looks for happiness where it is to be found, and then you punish her for your own stupid inadequacy, do you? – Ah! but I am here! Stop! Not so fast! He will have to tackle me first. Set your mind at rest, Nasie. Aha! he is fond of his heir, is he? Good! Good! I will get hold of his son. By heaven! isn't he my grandson? I can surely go and see the brat! I will tuck him away somewhere in the country; I'll take care of him, don't worry. That monster will capitulate when I say to him, "You must do a deal with me! If you want your son give my daughter back her property, and leave her free to do as she pleases." '

'Oh, Father!'

'Yes, your father, Nasie, a father first and foremost! That rascal of a great lord had better not ill-treat my daughters. Thunder and lightning! I don't know what fiery blood runs in my veins: I have tiger's blood in me, I could crunch the bones of those two men. Oh, children, is that what your life is? The thought of it is death to me. And what will become of you when I am gone? Fathers ought to live as long as their children. God, how badly Your world is arranged! And yet You have a Son, if what they tell us is true. You should save us from suffering through our children. My darlings, my darlings, to think that it should be sorrow that brings you to me. Your tears are all you let me know of you. Ah! well, yes, yes, you love me, I see that. Come and shed your tears here. My heart is big enough to hold all your troubles. Yes, even if my heart is broken each piece will make a father's heart again. If only I could take all your troubles on me and suffer for you! Ah! when you were little things, how happy you were! – '

'We were happy then as we have never been happy since,' said Delphine. 'Where are the days when we slid down the sacks in the great granary?'

'Father, that's not all,' Anastasie whispered to Goriot. The old man gave a violent start. 'The diamonds did not fetch a hundred thousand francs, and Maxime is hard pressed. We have only twelve thousand francs still to pay. He has promised me that he will be sensible and not gamble any more. His love is all I have left in the world, and I have paid too dearly for it to go on living if I lose him. I have sacrificed my fortune for him, my honour, peace of mind, children. Oh! do something to ensure that at least Maxime is not put in prison, not disgraced, that he can stay in the world where he is sure to make a position for himself. It's not only my happiness that is at stake now, we have children who would be left penniless. Everything will be lost if he is sent to Sainte-Pélagie.'

'I haven't got the money, Nasie. I've nothing left, nothing left, nothing, nothing, nothing. It is the end of the world. Oh! the world is tumbling into destruction, that's certain. Fly! Run away! Save yourselves while there is time! Ah! I have still my silver buckles, and half a dozen silver spoons and forks, the first I ever owned in my life. But I've nothing else except my life annuity, twelve hundred francs – '

'What have you done with your securities?'

'I sold them and kept just that trifle for my needs. I wanted twelve thousand francs to furnish some rooms for Fifine.'

'In your own house, Delphine?' said Madame de Restaud to her sister.

'Oh! what does that matter?' Goriot said. 'The twelve thousand francs are spent.'

'I can guess,' said the Countess. 'They're for Monsieur de Rastignac. Ah! Delphine, my poor girl, mind what you are about. Take warning by my plight.'

'Monsieur de Rastignac is incapable of ruining the woman he loves, my dear sister.'

'Thank you, Delphine! In my present dreadful troubles I expected better of you: but then you never did care for me.'

'Oh, yes, she cares for you, Nasie,' cried Goriot, 'she was telling me so not long ago. We were talking about you, and she maintained that you were beautiful while she was only pretty.'

'Pretty!' repeated the Countess. 'She's as pretty as a cold hard iceberg!'

'Even if I were what you think me,' said Delphine, reddening, 'how have you behaved towards me? You cast me off, you closed the door of every house I wanted to visit against me, you have never missed an opportunity of making me suffer. And when did I ever come as you did to screw our poor father's fortune out of him, a thousand francs at a time, and reduce him to the plight he's in now? That's your work, my dear sister. I have come to see my father as often as I could. I did not turn him out of the house and then come and lick his hand when I needed him. I did not even know that he had spent that twelve thousand francs for me. I am careful and economical and you know it! Moreover I never asked Papa for the presents he has sometimes given me, I'm not a beggar.'

'You were better off than I was: Monsieur de Marsay was rich, as you have some reason to know. You were always as sordid and mean as people who care for money are. Goodbye, I have neither sister nor – '

'Hush, Nasie!' cried Goriot.

'Only a sister like you could repeat what no one believes any more, you're a horrid unnatural creature!' said Delphine.

'Children, children, hush! or I will kill myself before your eyes.'

'There, Nasie, I forgive you,' Madame de Nucingen said. 'You are unhappy. But I am kinder than you are. How could you say that to me just when I felt ready to do anything to help you, even to making it up with my husband, which I wouldn't do for my own sake, nor for – ? But after all it's just like all the other cruel things you have done to me in the last nine years.'

'Children, children, kiss and be friends!' said their father. 'You are both angels.'

'No, let me alone!' screamed the Countess, shaking off the hand Goriot had laid on her arm. 'She has far less pity for me than my husband. Anyone would imagine she was the pattern of all the virtues!'

'I would rather people thought I owed money to Monsieur de Marsay, than confess that Monsieur de Trailles costs me more than two hundred thousand francs,' retorted Madame de Nucingen.

'Delphine!' cried the Countess, taking a step towards her.

'I only tell you the truth in return for your lies about me,' the Baroness said coldly.

'Delphine! you're a – '

She had no chance of finishing her sentence, for Goriot threw himself between the two sisters, laid one hand restrainingly on her arm and covered her mouth with the other.

'Goodness, Father! what on earth have you been handling this morning?' she said.

'Well, yes, I shouldn't have touched you,' said the poor father, wiping his hands on his trousers. 'I've been packing my things; I'm flitting, you know; I didn't know you were coming.'

He was happy at having drawn this reproach upon himself and so diverted the current of his daughter's anger.

'Ah!' he said, as he sank into a seat, 'you children have broken my heart. This is the end. My head is burning as if it was on fire inside. Be kind now, and love one another. This is killing me. Delphine, Nasie, come, there is right and wrong on both sides. Look, Dedel,' he went on, gazing at the Baroness with eyes full of tears, 'she needs twelve thousand francs, let us think where we can find them for her. Don't look at each other like that!' He slid from his chair, and dropped on his knees beside Delphine. 'Ask her to forgive you, just to please me,' he whispered in her ear. 'She is more miserable than you are, don't you see?'

'Poor Nasie,' said Delphine, alarmed at the wild, almost crazy, expression grief had drawn on her father's face. 'I was in the wrong, kiss me –'

'Ah! that is balm to my heart,' cried Goriot. 'But where are we to find twelve thousand francs? Suppose I offered myself as a substitute in the army?'

'Oh, Father!' they both cried, putting their arms round him. 'No! No!'

'God will reward you for that thought, our lives would not be enough to repay it, would they, Nasie?' said Delphine.

'And besides, Father dear, it would be only a drop in the ocean,' the Countess pointed out.

'But is there nothing a man can earn with his flesh and blood then?' cried the old man in despair. 'If anyone can save you, Nasie, I am his, body and soul; I will do murder for him! I will do what Vautrin did and go to prison for it! I –' He stopped abruptly, looking as if a thunderbolt had struck him. 'Nothing left!' he said, tearing his hair. 'If I only knew where to go to steal the money, but it is so hard to find a place to rob; and it would take time to rob the Bank, and I should need people to help me. Then I must die, there's nothing left for me to do but die. Yes, that's all I'm good for, I'm not worth calling a father now. No, no. She asks for my help in her need, and I, miserable wretch that I am, have nothing to give her. Ah! you bought yourself a life annuity, you old scoundrel, although you had daughters. Do you not love your daughters, that you could do such a thing? Die, die, miserably, like the dog you are! Yes, I am lower than a dog, a dog would not have behaved like that! Oh! my head! It is bursting!'

'Papa! Papa!' the two young women cried, clinging to him to prevent him from dashing his head against the walls. 'You must be reasonable!'

He broke into sobs. Eugène, horror-stricken, took the bill Vautrin had signed, the stamp on which was sufficient for a larger sum; he changed the figures and made it into a proper bill for twelve thousand francs payable to Goriot's order; then he went into the room next door.

'Here is the whole amount, Madame,' he said, handing her the piece of paper. 'I was sleeping, your conversation wakened me, and so I was able to learn what I owed Monsieur Goriot. This bill clears my debt, and you can convert it into cash. I will pay it off punctually on the proper date.'

The Countess stood stock-still for a moment, holding the document in her fingers. Then pale and trembling with mounting anger, rage, fury, she said,

'Delphine, I forgave you everything, as God is my witness, but who could forgive this? This gentleman was there all the time, and you knew it! You were petty enough to take your revenge and let me betray my secrets, my life, the lives of my children, my shame, my honour! There, you are nothing to me any more, I hate you, I will do you all the harm I can, I – ' She was too angry to go on; her throat dried up with rage.

'But he's my son, our dear child, your brother, your saviour!' exclaimed Goriot. 'Kiss him, Nasie! Look, I am kissing him,' and he strained Eugène to him in a frenzied clasp. 'Oh! my child! I will be more than a father to you, I will give you the love of a whole family. I wish I were God so that I could throw the universe at your feet. Why don't you kiss him, Nasie? He's not a man but an angel, an angel from Heaven.'

'Let her be, Father. She's mad at the moment,' said Delphine.

'Mad! Mad! And what are you?' cried Madame de Restaud.

'Children, I shall die if you go on like this,' cried the old man, and he fell on his bed as if a bullet had struck him. 'They are killing me!' he murmured to himself.

The Countess looked at Eugène who was standing as if paralysed, stunned by the violence of this scene.

'Sir? – ' she said to him, suspicion and inquiry in her gesture, voice and eyes, paying no attention to her father, or to Delphine who was hastily unfastening his waistcoat.

'Madame, I will meet the bill and hold my tongue about it,' he replied, to her unspoken question.

'You have killed our father, Nasie!' said Delphine, pointing to the old man lying apparently unconscious on the bed. Her sister fled.

'I forgive her with all my heart,' he said, opening his eyes. 'Her situation is frightful and would turn a better head. Comfort Nasie and be gentle with her, Delphine; promise this to your poor father who is dying,' he begged Delphine, holding her hand tightly.

'Oh, what's the matter?' she said, in great alarm.

'Nothing, nothing,' her father replied, 'it will pass off. There's something pressing on my forehead, it's just a headache. Poor Nasie, what a prospect lies before her!'

As he was speaking the Countess returned, and threw herself at her father's feet.

'Forgive me!' she cried.

'Come,' said Goriot, 'you are hurting me much more now.'

The Countess turned to Rastignac, her eyes swimming with tears.

'Sir,' she said, 'my misery made me unjust to you. You will be a brother to me, won't you?' And she held out her hand to him.

'Nasie,' said Delphine, putting her arms round her sister, 'little Nasie, let us forgive and forget everything.'

'No,' cried Nasie, 'I shall remember!'

'Dear angels,' cried Goriot, 'you are tearing away the dark curtain that hung heavy on my eyes; your voices bring me back to life. Kiss one another again. Well, Nasie, this bill will save you, won't it?'

'I hope so. See here, Papa, will you write your name on it?'

'Goodness! how stupid of me to have forgotten that! But I did not feel well, Nasie, so don't bear me ill-will. Send me a message to let me know as soon as your troubles are over. No, I will come myself. No, better not, I cannot risk meeting your husband again, I should kill him on the spot. As for the transfer of your property, I shall have something to say about that. Run along, child, and see that Maxime behaves himself.'

Eugène was too dumbfounded to say anything.

'Poor Anastasie has always had rather a violent temper,' said Madame de Nucingen, 'but she has a good heart.'

'She came back for the endorsement,' Eugène said in a low voice to Delphine.

'Do you think so?'

'I wish I weren't obliged to think so. Don't trust her,' he replied, raising his eyes as if to confide to Heaven thoughts he dared not put into words.

'Yes, she has always been a bit of a hypocrite, and my poor father lets himself be taken in by her airs.'

'How do you feel now, dear Father Goriot?' Eugène asked the old man.

'I feel inclined to have a sleep,' he answered.

Eugène helped him to bed, and he fell asleep holding his daughter's hand in his. Then Delphine prepared to go.

'This evening at the Italiens,' she said to Eugène, 'and you can tell me then how he is. You leave this house to-morrow, sir. Let's look at your room. Oh! how dreadful!' she exclaimed as she went in. 'You were even worse off than Father. Eugène, you have behaved very well. I would love you more than ever if it were possible; but, my dear boy, if you want to make your fortune you mustn't throw twelve thousand francs out of the window like that! The Comte de Trailles is a gambler. My sister shuts her eyes to that. He would have gone and found his twelve thousand francs where he has lost and won piles of money before.'

A groan from the next room brought them back to Goriot, whom they found apparently sleeping; but as the two lovers reached his bedside they caught the words: 'They are not happy!' Whether he was sleeping or awake, the tone in which these words were spoken struck so keenly home to his daughter's heart, that she leant over the pallet on which her father lay and kissed his forehead. He opened his eyes and said,

'Ah, it's Delphine.'

'Well, how are you?' she asked.

'Quite well,' he said. 'Don't worry. I shall go out presently. Don't stay, children, go and be happy.'

Eugène accompanied Delphine to her door, but he was too uneasy at the state in which he had left Goriot to dine with her as she suggested, and returned to the Maison Vauquer. He found Goriot downstairs, and just about to sit down to table. Bianchon had placed himself where he could examine the vermicelli-maker's face in a good light; and when he saw the old man pick up his bread and smell it to judge the quality of the flour, and noted that he seemed completely unconscious of what he was doing, the medical student shook his head ominously.

'Come and sit near me, young medico,' said Eugène.

Bianchon went the more readily because the change of place brought him near the old boarder.

'What's the matter with him?' Rastignac asked.

'If I'm not mistaken he's done for! Some grave abnormality must have affected his system: he looks to me as if he were about to be stricken with a serous apoplexy. The lower part of his face is calm enough, but the upper part is drawn and distorted – the skin looks as if it were pulled involuntarily upwards towards the forehead, do you see? Then the eyes show the peculiar condition that indicates the effusion of serum in the brain: look! you might think that they were full of fine dust, mightn't you? I shall know more about his state to-morrow morning.'

'Is there any cure for that?'

'No, none. It might be possible to prolong his life for a time if we could find a way of setting up a reaction towards the extremities, towards the legs; but if the symptoms have not passed off by to-morrow evening it's all up with the poor old fellow. Do you know what happened to bring the illness on? He must have received a violent shock, and his mind has given way under it.'

'Yes, you are quite right,' said Rastignac, remembering how the two daughters had struck blow after blow, without remission or respite, at their father's heart. 'But,' he said to himself, 'at least Delphine loves her father.'

That evening, at the Italiens, Rastignac took some care not to alarm Madame de Nucingen unduly: but he had barely begun to speak when she interrupted him.

'Don't worry about Father,' she said; 'he's very strong. He was a little shaken by what we told him this morning, that's all. Our whole fortunes hang in the balance, so you see how serious the matter is. I could not go on living if your affection did not make me insensible to calamities I should once have thought unendurable. Now only one anxiety can affect me, for only one misfortune that means anything can befall me – to lose the love that has made me feel the joy of being alive. I am indifferent to everything but your love, I no longer care for anything else in the world: you are the whole world to me. If I feel glad to be rich it is so that I can give you more pleasure. I am, I confess it to my shame, a better lover than a daughter. Why, I do not know. My whole life is bound up in you. My father gave me a heart, but you have made it beat. What does it matter to me if the entire world blames me if you exonerate me? and you have no right to think ill of me for sins I am driven to by an overwhelming love. Do you think me an unnatural daughter? Oh, no! it is impossible not to love a father so good as ours is. Could I prevent his seeing in the end the natural consequences of our deplorable marriages? Why did he permit them? Was it not his duty to think for us? Now, I know, he suffers as much as we do; but what can we do about it? Console him? Nothing we might say could console him. Our resignation hurt him and made him grieve much more than any reproaches or complaints we might have made. There are situations in life where all is bitterness.'

Eugène said nothing: this artless outpouring of sincere feeling filled his heart with tenderness. Parisian women are often false, intoxicated with vanity, selfish, flirtatious, cold: yet it is certain that when they truly love they are more ready than other women are to sacrifice all personal feelings to their passion; they rise above all their pettiness, and by this victory become sublime. Eugène was struck, too, by the keen and profound insight into natural feelings a woman shows when a privileged affection sets her, as it were, a little way off, and enables her to consider them with detachment. But Madame de Nucingen was not pleased at Eugène's silence.

'What are you thinking of?' she asked.

'I'm still thinking about what you said just now. Until this moment I was sure that I loved you more than you loved me.'

She smiled, and hardened herself to resist the pleasure she felt, so that their conversation might not go beyond the safe limits fixed by propriety. She had never before heard a young love express itself in all sincerity; a few more words, and she could not have guarded her self-control.

'Eugène,' she said, changing the conversation, 'you don't know what's been happening, do you? All Paris is to be at Madame de Beauséant's to-morrow. The Rochefides and the Marquis d'Ajuda have agreed to keep the whole thing dark, but the king is signing their marriage contract to-morrow, and your poor cousin knows nothing about it yet. She can't possibly cancel her reception and ball, and the Marquis will not be there. People are talking of nothing else but this affair.'

'And the world thinks a wicked sin funny, and winks at it! Don't you know that this will kill Madame de Beauséant?'

'No,' said Delphine, smiling, 'you don't know what stuff women of her kind are made of. But all Paris is going, and I shall be there! Of course it's really because of you I'm going.'

'But are you quite sure,' said Rastignac, 'that it's not just one of the silly rumours that are always flying about Paris?'

'We shall know the truth to-morrow.'

Eugène did not go back to the Maison Vauquer. He could not bring himself to forgo the pleasure of occupying his new rooms. The evening before he had been obliged to leave Delphine at one in the morning, but that night it was Delphine who left him to return home at two o'clock. He rose rather late next day, and waited for Madame de Nucingen, who came to breakfast with him about noon. In the greed with which, like all young men, he snatched at these enchanted hours of happiness he had almost forgotten old Goriot's existence. Getting used to all the elegant things that belonged to him was one long festival in itself; and then Madame de Nucingen was there, adding fresh lustre to everything by her presence. However, about four o'clock the lovers called Goriot to mind, and bethought themselves of the happiness with which he was looking forward to enjoying a new life in that house. Eugène pointed out that the old man ought to be moved there at once if he was going to be ill, and left Delphine to hurry back to the Maison Vauquer. Neither old Goriot nor Bianchon was at table with the others.

'Ha!' said the painter as Eugène came in. 'Old Goriot has crocked up; Bianchon is up there with him. The old chap saw one of his daughters, the Comtesse de Restaurama; then he insisted on going out, and made himself worse. Society is about to lose one of its brightest ornaments.'

Eugène leapt to the staircase.

'Hi! Monsieur Eugène!'

'Monsieur Eugène, Madame is calling you!' shouted Sylvie.

'Monsieur Eugène,' said the widow, 'you and Monsieur Goriot should have left on the fifteenth of February, that was three days ago, it's the eighteenth now. I ought by rights to have a month's money down for both of you; but if you'll answer for old Goriot I'll take your word for it.'

'Why, can't you trust him?'

'Trust *him*! If the old fellow went off his head and died his daughters wouldn't give me a farthing, and all his old things aren't worth ten francs. He took all that was left of his table silver away this morning, I don't know why. He was got up to pass for a young man. Lord forgive me, I believe he had rouge on, he looked quite young again.'

'I'll be responsible for everything,' said Eugène with a shudder of horror, feeling a dreadful premonition.

He went upstairs to Goriot's room. The old man was lying in bed, and Bianchon was with him.

'Good evening, Father,' said Eugène.

The old man smiled sweetly at him and asked, turning glassy eyes towards him,

'How is she?'

'She is quite well, but what about you?'

'I'm not too bad.'

'Don't tire him,' said Bianchon, drawing Eugène aside into a corner of the room.

'Well?' asked Eugène.

'Only a miracle can save him now. Serous congestion has set in; he has mustard plasters on, and fortunately he can feel them, they are working.'

'Can he be moved?'

'That's out of the question. He must stay here, and be kept quiet, and spared anything that might upset him –'

'Dear Bianchon,' said Eugène, 'we will look after him between us.'

'I sent for the senior physician of my hospital, and he's been in to see him.'

'Well?'

'He won't give his verdict till to-morrow evening. He promised me he would come round to have a look at him after the day's work was over. Unfortunately the contrary old creature did something silly this morning, and he's not willing to enlighten us about it. He's as stubborn as a mule. When I speak to him he pretends not to hear, and goes to sleep to get out of answering, or if his eyes are open he begins to groan. He went out some time this morning; he's been walking the streets, no one knows where in Paris, and he took everything he possessed of any value away with him. He's been out making some infernal bargain or other, and overtaxed his strength for the sake of it. One of his daughters has been here.'

'The Countess?' asked Eugène. 'A tall brunette with bright,

well-shaped eyes, a pretty foot and slender figure?'

'Yes.'

'Leave me alone with him for a while,' said Rastignac. 'I'll be his confessor, he won't keep anything from me.'

'Well, I'll go and have dinner meantime. But try not to excite him too much; there's still some hope.'

'Don't worry.'

'They'll have a good time to-morrow,' Goriot said, when he was left alone with Eugène. 'They're going to a grand ball.'

'What did you do this morning, Papa, to make you feel so poorly this evening that you have to stay in bed?'

'Nothing.'

'Did Anastasie come?' Rastignac asked.

'Yes,' said old Goriot.

'Now, don't hide anything from me. What else did she ask you for?'

'Ah! she was very unhappy,' he replied, gathering all his strength to speak. 'You see, my boy, Nasie hasn't had a penny to spend since the affair of the diamonds. She had ordered a gold lamé dress for the ball, which should set off her beauty like a jewel. Her dressmaker, a wretch of a woman, would not give her credit, and her maid paid a thousand francs on account for the dress. Poor Nasie, to have come down to such shifts! It made my heart bleed to think of it. But when the maid saw that Restaud was on such bad terms with Nasie she was afraid of losing her money and she came to an agreement with the dressmaker, and now the dressmaker refuses to deliver the dress until the thousand francs are repaid. The ball is to-morrow, the dress is ready; what was Nasie to do? She wanted to borrow my forks and spoons to pawn them. Her husband is determined she shall go to this ball, and flaunt the diamonds they say she sold in the face of the whole of Paris. Could she go to the monster and say, "I owe a thousand francs; pay the bill for me"? Of course she couldn't, I saw that at once. Her sister Delphine will be there in a magnificent dress. Anastasie should not be outshone by her younger sister. And then, poor girl, she was so drowned in tears! I was so humiliated at not being able to produce twelve thousand francs yesterday, that I would have given the rest of my miserable life to make up for the wrong I did her. You see, once I had the strength to bear everything, but lately lack of money has broken my heart. Oh! I didn't hum and ha about it, I assure you. I spruced myself up a bit and made myself look as good as new; and then I went out and sold my spoons and forks and buckles for six hundred francs, and I made over my claim to a year's payment of my annuity to Papa Gobseck for four hundred francs down. Bah! I can live on bread! It was good enough for me when I was a young man, so it should be good enough for me now. At any rate, my Nasie will have one happy evening. She will be smart. I have the thousand-franc note here under my pillow: it warms me to have it lying under my head, since it's going to bring pleasure to my poor Nasie. She'll be able to send that bad girl Victoire packing. Did you ever hear of such a thing as servants not trusting their masters? To-morrow I shall be quite well. Nasie is coming at ten o'clock. I don't want them to think I am ill, for they wouldn't go to the ball, they would stay and take care of me. Nasie will come and pet me to-morrow as if I were a child of hers, her tenderness will cure me. And, after all, I might have spent a thousand francs on physic, mightn't I? I would far rather give it to my Nasie, she's the doctor who cures all my ills. I can at least be of some comfort to her in her misery: that makes up for the wrong I did in getting an annuity for myself. She has fallen into an abyss, and I – I'm not strong enough to pull her out of it now. Oh! but I shall go into business again. I shall go to Odessa and buy grain; wheat is sold there at a third of the price we pay for ours. There's a law against importing grain in its natural state; but the honest fellows who make the laws didn't think of prohibiting wheat products. Aha! – I thought of that myself this morning! There's good business to be done in starch.'

'He's delirious,' Eugène said to himself, as he watched the old man. 'Come, you mustn't talk, you must rest – '

Eugène went down for dinner when Bianchon came upstairs again. During the night they looked after the sick man in turn, one student spending the time reading his medical books, the other writing home to his mother and sisters. Next morning the patient's symptoms were more hopeful, in Bianchon's opinion, but his condition demanded continual attention which only the two students could give. It would be an outrage upon the mealy-mouthed phraseology of these times to describe their work in detail: leeches were applied to the poor emaciated body, and poultices, footbaths and other medical treatment required the strength and devotion of the two young men. Madame de Restaud did not come; she sent a messenger for the money.

'I thought she would have come herself; but it's just as well she didn't, she would have been worried about me,' her father said, and he appeared to be content.

At seven in the evening Thérèse came, bringing a letter from Delphine.

What can you be doing, dear? Are you neglecting me already when you have only just started to love me? When we poured out our hearts to one another you showed me a soul too noble not to be true to love for ever, knowing love's infinite variety and range. As you said once, when we were listening to the Prayer in *Mosé*, 'For some it is the monotony of a single note, for others the infinite in music.' Remember I am expecting you this evening to take me to Madame de Beauséant's ball. It's quite true that the King signed Monsieur d'Ajuda's marriage contract this morning, and the poor Viscountess knew nothing about it till two o'clock. The whole of Paris is going to throng to her house, just as people crowd to the Place de Grève when there's going to be an execution. Isn't it horrible to go only to see if she can put a bold face on her misery and die courageously? I should certainly not go, dear, if I had been there before; but of course she won't receive society any more, and if I don't go now all the efforts I have made will be thrown away. My position is quite different from other people's. Besides, I'm going partly for your sake. I am waiting for you. If you are not with me within two hours I don't know if I could forgive such treason.

Rastignac took up a pen and wrote,

I am waiting for a doctor, and until he comes I shall not know if there is any hope of saving your father. He is desperately ill. I will bring you the doctor's verdict, and I am very much afraid it may be a sentence of death. You will see then if you can go to the ball. A thousand loving thoughts.

The doctor came at half-past eight, and although his opinion on the case was not hopeful he did not think that death was imminent. His prognosis was that there would be a series of alternate improvements in the good old man's condition and relapses, and his life and reason would depend on their degree.

'It would be better for him if he died quickly,' was the doctor's final pronouncement.

Eugène left old Goriot to Bianchon's care, and went to convey the sad news to Madame de Nucingen, such news as could not fail to plunge a heart still deeply sensible of family ties in mourning.

'Tell her she's to enjoy herself all the same,' Goriot called to him. He had appeared to be dozing, but started up as Rastignac was going out.

The young man presented himself before Delphine in grief and distress, and found her with her hair dressed and her dancing shoes on, ready except for her ball-dress – yet the finishing touches of her toilet, like the strokes with which an artist completes his picture, required more time than the whole ground-work of the creation.

'Why! You're not dressed!' she exclaimed.

'No, Madame. Your father – '

'My father again!' she interrupted him sharply. 'You don't need to teach me what is due to my father. I have known my father a long time. Not a word, Eugène; I'll only listen to what you have to say when you are dressed. Thérèse has got everything ready for you in your rooms. My carriage is waiting, take it and come back again for me. We will talk about Father on the way to the ball. We must leave in good time, for if we are held up in the line of carriages we shall be very lucky if we get there by eleven o'clock.'

'But, Madame! ...'

'Off with you! Not another word!' she said, darting into her boudoir for a necklace.

'Now, do go, Monsieur Eugène, you will vex Madame,' urged
Thérèse, trying to hurry the young man, who stood appalled by
the callousness of this elegant parricide.

He went to dress, with a mind full of the saddest, most dis-
heartening reflections. He saw the world as an ocean of mud into
which a man plunged up to the neck, if he dipped a foot in it.
'Worldly crimes are mean and ignoble!' he said to himself.
'Vautrin was greater than this.'

He had seen society in its three great aspects: Obedience,
Struggle and Revolt; or, in other words, the Family, the World
and Vautrin; and the necessity of choosing one of them dismayed
him. Obedience was boring, Revolt impossible and Struggle
hazardous. His thoughts carried him back to his home and his
family. He remembered the pure happiness of his uneventful life
there: he recalled the days spent among beings who loved him
dearly. Those dear creatures conformed to the natural laws of the
domestic hearth, and in so doing found a full and constant happiness there, unmarred by such torments as his. Yet for all his fine
thoughts he did not feel he had the courage to go to Delphine and
proclaim the creed of pure hearts, enjoining filial piety on her in
the name of love. His education, though barely begun, had borne
fruit already. He already loved selfishly. His powers of perception
were keen enough for him to recognize the nature of Delphine's
heart; he felt instinctively that she was capable of stepping over
her father's dead body to go to the ball; and he had not the
authority to play the part of mentor, nor the courage to cross her,
nor the strength of mind to leave her.

'She would never forgive me for putting her in the wrong over
this,' he said to himself.

Then he glossed the doctors' pronouncement, he gladly persuaded himself that old Goriot was not so dangerously ill as he had
thought; he went on to gather traitorous arguments to justify
Delphine. She did not know how serious her father's condition
was. The kind old man would send her to the ball himself if she
went to see him. The inflexible social law, true to a formula, so

often condemns where an apparent crime can be excused by those who know what palliation of it may be found in differences of temperament within the family circle, diversity of interests, changing circumstances, all the innumerable complications of family life. Eugène sought to delude himself; he was ready to sacrifice his conscience to his mistress. Within the last two days the whole orientation of his life had changed. A woman's disturbing influence had brought confusion to his world: she had eclipsed his family, and made his entire being subservient to her ends.

The circumstances in which Rastignac and Delphine had come together seemed expressly designed to afford them the keenest pleasure in each other. Their long-repressed passion had been inflamed by what is often passion's death-blow – enjoyment. When he possessed this woman Eugène knew that until that moment he had only desired her, he loved her only on the morrow of his happiness. Love is perhaps no more than gratitude for pleasure. It did not matter whether this woman was abominable or sublime, he adored her for the delight she had brought him as a dowry, and for the delight she took in him; and Delphine loved Rastignac as Tantalus would have loved an angel who had come to satisfy his hunger, or quench the thirst of his dry, parched throat.

'Well, how is Father?' said Madame de Nucingen, when Eugène returned, dressed for the ball.

'He's very ill indeed,' he replied. 'If you want to give me proof that you do really care for me, you'll hurry back with me to see him.'

'Yes, of course,' she said; 'but after the ball. Dear Eugène, be nice, don't read me a sermon. Come.'

They set off. Eugène sat in silence, and after a while Delphine said,

'What's the matter now?'

'I can hear your father's death-rattle,' he replied, with a touch of anger. And he began with the vehement eloquence of youth to tell her of the barbarous cruelty to which vanity had driven Madame de Restaud, of her father's desperate illness brought on by his supreme act of self-devotion, and what the cost of Anastasie's lamé dress would be. Delphine wept; and then she thought, 'I'm going to look a fright,' and that thought dried her tears.

'I will nurse Father, I will not leave his bedside,' she said.

'Ah! now you are as I wanted you to be,' cried Rastignac.

The lamps of five hundred carriages lit up the approaches to the Hôtel de Beauséant. On either side of the brightly lighted gateway a gendarme stood magnificently. The fashionable world hurried with such eagerness to see the great lady at the moment of her downfall, and came in such numbers, that the reception rooms on the ground floor of the mansion were already full to overflowing when Madame de Nucingen and Rastignac appeared. Never since the days when the whole court rushed to call on La Grande Mademoiselle, when Louis XIV tore her lover from her, had a disastrous love-affair made such a stir in Paris. Yet in this tragic situation, the youngest daughter of the quasi-royal house of Burgundy rose above her pain, and till the last moment dominated the social world, whose vanities she had acquiesced in only that they might serve the triumph of her passion.

The most beautiful women in Paris adorned the animated scene with their exquisite dresses and their smiles. The most distinguished men at court, ambassadors, ministers, illustrious men from every sphere, bedizened with decorations, stars, multi-coloured ribbons, thronged about the Viscountess. Orchestral music rose and fell in waves of sound under the gilded ceilings of this palace, which to its queen was desolate.

Madame de Beauséant stood at the door of her first salon to receive her so-called friends. She was dressed in white, and wore no ornament in her simply-braided hair. Her face was serene, and showed no sign of grief, or pride, or of forced gaiety. No one could read her heart: she looked like a marble Niobe. When she greeted her intimate friends her smile was sometimes mocking;

but she appeared to everyone so like her usual self, so exactly as she had been when radiant happiness adorned her like a jewel, that the most callous and insensitive admired her, as young Roman women applauded the gladiator who could smile at the moment of death. It seemed as if society had arrayed itself to bid farewell to one of its sovereigns.

'I was afraid that you might not come,' she said to Rastignac.

'Madame,' he said in a voice that shook with emotion, taking these words as a reproach, 'I shall be the last to leave you; that is why I have come.'

'Good,' she said, and she took his hand. 'You are perhaps the only one here whom I can trust. My friend, when you love, love a woman whom you can love for ever. Never forsake a woman.'

She took Rastignac's arm and went towards a sofa in the room where guests were playing cards.

'Go to the Marquis,' she said. 'Jacques, my footman, will go with you, and he will give you a letter addressed to the Marquis. I am asking him for my letters. He will give them all up, I like to think that. When you have my letters, go upstairs to my room. Someone will let me know.'

She rose to meet the Duchesse de Langeais, her best friend, who was coming to join them. Rastignac went out, and called at the Hôtel de Rochefide, where he knew the Marquis d'Ajuda was most probably spending the evening; and when he asked for him he was admitted. The Marquis invited the student to accompany him to his own house, where he handed over a box, saying as he did so,

'They are all there.'

He seemed to wish to say something more, to ask Eugène about the ball or about the Viscountess, or possibly to confess to him that he was even then in despair about his marriage, as later he was known to be; but a proud light flashed suddenly in his eyes, and with deplorable courage he kept his noblest feelings secret.

'Say nothing about me to her, my dear Eugène.' He pressed Eugène's hand affectionately and sadly, and turned away.

The student went back to the Hôtel de Beauséant, and the servant showed him to the Viscountess's room. There he saw preparations for departure. He sat down near the fire, looked at the cedarwood casket, and sank into a profoundly melancholy dream. In his eyes Madame de Beauséant had a more than human grandeur; she was like a goddess in the *Iliad*.

'Ah! my friend!' said the Viscountess. She went straight to Rastignac and laid her hand on his shoulder. He saw that his cousin was in tears, he felt her hand tremble: her other hand was raised to take the casket, and her eyes looked upward. Suddenly she took the box, put it in the fire and watched it burn.

'They are dancing. They all came very promptly, but death will delay its coming. Hush! my friend,' she said, and she put her finger on Rastignac's lips as he was about to speak. 'I shall never see Paris or this world again. At five o'clock in the morning I am leaving here, to go and bury myself in the remotest part of Normandy. I have been busy since three this afternoon making my preparations, signing documents, setting my affairs in order; there was no one I could send to –' She broke off. 'I knew he was sure to be at –' She stopped again, as grief overcame her. At such moments as these everything is agony, and certain words it is impossible to utter.

'In short,' she went on, 'I counted on you this evening to do me this last service. I should like to give you some token of my friendship. I shall often think of you. You have seemed to me to be kind and noble, unspoiled and open-hearted, in this world where such qualities are rare. I wish you to think sometimes of me. Ah!' she said, glancing about her, 'here is the box I used to keep my gloves in. Every time I took them out before going to a ball or a play I used to feel I must be beautiful because I was so happy, and I never handled it but I left some pleasant thought with it: there is much of myself in this, there's a whole Madame de Beauséant who no longer exists. Now it is for you; will you accept it? I will take care that it is sent to you in the Rue d'Artois. Madame de Nucingen looks very well this evening, you must love her tenderly. If we see each other no more, my friend, be sure that I shall pray for you, who have been so good to me. Let us go downstairs now, I do not want to let people think that I am weeping. I have eternity before me to weep in; I shall be alone, and no one will ask me the reason of my tears. One last look round this room.'

She stood there silently. Then after hiding her eyes for a moment with her hand, she wiped away the tears, bathed her face with cold water, and took the student's arm.

'Let us go!' she said.

No experience in Rastignac's life had ever stirred his heart so deeply, as this contact with suffering borne with such noble fortitude.

They returned to the ball, and Madame de Beauséant went through the rooms on Eugène's arm – a last graceful act of kindness on the part of this gracious woman. The student's eye soon picked out the two sisters, Madame de Restaud and Madame de Nucingen, from the throng. The Countess was magnificent in all the splendour of her diamonds. They must have scorched her: this was the last time she would ever wear them. Strong as her pride and her love might be, when she met her husband's glance her eyes fell. Such a sight was not calculated to lighten Rastignac's sad thoughts. Beyond the diamonds of the two sisters he saw again the mean pallet on which old Goriot lay. The Viscountess misunderstood his gloom, and withdrew her hand from his arm.

'Come,' she said, 'I must not deprive you of a pleasure.'

Eugène was soon claimed by Delphine, in high spirits at the impression she was making, and eager to lay at the student's feet the homage she was receiving in this new world which she was hoping would take her up.

'What do you think of Nasie?' she asked him.

'She has turned her father's very death into cash,' said Rastignac.

About four o'clock in the morning the crowd in the reception rooms began to grow less dense. Presently the music ceased, and a little later the Duchesse de Langeais and Rastignac were left alone in the great ballroom. The Viscountess, thinking that she would find no one there but the student, came back there when she had said goodbye to Monsieur de Beauséant, who said again as he went off to bed,

'It is quite wrong, my dear, to go and shut yourself up at your age! Do stay with us.'

When she saw the Duchess, Madame de Beauséant could not suppress an exclamation.

'I guessed what was in your mind, Clara,' said Madame de Langeais. 'You are leaving us, and will never return to us again; but you must not go without hearing what I have to say, without our understanding one another.'

She took her friend's arm and they went together to the next room; and there, looking at her with tears in her eyes, the Duchess clasped her in her arms and kissed her cheek.

'I will not part from you in coldness, my dear; I could not bear such a heavy burden of regret as that would lay on me hereafter,' she said. 'You can rely on me as if I were yourself. You have been truly great this evening: I felt I must show you that I too could rise to such heights, that I was worthy of our friendship. I have borne ill-will to you, I have not always been kind; forgive me, my dear: I take back all that may have wounded you, I wish I could unsay my words. Our hearts are now united by a common sorrow, for I do not know which of us is the more unhappy. Monsieur de Montriveau was not here this evening, do you understand what that means? No one who saw you at this ball, Clara, will ever forget you. I intend to make one last effort: if I fail I shall enter a convent. Where are you going, Clara?'

'To Normandy, to Courcelles. I shall love and pray there, until the day it pleases God to take me from this world. – Monsieur de Rastignac!' called the Viscountess in a voice that shook, as she recollected that the young man was waiting.

The student knelt and kissed his cousin's hand.

'Farewell, Antoinette!' said Madame de Beauséant. 'May you be happy. I need not say that to you,' she added, turning to the student; 'you are young, you can still trust and believe in something. As I take my leave of this world I am sustained, as a few privileged people are on their death-beds, by sincere and reverent feeling in those about me.'

Rastignac came away about five o'clock that morning, when he had seen Madame de Beauséant to her travelling coach, when he had received her last farewells, over which she shed tears: for the most exalted personages are not placed beyond the reach of the common emotions, and do not live without pain, as some who court the people would have them believe. Eugène walked back to the Maison Vauquer in the damp cold morning. His education was nearly complete.

'We're not going to be able to save poor old Goriot,' said Bianchon, as Rastignac entered his neighbour's room. Eugène gazed for a while at the old man sleeping, and then turned to his friend.

'Dear Bianchon,' he said, 'you are quite right to be content to stick to the modest career you have marked out for yourself; don't turn aside from it. I am in hell, and must stay there. Believe whatever evil you may hear about the world, it's all true! No Juvenal could adequately paint its gilded and bejewelled horror.'

Rastignac was wakened about two that afternoon by Bianchon, who was obliged to go out, and asked him to look after old Goriot whose condition had become much worse during the morning.

'The old fellow has not two days to live, perhaps not six hours,' said the medical student, 'but we must not stop trying to fight the disease. We shall have to give him expensive treatment, and we're going to need some money. We can do the nursing between us all right, but I haven't got a penny. I have turned out his pockets, and rummaged his cupboards: result – zero. I asked him about it when he had a lucid spell, and he told me he hadn't a farthing of his own. What have you got?'

'I have twenty francs left,' said Rastignac, 'but I will throw it on the roulette table, I am bound to win.'

'And if you lose?'

'I shall ask his sons-in-law and daughters for money.'

'And suppose they won't give you any?' persisted Bianchon. 'However, finding money is not the most urgent thing just now. We must wrap his feet and legs in a boiling-hot mustard poultice. If he cries out, there is still some hope for him. You know how to do it: besides, Christophe will help you. I'm going to call at the dispensary and ask them to give us credit for all the things we shall need. It's a pity we couldn't move him to our hospital; poor fellow, he would have been better off there. Come along now, and let me hand over my charge to you. Don't leave him till I come back.'

The two young men returned to the room where the old man lay. Eugène was dismayed by the change in Goriot's face: it was distorted, pallid and utterly exhausted.

'Well, Papa?' he said, bending over the wretched bed.

Goriot raised dull eyes to Eugène's face, and scrutinized him carefully without a sign of recognition. It was more than the student could bear: tears sprang to his eyes.

'Bianchon, should we not have curtains for the windows?'

'No, light and air do not affect him now, and it would be too good a sign to be true if he felt heat or cold. All the same we need a fire for heating drinks and preparing all the other things. I will send you in a few bundles of sticks to do till we get firewood. I burned yours yesterday and during the night, and all the peat he had, poor man. It was so damp the water was dripping from the walls; I could hardly keep the room dry. Christophe came in and swept it, it really is a pigsty. I burnt juniper to kill the horrible smell.'

'Good heavens!' said Rastignac. 'And just think of his daughters!'

'Look here, if he asks for a drink, give him some of this,' said the medical student, showing Rastignac a large white pitcher. 'If you hear him groan, and his abdomen is hot and hard to the touch, get Christophe to help you – you know what to do. If he should get wildly excited and talk a great deal, even if he is slightly delirious, don't worry: it will not be a bad sign. But send Christophe to the Hospice Cochin. Our doctor, or my fellow-student or I, will come and apply moxas. This morning, while you were sleeping, we had a grand consultation. A pupil of Doctor Gall's was here, and the senior physician from the Hôtel-Dieu, and our own chief. These gentlemen thought there were unusual features in the case, and we are going to study the progress of the disease, as it may throw some light on several rather important scientific problems. One of the doctors declares that he should show particular preoccupations according to the region of the brain affected by the pressure of serum. So listen to him carefully if he talks, and note to what category of ideas what he says belongs: whether he uses his memory, or his powers of perception or judgement; whether his thoughts are concerned with material matters or feelings; whether he makes plans for the future, or returns to the past; in short, be prepared to give us an exact report. It may be that the serum is invading his entire brain, in which case he will die in his present vacancy of mind. It is impossible to predict any normal course for these diseases. Suppose the shock came here,' said Bianchon, pointing to the back of the sick man's head, 'there are instances of very odd things happening: the brain may recover some of its faculties, and death is delayed. The matter may drain away from the brain, by channels that can only be determined by a post-mortem. At the Hospital for Incurables there's an imbecile old man in whose case the discharge took the direction of the spinal cord: he suffers horribly, but he's alive.'

'Did they have a good time?' said old Goriot, recognizing Eugène.

'Oh! he thinks of nothing but his daughters,' said Bianchon. 'He said to me dozens of times last night, "They are dancing now! She has her dress." He called their names. He made me cry, the devil take it! calling, "Delphine! my own little Delphine! Nasie!" in such a tone of voice! Upon my word,' said the medical student, 'it was enough to make anyone burst into tears.'

'Delphine,' said the old man, 'she is there, isn't she? I knew she was.' His eyes took on a wild restlessness, and he stared at the walls and the door.

'I'm going downstairs to tell Sylvie to get the poultices ready,' said Bianchon. 'It's a good time to apply them, now.'

Rastignac was left alone with the old man. He sat at the foot of the bed, and gazed at that shocking and pitiful face.

'Madame de Beauséant has fled the city, and this man lies here dying,' he said. 'Noble natures cannot long endure this world. How indeed should deep and noble feeling find a place in such a shallow, petty, mean society?'

Scenes from the ball the previous evening rose to his mind, to contrast strangely with the death-bed he was watching.

Suddenly Bianchon reappeared.

'See here, Eugène, I've just seen our senior doctor at the hospital, and I ran all the way back here. If he shows any signs of sanity, if he speaks, lay him on a long mustard poultice, and see that it covers him from the nape of his neck to the base of his spine; and send for us.'

'Dear Bianchon,' said Eugène.

'Oh! he's an interesting case from a medical point of view,' returned the medical student, with all a neophyte's ardour.

'Well, well,' said Eugène, 'so I'm the only one to care for the old man through affection for him.'

'You would not say that if you had seen me this morning,' Bianchon replied, without a sign of offence. 'Practising doctors after a while see nothing but the disease, but I can still see the patient, my dear fellow.'

He went away, leaving Eugène alone with the old man, and apprehensive of a crisis, which in fact was not long in appearing.

'Ah! is it you, dear child?' said old Goriot, recognizing Eugène.

'Do you feel better?' asked the student, taking his hand.

'Yes. My head felt as if it were gripped in a vice, but it's growing easier now. Did you see my girls? They're coming here directly, they will rush here as soon as they know I am ill; they always took such care of me in the Rue de la Jussienne! Good heavens! I wish my room was fit to receive them in. There was a young man here who burned all my peat.'

'I hear Christophe,' said Eugène; 'he is bringing up wood, sent you by that same young man.'

'That's good! But how am I to pay for the wood? I haven't a penny left, child. I have given everything away, everything. I'm a beggar, now. But at least the gold dress was lovely, wasn't it? (Oh! That pain!) Thank you, Christophe. God will reward you, my boy; I have nothing left, myself.'

'I'll pay you well, and Sylvie too, for what you are doing for him,' Eugène whispered to the man.

'My daughters told you that they were coming, didn't they, Christophe? Go back to them, I will give you five francs for your trouble. Tell them that I don't feel well, and that I should like to kiss them, to see them once more before I die. Tell them that, but don't alarm them more than you can help.'

Rastignac signed to him to obey the old man, and Christophe went.

'They are sure to come,' Goriot began again. 'I know them. Delphine has such a tender heart! If I die, what grief she will feel! Nasie too. I would rather not die, because I don't want to make them cry; and if I die, dear Eugène, I shall not see them any more. That's what death means. There where I am going I shall be very lonely. For a father Hell is to be childless, and I have already served my apprenticeship to that since they got married. My Heaven was in the Rue de la Jussienne. Tell me, if I go to Heaven do you think I may return in spirit to be near them? I have heard tell of such things. Are they true? I see them now in my mind as they were when we lived in the Rue de la Jussienne. They used to come downstairs in the morning: "Good morning, Papa," they would say. I took them on my knee, I had all sorts of teasing pranks to play on them, and they were delighted. They used to put their arms round me so sweetly. We breakfasted together every morning, they had dinner with me too: in short, I was a father then, I rejoiced in my children. When they lived in the Rue

282

de la Jussienne they did not question my authority in anything; they knew nothing of the world; they loved me dearly. Oh God! why could they not be children always? (Oh! my head! what racking pain this is!) Ah! ah! forgive me, children; I am in horrible pain, and it must really be pain, you have hardened me well to endure mere heartache. Oh, God! if I could only hold their hands in mine I should not feel my pain. Do you think they are on the way? Christophe is so stupid; I ought to have gone myself. He will get a sight of them. But you were at the ball yesterday. Tell me about them; how did they look? They didn't know anything about my illness, did they? They would not have danced, poor little things, if they had known. Oh! I must not be ill any longer. They still need me too much. Their fortunes are in danger. And to what husbands they are bound! Cure me! Cure me! (Oh! what pain! – Ah! ah! ah!) See here, you must make me well, because they need money, and I know where to go and get it. I'll go to Odessa and manufacture starch. I know the ropes, I'll make millions that way. (Oh! I cannot endure it!)'

Goriot was silent for a moment. He seemed to be summoning all his powers of endurance to bear the pain.

'If they were here I should not groan,' he said, 'so why should I groan now?'

A state of drowsiness supervened, and he lay quietly for a long time. Christophe came back, and Rastignac, thinking Goriot was asleep, did not restrain him from telling his story aloud.

'I went first of all to Madame la Comtesse, sir,' he said; 'but I couldn't get speaking to her, she was busy talking about something important with her husband. When I said I must see her, Monsieur de Restaud came himself and he said, "Monsieur Goriot is dying, is he? Well, it's the best thing he can do," he said, just like that. "I need Madame de Restaud to complete important business," he said, "she can go when it's all finished." He looked very angry, that gentleman did. I was just going to go out when Madame came into the ante-room through a door I hadn't noticed, and she said, "Christophe, tell my father I am discussing some matters with my husband, and I cannot leave him just now. It's a life-and-death matter for my children," she said, "but as soon as it's all settled I will come."

'As for Madame la Baronne, that's another tale! I didn't even see her, let alone speak to her. "Ah!" said the lady's-maid, "Madame came back from the ball at a quarter-past five, she is asleep now; if I wake her before twelve she will give me a wigging. I will tell her that her father is worse when she rings for me. Bad news will keep, I suppose," she said. It was no use begging and imploring that lady, oh dear no! though I tried it. And I asked for Monsieur le Baron, but he had gone out.'

'To think that neither of his daughters is coming!' Rastignac exclaimed. 'I'll write to them both.'

'Neither of them!' cried the old man, sitting up. 'They are busy, they are sleeping, they will not come. I knew it. You have to die to know what your children are. Ah! my friend, do not marry; do not have children! You give them life; they give you death in return. You bring them into the world, and they push you from it. No, they will not come! I have known that for the last ten years. I sometimes told myself so, but I did not dare believe it.'

Tears gathered and stood in his red-rimmed eyes, but did not fall.

'Ah! if I were rich, if I had kept my money, if I had not given it all to them, they would be here now; they would fawn on me, and cover my cheeks with their kisses! I should be living in a grand house; I should have fine rooms, servants, a fire in my room, all for myself; and they would be there all dissolved in tears, and their husbands, and their children. I should have all that. But I have nothing! Money buys everything, even daughters. Oh! my money! where has it gone? If I had riches to leave them they would comfort my pain, they would nurse me; I should hear their voices, I should see their faces. Ah! no, my dear child, my only child, it is better to be desolate and miserable! At least when a poor wretch is loved, he's quite sure that it is love. No, no, I wish I were rich, I should see them then. But who knows if I should? They both have hearts of stone. I loved them too much for them to have much love for me. A father ought always to be rich; he ought to curb his children as he would unruly horses, and I let them trample on me. Ah, the wretches! in this last act their conduct towards me during the last ten years reaches its proper climax. If you only knew how they plied me with little attentions in the early days of their marriages! (Oh, this pain is cruel torture!) I had just given them both nearly eight hundred thousand francs, they couldn't be disagreeable to me after that, nor could their husbands either. When I went to their houses it was, "My kind Father" here, "My good Father" there. There was always a place for me at their tables; and indeed I used to dine with their husbands, and they treated me with respect. They thought I still had something. What reason had they to think otherwise? I had said nothing about my affairs. A man who gave away eight hundred thousand francs to each of his daughters was a man to cherish, and they were very attentive to me; but it was for the sake of my money. Fine feathers don't always make fine birds. I found that out for myself! I used to go to the theatre with them in their carriages, and I stayed as long as I liked in the evenings at their parties. In short, they publicly called themselves my daughters, and owned me as their father. But I am still sharp enough, you know, and nothing escaped me. It was all calculated for a purpose, and that cut me to the heart. I saw very well that it was just a show and pretence; but what could I do about it? I did not feel at home at their dinner-tables as I do at the table downstairs. I could not join in the conversation. Some of those fine society folk would ask my son-in-law in a whisper, "Who is that gentleman?" "That's the father-in-law with the money-bags; he's very rich." "The deuce he is?" That was the way the conversation went, and they looked at me again, with the respect due to money-bags. Well, if I was sometimes a little awkward I paid dearly for my shortcomings! Besides, who is perfect? (My head feels like an open wound!) At this moment I am suffering what a man has to go through in order to die, my dear Monsieur Eugène; well, it's nothing in comparison with the agony that Anastasie inflicted upon me with the first look that made it clear to me that I had just said something stupid which made her feel humiliated: her look made me sweat blood. I should have liked to be an educated man, to know all about everything; but one thing I did know beyond the possibility of doubt – I was not wanted here on earth. Next day I went to Delphine for consolation, and what should I do but commit some blunder there, and make her angry with me! I nearly went crazy because of it. For a week I did not know what I ought to do. I did not dare to go and see them for fear of their reproaches. And there I was outside my daughters' doors.

'O God! since You know the misery, the suffering I endured, since You have counted the wounds inflicted in these years which have aged me, changed me, broken my heart, turned my hair white, why do You make me suffer now to-day? I have expiated to the full the sin of loving them too much. They themselves have been the instruments of vengeance, they have tortured me like executioners.

'Yet fathers are such simpletons! I loved them so; I returned to them as a gambler does to the gaming-table. They were my own particular vice; they took the place another man fills with his mistresses, that's the whole story!

'They were both always needing some frippery or other; their maids would tell me what they wanted, and I would give it to them for the sake of being met with smiling faces. But they gave me a few little lessons, all the same, on how I should behave in society. Oh! they lost no time about it! They were beginning to be ashamed of me; that's what comes of bringing your children up well. At my age, however, I could not go to school. (Oh, God! this pain is terrible. Doctors! Doctors! If they opened my head it would hurt less!) My daughters! My daughters! Anastasie! Delphine! I must see them. Send the police to fetch them, compel them to come! Justice is on my side, everything is on my side, natural affection, and the law as well. I protest! The country will go to ruin if the fathers are trampled underfoot. The thing is clear as day. Society, the whole world, turns on fatherly love, everything falls to pieces if children do not love their fathers. Oh! if I could only see them, hear them, no matter what they have to say; just the sound of their voices would soothe my pain – especially Delphine's voice. But tell them when they come not to look so coldly at me as they do. Ah! Monsieur Eugène, my good friend, you do not know what it is to see the radiant gold of a look change suddenly into dull chilling lead. On the day when the sunshine of their look clouded over for me, the winter of my life set in; disappointment has been my daily bread, and I accepted it; I have lived on humiliation and insult. I love them so much that I swallowed all the affronts with which they sold me a few poor little clandestine moments of joy. Think of it! a father hiding himself to catch a glimpse of his daughters! I have given them my life, and they will not give me one hour to-day! I hunger and thirst to see them, my heart is on fire within me, and they will not come to soothe the pangs of death, for this is death, I feel that I am dying. Don't they know, then, what it means to trample on one's father's corpse? There is a God in Heaven, and we fathers are avenged whether we wish it or not. Oh! but they will come! Come, my darlings, come and kiss me once more, give me one last kiss, the *viaticum* for your father, who will pray to God for you in Heaven, who will tell Him that you have been good daughters, who will plead for you! After all, it is not your fault. They are innocent, my friend! Tell everyone that; let no one be distressed on my account. It is all my fault; I taught them to trample me underfoot. That was how I liked it to be, and it's nobody's business but mine, it's no concern of human justice or God's justice. God would be unjust if he condemned them for their behaviour towards me. I did not know how to treat them; I was stupid enough to resign my rights; I would have humbled myself in the dust for them! What could you expect? Such weakness on the part of a father would have corrupted the finest nature, the noblest soul. I am a wretch, and I am justly punished. I am the cause, and the only cause, of their unfilial conduct; I spoilt them. To-day they want pleasure, as they used to want sweets. I always indulged them in all their childish whims. They had a carriage of their own when they were fifteen! Nothing was denied them. I, and I only, am to blame; but I sinned through love of them. Their voice melted my heart.

'I hear them, they are coming. Oh! yes, they will come. The law demands that they should come to see their father die; the law is on my side. Besides, it will only cost the hire of a cab for one drive, and I will pay for it. Write and tell them I have millions to leave them! On my word of honour it's true. I am going to Odessa to manufacture Italian wheaten-paste foods. I know how to do it. I have a scheme, and I shall make millions out of it. No one else has thought of it. You see, the stuff does not get damaged in transit as grain or flour does. Heh! Heh! starch too; there are millions to be made in starch. Millions, tell them; you will not be telling a lie; and even if it's greed that brings them, I would rather shut my eyes to that, at any rate I shall see them. I want my daughters! It was I who made them, they are mine!' And the old man suddenly sat up and presented to Eugène's gaze a defiant head, crowned with scanty white hair, and a face that expressed a threat in every line.

'There, there,' said Eugène, 'lie down again, dear Father Goriot. I will write to them now. As soon as Bianchon comes back I will go for them if they do not come.'

'If they do not come?' repeated the old man, sobbing. 'But I shall be dead by then, dead in a burst of rage, rage! Rage is getting the upper hand of me! Now I see my life whole. I have been duped. They do not love me – they have never loved me: that is clear as day. If they have not come by now, they will not come. The longer they delay, the less easily will they bring themselves to give me this joy. I know them. They have never had any perception of my disappointments and sorrows, or my need of them; they will not be able to imagine my death either. It is just that their minds are shut to the nature of my tenderness for them. Yes, I see it now: because I always gave away my whole heart as a matter of course, my gifts were cheap in their eyes. If they had wanted to put out my eyes, I would have told them to do it. I was a fool. They think all fathers are like theirs. You should never allow yourself to be held cheap. Their children will avenge me. You see, it is to their interest to come here. Warn them that they are imperilling the peace of their own death-beds. They are committing every crime when they commit this one. Go and tell them that not to come is parricide! They have enough on their conscience without adding that sin. Go and shout like this, "Nasie! Delphine! Come to your father, who has been so good to you, and who is now suffering pain!" No answer; nobody comes! Am I to die, then, like a dog? So this is my reward, to be forsaken. Oh! they are vile, stony-hearted women, my curse upon them; I abhor them! I shall rise from the grave at night to curse them again; for indeed, my friends, don't you think I'm right? They are behaving very badly, aren't they? What am I saying? Didn't you tell me that Delphine was here? She has more heart than her sister. You are my son, Eugène; you must love her, be a father to her. The other child is very unhappy. And what about their fortunes? Ah! God! I am dying, I cannot endure this pain! Cut off my head, leave me only my heart.'

'Christophe!' shouted Eugène, alarmed by the increasing desperation of the old man's groans and cries. 'Go and fetch Bianchon, and get me a cab. – I am going for your daughters, dear Father Goriot. I will bring them back to you.'

'Compel them, make them come! Call out the Guard, troops of the line, everyone, everything!' he said, looking at Eugène with eyes that still held the last gleam of reason. 'Tell the Government, the Public Prosecutor, that they must be brought to me. I demand their presence!'

'But you have cursed them.'

'Who said that?' said the old man, in dull amazement. 'You know very well that I love them, I adore them! If I see them I shall be cured – Fetch them, my good neighbour, my dear child, you are a kind boy; I wish I could show how grateful I am to you, but I have nothing to give but a dying man's blessing. Ah! if I could only see Delphine I would tell her to pay my debt to you. If her sister cannot come, bring Delphine to me. Tell her you won't love her any more if she will not come. She cares so much for you that she will come then. Give me something to drink, I'm on fire inside! Put something on my head. I know my daughters' hands could save me, I feel it in my bones – God! who will build up their fortune again if I go? I must go to Odessa for their sake, go to Odessa and manufacture vermicelli.'

'Drink this,' said Eugène, raising the dying man and holding him in his left arm, as he held a cup of tisane to his lips.

'It's easy to see that you love your father and mother!' said the old man, clutching Eugène's hand with both his feeble, trembling hands. 'Do you understand that I am going to die without seeing them, without seeing my girls? I have been thirsty for ten years, and *they* have never quenched my thirst. My sons-in-law killed my daughters. Yes, I was bereaved of daughters when they got married. Fathers, tell the Chambers they must pass a law against marriages! Don't let your daughters marry, if you love them. A son-in-law is a scoundrel who spoils everything in a girl's heart, he corrupts her whole nature. Let there be no more marriages! They carry off our daughters, and rob us of them, and we are left alone when we come to die. Pass a law for dying fathers. It is shocking! It cries for vengeance! They would come if my sons-in-law did not prevent them. Kill them! Strike down Restaud, kill the Alsatian, they are my murderers! Death or my daughters! Ah! this is the end, I am dying and they are not with me! Dying without them! Nasie, Delphine, why do you not come? Your father is going – '

'Dear Father Goriot, keep calm, there, there, stay quiet; set your heart at rest; don't think.'

'Not to see them – there is death's sting!'

'But you shall see them.'

'Truly?' cried the distracted old man. 'Oh! shall I see them? I shall see them and hear their voices. I shall die happy. Ah! indeed, I don't ask to live any longer; I could not stand this; my pain gets worse and worse. But just to see them, touch their dresses – ah! just touch their dresses, that's not much to ask – let me feel something that is theirs. Let me lay my fingers on their hair – hair – '

His head fell back on the pillow as if he had been clubbed. His hands moved on the coverlet as if they were groping for his daughters' hair.

'My blessing on them – ' he said, with an effort, 'bless – ' His voice suddenly failed.

At that moment Bianchon came into the room.

'I met Christophe,' he said, 'he's gone to fetch you a cab.'

Then he looked at the sick man, and pulled back the closed eyelids with his fingers, revealing, as the two students watched, eyes grown cold and lustreless.

'He will not come round from this,' said Bianchon; 'at least, I think it's unlikely.' He felt the old man's pulse, and then laid a hand on his heart.

'The mechanism still works; but in his case it's a pity; it would be far better if he died.'

'Oh! yes, indeed it would!' said Rastignac.

'What's the matter? You're as pale as death.'

'Oh, Bianchon, you don't know what cries and lamentations I've been listening to. There is a God! Oh! yes, there is a God! and he has made a better world for us, or this earth is blank and meaningless. If it had not been so tragic I should weep and feel better, but the thing lies like a dreadful weight on my heart.'

'We're going to need a lot of things, you know; where can we get money?'

Rastignac pulled out this watch.

'Take that, and pawn it as soon as you can. I don't want to stop on the way to the Rue du Helder, for I'm afraid to lose a minute, and I must wait here for Christophe. I haven't a farthing;

my cabman will have to wait for payment till I come back again.'

Rastignac rushed down the stairs, and drove off to Madame de Restaud's home in the Rue du Helder. In his imagination, as he went, he lived again the terrible scenes he had witnessed, and his indignation rose to boiling-point. When he arrived at the house and asked for Madame de Restaud, he was told that she could not see him.

'But I come from her father, who is dying,' he told the footman.

'Monsieur le Comte has given us the strictest orders, sir.'

'If Monsieur de Restaud is at home inform him of his father-in-law's condition, and tell him that I must see him at once.'

Eugène was kept waiting a long time. 'Perhaps he is dying at this very moment,' he thought.

The man came back and showed the student to the smaller drawing-room, where Monsieur de Restaud was standing before a fireless grate. He did not invite his visitor to sit down.

'Monsieur le Comte,' said Rastignac, 'Monsieur Goriot, your father-in-law, lies dying at this moment in squalor, in a mean, poverty-stricken room, and he has not even a farthing to buy firewood. He is at the point of death, and is calling for his daughter –'

'Monsieur,' the Count replied stiffly, 'as you may have had occasion to note, I feel very little affection for Monsieur Goriot. He has shown himself in an extremely discreditable light in connection with Madame de Restaud. He is the author of misfortunes that have ruined my life, and destroyed my domestic happiness. It is a matter of complete indifference to me whether he lives or dies, and there you have my feelings with regard to Monsieur Goriot. Public opinion may blame me, but I care nothing for that. I have more important things to do at the moment than to worry about what fools and strangers are going to think of me. As for Madame de Restaud, she is not in a fit state to go out. Besides, I do not wish her to leave the house. Tell her father that as soon as she has done her duty by me and my child she shall go to see him. If she loves her father she can be free in a few moments, it's as she chooses –'

'Monsieur le Comte, it is not for me to criticize your conduct, you are master in your own house, but can I count on your keeping your word to me? Well, then, promise me you will tell her that her father has not a day to live; that he looked to find her at his bedside, and cursed her when she did not come.'

'You may tell her that yourself,' Monsieur de Restaud answered, impressed by the fierce indignation expressed in Eugène's voice.

Rastignac followed the Count to the drawing-room the Countess habitually used. He found her drowned in tears, crouched in the depths of a large armchair as if she was in despair and longed for death. She was a pitiful sight, and he felt sorry for her. She did not look at Rastignac, but darted timid glances at her husband which showed her complete prostration, body and soul, under the weight of her husband's tyranny. The Count nodded, and she took this as permission to speak.

'I heard all you said, Monsieur. Tell my father that if he knew my plight he would forgive me. I did not expect to have to bear such torture as this, and it is more than I can stand, Monsieur – but I shall never give in,' she added, turning to her husband. 'I am a mother. Tell my father that I am not to blame for the way I have treated him, in spite of appearances!' Her voice had the heavy vehemence of despair.

Eugène bowed to the husband and wife and went away, feeling stunned. He guessed at the horrible dilemma that confronted Madame de Restaud. Monsieur de Restaud's tone had shown him the uselessness of his errand, and he understood that Anastasie was no longer free to act as she chose. He hurried to Madame de Nucingen, and found her in bed.

'I am ill, my poor dear,' she said. 'I caught a chill coming back from the ball, and I'm afraid of inflammation of the lungs. I'm waiting for the doctor –'

'Even if you are at death's door,' Eugène broke in, 'you must drag yourself somehow to your father's bedside. He is calling for you. If you could hear the faintest of his cries you would not feel ill any longer.'

'Eugène, Father is perhaps not quite so ill as you say; but I should hate you to disapprove of me even the least little bit, and I will do exactly as you want me to. Father would die of grief, I know, if I made my illness much worse by going out to see him. Oh, well, I'll go as soon as I've seen my doctor. – Ah! why are you not wearing your watch?' she cried out, as she noticed that the chain was missing.

Eugène reddened.

'Eugène, Eugène! if you have sold it already, or lost it – oh! it will really be too bad of you.'

The student leant over Delphine's bed, and said in her ear.

'Do you want to hear the truth about it? Well, here it is! Your father has not enough money to pay for the shroud in which he will be laid this evening. Your watch is at the pawnshop. I had nothing left.'

Delphine at once sprang out of bed, ran to her desk, took her purse from it, and held it out to Rastignac. She rang, exclaiming as she did so,

'I'm going, I'm going at once, Eugène. Just give me time to get dressed. Oh! I should be a monster if I did not go! Go back to him; I will be there before you. Thérèse,' she called to her maid, 'ask Monsieur de Nucingen to come upstairs and speak to me this very minute.'

Eugène was so glad to be able to tell the dying man that one of his daughters was coming, that he felt almost happy when he reached the Rue Neuve-Sainte-Geneviève. He fumbled in Delphine's purse for money to pay his cabman at once, and found that the purse of this wealthy young woman of fashion contained exactly seventy francs.

He went upstairs, and found old Goriot sitting up, supported by Bianchon, while the house-surgeon from the hospital was applying moxas to his back, under the supervision of the physician. It was the last resort of medicine, and, in this case, useless.

'Can you feel them?' the physician asked. But old Goriot had caught sight of the student, and only said,

'They're coming, aren't they?'

'He may rally,' said the surgeon, 'since he can speak.'

'Yes,' Eugène answered the old man, 'Delphine is on the way.'

'That doesn't mean anything,' Bianchon said to the surgeon. 'He was talking about his daughters. He's been calling for them as a man impaled on a stake cries, so I've heard, for water.'

'There's no use going on,' said the physician; 'there's nothing more we can do; he's finished.'

Bianchon and the surgeon laid the dying man down again at full length on his revolting bed.

'All the same, his linen ought to be changed,' the physician said. 'Even though there is no hope, some respect is due to suffering humanity. I shall come back again, Bianchon,' he went on, turning to the student. 'If he complains again, rub laudanum on his diaphragm.'

The physician and the house-surgeon went out together.

'Come, Eugène, cheer up, my boy,' said Bianchon, when they were left alone. 'We must put a clean shirt on him, and see about changing his sheets. Go and tell Sylvie to bring up sheets, and to come and help us.'

Eugène went downstairs, and found Sylvie helping Madame Vauquer to lay the table. Rastignac had hardly opened his mouth before the widow bore down on him, with the acidly sweet graciousness of a wary shopkeeper who is anxious neither to lose her money nor to offend her customer.

'My dear Monsieur Eugène,' she said, in answer to his request for sheets, 'you know as well as I do that old Goriot hasn't got a sou left. It's just throwing sheets away to give them to a man who's on the point of turning his toes up, especially as one will have to be used for the shroud, I suppose. And then you owe me a hundred and forty-four francs as it is; add forty francs to that for sheets, and there are several other little things; the candle Sylvie will give you is just one of them; altogether all that amounts to at least two hundred francs, and a poor widow like me can't afford to lose so much money. Come now, Monsieur Eugène, you must see what's right, I've lost quite enough in the last five days, since fortune took a spite at me. I would give ten crowns to have had the old fellow move out of here, as you said he was going to. The other boarders don't like it. For two pins I would get him taken to the workhouse. Put yourself in my place, Monsieur Eugène. My establishment must come first, it's my living, after all.'

Eugène ran upstairs to Goriot's room.

'Bianchon, where's the money for the watch?'

'There, on the table; there's three hundred and sixty odd francs left. I paid off what we owed out of what I got for it. The pawn-ticket is under the money.'

Rastignac hurried downstairs again.

'Here, Madame,' he said, with disgust, 'let us settle our accounts. Monsieur Goriot has not much longer to stay under your roof, and I – '

'Yes, he will leave here feet foremost, poor creature,' she said, counting out two hundred francs, with a half-complacent half-lugubrious expression on her face.

'Let's get done with this,' said Rastignac.

'Bring the sheets, Sylvie, and go and help the gentlemen upstairs. You won't forget Sylvie?' she continued in a whisper to Eugène. 'She's been sitting up two nights now.'

As soon as Eugène's back was turned the old woman ran after her cook.

'Take the sheets from number seven, the ones that were turned sides to middle,' she muttered in her ear. 'Goodness knows, they're quite good enough for a corpse.'

Eugène was by this time half-way upstairs, and did not over-hear the old boarding-house keeper.

'Come on,' said Bianchon, 'let's change his shirt. Hold him up straight.'

Eugène went to the head of the bed, and supported the dying man, while Bianchon pulled his shirt over his head. Goriot made a movement with his hands as if he were trying to protect something he held against his chest, and uttered mournful inarticulate cries, like some dumb animal in overwhelming pain.

'Oh, yes!' said Bianchon, 'I know what he wants – it's a little locket and a chain made of hair we took from him when we were putting on the moxas. Poor fellow! we must give it back to him. It's on the mantelshelf.'

Eugène went to fetch the chain of plaited hair, which was ash-blond in colour, and was no doubt Madame Goriot's. On one side of the locket he read 'Anastasie' and on the other 'Delphine'. It was a symbol of Goriot's own heart that rested always on his breast. The curls of hair inside were so soft and fine that they must have been cut when the two girls were tiny children. When he felt the locket touch his chest the old man heaved a long-drawn sigh of satisfaction. It was awe-inspiring to watch. This was one of the last signs of his capacity to respond to the outside world, as his sensibility withdrew itself to that mysterious centre within from which all power of feeling comes, and to which all emotions appeal. His distorted face shone with delirious joy. This vehement manifestation of a force of feeling that had survived the power of thought affected the two students so deeply that scalding tears fell on the dying man, who gave a piercing cry of delight.

'Nasie! Fifine!'

'He has not done with life yet,' said Bianchon.

'And what does he go on living for?' said Sylvie.

'Only to suffer,' answered Rastignac.

Bianchon, making a sign to his friend to follow his example, knelt down and passed his arms under the sick man's thighs, and Rastignac, kneeling on the other side of the bed, supported his back. Sylvie stood ready to pull away the sheet from underneath, and replace it by one of those she had brought. Deluded no doubt by the tears he had felt, Goriot gathered all his remaining strength to stretch out his hands, which on either side of the bed encountered the students' heads. He clutched at their hair convulsively, and they heard a faint whisper,

'Ah! my angels!'

Two words, two murmurs given meaning by the soul which fled as they were spoken.

'Poor dear man,' said Sylvie, touched by that exclamation, the expresssion of a supreme tenderness, aroused for the last time by a most ghastly, most involuntary lie.

The last sigh of this father was to be a sigh of joy, a sigh that epitomized the feeling of a lifetime: he was cheated to the end.

They laid old Goriot reverently down again on his wretched bed. From that moment his face held only painful reflections of the battle life and death were fighting in what was now no more than a machine, for the consciousness in the brain that makes the human being aware of pain and pleasure had gone. Total destruction was now only a question of time.

'He will lie like this for several hours, and die by imperceptible degrees. There will not even be a death-rattle to tell us when he goes. The brain must be completely overrun.'

As Bianchon spoke, a young woman was heard coming panting upstairs.

'She comes too late,' said Rastignac.

But it was not Delphine, it was her maid Thérèse.

'Monsieur Eugène,' she said, 'there's been a terrible scene between Monsieur and Madame about some money my poor mistress wanted for her father. She fainted, and the doctor came, and she had to be bled, and she kept screaming: "My father is dying! I want to see Papa!" Oh! cries and screams that would have broken your heart to hear.'

'That will do, Thérèse. It would be useless for her to come now. Monsieur Goriot has lost consciousness.'

'Poor dear gentleman, is he as bad as that?' said Thérèse.

'You don't need me any more, I must go and see about my dinner; it's half past four,' interposed Sylvie. She bustled out, and barely missed colliding with Madame de Restaud at the top of the staircase.

The Countess appeared in the doorway like some sombre and terrible spectre. She looked at the death-bed, in the dim light shed by the single candle, and wept at the sight of her father's mask-like face, where only an occasional tremor revealed the last flickerings of life. Bianchon tactfully left the room.

'I got away too late,' she said to Rastignac.

The student bowed sadly in answer. Madame de Restaud took her father's hand, and kissed it.

'Forgive me, Father,' she said. 'You used to say that my voice would call you back from the tomb; oh! return to life for one moment now to bless your penitent daughter. Oh, Father, hear my voice. Oh, this is dreadful! No one in the world will ever bless me now but you; everyone hates me, you are the only one on earth who loves me. Even my own children will hate me. Father, take me with you, I will love you, I will take care of you. He cannot hear me now – oh! I'm out of my mind –'

She fell on her knees, and stared wildly at the poor ruined body before her.

'My cup of misery is full,' she said, looking at Eugène. 'Monsieur de Trailles has gone, leaving enormous debts behind him, and I have found out that he was deceiving me. My husband will never forgive me, and I have left my fortune at his disposal. I've no illusions left, I can see with clear eyes now. Alas! for whose sake did I betray the only heart where I was worshipped?' She gestured towards her father as she spoke. 'I slighted him, turned my back on him, treated him unkindly times out of number, miserable wretch that I am!'

'He knew it,' said Rastignac.

Just then Goriot opened his eyes; but it was only the effect of a muscular contraction. The Countess's quick movement of awakened hope was a sight no less terrible to see than the sight of the dying man's eye.

'Can he hear me?' the Countess exclaimed. 'No,' she said to herself, sitting down beside the bed.

Eugène understood that Madame de Restaud wished to watch by her father's side, and went downstairs to take some food. The boarders were already assembled.

'Well,' said the painter, in a tone of inquiry, 'it seems we're going to have a little deathorama up there, eh?'

'I think you might choose a less painful subject for your jokes, Charles,' Eugène said.

'So we're not allowed to laugh here any more?' retorted the painter. 'What difference does it make? Bianchon says that the old man is incapable of taking anything in now.'

'In that case,' said the official from the Muséum, 'he will die as he has lived.'

'My father is dead!' shrieked the Countess.

At that terrible cry, Sylvie, Rastignac and Bianchon ran upstairs, and they found Madame de Restaud had fainted. When they had revived her, they carried her down to the cab that was waiting at the door. Eugène confided her to Thérèse's care, and told the maid to take her to Madame de Nucingen.

Bianchon joined them again.

'Yes, he's dead,' he said.

'Come, gentlemen, sit down and let's have dinner,' said Madame Vauquer. 'The soup will be getting cold.'

The two students took their places together.

'What's to be done now?' Eugène asked Bianchon.

'Well, I've closed his eyes and arranged him decently. When we have reported the death at the Mayor's office, and the doctor there has duly certified it, we'll sew him in his shroud and bury him. What else should we do with him?'

'He'll never sniff at his bread like this again,' said one of the boarders, mimicking the old man's trick of puckering up his face.

'For goodness' sake, gentlemen,' cried the tutor, 'lay old Goriot on the shelf, and let's have some other sauce with our supper, for we've had him rammed down our throats for the last hour! It's one of the privileges of the good city of Paris that you can be born, live, die there, without anyone paying the least attention to you, so let's take advantage of civilization's blessings. Sixty men at least have died to-day; do you want us to sit down and cry over every member of the whole hecatombs of Parisian dead? If old Goriot has popped off, well, so much the better for him! If you are so fond of him, go and look after him, and let the rest of us eat our meal in peace.'

'Oh! yes,' said the widow, 'it's true enough that it's all the better for him that he's dead! It seems that the poor soul had a great deal of unpleasantness while he was alive.'

Such was the sole funeral oration of a being who in Eugène's eyes was Fatherhood itself.

The fifteen boarders began to chat as they ordinarily did. When Eugène and Bianchon had satisfied their hunger, the clatter of forks and spoons, the noisily cheerful conversation, the various unconcerned expressions on those greedy, indifferent faces, everything about them shocked and nauseated them. They left the house to find a priest to watch and pray by the dead man's side that night. It was necessary to dole out the good old man's last rites according to the scanty means at their disposal. Towards nine o'clock in the evening the body was placed on the bare sacking of the bedstead in that desolate room. A candle burned on either side, and a priest came to watch there. Before going to bed, Rastignac, who had made some inquiries of the priest about the cost of the funeral, wrote a note to the Baron de Nucingen and to the Comte de Restaud, requesting them to send their representatives to defray the expenses of interment. He sent Christophe with the letters, then went to bed, completely exhausted, and slept.

Next morning Bianchon and Rastignac were obliged to go themselves to notify the death, and it was registered about twelve o'clock. Two o'clock came, and the sons-in-law had still sent no money, nor had anyone presented himself in their name, and Rastignac had already been obliged to pay the priest. Sylvie asked ten francs for laying out the old man and sewing him into a shroud, and Eugène and Bianchon calculated that they had barely enough to cover the expenses if the dead man's family refused to take any responsibility for them. The medical student, therefore, undertook to lay the body himself in a pauper's coffin, brought from his hospital, where he got it at a cheaper rate.

'Play those rascals a trick,' he suggested to Eugène. 'Buy a grave for five years at the Père-Lachaise, and arrange with the Church and the undertaker for a third-class funeral. If the daughters and their husbands refuse to pay up, you can have this legend carved on the tombstone – "Here lies Monsieur Goriot, father of the Comtesse de Restaud and the Baronne de Nucingen, interred at the expense of two students."'

Eugène took part of his friend's advice, but only after he had paid a fruitless call first on Monsieur and Madame de Nucingen, and then on Monsieur and Madame de Restaud. He got no further than the door in either house. Both porters had received strict orders.

'Monsieur and Madame are receiving no one,' they said; 'their father is dead, and they are plunged in the deepest grief.'

Eugène had experience enough of Parisian society to know that he must not insist. A strange pang shot through his heart when he saw that it was impossible for him to reach Delphine.

'Sell one of your ornaments,' he wrote to her in the porter's room, 'and let your father be decently laid to his last rest.'

He sealed the note, and begged the porter to give it to Thérèse for her mistress; but the man handed it to the Baron de Nucingen, who threw it in the fire.

It was now about three o'clock, and Eugène, having done all he could, returned to the boarding-house. Tears came to his eyes in spite of himself when he saw the coffin, barely covered by a scanty black cloth, standing on two chairs outside the wicket gate in the deserted street. A shabby sprinkler lay in a silver-plated copper bowl of holy water, but no one had stopped to sprinkle the coffin. No attempt had been made even to drape the door with black. The dead man was a pauper, and so there was no display of grief, no friend, no kinsman to follow him to the grave.

Bianchon, who was obliged to be at his hospital, had left a note for Rastignac to let him know what arrangements he had made for the funeral service. The medical student's note told Rastignac that a mass was beyond their means, that they would have to be content with the ordinary vespers service, which cost less, and that he had sent Christophe with a note to the undertaker's. As Eugène looked up after reading Bianchon's scrawl he saw Madame Vauquer fingering the little round gold locket that held the hair of Goriot's two daughters.

'How could you dare take that?' he exclaimed.

'Bless me! was it to be buried along with him?' retorted Sylvie. 'It's made of gold.'

'Of course,' answered Eugène indignantly, 'let him at least take the only thing there is to represent his two daughters with him to the grave.'

When the hearse came, Eugène had the coffin taken up to the house again, unscrewed it, and reverently placed on the old man's breast the token that recalled the time when Delphine and Anastasie were young, unspoiled and innocent, before they had learned to question his authority in anything, as he had remembered in his dying agony.

Rastignac and Christophe, with two undertaker's men, were the only mourners to follow the funeral to the Church of Saint-Étienne du Mont, which stands not far from the Rue Neuve-Sainte-Geneviève. There the coffin was carried into a low-roofed and dark little chapel. The student looked round it in search of Goriot's two daughters or their husbands, but in vain; he was alone except for Christophe, who had thought he was bound to attend the funeral of a man through whom some handsome tips had come his way. As they waited for the two priests, the choir-boy and the beadle, Rastignac grasped Christophe's hand; he could not have uttered a word at that moment.

'Yes, Monsieur Eugène,' said Christophe, 'he was a good and kind man, who never said one word louder than another; he bothered nobody, and never did any harm.'

The two priests, the choir-boy and the beadle came and said and did all one could expect them to for seventy francs in an age when the Church is not rich enough to pray for nothing. The clergy chanted a psalm, the *Libera* and the *De profundis*. The service lasted twenty minutes. There was only one mourning coach, which was for one of the priests and the choir-boy, and they agreed to share it with Eugène and Christophe.

'There's no one to follow us,' said the priest, 'so we may as well go fast; we don't want to spend time on the way; it is half-past five.'

However, just as the coffin was placed in the hearse, two empty

303

carriages painted with the coats of arms of the Comte de Restaud and the Baron de Nucingen arrived, and followed in the procession to the Père-Lachaise. At six o'clock Father Goriot's body was lowered into his grave in the presence of his daughters' servants. When the short prayer was said which was the old man's due in return for the student's money, priest and servants went away. The two grave-diggers flung a few shovelfuls of earth on the coffin and hid it from sight; then they straightened their backs and one of them asked Rastignac for their tip. Eugène searched his pocket but found nothing there, and he was obliged to borrow five francs from Christophe. The incident, so trivial in itself, overwhelmed Rastignac, and a wave of desperate sadness swept over him. Night was falling, and a damp half-light fretted the nerves. He looked at the grave, and in that place the last tear of his youth was shed. It was a tear that had its source in the sacred emotions of an innocent heart, one of those tears whose radiance springs from the ground where they fall and reaches the gates of Heaven. He folded his arms, staring at the clouded sky, and Christophe, seeing his mood, left him.

Thus left alone, Rastignac walked a few steps to the highest part of the cemetery, and saw Paris spread out below on both banks of the winding Seine. Lights were beginning to twinkle here and there. His gaze fixed almost avidly upon the space that lay between the column of the Place Vendôme and the dome of the Invalides; there lay the splendid world that he had wished to gain. He eyed that humming hive with a look that foretold its despoliation, as if he already felt on his lips the sweetness of its honey, and said with superb defiance,

'It's war between us now!'

And by way of throwing down the gauntlet to Society, Rastignac went to dine with Madame de Nucingen.

Saché, September 1834

～ THE END ～